VERBENA

ALSO BY NANCI KINCAID

Crossing Blood, a novel

Pretending the Bed Is a Raft, stories

Balls, a novel

Verbena

a novel by

Nanci Kincaid

A SHANNON RAVENEL BOOK

Algonquin Books of Chapel Hill 2002

ℝ

A SHANNON RAVENEL BOOK

Published by
ALGONQUIN BOOKS OF CHAPEL HILL
Post Office Box 2225
Chapel Hill, North Carolina 27515-2225

a division of
Workman Publishing
708 Broadway
New York, New York 10003

Published simultaneously in Canada
  by Thomas Allen & Son Limited.
Design by Anne Winslow.

This is a work of fiction. While, as in all fiction, the literary perceptions and insights are based on experience, all names, characters, places, and incidents are either products of the author's imagination or are used fictitiously. No reference to any real person is intended or should be inferred.

Library of Congress Cataloging-in-Publication Data
Kincaid, Nanci.
    Verbena : a novel / by Nanci Kincaid.
      p. cm.
    "A Shannon Ravenel book"—T.p. verso.
    ISBN 1-56512-348-4
      1. Women—Southern States—Fiction.   2. Single-parent families—
    Fiction.   3. Southern States—Fiction.   4. Widows—Fiction.   I. Title.
    PS3561.I4253 V47 2002
    813'.54—dc21   2001056531

10 9 8 7 6 5 4 3 2 1
First Edition

For Tomey

We love because it's the only true adventure.

NIKKI GIOVANNI, 1982

One's real life is often the life that one does not lead.

OSCAR WILDE

• ◆ •

Nothing is a stronger influence . . . on their children
than the unlived lives of their parents.

CARL JUNG

• ◆ •

Experience is what you get when you didn't get
what you wanted.

ITALIAN PROVERB

CONTENTS

PART I: 1

An Accidental Life

• ◆ •

PART II: 125

The Gift of Weeping

• ◆ •

PART III: 247

One Thing and Then the Other

• ◆ •

EPILOGUE 328

VERBENA

I

AN ACCIDENTAL LIFE

I

Looking back, it seemed Bena's life had more or less belonged to her right up until Bobby died and took it away. With Bobby in the grave Bena's life had quickly become doing what Bobby wasn't there to do. Get the lawn mowed, keep the car running, pay off the mortgage, and raise his kids right so that they'd all turn out decent, reasonably athletic, and basically honest—which she'd done. Not a criminal among them. They were serious children—maybe that was true. When Bena looked back she worried that probably they hadn't laughed enough or ever found the pleasure of pure out-and-out silliness and she was sorry about that. But on the other hand, not a one of them was mean.

It was more than five years ago now, but sometimes it still seemed like just last week. The news—which is how they talked about it still. The night we got *the news*. When he told Mama *the news*. When *the news* hit school. Marcus Langley, one of Bobby's fishing buddies, was standing at the door in his Alabama state trooper uniform looking like a total stranger. He had on his official law enforcement expression, which Bena had never seen before. Beside him was his nervous partner whose eyes were darting wildly like he was afraid to take a hard look at Bena under the circumstances.

"Bena, honey," Marcus said. "There's been an accident. It's Bobby. Killed in a rollover. And Bena, now, he was not alone. There was a woman." The news had come at once like that, packaged in sentence fragments.

She'd been at home with the kids that night, the five of them. Eddie, the baby, was almost ten and Sissy, the oldest, was a sophomore in high school. The TV was on and every radio and stereo in the house was blaring out some competing noise. Bena was grading papers at the kitchen table. She had the kind of mind that could cut right through the distractions of life and stay focused on her task. She was a sixth-grade teacher then, a good one. That was before she found out they would pay her better money to fill out government forms than they would to teach the children anything about the government. They'd let her do it in an air-conditioned office too and not a sweatbox classroom where all the papers were turned in wet and smeared since it was way too hot for anybody to get a grip on their pencils—or their thoughts.

Then there came the knock on the door that changed everything. The Alabama state trooper car with its flashing light parked in the yard making their dog, Elvis, howl as if he knew exactly what had happened just by pure instinct. And all five of her golden children wild-eyed and frozen at the news that Bobby Eckerd, their daddy, was dead.

Two afternoons earlier Bobby had told Bena he was going to a meeting in Montgomery. His company was trying to get a bid in on paper supplies for Maxwell, the air force base. He said it would take him a day or two and kissed Bena good-bye. And she had let him go off being believed.

THE STATE TROOPERS said Bobby's car went off the embankment up on that twisty part of Highway 82. They said it looked like he just forgot to take the curve like maybe he thought for a minute his car was an airplane and it would just lift off and sail him through the air, like he was a jet pilot, like he could take wing and fly. There were no skid marks, the state troopers said. No signs of braking. Car rolled over six or eight times. Bobby was killed instantly.

They found the woman in a ravine with her skull mostly crushed. She was still breathing. They took her to Jackson Hospital and called all her next of kin. "We're sorry, Mrs. Eckerd, to have to bring you this news," the nervous officer kept saying to Bena. "We're sorry, ma'am."

The day after the accident the newspaper ran the pictures of Bobby and the woman together, side by side, like a pair. ACCIDENT TAKES LO-CAL MAN'S LIFE, the paper said. WOMAN IN CRITICAL CONDITION.

Bena's daughter Ellie, who was eleven, brought the newspaper into Bena's bedroom to show it to her. "Mama," she said, "you want to see what the woman looked like?" Bena sat up in bed and studied the picture of the woman. Her name was Lorraine Rayfield. She was only twenty-four. Bena had never laid eyes on her before. Her hair was dark and curly and Bena remembered thinking she probably dyed it to get it so black. Bena's own, once auburn, hair was a non-color brown. Bena searched the woman's face and decided that her people might be foreign or something. Italian maybe. Or Puerto Rican. She had the looks of a stranger just passing through on her way someplace else. It was clear she was not someone who belonged in Bena's—or Bobby's—life.

"She's not as pretty as you, Mama," Ellie said.

"Pretty is as pretty does," Bena said.

"I bet she's not as nice as you either."

"There's more important things than being pretty—or nice, Ellie. You remember that, okay?"

"Yes, ma'am," Ellie said. "Like what?"

"I don't know for sure right this minute. You'll have to ask me later, okay?"

"Like being alive," Ellie said. "It's more important to be alive. Right?"

BOBBY'S FUNERAL WAS well attended because nearly everybody loved Bobby Eckerd. His children were scrubbed and good-looking and behaved in a way that would make any father proud. His wife, Bena, was composed and gracious. Anybody that pitied her was wasting time—at least that's what she told herself at the time. Bena had entered the church with her two sons and three daughters flanking her like clear skinned, blue-eyed soldiers, and she had felt strong in the midst of them. What Bobby Eckerd had needed with Lorraine Rayfield Bena might never know. But she was not going to let her children become ashamed of their father. She was going to insist that they look beyond the obvious. That's what she had always tried to do herself.

BENA'S OWN DADDY had died when she was fifteen. Afterward once a month she and her mother had gone to his grave with garden shears and spray cleaner. Her mother washed the bird droppings off his marker while Bena clipped the grass from around his grave. They never talked during this time. Bena liked to think it was a labor of love they'd shared.

Bena's mother died the year after Bena and Bobby married. She was buried beside Bena's daddy, her name etched on the other half of his marker. Bena and Bobby had moved to Baxter County by then so Bena had had to let the tending of their graves go. It didn't bother her though, since it didn't seem as sad, her two parents together again in the bowels of the earth, where their late-life child had no choice but to let them rest in peace.

Bena had been a surprise baby. Her mother was forty-seven and childless when she thought she was going through *the change*—and she was. The change was the baby she'd stopped wanting years before. She named her Verbena because the verbena was in bloom then. Bena had always thought it was an old-lady name, which made sense because her mother was an old lady when she named her. It was her daddy who'd call her *Baby Bena,* the second part of which stuck. Thank goodness. A half name suited Bena better.

Once when she was a little girl Bena remembered hearing a lady at church tell her mother, "My verbena is giving way to weeds."

"This is my Verbena." Her mother patted Bena's head.

"You're named after a pretty little flower, honey," the lady said. "It grows wild lots of places. Same as a weed."

Bena had thought then that her name was misleading. She'd never felt like a flower. From the beginning she'd felt more like a weed that had sprung up hearty and uninvited.

Bena's mother was old enough to be a grandmother—or in Alabama even a great-grandmother—when she delivered Bena. She was hospitalized over a month after the birth, just from the shock of it all. She'd tried to be a thankful and loving mother, but mainly she was tired and very disappointed in God's imperfect sense of timing. It made her question His divine plan.

Bena's parents had been each other's entire lives until Bena burst onto the scene screaming and needing—disturbing the peace and order her parents had fine-tuned in their long, sterile years together. It had never seemed possible to her that the product of a loving union could be the very thing to destroy that loving union. What kind of plan was that? She'd always felt like a rude interruption in her parent's very polite lives. It was a terrible way to think about herself. An accident, living an accidental life.

Then the proof came: her daddy's heart attack—or drowning. They'd found him floating facedown in a lake and both things had happened. One, they said, had caused the other. Accidents lead to accidents. Afterward her mother had medicated herself into an early death. The past had started swirling through her head, and everything got out of order like a family album with all the photos spilled on the floor. She could take a pill and there was no present anymore

—no future either. She couldn't recall whether or not she'd taken her medicine. The more she took, the less sure she was. Bena sorted her medicine and wrote out a schedule for her, tried to call and remind her, but then there was the day her mother didn't answer the phone. Bena was pregnant with Sissy when she watched the ambulance carry her mother away with a pink bedsheet pulled up over her head.

Now, for the first time since they'd been laid to rest Bena wished for her parents. She wanted them to put their arms around her and promise that everything would be okay—something they'd never really done. She wanted them to kiss her children and hold their hands and be strong and wise for them—because she might not be able to be either. It was odd that on the day of Bobby's funeral instead of wishing for him, she was wishing for her dead parents, who'd been gone such a long, long time. On this day, more than any other, Bena desperately longed to be somebody's much loved child.

Bobby's mother wept uncontrollably through the funeral. There was a sort of anger in her grief that was frightening. Bobby's daddy had taken off years ago—nobody knew where. Afterward, for a while, Bobby's mother had focused on Bobby, her oldest son, nearly smothering him in love and expectations. Then his stepdaddy, Kyle, came along and distracted her. Kyle owned a construction company. He moved Bobby's mother into a big, fine house and put the boys to work in the summertime to keep them out of trouble. One by one they'd begun to call Kyle *Daddy*. Several years back he'd moved the business to Georgia, just outside Atlanta. Now they only rarely saw them or heard from them. Two of Bobby's brothers still worked for Kyle though. But to this day they insisted Bobby was their mother's favorite. It had become a family joke. *Mama, if we were on a ship and it was sinking, who would you save after you saved Bobby?*

Kyle brought Bobby's mother by the house before the service. Bena was lying down in the bedroom with the lights off. Bobby's mother eased into the room and sat down on the bed beside her. She shook her head *no, no, no,* and wept into her handkerchief. Bena had tried to comfort her the best she could.

"You don't understand." Bobby's mother blew her nose. "Bobby wasn't happy. That's what breaks my heart. He wouldn't be off with a young girl—not if he was happy at home. On some level, Bena, you have to know that."

"It might not be like it seems," Bena said.

"That's the trouble with the truth," Bobby's mother said. "Nobody wants to tell it—and nobody wants to hear it."

"You don't know the whole story," Bena said. "Nobody does."

"I know Bobby is dead," she sobbed. "I know he was searching. He wasn't at peace."

"Maybe he was," Bena said. "He got saved."

Bobby's mother closed her eyes and shook her head. "You don't understand, do you? It was the same when Bobby's daddy left us. I didn't want to admit it either."

"Admit what?"

"That something was missing."

"What was it?" Bena asked. "What do you think was missing?"

Kyle knocked on the door. "I pulled the car around," he said. "It's time to go."

Bobby's mother squeezed Bena's hand and looked at her, "We got to live with this the rest of our lives," she whispered. "Bobby's unhappiness." She shook her head as if she was furious about it. "You okay, honey? I know this isn't easy for you either."

It RAINED WHEN Bobby was laid in the ground. Black umbrellas surrounded the grave like gnats clustered on a wound. It was muddy and messy and the coffin slipped and sank while the men tried to steer it into place. *Amen,* people said. Bena watched it all as if she were a person in the audience at a really sad movie.

That night her son Joe said, "Daddy ruined everything, didn't he, Mama?"

"He changed everything," Bena said. "We're not going let things be ruined."

• • •

It was two weeks after Bobby had been buried that Bena got the phone call from Lorraine Rayfield's mother. "Mrs. Eckerd," she said, "please forgive me for intruding on your terrible grief."

Bena was too stunned to speak.

"I'm calling to ask you something," Mrs. Rayfield said. "It's hard for me and I hope you'll forgive me."

"What is it?" Bena asked.

"It's Lorraine," Mrs. Rayfield said. "She's not doing so good. The doctors say it's only a matter of. It's her brain. The damage is. She needs the last rites."

"I'm sorry," Bena said.

"So, what I'm wondering is. I was thinking if you might. I'd like Lorraine to die in peace, you know. Do you think you might be able to forgive her?"

"Forgive her?"

"I didn't raise Lorraine to be off with somebody's husband. I know in her heart she's so sorry. It's just that, if you could forgive her, then maybe she could go, you know. Die. I think she's lingering until she gets the forgiveness."

"What do you want me to do?" Bena asked.

"Can you come to the hospital?"

It sounded to Bena like the woman must be Catholic or something, all that talk about forgiveness and last rites. Bena was a Baptist. She knew nothing about all the rigmarole the Catholics put their dying loved ones through. She had no idea what they expected from her. *Forgiveness,* Lorraine's mother had said.

Bena drove to Montgomery without telling anyone where she was going. She couldn't have said why she was doing this exactly, except that she'd been asked to. For the most part, when she could, Bena tried to do what people asked her to.

Mrs. Rayfield, Lorraine's mother, didn't look much older than Bena. She looked like she could just as easily have been the woman in Bobby's car. A woman, maybe like her daughter, so compelling that Bobby would be unable to keep his eyes off her and on the road. "Thank you for coming," she whispered.

"It's okay," Bena said.

"I'll show you where she is." Mrs. Rayfield took Bena's arm and led her down the intensive-care hallway and into a cold, well-lit room with a roll-up bed in the middle of it. A bandaged, wired Lorraine Rayfield lay there looking as small as a child. "She can hear you," Mrs. Rayfield said. "The doctors might think she can't, but she can." Mrs. Rayfield leaned over the bed and whispered, "Lorraine, honey, Bobby's wife is here to see you. It's okay. She's not mad." Then she kissed the bandaged head and stepped away from the bed. "I'll give you a few minutes alone," she said. "I'll wait outside the door."

For an instant Bena didn't want to be left alone with this small, dying woman. She stared at the swollen face of a person she didn't know at all. Lorraine's eyes were sealed closed and her face was purple and distorted. It occurred to Bena that the dark curly hair in the newspaper picture had been shaved so that the doctors could try to stitch her head together.

Bena pulled a tall stool to the bedside and sat on it. She touched Lorraine's hand. It was dry and papery. "Your mother called me," she said.

For a minute Bena just sat and stared at the tiny figure in the bed. She could be one of Bena's daughters. Sissy maybe. Sissy was a child with a wild streak too, wasn't she? She tried to imagine Bobby in a car with this woman but she couldn't think of it, what they would say to each other, where they might be going, what Lorraine had been wearing or planning. It was all dark and impossible.

"Okay." Bena took a deep breath. "Your mother says you can hear me. I don't know how you knew Bobby—how long or how well. But, look, Bobby was an easy guy to love. You should have seen his funeral. Everybody came. Practically the whole county. So you shouldn't feel bad because you loved him too, okay?"

EVEN AS SHE SPOKE Bena wondered if she meant a word she was saying. The words just came to her as if she'd been rehearsing for this scene all her life. She'd have laid hands on and healed Lorraine Rayfield if she'd known how. She'd have commanded her to rise from her bed and go forth and sin no more. It was odd how connected she felt to this woman, the one whose hand she kept instinctively reaching for. Before leaving she leaned over and kissed Lorraine's swollen face just like her mother had done—as if Lorraine was a daughter both women loved. As if she were every woman's daughter. Later Bena would accuse herself of simply having been curious to see what Lorraine looked like—this woman who'd been with Bobby when he died. This woman who—dead and alive—had altered Bena's life forever.

Before Bena left the hospital Mrs. Rayfield said, "Mrs. Eckerd, if you have any questions about Lorraine and Bobby. Their relationship. I'll tell you what I know. If, you know, that would make things any easier for you. Knowing the truth."

"No, thank you," Bena said.

SOME OF THE TEACHERS at school told Bena that lots of times a dead person will appear to have a last word with you or—in Bobby's case—to explain things and beg for understanding. They said, "You'll think you're dreaming, but you won't be."

One of the other sixth-grade teachers, Mayfred Piper, who lived a life even messier than Bena's and whom over the years Bena had come to love for exactly that reason, told Bena that her own dead mother had appeared one night in a white nightgown at the foot of her bed and had reached out and touched Mayfred on the leg. "It was as real as anything." Mayfred cried telling it and Bena believed her.

But Mayfred was a black woman, and so to Bena that meant she was bent more toward the spiritual in the first place and therefore God might naturally be more inclined to give her some sort of dramatic sign like that. Make her rise up out of the bed singing "I Go to the River" and then fall to the floor in total submission and gratitude. That's how Mayfred told it, that she lay sprawled on the floor in a humble prayer posture, giving nonstop thanks, until morning came. Bena didn't personally know any white people who did things like that.

Afterward Mayfred said she knew God had called her to His service and now she was a self-appointed missionary of sorts. "The trouble with Jesus," Mayfred liked to say, "is that He was just so perfect. A lot of people, they aren't attracted to somebody perfect. That's why God's got to get all the mileage he can out of sinners— like me. I'm like a lightning rod for sinners because I don't claim to be perfect like a lot of religious people. Nothing like one sinner to attract another sinner. God's got sense enough to know that. It's just certain *people* that don't."

Mayfred drove some people crazy being so religious, but Bena didn't mind it. She wondered how it would be to have God pick you out from the multitudes and assign you a holy task like that. God was always telling Mayfred to do this or that and she was always hell-bent on doing whatever He said, even if it didn't seem to make a bit of sense.

God didn't seem as inclined to do white people that way. Bena was secretly glad. She was sure He had His reasons why. But no sooner did she start to think like that than a new teacher at school, one who'd only recently moved to Baxter County from over in Phenix City, and who was every bit as white as Bena, gave her a dose of hope. The woman's only son had shot himself in the face with his daddy's gun. She was the one that found him, folded in a knot on his bed, like somebody sleeping in a river of blood. She said her soul came loose from her body at the sight of her boy, self-murdered. It was the same as if he'd shot her too, left her to go through life dead-hearted. Then she swore that about a month later her dead son woke her up from a deep sleep to say he loved her. He wanted her to know it wasn't her fault. *I don't blame you,* he'd said, *so stop blaming yourself.*

She told Bena that at first she thought she was in a dream, but then she felt something heavy lift off her chest, like a piece of fallen furniture or the foot of a really big man—and suddenly she could breathe easy again, the way she used to before everything happened. She was not so crushed underneath anything anymore. She swore her boy coming to her like that gave her the only moment of true peace she'd known since the accident. But in this woman's case, it was a one-time thing—no repeats. God didn't enlist her to His eternal service like He did Mayfred. All God did was tell the woman she needed to divorce her boy's father, which she'd been wanting to do for the longest time anyway. Then she moved to Baxter County to start her life all over. "One miracle," the woman said, "can set you free forever."

Bena hoped this was true. She was ready to believe it because she needed a last word with Bobby—to know for sure that his sin hadn't backfired so bad that he'd completely lost his salvation. Bena herself had witnessed his being saved. He'd walked the aisle for Christ and the preacher shook his hand and patted him on the back. There was no doubt at the time that it was for real too. It had been all he could do not to sob his eyes out in front of everybody. He said so himself. As it was, his voice trembled and his hands shook so bad Bena thought for a minute he might be having a heart attack. It scared her. For days afterward he'd gotten so quiet it was spooky, maybe just from pure relief, knowing now he could quit worrying about living and dying and heaven and hell and put that energy toward something else. Knowing he was saved for all eternity. Some people said they could see a change in him afterward.

Bena had never been a religious person really. Originally religion was a favor she did for her mother to provide the woman some peace of mind. Everybody who wanted to be normal went to church. Bena's friends were all going to church pretty much for the same reasons she was—because their mothers had got religion somewhere along the way and were sort of panicked about it. After a while it got to be a habit, church. The Sunday shoes, the church dresses, the little New Testament with her full name embossed on it in gold.

By the time she was grown Bena was taking church more seriously—some might say too seriously. Maybe she'd started to actually listen to the preacher or something, because the whole thing stirred feelings in her that made her unspeakably sad. This big world full of sinners, most of them wishing desperately to be something better than what they were. Herself included. It could rip you to pieces if you thought about it too much. So Bena had found a way to go through all the motions without dwelling on the big questions too much. In this way she was absolutely born to be Baptist because nearly everybody she knew operated pretty much the same way. It was just that now that Bobby was gone and the afterlife seemed her only hope of ever seeing him again, it made her want to truly believe all the things she'd only pretended to believe before. If Bobby could get himself let into heaven, then Bena ought to be able to too. For a while after Bobby's funeral she got her mind set on it.

Bena went to bed night after night in a state of waiting, praying that Bobby's spirit would come to her—just once. She'd say, *Bobby, is heaven real?* She'd say, *Look what a mess you've made of everything!* Some nights she fell asleep imagining Bobby and Lorraine appearing together, sitting on the edge of her bed, their wings fluttering like a couple of lovesick angels.

IT WASN'T UNTIL Bena got the call from Mrs. Rayfield more than a month later, saying that Lorraine had died without ever opening her eyes, that Bena began to comprehend death, the finality of it. It was only then, when she knew for sure that Lorraine was buried more than sixty miles away from where Bobby was buried, that she finally stopped looking for Bobby to come up the drive at the end of the day, blowing his horn like a public service announcement—or a warning to any children who had a talking-to coming that their daddy was home.

When Bena looked back at her marriage, for the life of her, she couldn't remember a single time when she hadn't been glad to see Bobby come home. He'd sling his briefcase on the coffee table, walk across the room in his wilted white short-sleeved shirt, loosening his necktie along the way, give her a little automatic kiss, and say, "How's the Queen doing?" That was what he'd called Bena—the Queen.

He'd head for the bedroom and change into shorts and a T-shirt, and if it was summer he might mow the grass, or if it was winter he might rake the pine straw into mounds and cushion the flower beds with it. Or throw the ball with Joe and Eddie until Eddie got frustrated and started to cry. Or watch Sissy practice her baton twirling, figure eight after endless figure eight. Or talk Leslie into setting free the turtle she'd caught, convincing her that life in a cardboard box wasn't worth living no matter how loved one was. If Leslie couldn't be convinced then it was Bobby who dug the turtle's grave and put the dogwood blossoms on it.

Bobby might fill up all the bird feeders with sunflower seed or pour kerosene on fire-ant beds dotting the yard or spray the wooden deck with water repellent to prevent rot or put sand on oil spills blighting the carport floor. Bobby was always doing something— with Elvis trailing him every step he took.

Bobby claimed he'd gotten Elvis for the kids, but Elvis had never belonged to anybody but Bobby. It was Bobby who picked him out of the litter. It was Bobby who named him. Bena had protested. *Elvis?* she'd said. *No way.* But Bobby had insisted, saying, *Look how black his fur is. It's so black it's blue. Like Elvis's shoe-polished hair.* Bobby had always loved the story of Elvis putting black shoe polish all over his hair, then getting rained on, all that black washing down his face and staining his clothes and everybody laughing at him, thinking he was a weirdo. It was stories like that that made Bobby love Elvis. He loved him as much as any girl ever did, maybe more. It embarrassed Bena too, having a husband who worshiped Elvis like that. She'd wished Bobby would get more current.

After he got saved, sometimes on Sunday nights Bobby would put

Elvis's gospel music on the stereo and play it full blast. When the kids came and gawked at him in horror, saying, *Daddy, stop it!* he'd smile and say, *The Catholics—now, they may have the Pope with that crown on his head, but us Baptists, we got Elvis. We got the King.* He'd get tears in his eyes when Elvis sang "Amazing Grace," like that was the one song in the world that made Bobby believe in the Holy Spirit for real. Bena had asked the preacher to play Elvis's "Amazing Grace" at Bobby's funeral too, which he did. After which she never could stand to listen to it again.

Ordinarily Bobby was not the kind of man who let himself get bored, although on rare nights he might just sit in the den and watch the news like he was in some kind of trance, waiting for Bena to get supper on the table. Bobby had been a casserole man. Chicken casserole was his favorite—the one with the spaghetti noodles, cheese, and almonds. Most men are meat-and-potatoes guys, but Bobby was different that way. He liked everything all mixed together from the beginning.

After supper sometimes Bobby would sit in the yard with Elvis under his chair and smoke a cigar. *The cigar stink keeps the mosquitoes away,* he liked to say. But it did not keep the children away. When the children were little they practiced their headstands and backbends in the grass where he sat, saying, *Watch this, Daddy.* Bobby would watch them tirelessly, his cigar smoke settling like a gray cloud around his head. Some nights he'd send the children to the kitchen saying, *Go tell the Queen to come out here. Tell her there's a handsome traveling salesman out here who's craving her company.* Minutes later the children would run back to him, saying, *Daddy, Mama's coming as soon as she cleans up the kitchen.* But sometimes it took longer than she expected and Bobby would come inside before she could make her way outside. She regretted that now.

Bena had relived their early life from a million different angles since Bobby died. She remembered him the same way you remembered a magic trick—all the pleasure was in the bewilderment.

But she knew this. When Bobby had walked through the door at the end of the day, Elvis panting at his heels, Bena's life had made perfect sense. The meatloaf she was slapping into shape made sense. The laundry she would rotate from washer to dryer to dresser drawers all evening long made sense. The children arguing and telling on one another and all their lamentations and denials made sense. The car payments made sense. Her menstrual cramps made sense. The toilet whose handle had to be jiggled just right to stop its whining made sense. Even her students who, try as she might, she could not quite reach, who'd leave her class still unable to read a standard paragraph and make sense of it—even they made a sweeter, gentler sense. Bobby had had a way of putting the sense into everything. That had been his gift to Bena. Marriage to Bobby had kept her very sane.

FOR THE FIRST FEW months after Bobby was killed in the car accident Lucky McKale, their mailman, walked up the long drive and delivered the mail to Bena by hand so she wouldn't have to make her way down to the mailbox just to get a fistful of overdue bills and sympathy cards. "Anything I can do to help out?" he asked Bena nearly every day in the beginning of her widowhood. Later he got bolder, "You'll get over this, Bena. It might not seem like it now, but time is a great healer."

"I haven't noticed time healing Sue Cox," Bena said. Sue Cox was Lucky's wife. Lucky just stood and looked at Bena like she'd slapped his face. Afterward he stopped hand-delivering her mail, just stuffed it in her mailbox the way he was required by law to do.

For weeks at a time Bena wouldn't take in the mail just because she couldn't stand to. She thought people shouldn't be allowed to intrude on her life simply by licking a stamp. Depending on the feel of the mail she might just dump a whole handful straight in the trash and never so much as glance at the return addresses. Most of the summer she did this. It was good when school started again and she was forced back to work. It seemed easier to make the transition from wife to widow at school, where it was part of her job to be mature and appropriately distant.

At home she remained a wife for the longest time, years really. A wife with no husband—but with five children to concentrate on, which she did. She watched for signs of lingering sadness or loneliness or anger or any of the natural by-products of grief—and for normal rites of passage. There were plenty of both. Joe tried to help her police the others, but he was almost too perfect to make a good enforcer. He set the bar too high for the rest of them. There was that thing with the stolen exam, but he had managed to get that straightened out. Any of the rest of her kids would probably have been kicked out of school, but Joe had a way about him. He was an example setter. Unlike Sissy, who was always one step from disaster. Or Leslie, who for a while after her daddy died talked of nothing but finding a way to be with him again—which kept Bena terrified. She checked on Leslie while she slept—two or three times a night— touching her to make sure she was still breathing. Or Ellie, who loved everybody and everything with no radar for danger or deceit. It would take a while longer to know if this would be a blessing or a curse. Or Eddie, for the longest time a loner, always locked in his room with the dog, doing Lord knows what. He swore he just needed peace and quiet—so he could sleep. It seemed Bobby's death had tired him out something awful.

ONLY ONCE, ABOUT two years after Bobby died, did Bena fold beneath the enormity of his death. It sat on her shoulders like a huge gray past world, heavy and unbalanced. If she'd known how to squeeze out from under it—even if it meant the world would crash around her—she might have done it. Instead her life was like an involuntary game of piggyback with a dead man twice her size. Twice, at Mayfred's suggestion, Bena went to church to turn her life over to Jesus, in hopes He'd lift Bobby's dead weight off her shoulders, keep her from collapsing beneath the memories and misery.

"I don't care what the Bible says," Mayfred told Bena, "God ain't gon' answer every prayer you pray. He don't have time for all that, for one thing. But just saying the words, you know, that can carry you a long way by itself."

To THIS DAY none of her children had ever confessed to knowing anything about the field of pot growing in the yard. A Baxter County sheriff's deputy had come to talk to Bena's sixth-grade class about the dangers of drugs and had brought samples of marijuana with him. It was weird, because Bena could swear a weed looking just like that was growing wild in the back of her yard out by the woods. She asked the deputy if it was possible for the stuff to grow wild and he said he'd like to come home with her to take a look. The deputy had been flirting with her all afternoon and she thought he probably just wanted the chance to get to know her better.

When they got to her house and she showed him the patch of look-alike plants he said, "Ma'am, I'd say some of your kids has got them a heck of a side business going here. Look here, these are planted in rows. Hand-planted."

Before she could think about what he was saying, Bena ran to the house and got her kitchen matches and ran back. She was swallowing terrible screams like somebody drowning in scalding water. While the deputy walked to the woods to see how far back the plants went, Bena lit one match after another and it was a dry spell too, so the flames took hold fast. She was mumbling like a madwoman, *her children, kill somebody, destroy everything, hateful, hateful, hateful,* cursing each match as she scratched it across the box and flung it at the dry leaves.

Before the deputy could stop her she had a blaze going that drew all her kids out of the house, except Joe, who was at baseball practice. Elvis darted out too, straight to the edge of the flames, where Bena was standing like a woman in a trance. "Mama!" the kids started yelling. "Stop it, Mama." The fire was spreading fast, burning up everything it touched. It smelled so sweet.

"Who did this?" Bena, red-faced, pointed at the rows of plants. Her hair was wild. Her eyes shot them dead where they stood. She struck a match and held it toward them. "I hate you for doing this."

Leslie ran and called the fire department. The deputy got the lawn hose and tried to drown the flames the best he could. Sissy ran to the front to get a second hose. Eddie tried to get Elvis in the house. The dog was going crazy, running back and forth, barking at the fire, growling the way he did when the garbageman came. Ellie kept screaming, "Mama, please. Stop it." Every time Ellie came near Bena, the deputy yelled at her, "You kids stay back. Get out of the way." He grabbed Bena, shook her by the shoulders, and snatched the matches out of her hand as if she were a child. She stared at him like he was a million miles away, like she had no idea who he was putting his hands on her like that.

By the time the volunteer fire department got there the fire had spread to nearly a half acre. Bena was starting to imagine her house burning down too. She wished it would. The fire crew hosed, chopped, doused, and struggled with the fire. They shouted orders, their voices so strong, their spirits high. It occurred to Bena that they might thank her later, for the battle, for the chance to conquer the enemy, for the thrill of trial by fire to which they were so devoted. Their exhilaration was terrifying. Bena stood and watched, kicking dirt and tufts of grass at the flames in a useless gesture. She was covered with soot. Sweat poured down her face in broken black lines. But she was not crying.

A knot of cars had gathered at the end of the driveway. People who'd come to watch the fire destroy what it could. People who'll love hell when they get there, Bena thought, all that excitement and destruction—those eternal flames. Bena cursed them, the same neighbors who'd crowded into her kitchen with sliced ham, green-bean casserole, and macaroni and cheese—love offerings—when Bobby died. What would they offer her now? What would they say about this other kind of grief? "Bena Eckerd is crazy. It's no wonder Bobby did what he did." It had been two years since they'd all gathered around to lower his coffin into the ground.

Bena saw the mail truck weaving through the mess of stopped cars, determined to get to the house. Maybe Lucky was bringing her a fistful of urgent past-due notices. That seemed to be what he was best at. He pulled all the way up into the front yard and parked on the grass. Bobby's grass. Bobby used to love working in the yard. He used to say their grass looked prettier than any putting green. And it had. Now it was riddled with crabgrass and bare spots and she couldn't remember if anybody had bothered to mow it since summer. She saw Lucky jump out of the van and run where the deputy was hosing down hissing embers. "What the hell happened here?"

"Trash fire got away from us," the deputy shouted. He didn't say a crazy woman went haywire with a box of kitchen matches.

"Damn, if it didn't," Lucky said. He'd been friends with Bobby before everything. Who names a human being Lucky anyway? A curse for sure. A lie if you knew him at all. Bena watched as he ran to the toolshed, grabbed one of Bobby's old shovels, and started slinging dirt at the fire. You'd think his own house was about to burn down the way he went at it. If you asked Bena, he was enjoying himself. She hated people who were their best in crisis.

She looked upward, where black smoke swirled into a dark, ominous cloud. It made her think of spirits rising, ghosts or something. It made her think of Indian smoke signals and what this one might say. *Family going to pieces. Hopes and dreams going up in smoke.* She wondered if Bobby was watching. She wondered what he thought of the terrible mess she was making out of the mess he had made.

When the fire was finally out the firefighters were weary and satisfied. They were like soldiers who, in their victory, were kind to the captors. "That was a close call, ma'am," they said. "You're lucky, lady." They were trying to make the onlookers go home, clear the drive so the fire trucks could turn around.

Bena turned to face her silent children, huddled together in the carport. Joe had come home from baseball by now too. He looked stricken standing with the others, trying to think what to do. The deputy ordered them to move out of the way—Bena's kids—their arms folded, their faces sooty and fearful. She was full of such fury that it would have felt wonderful to slap their faces. She wanted to hit them again and again until they understood her pain. She was shaking. They could see that.

"I don't know who is responsible for this." Bena waved a charred twig. "But if this is the best you know how to do, then I give up. I quit." Bena crumpled the twig in her fist and threw it at them. "I'll forget I ever had any children." She spit the words. "I swear to God, I don't need this. In a real family people look out for each other. They don't do stupid, selfish things that can destroy everybody. You're just like your daddy," she said. "Every sorry one of you."

"Mama." Ellie reached for Bena.

"Stay away from me," Bena snapped. "Don't come near me. I hate you all." Then she turned to go toward the house.

The deputy who'd been standing by listening to Bena came forward then and pointed his finger at Bena's children a full minute before thinking of what to say. "Damn it." He was looking mostly at Joe because he seemed the oldest. "It's a good thing your daddy is not here to see this. If I ever hear of any of you giving your mama any kind of trouble again I'll personally come after you and make you sorry. I'll make it my personal business. You understand me? Don't you think your mama has been through enough?"

Leslie and Ellie were nearly crying and Sissy had covered her face with her hands. Joe was stoic and Eddie was trying to be.

Out of the corner of her eye Bena saw Lucky McKale coming toward her. How dare he try to talk to her at a time like this. She ran the last steps to the house and closed the door behind her before he could catch up.

FOR WEEKS AFTERWARD Bena waited for some form of legal action against her or one of her children. She was terrified to get the mail. Every time the phone rang her heart slammed into her ribs. She imagined everything awful. Her children in handcuffs, locked up for years in dungeon prisons like she'd seen on a TV special. The others scattered about in the worst sorts of foster homes, where they'd be so mistreated they'd have no choice but to run away, hitchhike to Panama City or Gulf Shores and get raped and murdered on the way. Their bodies would be found facedown in a grove of peach trees. The boys wearing only their T-shirts. The girls wearing only their shoes. It would be so bad they'd have closed casket funerals and be buried someplace down in Florida, which was not even their home state. It haunted Bena, the family coming loose from each other and falling apart—disintegrating right before her eyes. And it would be her fault.

The only thing official that ever came was a request for a donation to the volunteer fire department. Bena wrote them a check, even if it meant skipping the car payment one more month.

WHEN BOBBY HAD been alive Bena'd never thought of herself as something entirely separate from him. They were like a pair of bookends, their children the rare collection they struggled to keep together, standing upright. But now with Bobby gone Bena longed to be more than the pitiful lone bookend against which her children leaned and leaned and leaned.

In a secret room in her head she was wonderfully alone. It was a cool, well-organized place that she hadn't known about before, like finding a sunroom in the attic of a dark, gloomy old house. No husband there. No children. In that one private, orderly space in her head everything was different. She lived in a nice apartment somewhere away from Baxter County. Florida maybe. By the ocean. She had a different job—a better one—that paid her more and worried her less. She took care of herself, conditioned her hair, filed her nails, steamed her vegetables, listened to music, took walks at sunset, made new friends whose lives were clean and simple, not full of sad stories and hopeless patterns. She laughed often and slept soundly. In the beautiful recesses of her mind, Bena was a completely different woman, the one she might have been if Bobby had never come along. She was who she should have been all along, who she wished she were right now, who she swore she would be if her children ever really did grow up and go away—letting her have her life back.

It was Joe who finally came to her, "Mama," he said, "look. We're all sorry this happened. It was stupid. You don't have to worry about anything like that ever happening again. I swear."

"Good," Bena said.

"So do you think you can stop being mad all the time?"

"I don't know."

"Could you try?"

The TV was on in the den and Bena could hear the voices of her children mingling with the canned laughter. She went to the hall and looked at them. Joe sat like a king in his father's La-Z-Boy, throwing cheese curls at the girls, who ordered him to stop. Eddie was lying down, taking up the whole sofa, trying to watch TV, saying to his sisters every few minutes, "Y'all shut up. I can't hear." The girls, lying around on the floor, legs propped up on the coffee table, talked to one another in their wise sister voices, ignoring their brothers, as if they were just familiar pieces of badly designed furniture in the room.

"Can I come in?" Bena asked.

They sat up—snapped to attention—unsure which version of their mother prowled the house this night.

In their silence they looked strangely innocent to Bena. She saw the babies they used to be. Her babies. She sat down on the sofa next to Eddie, who scooted over as far as he could. God had never been as real to Bena as her children.

"Is something wrong?" Sissy asked. She was hugging her knees to her chest.

"Me," Bena said.

No one spoke. They just looked at her.

"I lied to you."

"It's okay, Mama." Ellie touched Bena's arm with one finger, the way you touch a burner on the stove.

"What'd you lie about?" Joe asked.

"I said I hated you all."

"Oh," Joe said. "Thought you were going to tell us we're adopted or something."

"Shut up, Joe," Sissy said. "Nobody in their right mind would adopt you."

"I'm a lucky woman," Bena said. "If I forget it, you all remind me, okay?"

"Could you say it like you mean it, Mama?" Leslie said. "You sound so sad trying to convince us you're lucky."

Bena laughed.

"She laughed," Joe said. "She cracked a smile."

"You can be pretty mean when you want to, Mama," Sissy said.

"You're one to talk." Eddie kicked Sissy.

"So, Mama, does this mean we won't have to be taking you over to Bryce after all?" Joe teased. "They got a ward there just for py-romaniacs, you know."

"Do they have one for smart-asses?" Leslie asked.

"Eddie." Joe pointed to the phone. "Go call Bryce and get Mama's name off the waiting list."

"It's a wonder I'm not any crazier than I am," Bena said.

"We're all a little bit crazy, aren't we?" Sissy said. "That's what keeps us from killing ourselves, right?"

"That's what keeps us from killing each other," Leslie said.

Bena took Leslie's hand because she was sitting closest. "In the future just remember that if I ever say I hate you, it's just because I love you so much. Okay?"

"That's female logic if I ever heard it," Joe said.

"Like you know anything about females," Leslie said.

To celebrate Bena's return to the fold Sissy and Ellie fried bacon and sliced tomatoes for sandwiches. In Baxter County food is love. It is how you prove forgiveness. Breaking bread will stand up in the court of public opinion. *She fried up some bacon. That's how sincere she was. He asked for seconds, so I knew he was truly sorry*. It was right to cook something good now. Afterward it would be right to bake a pan of brownies or rip into a box of ice-cream sandwiches.

When the phone rang Joe answered it. "Mama, it's for you. Some guy named Smokey. Says he got your number off the firehouse wall." It wasn't really funny, but Bena laughed because it was part of the way back to normal. Trying to laugh your way back to the place where maybe things can really be funny again.

Sissy yelled from the kitchen, where she stood over the sizzling frying pan: "Since you're in such a good mood, Mama, does this mean Barrett can come over?"

"Like he hasn't been sneaking over here every night anyway," Leslie said.

Bena went to bed high on forgiveness—on the rush of being forgiven. It was like at somebody's wedding when you drank so much champagne that all the doubts you'd accumulated about marriage subsided and you got carried away with hope and love and the possibility of happiness ever after. At weddings you danced with strangers and said, *Aren't they a perfect couple,* and meant it a thousand times over.

2

Another three years crawled by and Bena didn't think about Lucky McKale much. She sometimes saw him go by in his U.S. Mail van, but didn't wave or honk her horn in recognition the way she once would have—when Bobby was alive. Bobby and Lucky had been buddies in high school. Lucky was a big-time athlete, and Bena supposed it was only when he was required to wear his mailman's uniform that he'd finally given up wearing his letter jacket. He'd played college ball until he hurt his knee. As far as she could tell, he'd been one of those boys cursed with the great expectations of others. Including Bobby. Bobby'd never stopped being disappointed for Lucky and the way his career had failed to materialize. *Tough break,* he used to say when they saw Lucky. *He was one of the best.*

The one notable thing Lucky McKale had done was marry Sue Cox Miller. She was a year older than Bena and had been the girl that other girls assumed all the boys secretly wanted to marry. Her daddy was rich. He owned a car dealership, and nearly every car in

Baxter County said MILLER AUTO on its rear bumper. That would have been enough by itself, but she was beautiful too. Even now, when middle age had her in its clutches, it was gentle with her.

As a girl Sue Cox had been free-spirited in a way that had set her apart from most all the other girls, who had set their sights on going to heaven—you know, waiting until they died to do it. It wasn't just the drinking and the wild partying that Sue Cox did better than anybody else, but it was her bold, vulgar style that made her so universally appealing to everybody. Like getting arrested for suggestive dancing on the roof of Lucky's car after their junior prom and spending the night in jail for disturbing the peace and public drunkenness. Or like cutting her hair short when everybody else's hair was long and she was crazy drunk and somebody dared her to. Even with her dark hair in little butchered tufts, she was still beautiful.

Everybody knew that Mr. Dickey, the math teacher, used to take Sue Cox out to lunch during his planning hour on school days and simply write her a pass to get back into class afterward. There were rumors that they didn't really go to lunch at all, but to his apartment, which had mirrors on the ceiling. In her purse Sue Cox carried a whole book of passes that Mr. Dickey had signed for her —just in case a need ever arose. Sue Cox believed in moving about the school—and the world—freely. It was a revolutionary way to think. She went about handing the passes out like she was freeing the falsely imprisoned. She was her own sort of suffragette. Nobody ever accused her of being stingy.

In high school Sue Cox's drinking had seemed rebellious and full of style. Something she would look back on someday and be happy about—while most of the other girls would be full of regret over how careful they'd been, how worried about their imaginary reputations and what *people* would think. Even in high school, Bena understood the sorts of regrets that would come later about having played it too safe and been too sweet. She knew those regrets lay in wait for her. Even so, she'd been unable to set herself free the way Sue Cox had. Bena both admired and hated Sue Cox for this.

That Sue Cox would choose Lucky McKale to love and marry didn't really surprise anybody. In high school he was handsome and destined for gridiron glory—and he was funny too. He came from a mess of a family, but nobody much held it against him, because back then in Baxter County, Lord knows, who didn't? His daddy was known to be no-count, but for the most part folks were nice to the old man on Friday nights, when he came out to the ball games drunk as a coot to claim Lucky as his son. Sue Cox, bouncing around on the sidelines in her skintight cheerleader outfit, would spot old man McKale and wave to him enthusiastically, which was more than Lucky ever did. "Hey there," Sue Cox would shout, waving her pom-pom. "Aren't you just so proud of Lucky you could die?"

That Lucky loved and married Sue Cox was even less of a surprise. As wild as she was, everybody knew she had the power to make Lucky McKale respectable—and happy too. She seemed more than willing. She came from a family so well-to-do that anything she did became instantly acceptable. Even marrying one of the McKale boys. Lucky and Sue Cox ran away and got married right out of high school.

The surprises had come years later, when Lucky ended up without the pro career everyone was counting on and instead became a civil servant, just like any ordinary federal postal employee earning his government paycheck. And Sue Cox had discovered for herself—and revealed to all—that she wasn't, after all, a bold and beautiful party girl simply sowing the wild oats to which she felt entitled, and with which she entertained and thrilled everyone around her. She was, instead, a relentless and chronic drunk—referred to by those who loved her most as an alcoholic who suffered an insufferable disease. Booze had kept Sue Cox from holding a job, or having any babies, or—after three DUIs—driving a car in Baxter County.

There was still debate about whether or not the accident was really Sue Cox's fault, but there was no debate about the fact that it left the other driver so mangled that her left leg had had to be amputated in order to get her out of the smoldering car. The only reason Sue Cox didn't go to jail was because the woman with the amputated leg had had a higher blood alcohol level than Sue Cox and she'd been the one who'd sped through the stop sign and smashed headfirst into the rear end of Sue Cox's expensive car.

Once things got bloody and people began losing body parts, the thrill was gone. Overnight Sue Cox was not as powerful as she was pitiful. Besides, booze was the old-fashioned way to lose your mind and forget what you needed to forget. Booze dated Sue Cox. Now they had slick new designer drugs to do that for you. Drugs with catchy little names that Bena's kids swore they could buy at school any day of the week. (And on at least two occasions, she suspected they had.)

People said you could buy drugs behind the old Texaco station from boys in sunglasses who lived in the housing project and whose baggy pants were falling off their behinds. Or you could buy them from that lawyer up at the courthouse—the one who had represented Sue Cox when she had her wreck and who was almost as rich as her daddy and had been married to three different women, all from Atlanta. Or, people said, there were two orderlies out at the hospital who could sell you a little bliss or insanity, either one, depending on what you craved.

Sue Cox was sentenced to public service. It's what she did instead of going to jail. She had to speak to the kids at the high school about the evils of alcohol. She'd titled her talk "It's Not Cool to Be a Fool." They put an article in the newspaper with a picture of Sue Cox like she was a preacher standing behind a pulpit. But most people knew better. Even so, she spoke all around Baxter County, at church youth groups, Girl Scout meetings, the Kiwanis Club, Needle Arts, the Garden Club, and the Ladies League. She liked to end her talk with a prayer she'd copied out of a book. She was so sincere, people said, that she couldn't help but break your heart.

Now, years later, Sue Cox's life was a series of trips to rehab, where she'd dry out and explore the depths of her heart and history in search of some new reason why, or some further evidence of an indestructible soul from which she could draw strength in the future. After which she'd be sent home to slowly forget all that she'd unearthed. In a matter of months, as a matter of course, she'd begin to self-medicate again—one beer at a ball game, one sip of champagne at a wedding, one shot of vodka to get her going in the morning. It was all a matter of public record.

It was generally agreed that life had been cruel to Lucky and Sue Cox—first by blessing them so singularly, making them the envy of all. And then by allowing those same blessings to sour on them and become curses. Now they were reduced to living lessons for the young people in the county. Their lives provided perfect examples of why it's better to study than to be popular. Nobody was envious anymore. But nobody ever really thought badly of either Lucky or Sue Cox either. It was like they were living proof that life might actually be fair after all.

So WHEN THE DOORBELL rang late one afternoon, too late for a mail delivery, Bena was not expecting to see Lucky McKale standing there, smiling. "Hey," he said. "Got something here for Joe. A graduation present, I guess. Saw his picture in the paper. Knew he was a heck of a baseball player—I follow legion ball. But didn't know you had you a honor student. Saw where he got a real good scholarship to the university. Guess you're mighty proud of him?"

Bena looked first at Lucky's face, then at the large box at his feet.

"Pretty heavy, so I thought I'd drop it by on my run home," he said. "Nobody around here midday to sign for it."

"That's real thoughtful." Even though it was a long time ago, Bena looked at Lucky for some sign that he remembered why he'd stopped extending courtesies to the Eckerd household in the first place. But he just smiled at her.

"Come in." She held the door open while Lucky hoisted the box and carried it over the threshold.

"A computer, huh?" He read the lettering on the box.

"Joe's been saving for it," Bena said.

"Nice. It's the way of the future—computers."

"Right," Bena said.

"You want me to put this in Joe's room? It's heavy."

"Joe can get it. He'll be home soon."

"Okay, then. I got my clipboard out in the van. Need to get you to sign the paperwork. I'll be right back."

Bena watched him go down the walk to his van. She felt a wash of regret. When Lucky came back with his clipboard Bena signed the papers. "Can you stay and have a cup of coffee?" she asked. "It's the least I can offer you for your trouble?"

Lucky smiled. "You got any ice tea? I'm not much of a coffee drinker. Tears my stomach up."

"Sure," Bena said.

He followed her to the kitchen, where she poured them each a glass of tea. He sat down in the den in a chair across from where she sat. "It's already getting hot," he said. "Mosquitoes be hatching next thing you know."

Bena ran her finger around the lip of her tea glass. "When you were so good to me after Bobby died, I behaved awful. I'm real sorry."

"It was a long time ago. You were going through a bad time."

"That's no excuse."

"No, but it's a good explanation. Otherwise I might just have to think you were a pure-T bitch." Lucky grinned.

Bena laughed. "I guess I was."

"No," Lucky said, "I knew Bobby pretty good, remember? He wasn't the kind of man to love a bitchy woman. And it was clear he loved you to death."

"Not everybody would say it was so clear." Bena smiled.

"What, because of that woman? Lorraine? Shoot," he said. "I hope you got better sense than to go reading a bunch of stuff into that. Men do stupid things sometimes. I'm a man, so I know."

"It's all in the past now." Bena wanted to drop the subject before one of the children wandered in. Although the children weren't really children anymore. Sissy had graduated two years ago and moved into a paper-walled apartment with two girlfriends. She talked non-stop about going down to Miami and getting a job on a cruise ship. Maybe going to Europe or somewhere.

Sissy had a boyfriend that Bena hated. Barrett. Sissy could do so much better than Barrett. Bena thought he treated Sissy like a slave, but no amount of saying so could bring Sissy to her senses, so Bena felt she had no choice but to turn the child over to God—something she didn't feel as good about doing as she once might have. She'd turned Bobby over to God too, and look what had happened. But God was supposed to see all, wasn't He? And Bena went weeks sometimes and didn't see Sissy the first time. Consequently Bena never discouraged Sissy from dreaming her way to Miami or Europe or any place that was far away from Barrett. Bena worried that Sissy losing her daddy like she did, when she did, had made her almost desperate to have a man back in her life—even a sorry-dog boy-man like Barrett. It could worry Bena to death if she let it.

Now Joe would be the second to graduate. When he left for college this summer she'd be down to just three children in the house —Leslie, Ellie, and Eddie.

"Tell me this," Bena said. "I'm asking respectfully—okay? How is Sue Cox doing? I heard she's been in the hospital."

"She's over in Atlanta. Checked herself into Hastings Rehab again." He shook his glass a little so the ice rattled. "It's her fourth time over there."

"I'm sorry," Bena said.

"Sometimes she needs more help than I can give her. Usually does her good to get away and get herself back on a good track. It's hard —I won't lie to you. Alcoholism is a bastard of a disease, Bena."

"Well, she's lucky to have you."

"Not really." He smiled. "If anybody's lucky, I guess it's me." He handed Bena his ice-tea glass. "Thanks for the drink. I better get the van back to the lot before they start to wonder what happened to me."

THREE DAYS LATER Bena called Lucky on her lunch break from school. She looked up his number in the phone book and left a message on his home machine. "Hey," she said. "This is Bena. I just want to thank you again for going to so much trouble to bring Joe his computer. Oh, and also, I hope Sue Cox is doing well too, you know, over at Hastings. You take care now." Bena hung up and wondered if she'd maybe lost her mind. But she felt alive for a moment there, so she didn't let herself regret one small gesture. A kindness at that.

The following week Lucky rang Bena's door late in the afternoon. Eddie answered the door and yelled, "Mama, the mailman wants you."

There was Lucky with a fistful of mail. "Something else for Joe?" she asked.

"No. But I got a special letter for you." He handed her the stack of letters, which she began shuffling through, looking for the special one he was talking about.

"Something smells good," he said.

Bena looked at him. "Chicken casserole. It used to be Bobby's favorite."

"Is that right?"

"You don't want to stay for supper, do you? We can put on another plate."

"No. I've got the van out here—government property. But thanks anyway."

He took a couple of steps, backing up. "So I'll be seeing you. If I've handed you any junk mail or anything you just throw it in the trash, okay?"

Bena closed the door and walked back toward the kitchen. Eddie yelled from his room, "What did that guy want, Mama?"

"Nothing," Bena said.

"Why was he here then?"

"He's the mailman," she said. Then she saw it. The small white envelope with her name, *Bena,* scrawled across it hurriedly. No address, no stamp. Her heart pounded foolishly, the way it did when she saw a police car come up behind her with its lights and sirens going—as if she were about to be arrested. Or as if it were the same policeman who'd brought her *the news* was tracking her down again just to be absolutely sure she'd gotten the full impact of the message: *Bobby is gone.*

She put the letter in the pocket of her jeans and finished setting the table for supper. Joe had baseball practice as usual. Leslie said she was staying late to decorate for senior day, but Bena wasn't sure she believed her. Leslie had a sneaky streak—she and Sissy both. Supper would just be Eddie and Ellie and Bena. She put out place mats and mismatched cloth napkins just for the heck of it, so the table would look nice. Eddie wouldn't notice, but Ellie would. "Mama," she'd say, "what's the special occasion?"

"No occasion," Bena would answer.

AFTER DINNER BENA cleaned the kitchen, although it really didn't look much better when it was clean than it did when it was a mess, but the cleaning up afterward was a ritual that she depended on to prove to herself that she was a normal woman and this was a normal house. Then Bena went back to her bedroom and ran a hot bath. She put shampoo in the water to make suds, something she hadn't done in a long time. She locked the door and sank into the bathtub slowly and read the letter.

Dear Bena:

It sure was nice to come home from work and hear your voice on my machine. Thanks for the nice message. I didn't tell you this, but part of Sue Cox's treatment is that her family (me) is not allowed to be in contact with her for six weeks. No phone calls, nothing. So it gets lonely around here. Sometimes I get tired of watching TV and start to wish I had somebody to talk to—like you. This might be way out of line and if so you just tell me so, but I was wondering if you might consider coming over to my place one night for supper. I'm a decent cook. I could barbecue some ribs. Make up a salad. Get a pint of ice cream for dessert. We could just talk. That's all. I believe we have some things in common—just the way our lives have not turned out exactly right —excuse me for saying that about your life in case you feel differently—but I think you know what I mean. I also know you have no reason in the world to think very well of men after what happened with Bobby and Lorraine Rayfield—but I swear to God I'm just looking for a friend—and the fact that you are good looking has nothing to do with it—ha, ha. Let me know what you think about this idea.

Sincerely,
Lucky

P.S. The reason I say my house is because that way you don't have to upset your kids or explain to them who I am. Also, I live out from town on six acres where nobody will have to see you come or go. You know how folks talk in this county. I guess we both have been the subject of enough talk already. I hope you can come.

Bena waited three days before answering even though she'd known instantly what her answer would be. The three-day waiting period was a by-product of being a woman of her era and inclination. Not an unspoken rule exactly—more like instinct. It wouldn't hurt for Lucky to spend a few days wondering if he'd made a terrible mistake or done something brave for which he'd be richly rewarded. The same things Bena was wondering. It wouldn't hurt for Lucky to have Bena on his mind for a few days, sort of building up to the moment when the answer would come. She bet he'd already decided what he would do in case he got a *yes* and what he would do in case he got a *no*. None of this was something she consciously thought about. It was all just sort of coded in her blood—which hadn't stirred much in several years.

SHE CALLED LUCKY while she knew he was out on his route. This seemed better because she was a little nervous. This way she could erase her message if it sounded stupid and redo it until it came out close to right. "Hey, Lucky," she said. "This is Bena. Supper at your house sounds nice. I'm free Friday night if that works. Let me know."

Lucky didn't share Bena's feelings about the answering machine. He called her back less than an hour later at school and had the secretary get her out of class, which scared her half to death. All she could think was that Eddie'd gotten hurt at his end-of-school picnic, which was this very day—probably doing something foolish to impress girls, whom he was beginning to discover in an all-encompassing way. Bena pictured him in a cast or with his eye poked out. Or maybe Ellie'd gotten suddenly sick and been rushed to the hospital. Or Leslie'd been in a motorcycle wreck—lots of reckless boys had motorcycles at the high school and Leslie'd been known to take a forbidden ride with a forbidden boy. She was easily dazzled by shiny chrome and a racing motor. Or maybe Joe'd gotten bad news from the university and now his scholarship was seriously compromised. Or Sissy'd gone completely crazy and married Barrett and was calling her to say so. Lord, she hoped to heaven that wasn't it. What if Barrett had gotten her pregnant?

"Hey, there," Lucky said.

"Heavens," Bena said. "I thought you were one of my kids."

"Got your message. Friday is great. I'll write out the directions and put them in your mailbox this afternoon. You like chicken, don't you? Forget the ribs. I'll barbecue some chicken. How does that sound?"

"Good," Bena said.

"Thanks for calling back, Bena. I wasn't sure you would."

She hung up and saw the secretary staring at her. "Everything okay, Bena?"

"I hope so," she said.

WHEN FRIDAY NIGHT came Leslie spent the night out. Ellie had her friend Liz over for the weekend because Liz's parents were out of town. Bena was the one mother other parents could usually count on not to be going anyplace or doing anything. She was both the working mom *and* the stay-at-home mom. "Liz is always welcome," she'd said for the thousandth time.

Eddie was catching a ride out to the mall, after which he'd no doubt come home and call girls on the phone. He usually locked himself in the laundry room to do it. Girls had recently become interesting to Eddie. Not his sisters and their friends, of course. Other girls. Real ones. He'd begun to refer to all females outside his family as *normal* females. He seemed relieved to discover that there were some.

Bena told her kids she was meeting a friend for supper, knowing that they'd conjure up visions of Shoney's Slim Jims and strawberry pie—or the Golden Corral salad bar with Bena's friend Helen, who taught third grade and was always clipping coupons. Or maybe Leeanne Sims, whose husband had divorced her six months ago and who was constantly looking for a friend to take to supper in exchange for some simple listening—again—to the whole sordid story of the tragic betrayal. Oddly enough, divorce was interesting to Bena, so she never minded listening.

More than once she'd wondered what would have happened to her marriage if Bobby hadn't been killed. Would he eventually have left her for Lorraine Rayfield? Or would he have dumped Lorraine and taken up with some other unlikely woman—maybe this one just twenty-two, maybe a redhead this time? Would it be better if rather than just one woman that he'd really loved there'd been lots of women, all of them just notches on his proverbial belt? What then? Would she be the one calling friends to go to supper so that she could explain to them again and again what had actually happened and how totally surprised she'd been and how Bobby had turned from being such a good and decent man to becoming not just the worst kind of traitor, but also her lifelong enemy—who was, from this moment forward, devoting himself to assuring her misery in every way possible: fighting her for the children, the house, the car, the bank accounts, the retirement fund, the vacation time-share every July. Bena had heard of everything terrible.

Maybe something terrible like that might have happened to her if Bobby'd had more time to make mistakes, although Bena couldn't really imagine it. Not Bobby. Bobby really had been a good and decent man—mostly. But she'd stopped trying to convince her friends of that because whenever Bena tried to praise Bobby they just looked at her like she was—you know—either a liar or a fool.

The other scenario Bena liked to toy with was this: What if she'd been the one? What if she'd gotten tired of her life with Bobby? What if she'd met a more interesting man who made her feel like a more interesting woman? What if she'd wanted out? What then? Would she ever have left Bobby or would she simply have done what her mother did and Bobby's mother too. Stay. Stay because people expect you to and it's easier and it holds the family together and the finances are better that way and it happens to almost everybody anyway if they stay married long enough, this inertia, this mild death that sets in prior to the literal ones, sort of numbs you up in advance, foretelling the end times.

Staying was something that Bena'd observed not just in her mother and her mother-in-law but also her friends. Hadn't she heard everything imaginable during all these years of fifteen-minute breaks in the teachers' lounge at school, where women took time out from educating the children to educate one another? Overall, men had never fared very well in the teachers' lounge—neither the two who occasionally appeared in person to get a Coke from the machine nor the dozens who appeared through detailed personal anecdote followed by group analysis of the detailed personal anecdote.

Bobby's death was like if you'd spent nearly twenty years reading a book and were only halfway through when the book got lost or taken away from you. For the rest of your life, all you could do was guess the end. Bena would have to wonder forever how things might have turned out. She was less sure than ever that she believed in happy endings.

Bobby'd been dead more than five years and yet Bena felt a lot luckier in love than many women whose husbands were alive and well—and to whom they still went home night after night. She bet some of her friends wished they could lose the book they were reading, a horror story that got worse with every page—or more and more boring. Sometimes the loneliness of married women caused Bena's own loneliness to pale in comparison. Really. That's what she told herself.

BENA TURNED OFF the highway and onto the gravel road that would take her to Lucky's house. She was clutching the directions so tight her hand was sweating. She drove slowly, just to prove to anyone who might wonder that she wasn't unduly anxious. It was peaceful out here. Green pastureland and blue woods and crickets singing country music at a deafening volume. This was a way of living a life Bena knew nothing about. Seclusion and privacy weren't even concepts when you had five children. She could see lights ahead, and when she went around a last curve she came upon the house. She thought for a minute that it had to be the wrong house. The thing that changed her mind was that it was the *only* house. It seemed too nice a place for Lucky McKale to live. Didn't Bobby used to say that Lucky was the salt of the earth? If he really was the salt of the earth, wouldn't he live in a double-wide or one of those build-it-yourself-over-a-lifetime projects so many people in Baxter County lived in? Did Bena think that just because Sue Cox was off at a detox it meant she didn't have a nice home? Sue Cox's house looked like a place you'd try to escape to—not from. It didn't seem right that Sue Cox's house was much nicer than Bena's. And Bena had been cold sober every minute of her life.

Bena eased ahead and parked her car behind Lucky's truck. She wasn't nervous until she saw Lucky sitting on the porch, watching her.

"Hey, lady," he smiled. "Any trouble finding the place?"

"You give good directions." Bena got out of the car and glanced around. "It's nice out here."

"As near to heaven as I'm likely to get," Lucky said.

Bena stood awkwardly beside her car thinking maybe she shouldn't have come.

"Come on in," Lucky said. "I'll introduce you to Tom."

"Tom?"

"Man's best friend."

"Why do I feel like I'm walking into a *Lassie* rerun?"

"God, I used to love that show when I was a kid." Lucky was wearing an ironed shirt and Bena wondered if he'd ironed it himself. "Trouble was it came on Sunday nights right in the middle of Training Union, remember? Boy, that used to kill me. My mama making me miss *Lassie* to go to Training Union over at the Baptist church. I used to give her a fit."

"Did it take?" Bena asked. "Training Union?"

"Now, what do you think?"

"I think your mama probably knew best."

"Lord knows my mama tried. But she didn't have all that much to work with."

By the time she made her way to the porch Bena could smell the barbecue. Lucky had put on some music too, George Jones, she thought. Or maybe it was B. J. Thomas. One of those sad, moody types where the only luck is bad luck. Tom was waiting just inside the screen door to lick her. He looked like a golden retriever but Lucky said no, he was a mutt. "The best mutt in the world," he said. "But still a mutt." He reached down to pat Tom's head. "You might say me and Tom are both a couple of mutts. Ain't that right, Tom?"

"Excuse me for asking," Bena said, "but shouldn't the dog be named Lucky and the man be named Tom? You two ever think of changing names?"

"Shoot, between us me and Tom have thought of everything you can imagine. Like once we had this plan where I was going to disguise myself as a woman and Tom was going to disguise himself as a cat and we were going to take off and go cross-country incognito. You ever want to be just the exact opposite of what you are? Probably not. Not in your case. But me and Tom, we get in moods like that."

"Not a pretty thought."

"As for me and Tom changing names, it'd never work. You can't have a dog going around named Lucky. Wouldn't want to put a curse like that on a good dog."

"And can't have a complicated man going around with a simple name like Tom. You definitely need a name with more than three letters."

"See, Tom," Lucky said, "I told you she was smart."

INSIDE, THE HOUSE was really striking, like something you'd see in Atlanta, nice upholstery and antiques. "Looks like something out of *Southern Living,*" Bena said.

"Yeah, Sue Cox rather read that fool magazine than the Holy Bible."

"You collect antiques?" Bena asked.

"Most of the good stuff was in her family," he said. "When her daddy died he pretty much left everything to Sue Cox since she's an only child. You know her old man came from nothing, but he was pretty well fixed in the end, after he sold his dealership. So now I guess you could say Sue Cox is pretty well fixed."

"It sure looks like it," Bena said.

"And she's nice enough to let me and Tom live here with her as long as we don't mess up too bad. Ain't that right, boy?"

Lucky went to the refrigerator and got two beers, poured one in a glass for Bena, and handed it to her wrapped with a paper napkin. "Come on. I'll show you around."

The house was small, but interesting. There was a master bedroom with a garden bath where you could walk right out of the shower through some French doors and onto a little patio with lounge chairs and white cushions and plants everywhere. "Sue Cox calls this her meditation garden," Lucky said. "But she don't really meditate. She just sits out here naked when she suntans—calls it meditating."

There was one guest bedroom but the bathroom wasn't as elaborate and didn't provide a place for meditation or nude sunbathing, either one. Otherwise there was the main room with high ceilings, and two rock fireplaces and linen-and-down sofas, which Bena was afraid to sit on for fear they'd wrinkle. A perfect kitchen opened up to the main room. The kind of kitchen where the dish towels looked brand-new, didn't have tomato-sauce stains or burn spots everywhere. It was kitchen enough to make you think that you might actually want to cook something.

Throughout the house were hardwood floors and Oriental rugs that looked old and real. Bena didn't know much about rugs. Her house was carpeted and, now that she thought about it, it badly needed recarpeting. She'd chosen the brown-and-rust tweedy look years ago, not because she liked it but because it wouldn't show dirt.

When the kids had been little that had been one of the themes of her life. Dirt.

Maybe in a few more years, when Eddie graduated and moved out, she'd redo her house so that it could look this way—clean and beautiful, like a place where well-behaved, civilized people lived. Maybe she'd carpet the whole thing in a white wall-to-wall. Maybe she'd throw out the old furniture and get new. Shoot, maybe she would just sell her stupid house and start all over.

Lucky led her through a tiny den with a huge TV built into the wall and a sectional sofa. "This is my game-watching room."

"Auburn or Alabama?"

"Now, what the hell kind of question is that?"

"Stupid question," Bena laughed. "I forgot you are a Baxter County living legend—to this day. War Eagle!"

"Sue Cox built this room so she could put me in here and lock the door during football season. She says, *Only thing worse than Auburn losing is Auburn winning.*"

"It's real nice," Bena said. "Everything is real nice."

"The nice part is Sue Cox's doing. But the barbecue chicken, that's my doing. Come on and I'll fix us some plates and we'll eat out on the porch."

Bena watched Lucky serve the plates with chicken, tossed salad, and squares of white cornbread. "You're in for a treat," he said. "This is my secret recipe right here." He held a plate under his nose, closed his eyes as if in prayer, then shook his head and looked at Bena. "A work of art," he said. "Damn if I'm not an arteeest! Grab us two more beers out of the fridge and follow me."

HE HADN'T EXAGGERATED his cooking skills. Or maybe Bena just couldn't remember when a man had ever cooked her a nice dinner. Bobby hadn't been a cook, and she didn't count the time Joe made her that fish-stick dinner to get his Boy Scout badge or Eddie's willingness to split a can of SpaghettiOs. From the back porch you could look out over a blue-green slope and see the hint of lights far off below you. Bena took a lot of comfort in the sight, the lights and their distance.

"I'm going to light us some candles," Lucky said, "but don't be thinking I'm trying to get romantic on you or anything. It's just the damn mosquitoes. Can't put on the porch light cause it will draw them. So I have to light these things. These are special candles, full of poison."

"Very appetizing." Bena smiled.

"Looks pretty though, don't it?"

The chicken was burned crisp and black on the edges, just exactly right. And the secret recipe had two not so secret ingredients, honey and Tabasco sauce. It was past delicious. Clearly Lucky was a man who knew his barbecue. They ate slowly, pausing to lick their fingers and forcing Lucky back to the kitchen for a second fistful of napkins. Tom lay under the table hoping they'd drop something. "It was nice of you to come tonight, Bena," Lucky said.

"How could a woman in her right mind turn down an evening like this." She smiled. "A nice man, a nice dog, and a nice chicken."

"Can't hardly beat it." Lucky grinned. "You know, Bena, I always liked you."

"You don't even know me," she said. "Not really."

"No, but I knew I'd like you if I got a chance to know you. When all that shit happened, you know, Bobby and Lorraine—I just felt awful. You didn't deserve to go through all that. Me and Bobby were friends a lot of years, but let me tell you what, Lorraine—she was a sweet girl, all right, but she didn't hold a candle to you. Not that I mean to be speaking ill of the dead or anything."

"The way you talk it sounds like you knew her—Lorraine?"

Lucky seemed to consider her question, then said, "You ready for some ice cream? I got Cherry Garcia."

"Did you?" she asked.

"Did I what?"

"Know Lorraine?"

Lucky ran his hand through his hair, which had curled in the humidity, giving him an uncorked look. "Shit. Do you really want to go down this road, Bena? I didn't mean to start in on this. That's for damn sure."

"So you did know Lorraine?"

"I met her."

"Where?"

"Shit, Bena. What difference does it make?"

"Listen to me, Lucky," Bena put her fork down harder than she meant to. It clanged against the plate. "For years I never asked questions because I didn't want to know and I didn't know anybody to ask. But now I do want to know—and I'm asking you." She took a drink from her Bud Light. She didn't really even drink beer.

"The truth has a way of backfiring on folks, Bena. But if you want the truth I'll try to tell it—what I know of it. But you ain't gonna like it. I can tell you that up front. Just promise me one thing. Promise me you ain't gonna get the messenger here mixed up with the message. Okay?"

"I'm listening," Bena said.

"I met Lorraine at your house."

"My house?" Bena stared at him a minute, letting the words sink in, then took another drink of beer. "Go on."

"The first time was when I took a package up to the house. Remember when y'all ordered all those bulbs from Connecticut?"

"They were from Holland."

"Holland via Connecticut. Well, I brought them up to the house just about the time Bobby walked out with this woman—Lorraine. It seemed harmless at the time. I didn't think much of it. He introduced me—you know how he used to do, *This is Lucky who never made it to the pros*— but damn he used to be good. So Lorraine said hello and Bobby signed for the bulbs and I went about my business."

"What else?"

"She drove a red Honda Civic. Later I used to see it parked up at your house. Hard to see your house from the road in the summer, but in the winter, well I could see she was there pretty often. Or you know, once in a while."

"He brought her to our house?"

"I guess he figured you and the kids were gone to school all day. Maybe he thought it was the safest place. Better than parading her all over town, wasn't it?"

"And you never thought of mentioning any of this to me?"

"Like you said, I didn't really know you, Bena."

"Who else knew?"

"I couldn't tell you. Maybe nobody." Lucky pushed his plate aside and picked up a spoon and started tapping it against his beer bottle. "Damn, Bena, I'm a mailman. If you're a mailman you know the lives of everybody on your route. You see the bills that come and go, letters from who, what, and where. You ride by folks' houses six days a week, watch them coming and going, notice if they have company, if they close the blinds certain times. You get their kids' names memorized, carry treats for their dogs. A mailman is like being a policeman or a psychiatrist. You start to know a family's story. I mean it's like doing involuntary surveillance or something. I'm just doing my job. But I don't do it with my eyes closed."

"Obviously."

"Shit, you're not mad are you? You wanted me to tell you what I know."

"I'm not mad," she said. "But I am a fool."

Lucky squeezed her hand. "See, I told you we had a lot in common—me and you." He grinned. "Although, if you ask me, I think Bobby was the real fool."

"What was I doing all those years—married to a man I didn't even know?"

"Hell if I know." He smiled. "But I'm gonna get us some ice cream. An occasion like this calls for some Cherry Garcia, don't you think?"

WHEN BENA GOT HOME neither of her children were even slightly suspicious. They asked no questions. As she expected, Eddie was sprawled out on the dirty towels in the laundry room whispering into the phone. For one creepy second the sight of him made her think of Bobby—that instinctive sneakiness that Eddie must have gotten from his daddy. She imagined all the whispering phone calls Bobby probably made. Why had nothing ever seemed out of the ordinary? Maybe because it *was* so ordinary—what she and Bobby had together. Maybe that was why he was on the phone to Lorraine in the first place—because he was searching for something that was not so damned ordinary.

SCHOOL WAS OUT for the summer. When Joe left for summer school at the university he and Bena both cried like babies. She could see how happy he was to be moving into the future—which he had reason enough to believe would be bright. Of all Bena's children Joe was the one most hell-bent on making something of himself. He'd do it too. He was like his daddy that way.

"Promise me you'll call home, honey. On Sundays, when the rates are low."

"Yes, ma'am," he said.

Bena touched his hair as if it was something she'd never done before—but had always wanted to. "I don't know what I'm going to do without you."

"I'm going to make you proud, Mama. I swear I am."

"I'm real proud of you already. I always have been."

He drove off in a piece-of-crap pickup truck he'd bought from a classified ad. "Don't matter what it looks like—long as it runs," he'd told her. He waved good-bye trying not to let Bena see how bad he was crying—which he hadn't done much since his daddy's funeral. When the old sadness got all mixed up with the new happiness waiting for him up in Tuscaloosa, this was the way it came out.

Bena loved this boy so much it scared her. She was struck by the thought that maybe she hadn't told him so often enough. That she needed one more chance to make him understand that he was precious to her. You can't just assume that men, especially young men, know things like that, can you? Don't they need you to make the point again and again? Her beautiful boy going off into the world to turn himself into a man. She wouldn't be there to watch it happen. She'd have to put it all together from the clues that came her way in the Sunday phone calls. Any ways she'd failed him she'd have to live with now. It was too late to explain anything more—not unless someday he decided to ask her some particular question about things. But Bena thought probably he'd try to put together his own answers and not bother her to do it for him.

Joe laid on the horn all the way down the drive and out to the highway. It sounded like part scream, part Glory-hallelujah-praise-the-Lord.

THE THREE OTHER KIDS had part-time summer jobs. Leslie was baby-sitting for the young doctor Sissy had worked for part-time. He and his wife had three children and dreaded summer for the same reason Bena loved it—because school was out. They made it worth Leslie's while to give up her summer. Leslie was saving for college because her chances at a scholarship were nowhere near as good as Joe's had been. Joe had mastered the concept of studying, whereas Leslie had mastered praying for miracles. Overall it had served her pretty well, except in the scholastic arena.

Ellie had gotten a job lifeguarding at the country club swimming pool and she'd gotten Eddie a job working there at the concession stand. "You don't have to be a member of the country club to work there, Mama," Eddie said when he got hired, like it was some of the best news he'd ever heard. Lots of boys caddied at the country club, but their daddies belonged, so that kept Eddie from even trying to do it. He figured a father and a membership were probably required, and he lacked both. But the concession stand, shoot, that was a long shot better because it was air-conditioned for one thing and because girls paraded back and forth all day in their bathing suits to get soft cones and cheese fries, which he'd be preparing with his own two hands. Eddie was born for this job.

What this meant was that Bena, for the first time, had the summer to herself. The first week all she did was sleep. The second week she grew restless and decided she needed a project. She needed to change something. It's something that happens to a woman when some personal change is on the brink of revealing itself, and to hurry it up you go to work on your house—painting a room or reupholstering a chair. A woman's house is a stand-in for her body, it's interior a stand-in for her interior. Women usually know this about each other. But Bena actually knew it about herself too. Ever since she'd had supper at Lucky's she'd felt unsettled. She told herself it was because Sue Cox's house was so nice and hers was so—not.

Women without children don't really understand houses. That's what Bena thought. You have to have been a house to really understand a house. And she'd been that—had housed all five of her children, wrapped them in her skin and cradled them in the curve of her bone. They swam in her blood, read her mind (which she'd never intended), and bruised her heart—sometimes kicking it, punching it with a sudden fist or banging their heads against it. A real house bears scars, Bena told herself. Where were Sue Cox's pencil marks on the woodwork, measuring her children as they grew? Bena thought she'd like to see Sue Cox's house after five kids and a dog lived there for almost twenty years. That's what she'd like to see.

The idea came to her like a name she'd forgotten, even though she could see the face before her. It was her own face all these years later. *Verbena Martin Eckerd,* who'd given her life away—and had now decided that maybe she wanted it back. So she'd clean out the attic and all the closets in the house and give everything useless to somebody who would know what to do with useless stuff.

Sue Cox, off at the drug rehab (which to Bena's way of thinking was just like an expensive summer camp for adults), unavailable for intrusive calls or visits from friends or family, busy sorting out once more the sordid details of her perfectly furnished and accessorized life, had somehow inspired Bena to do some sorting out of her own. She wanted closets like the ones Sue Cox had. Neatly organized with just stuff you really use in them. No worn-out, torn-up stuff either. No more letting Ellie fold the linens and shove them into the hall closet in little rolled heaps. No more never finding a top sheet that matched a bottom sheet. From now on any single item that should be part of a set would have to go. Maybe she'd drive over to the West Point Pepperill mill outlet and buy some new bedsheets and dish-towels and whathaveyou and she'd start to live differently, to cook differently, to sleep differently. It would be a start. It's amazing, she thought, what you can learn from the good example of a bad alco-holic. No more of this hanging on to old stuff in case you might ever need it—someday—in the future. Whose idea was that anyway?

Bena would start with Bobby's stuff, most of which had made its way to the attic over time. She must have been crazy to think that someday Joe and Eddie would grow into Bobby's old clothes—and actually want them. His wide ties? His black nylon knee-high socks coupled and knotted? His threadbare white short-sleeved cotton shirts with the subtle stripes? His lightly mildewed wing-tip shoes?

Bena spent the morning in the attic, which had the therapeutic ef-fects of a sauna. Box after box labeled *Bobby* she carried down the spring ladder and stacked in the hall. It must have been 120 degrees in the attic, the air so hot it was like climbing in and out of hell all morning. The boxes were heavy, but Bena felt strong and refused to give up on any box, refused to set it aside and wait until one of the boys could carry it down for her. That had been one of the big mis-takes in her life, setting things aside—for later.

Her fury gave her energy, and she'd get all of Bobby's stuff out of the attic this day or die trying. If worse came to worst she'd just position the too heavy boxes and push them out of the attic, letting them tumble and thud their way to the floor. So what if something broke? So what if the sides split and the contents spilled?

When the doorbell rang her drenched hair was pinned on her head with a couple of Bobby's old tie clips. She was barefoot, her blouse was soaked, and her shorts stuck to her like they were pasted. She hadn't stopped all morning—into the hellish attic heat, find a *Bobby* box, push, pull, or shove it down the ladder, and get another one, another one, another one. It gave her that good feeling she imagined a soldier must feel when he went to combat with strength of conviction and courage. Like when you can do anything because you're not afraid to die.

She opened the door. There was Lucky. "Looks like I came at a bad time."

"I don't know why you say that?" Bena wiped her face with her shirttail.

"Why didn't you say the back forty needed plowed? I'd have done it for you."

"Very funny."

"You haven't answered any of my notes."

"I've been really busy," Bena said.

"I can see that."

"You want to come in?" She swung the door wide open.

"Is that an invitation?"

"I'll pour us some tea? Come on."

"I'm just relieved to know you're not dead, woman." Lucky followed Bena to the kitchen. "Didn't you get my note that said *Are you dead or alive? Check one.*"

"Maybe I didn't know the answer."

"Bullshit."

"Here." Bena handed him a glass. She went to the refrigerator and got a fistful of ice and dumped it into their glasses. She got the pitcher of tea and poured his glass so full it overflowed and splashed on the floor. "I know," Bena said. "That's not the way Sue Cox does it, is it?"

"Sue Cox?" Lucky looked around like maybe he thought Sue Cox was going to make a sudden appearance. "What the hell? What you got in that ice tea? LSD?"

"Excuse me, but I'm not the one who's into substance abuse, am I?"

Lucky put his tea glass down on the counter and took Bena's glass out of her hand too. "Look at me," he said. "What the hell is going on?"

"Nothing."

"Oh, that's good. That's priceless. You acting mad as a hornet, looking like you just built a barn with your bare hands, but trying to tell me nothing is wrong. Damn if I'm buying it."

Bena pulled away from him. "I don't care if you believe me or not. I don't have to explain anything to you anyway."

"No," Lucky said, "but I got the feeling you want to. So I tell you what—I'm going to get out of here and deliver the mail come rain or come shine because Joe Public, he's depending on me. I'll leave you here to enjoy your misery. But come eight o'clock tonight I will be expecting you out at my place. A little dinner and a lot of conversation. And you better show up too. Because if you don't I'm going to come looking for you, kids or no kids. I'm not sure what's got you upset, but you are dealing with a guy who can't be scared off by an upset woman. Tell you the truth, a woman scares me most when she's not upset. That's when I start to worry. So I'll see you tonight." Lucky smiled at Bena. "Don't you be late."

Bena just stared at him.

Before he closed the door he said, "Be sure you clean up a little too. I don't want you scaring Tom." He winked at her and walked out the door.

. . .

By LATE AFTERNOON Bena had every scrap of anything that had belonged to Bobby out of the attic and strewn in the hall—his fishing stuff (Joe and Eddie didn't fish), the boxed contents of his desk that they'd brought over from his office and she'd never bothered to look through. (Were there pictures of Lorraine in there—or notes she'd written him or hotel receipts or birthday cards she'd signed with love?) All evidence or lack of it that Bena might ever need was going out with the rest of the garbage.

There was his footlocker full of college memorabilia and letters from his mother, old scrapbooks and photo albums that had belonged to his family—some pre-America photos dating all the way back to Scotland, where the Eckerd men looked satisfied but most of the women looked worried sick. Every pair of shoes he'd ever had. All the little doodad Father's Day and birthday gifts the kids had made or selected for him. A couple of nice wool sweaters she'd given him that he never wore. His briefcase. His file cabinet full of old bills and insurance information. Nicked and scarred golf balls. All the bottles of cologne he'd accumulated and never used. The Bible they read from at his funeral. And dozens of magazines he'd saved, *Field & Steam, Sports Illustrated, Golf Digest, Time, Newsweek, Life*. These might be worth something. Maybe she'd give them to the librarian at school.

She'd let the kids take what they wanted (and insist that one of them take the old family photos because no right-minded Southerner could allow old photos to be thrown away) and the rest she'd call the Salvation Army to come get. That a life could be reduced to a half a truckload of charitable donations seemed wrong to Bena. But that Bobby's clothes and possessions be left to haunt the attic any longer seemed even worse.

The only thing Bena saved from it all was Bobby's Hawaiian shirt. He'd bought it when his company rewarded his high sales with a trip for the two of them to Hawaii. His mother'd kept the children. Bena'd been so proud of Bobby then, had known he was destined for big success. It was the only real vacation the two of them had ever taken together. She remembered Bobby picking out that bright blue shirt with the hula girls dancing under palm trees. She'd said, "Where in the world will you wear that?" But he'd loved that shirt and wore it everywhere. So maybe she'd hold on to it a little longer.

BY A QUARTER to eight Bena was bathed and dressed in clean slacks and a white shirt with the sleeves rolled up. She'd painted her toenails and put on a pair of sandals. "Going to run a few errands and get a bite to eat," she told her kids on her way out the door. Eddie didn't even look up as she left. He didn't notice that she was carrying his daddy's old Hawaiian shirt with her.

When she pulled up at Lucky's he was standing in the driveway, waiting for her, Tom at his side. He walked over and opened her car door. "You came," he said, as if he was surprised, which Bena knew he wasn't.

"Brought you something." She handed him the Hawaiian shirt.

"What's the occasion?" he said, looking a little bewildered.

"It was Bobby's," Bena said. "Thought you might like to have it?"

Lucky looked at Bena, squinting like he was studying something. "Thanks." Then he smiled and said, "You clean up pretty good, lady."

"Where's the food?"

"Before we eat," Lucky said, "I got something I want you to see. Come on, it's around back." Bena followed him around the side of the house and across the backyard grass and into the edge of a grove of pine saplings.

"Where're we going?" Sandspurs stuck to Bena's slacks and pricked her ankles as they made their way through the weeds, after which they wove through a massive patch of blackberry bushes heavy with berries, Lucky holding the branches back as if they were doors he was opening.

"You ought to pick these." Bena detangled the stickers from her shirt, eating a few ripe berries, her fingers black with the juice.

"You know one thing I've wanted all my life?" Lucky said. "Since I was a kid. I wanted a fishing pond close to the house. You know, where I could fish a little bit in the cool of morning before I go off to work and fish a little bit more when I come home in the evening. Fishing is the finest hobby a man can have, Bena. I know. I tried them all—golf, tennis, waterskiing, hunting, biking, even drove a race car once over at Talladega. But fishing, it's not a hobby for the mind and body—it's a hobby for the soul. I mean it. Bobby liked to fish didn't he?"

"Sometimes," she said.

"You ever fish?"

"When I was young. Later on I stayed too busy trying to keep my kids from falling in the water and drowning to enjoy it. I never had the peace of mind to fish."

"That's it," Lucky said, "peace of mind. See here." He pointed to a clearing just below where they stood. "I'm gonna put a pond in right there. All the way from that fence over there to that stand of trees there. That way you can see it from the house. We designed the house to look out over the pond—so all we got to do now is just put the pond in. I'll stock it with bream and bass and maybe even some catfish later on. I'll get me a little rowboat, see, and float out on my pond with a couple of cold beers and half a lifetime of mistakes to contemplate. There's nothing like it, the things you can think of when you're out here floating on this pond with your line in the water, getting a nibble here and there. You throw back what you catch. Just eat the big pounders, you know. It's the catching that's the thing. That's the thrill."

"Not the fish fry? The hush puppies?"

"Shoot, frying up the fish is the anticlimax."

"Water makes me nervous," Bena said. "I'm not a good swimmer."

"Oh, I'll have some life vests for folks like you." He smiled. "We not going to have anybody drowning out here in this pond."

"Water draws snakes, you know," Bena said.

"I ain't got nothing against snakes," Lucky said. "This pond is going to be a place where all God's creatures are welcome. The deer will come to drink and maybe some bobcats and all the raccoons and possums from miles around. It ain't impossible that a black bear might find its way down here. So you know I can't be worried about a couple of snakes taking a swim. What? You scared of snakes?"

"Scared out of my mind," Bena said.

"So is Sue Cox. I don't know what it is with women and snakes? Sue Cox says it's right out of the Bible, you know. Women never will forgive the serpent for what he did to Eve. You believe that?"

"Maybe," Bena said. "Mostly I just think they're creepy—like a bunch of you-know-whats crawling around everywhere. About half of them are poisonous too."

Lucky laughed. "Shoot."

"So when are you putting the pond in for real?" Bena asked.

"I'd love to have done it while Sue Cox is away, you know. Let her come home and have the pond for a surprise. She don't care too much about a pond, but I swear to God if she sees it she'll love it. I'd paddle her around in the boat after supper. Maybe we'd get some ducks or something out here. She could feed the ducks. One of the reasons we bought this land was because it had this perfect spot for a pond. She knows I been dreaming of a pond a long, long time."

"Well, just do it then," Bena said. "You ought to."

Lucky whistled for Tom. "You ever scared to let a dream come true, Bena? I have a good time thinking about my pond—I sit out here sometimes and imagine the whole thing. The dock I'll build. The picnic table I'll put over there under that tree. The salt lick I'll get for on that ridge. In my mind it's as real as you are, standing there."

"Maybe that's all you need then," Bena said. "There're people like that. All they need is something to dream about, but they don't necessarily need to take any action to make the dream come true."

"You talking about yourself?"

"No," she said. "Am I talking about you?"

"Maybe." He smiled. "Come on, let's go to the house and put supper on the table. Mosquitoes about to eat me alive out here."

THEY ATE HAMBURGERS and potato salad out on the porch, surrounded by flickering bug-killing candles and a yard full of fireflies and mosquitoes. At the edge of the yard the crickets wailed. "You're not eating much," Bena said. "Makes a person nervous when the cook won't eat."

"My stomach is acting up." He took a long swig of his beer.

"It's none of my business, but should you be drinking beer, you know, in Sue Cox's house?"

"She's the alcoholic, not me. I'm purely a social drinker—more social than drinker. By the time Sue Cox gets home the only alcohol in this house will be rubbing alcohol, and maybe not that."

"You worried about something?" Bena pushed her plate aside.

"Tell me what's going on with you," he said. "Why the meltdown today?"

Bena pressed the cold glass to her face, paused a minute, then said, "Why didn't you and Sue Cox ever have kids?"

"God knows we tried," he said. "Not that it's any of your business, of course."

"I'm sorry," Bena said. "I just felt like I wanted to know if it was a decision you made—or one, you know, God made."

"I'd say ole God, in his vast wisdom, knew me and Sue Cox would be a sorry pair of parents no matter how much we lied to ourselves about it."

"I think you'd have been a good daddy for a child," Bena said.

"A kid don't need a moody sonofabitch like me for a daddy. Or a mama who's off on a binge or checked into the loony bin every time you turn around. God knows Sue Cox wanted a kid so bad it about tore me up not being able to give her one. I got her Tom here as a substitute, you know. But she wasn't too impressed with Tom. I went and did all those damn tests too. Found out I had some good sperm. You know, quick and agile, not a quitter among them— tough as nails, like their daddy." He smiled. "Trouble was there weren't as many of the little guys as there ought to be. Damn if one test don't lead to another. Doctors, they get hell-bent on finding something wrong with a person, won't stop until they got you convinced you won't live till the end of the week. They get you to thinking you don't even deserve to live that long. I swear to God those assholes had me convinced my time was up."

"So what happened?"

"Went to work building my sperm count. Damn if I didn't get up a regular army of sperm. That almost killed Sue Cox too. My sperm count skyrocketing like that. Because then it meant she was the infertile one. That's how she took it. Like one more reason to hate herself. And me too."

"I'm sorry," Bena said.

"It's not your fault."

"If there's anything you can't blame me for"—Bena tossed her balled-up napkin at him—"it's infertility. Bobby could look at me a certain way and I swear I'd come up pregnant."

"I believe he was doing more than looking, Bena," Lucky said, "but maybe not enough for you to notice."

"Ha-ha," she said.

"So tell me something. Why you want me parading around in one of your dead husband's old shirts? Isn't that a little kinky?"

"Who said anything about parading around? It's a gift. That's all. Think of it as a token of my esteem or something. I don't care what you do with it. Use it to wax your truck if you want to." Bena stabbed her potato salad.

"So let me ask you something else. How you feel about Bobby these days? Still hanging on to the guy's clothes? That means something, don't it?"

"You know what I was doing when you came by today? I was digging all Bobby's stuff out of the attic—getting rid of it. Tomorrow the Salvation Army is supposed to come and haul it away."

Lucky was leaning back in his chair listening, his eyes gone soft in a way that made Bena uneasy. He looked at her so long she reached over and punched him, "Well," she said, "say something."

Lucky smiled. "You not going to give away his tackle box, are you? He had some mighty fine hand-tied lures in there. I wouldn't mind having some of those lures, you know, for when I get my pond put in."

"You can check with the Salvation Army after tomorrow," Bena said. "Maybe they'll make you a deal."

Lucky laughed loud. "You're a mess, Bena," he said. "So tell me this: how does it feel, getting rid of the old man's goods?"

"Like brushing your teeth, you know, after years of forgetting to. Or like adding a room onto the house—a nice empty room. Does that make sense? It just feels, I don't know, sort of exciting."

"Lord, if cleaning out an attic excites you like that, I'm going to have to get you over here and turn you loose. Didn't know you were that easy to please." Lucky grinned and leaned forward in his chair, looking Bena square in the eye. "Seriously, Bena, I'm proud of you, lady. No kidding. You are moving headfirst into the big tomorrow. Next thing you know you'll be out dating—and when the word gets out, all the men in the county will be lined up after you—and then you'll have you a regular steady boyfriend—and then before I know it, you'll be coming over here dragging your second husband."

Bena laughed.

"You like that notion, don't you?" Lucky said.

"I've been out on some dates since Bobby died. I haven't been just sitting in the house like a shut-in or something, no matter what people think. I went out with Lawrence Jackson for one. You know, at the bank."

"Get out of here," Lucky said.

"I did," Bena insisted. "He liked me too."

"Who else you been out with? Give me a rundown."

"Let's see, Johnny Johnson. You know him."

"He's my dentist. At least he was before he got in that trouble."

"Yeah, well, I went out with him for about two months. He was pretty nice. And Mr. Sargeant, up at the high school. Sissy fixed me up with him. My kids went through a spell of trying desperately to find me a new man. It was awful, like being the only client at a live-in dating service. Oh, and Edward Lincoln—dear Lord, that was one man who could not be discouraged."

"Elizabeth's ex-husband?"

"The one and only."

"How many times has he been married?"

"Four, I think."

"But you didn't think twice? Even in baseball you don't get but three strikes."

"He's a handsome man," Bena said. "He knows how to talk too."

"Good God, woman." Lucky held his hand up like a signal. "Stop. You're breaking my heart here. Next thing you know I'll go into a jealous rage."

"I was just doing it, going out, because, you know, I thought I should. People said it was the healthy thing. *You got to get out more, Bena.* All that."

"Shit," Lucky said, "I prefer to think of you as a shut-in, if you don't mind."

It was amazing to Bena, to find herself talking about this. She almost never told anybody about the men she'd dated, not even the teachers at school, who were more than interested in the details of her personal life. Not even her daughters, who waited up for her to come home from dates and begged for details, knowing that Bena wouldn't give them any, ever, and who she imagined were grateful for that. The details were so embarrassing that Bena didn't even like to think about them. She wasn't telling Lucky this part either. She

hadn't told anybody. She convinced herself that she'd just started trying to date too soon—that it was for all the wrong reasons too. She
didn't even know what the reasons were.

It was like she was testing herself, and failing over and over again.
She wanted to see if she could feel something for someone again. To
see if she could get that alive feeling back. But all she could remember was the night Edward Lincoln had taken his shirt off. They'd
been kissing and stuff, she'd liked being held by him, had liked his
slow ways. Bena thought maybe things were going along okay, that
maybe she could feel something for him if he just held her a little
longer, kept up the love talk and touching. She was doing okay
up until he took off his shirt. He'd carefully draped it over a chair so
it wouldn't get wrinkled, and that sort of ruined the moment. It
didn't seem right for him to worry about wrinkling his shirt in what
was supposed to be a passionate moment. What kind of man worried about a thing like that?

But then, oh God, she noticed that—even though he was handsome and knew it and operated with the confidence of a handsome
man—he didn't have any shoulders. Not really. Well, of course he
had shoulders, but they were narrow and small, like her own. Bena
had never seen a man with such delicate shoulders and it made her
want to leap up and run from the room. It wasn't that Bobby'd necessarily been Mr. Body Beautiful, but he was big boned and had had
strong shoulders. She'd taken comfort in that. That he could carry
the world on his shoulders if he had to, or something like that. But
Edward Lincoln—it was clear—could not carry the world on his
shoulders. For one thing, it might wrinkle up his shirt. For another,
he didn't seem physically designed to be a lean-on-me sort of guy.
It wasn't because he wasn't Bobby. It was because Bobby's was the
body she'd known. And here was Edward Lincoln, his body very different. She'd forced herself to try to be tender, to return his tenderness, but it was impossible. There she was, mother of five, not

magazine quality herself. *Feel something,* she ordered herself. This man is kissing you. *Feel something.* But she didn't. Not that night. Not any night afterward.

LUCKY AND BENA carried the dishes inside to the kitchen and cleaned up. Lucky was quiet. It was sort of nice, doing a domestic chore with a silent partner. It was the sort of small thing that Bena really missed. Maybe Lucky did too. "How much longer until you can hear from Sue Cox?"

"Three weeks." He poured Tom's food into his bowl.

"That's good," Bena said.

LATER, WHEN BENA picked up her car keys to leave, Lucky took her arm and said, "Braves are playing. I know you like baseball. I used to see you at Joe's games screaming like somebody just let out of Bryce. Stay just a couple of innings."

"I don't think so."

"Pretty please? With sugar on it?"

"Lord knows I love to see a man beg." Bena smiled.

The Braves were ahead by two runs. Bena knew the names of nearly every player on the team because Joe and Eddie always kept the Braves games going full blast on the TV at home even if neither one of them was around to watch. Over the years the players' names had sort of filled up Bena's house with artificial activity. When the Braves drove in a third run Bena shouted and crooked her arm to do the tomahawk chop in celebration.

"I hear it makes the Indians mad when you do that," Lucky teased.

"What?" Bena said. "This is my Jane Fonda imitation, mister."

Lucky looked hard at Bena. "I like you, Bena, one hell of a lot. I think about you too." He paused. "Do you ever think about me?"

"A little bit," she lied.

He grinned. "Good enough. I'll take it."

The conversation made Bena nervous. She excused herself and

went to the bathroom—Lucky's and Sue Cox's, not the guest bath-room—and she locked the door and proceeded to explore. She'd never done anything like this in her life. She didn't even know what she was looking for. The medicine cabinet had all the basic medicine-cabinet contents, nothing noteworthy. Some prescription medicine for Lucky's nervous stomach. That kind of thing. One drawer had Lucky's toothbrush and shaving stuff, some Band-Aids and Q-Tips and contact lens solution. It was the only messy drawer. Another one had Sue Cox's makeup and hair clips. The cabinet below had the usual Tampax, toilet paper, air freshener, and Lysol spray cleaner.

In the closet the towels were perfectly folded and arranged by color. There were hand towels and washcloths to match, and they were all monogrammed with SCM, which struck Bena—as if she were discovering a small injustice. Didn't Lucky live here too? Didn't he have any towels with his initials on them? So she searched the cab-inet to see, but no. It was like a tiny insight into their marriage.

In a basket on the floor were magazines, dull ones. One about building decks, one about fishing, one about automobiles, and sev-eral catalogs where you could order special hardware and lawn equipment and car accessories and doghouses. Bena flushed the toi-let, ran the water a minute, then went back to the TV room.

"You okay?" Lucky asked.

"Yes," Bena said. "It just took me a while to look through all the drawers and cabinets in your bathroom."

Lucky looked up from the game. "You looking for anything special?"

"Clues," she said.

"You solving a mystery?"

"I never look through people's personal stuff. I swear. I don't know why I looked through your stuff, and I don't know why I told you I did it either."

"I guess you wanted me to know," he said. "You find anything interesting?"

"No."

"You're disappointed, aren't you." He grinned. "I tell you what. Next time you come over I'll have you some stuff tucked away in there, you know, good stuff. It'll make it worth your while to snoop."

"Sorry," Bena said.

"Don't be." Lucky ran his hand over her head. "I love a nosy woman."

By the time Bena left to go home the Dodgers had come back and tied the game, 6–6. "No real fan ever leaves a tie game, Bena," Lucky said in mock alarm. "Man, do you have a lot to learn."

"I'll let you in on a secret," Bena whispered. "I'm not a real fan. I'm faking it just to make you happy."

"You do," he said. "Make me happy."

THE NEXT FEW WEEKS Lucky put a note in Bena's mailbox every day. Sometimes he would include a newspaper clipping, once of an armed robbery where the defendant was sentenced to seventeen years. Lucky wrote in the corner, *I used to go to Training Union with this guy when we were kids.* Sometimes he'd send her a write-up of a Braves game *since I know you forgot to watch it last night* or some fast-food coupons *enough for your kids too* or an announcement of an antique-car show that was going on at the mall *which you should take Eddie to see.*

Or once the story of a local man who'd locked his wife in the trunk of his car and just kept her there. He gave her a pillow and some blankets and stopped now and then to give her food and water, always parked her in the shade. Sprayed her down with the hose when she begged for a bath. When they finally arrested him he said it was the only way he could be sure she wouldn't run off. She was pretty messed up when they finally found her. She'd been living in his trunk for nearly a month, sleeping in her own feces, lost all sense of day and night. *Read this,* Lucky said. *What the hell is wrong with people?*

Bena began to look forward to the mail each day, to the white envelope that would have her name on it and a couple of sweet sentences scrawled inside along with some social commentary or unsolicited advice. Some mornings she went to the mailbox early to put a note for Lucky in there. Once she left him a homemade cinnamon roll wrapped in tin foil, and another time she left him an article on stocking fish ponds that she found in a magazine at her doctor's office when she went for her Pap smear. She'd ripped out the article right there in the waiting room and no one seemed to care. Afterward he'd drawn her a sketch of how the pond would look when he actually installed it, where it would sit on the land in relation to the house. It was funny to Bena, the arrow pointing to *Sue Cox's House,* and the arrow pointing to *My Pond*. He drew an assortment of wildlife gathered around the pond, each of them identified with an arrow too, in case she could not decipher his artistic rendition of paradise. *Turtle, wildcat, raccoon.*

WHEN BENA'D FINISHED cleaning out the attic she'd moved to the kitchen. Oh my God. She'd taken everything out of every cabinet and drawer. As she'd promised herself, she put in the give-away pile any single item meant to be part of a set. No more mismatched spoons and forks. No more odds and ends pots and lids or jelly-jar drinking glasses or chipped casserole dishes that had come into the house as love offerings when Bobby died, but whose owners had failed to write their names on masking tape and stick it on the bottom of the dish so that in the end, after everything had been half eaten, frozen, defrosted, and reheated, Bena couldn't remember whose dish was whose. So she'd simply adopted them.

Before she knew it she had twice as much in the give-away pile as she had left in her kitchen, so she did an unlikely thing. She went to Gayfer's and bought new, plain white dishes, four boxed sets of service for four. Sixteen of everything. Just in case she ever had sixteen people over for supper sometime, which so far in her life she never had. While she was at it she bought new drinking glasses, twenty in all, and an economy pack of ten dish towels and ten dishcloths, solid white, so she could bleach them clean when she needed to without any stripes or designs fading on her. She debated a long time over replacing her silverware, such as it was, but decided to wait on that, maybe get it next time they had a sale. Already she was spending more money than she should. Charging it to her Visa. That was one thing she'd learned from Bobby. Never charge anything you can pay for. And never charge anything at all if you can help it. In this case Bena felt more than justified. She spent three hours in Gayfer's, making her selections, adding and subtracting to see how much she could get today and planning for what she'd get next month. It was one of the most satisfying days she'd spent in a long time.

When she got home she arranged the new white dishes in the cabinet very artistically. Large plates on the bottom shelf with the bowls. Salad plates and saucers on the second shelf, the cups hanging on hooks. It was going to look wonderful. Eddie came in looking for the peanut butter, and Bena pointed to the table where she'd piled up all the contents of the pantry. "Right there," she said.

"What are you doing, Mama? Everything is empty."

"*Empty* is just another word for possibility," she said.

"You been reading some kind of book, haven't you?" he said. "One of those change-your-life books. Right?"

"No," Bena said.

"You saw something on *Oprah*? Right?"

"Eddie, Eddie," Bena teased, "you don't think your mama can think for herself and make changes without outside interference? I'm hurt."

"Yeah, sure." Eddie stuck his finger in the peanut butter jar and hooked a big glob, which went straight to his mouth.

"For heaven's sake, use a spoon," Bena said.

"Where is a spoon?" he said. "The spoon drawer is empty."

Bena stopped her dish arranging to find him a spoon. "Here," she said. "What do you think?"

"About what?" Eddie said.

"That." Bena pointed to the cabinet she'd just organized.

"They're dishes," Eddie said.

"New dishes."

"What was wrong with the old dishes?" Eddie ate peanut butter from the jar with his spoon.

Bena turned and stared at him. "I feel like you're your daddy's ghost come back to haunt me."

Eddie looked a little freaked. He didn't like Bena to ever mention his daddy. Not even if she was trying to say something nice, which in this case, she wasn't.

"That's exactly the kind of thing your daddy would say." She smiled.

"Yeah, next thing you know I'll be driving headfirst off the side of a mountain."

"Eddie!" Bena said. "Don't talk like that."

"Well, don't tell me I'm like him then."

"You're like you," Bena said. "Okay? I just wanted you to ooh and aah a little over these dishes. We're reorganizing around here. We're cleaning up our act."

Eddie winced to hear Bena talk this way. "Mama, a bunch of new dishes cannot change our lives or anything. They're just dishes."

Bena kissed his face but didn't try to explain to him how wrong he was.

In her excitement to get to Gayfer's, Bena had forgotten to get the mail. She rushed down the drive only to find two credit-card offers, a furniture store flyer, the water bill, and the thing she was looking for—the note from Lucky. *Gone to Hastings to get Sue Cox. Her time is up.*

ON SUNDAY NIGHT Bena got a call from Joe. "I'm not going to call you every week, Mama. Just when I have something to say."

"So you've got something to say now?"

"Not really."

"How are your classes? Is baseball going okay? Tell me what's going on."

"Well." Joe paused. "I met a girl . . ."

MORE THAN A WEEK passed and Bena didn't hear a word from Lucky. *So this is it,* she said to herself. *It's over. No more notes. No more dinners. No more talks.* She told herself that she was happy for Lucky. He'd been lonely, that was why he'd reached out to her in the first place—because he thought she was too. But now Sue Cox was back and he had his real life back the way he wanted it and for all she knew they were at home right this minute. Maybe he was planning the pond, calling for the backhoe to come dig the hole. Maybe Sue Cox was healed and lying naked in her suntan garden, meditating. Bena didn't mind feeling foolish so much, but she refused to feel jealous too.

What was the big deal anyway? Lucky had never so much as hugged her neck or patted her back. He'd barely ever touched her at all. Why didn't he ever kiss her when he had the chance? When they were hiking through the underbrush to see the pond site, when they were watching the Braves, when they were talking and eating hamburgers out on the porch?

Because he didn't want to. That was why.

ONE EVENING IN a rash moment when Bena was going over to J. C. Penney's to look at their pots and pans on special, she made a calculated wrong turn and drove out to Lucky's place. She just wanted to see if they were home. She stopped at the Seed and Feed on her way and bought a nice hydrangea in a pot. That way, if they were home and saw her drive up, she could give Sue Cox the plant and say, *Welcome home. I heard you were back.* Like that.

Bena wanted to know if Lucky was just going to go on with his life like the two of them had never become friends. She knew men could do stuff like that. It was just so hard to believe. Wouldn't he miss her at all?

It was a nice little drive out to Lucky's place, time to give herself a good talking to, and when Bena turned off on the road leading up to Lucky's house it was eerie—not a light on anywhere except the light on the telephone pole that lit the backyard. Where was Tom? Who was feeding him? Lucky's truck was nowhere to be seen either. Clearly, he and Sue Cox were not back from Atlanta yet. Maybe it had taken a few extra days to sign Sue Cox out—or maybe they'd checked into a nice hotel in Atlanta to celebrate Sue Cox's freedom and Lucky's life returning to normal. Bena pulled her car back out on the highway and rode home with the feeling that their empty house was a signal that her own life was about to feel very empty too. It was going to be hard to give Lucky up. But even harder to be given up by him.

WHEN BENA GOT home Sissy and Barrett were waiting in the den. They'd come to tell her good-bye. Earlier that day they'd driven back from Dillon, South Carolina, where they'd gotten married and spent their first night together as man and wife at some kind of Mexican wonderland–type place on the South Carolina border.

"Be happy for us, Mama. Please." Sissy hugged Bena, who stood like a lone pine in the wind, about to be blown over by the news.

"See, Mrs. Eckerd," Barrett explained, "I got laid off over at the lumberyard. Last hired, first fired, you know. So I said, what the heck, Sissy's always talking about going down to Miami and getting a job on a boat down there."

"A cruise ship," Sissy interrupted.

"Right," he said. "So I said, what the heck. I'll just go with her and we'll both hire on to a ship. It'll be like a honeymoon. We'll go wherever it takes us. There's nothing to tie us down here. So, we just said, you know, what the heck, let's get married."

Bena sat down in a chair, like a net catching her as she fell off an invisible tightrope. This was exactly what she'd most feared happening to Sissy's life. Barrett.

"We're all packed, Mama," Sissy said. "We're heading out tonight. It will take us a good two days at least. We just came to say goodbye."

Bena began to cry.

Sissy kneeled on the floor and put her head in Bena's lap. "Don't cry, Mama. Be happy. I'm happy."

"What's going on?" Eddie was coming in from his nightly prowl out at the mall. "What's wrong with Mama?"

Sissy flashed her new wedding ring, which Bena thought looked like a toy. It was just all so tragic and stupid. Why couldn't Sissy see Barrett for what he was?

"Y'all got married?" Eddie said.

Sissy leaped up and hugged him. "Isn't it wonderful?"

"We're going down to Miami," Barrett said. "Relocating."

Bena looked at those glassy eyes of Barrett's and wanted to jump up and slap his face until he turned into a mature, responsible, hardworking person. How could Sissy go off with this boy who'd never —as far as Bena knew—shown her even the basic courtesies, like showing up when she expected him, paying up when he owed her, giving up his selfish little-boy ways in honor of her. Was Sissy blind? Was she going to devote her life to proving to the world one more time that love is blind? If so, it'd be another wasted life. One more wasted life.

While Sissy and Barrett went back to the bedroom to tell Ellie and Leslie the news, Bena got up and splashed water on her face and tried to think what to do. If she could have, she'd have called Lucky. *Hello, Sue Cox?* she'd say. *May I speak with your husband, please? It's very important.* Lucky would know how to make sense of this. He'd say, *You got to set Sissy free, Bena. She's already set herself free. You just love her and try to talk to her the best you can. The rest is hers to work out.* Something like that. But for God's sake, Lucky didn't even have any children—so what would he know anyway?

"It could be worse, Mama," Eddie said. "Sissy could of married a serial killer or something. Barrett's not so bad. I mean, he's okay."

Bena tried to smile. When Sissy and Barrett came back with their arms entwined, followed by Leslie and Ellie in their pajamas, giddy and excited that their sister was leading the way—away from home, out into the big world better known as Miami. She was blazing a trail they could follow, and it was clear they were grateful.

"We got to go, Mama," Sissy said. "We'll call you when we settle in, okay?"

"One thing," Bena looked at Barrett, by all accounts a handsome boy, but nothing near a man—not as Bena understood a man to be. "I want to know one thing, Barrett. Do you love Sissy?"

"Mama!" Sissy wailed. "Of course he does."

"I'm asking him," Bena said. "Do you love Sissy, Barrett?"

The room fell silent. It wasn't like their mama to put people on the spot this way. It was so rude, but there she was—waiting for him to answer.

He looked at Eddie, guy to guy, like a call for a little help. Then he looked at Sissy, who wanted desperately for him to pass this test. "Well, sure I do."

"Let me hear you say it then," Bena said. "Say it."

"I love Sissy."

Sissy hugged his neck and kissed his face. Ellie and Leslie practically broke into a cheer over the sheer romance of it all. Eddie looked relieved.

"That's good," Bena said. "That's real good." She put her hand on Barrett's shoulder and looked at him as hard as any man could. "I know Sissy doesn't have a daddy for you to answer to. But she's got me and her brothers and her sisters and let me tell you one thing: if you ever even think about mistreating her we'll all be down to Miami after you so fast your head will spin. Isn't that right, Eddie?"

Eddie was ashamed that his mother was talking like this to Barrett, but he liked what she was saying—that, messed-up family that they were, they'd still stick together in times of trouble. It was something he'd always wanted to believe. "Yes, ma'am."

"Sissy is the sweetest girl in the world," Bena said. "And I would say you're about the luckiest boy in the world right about now. Don't you ever forget that."

"Sure," he said. "I won't."

When all the good-bye hugging started, Bena took Sissy's hand and led her into the laundry room and shut the door. "I love you," she said. "But this is your life. This is the boy you love. So I'm going to say a prayer every night that everything works out for the best. But listen to me, Sissy. You're a beautiful girl—sweet, smart, and kind. Barrett is not the only man in the world who'll ever think so. If he's not good to you, there are other men in this world who will be. A woman has got to hold out for a good man. If Barrett turns out to be different from what you're expecting, mean to you or anything— you leave him. Do you hear me?"

"Mama," Sissy whispered, "I just barely got married and you're already talking about me leaving him."

"I don't want to be saying this, Sissy. But you're about to go almost a thousand miles away and I won't have any way of knowing how you're doing. Barrett has some strikes against him going in. You know that."

"Mama, he's not like you think. That trouble was a long time ago."

"Promise to call me, collect, anytime," Bena said. "I love you, Sissy Eckerd."

"Sissy Carter." She grinned.

"Mrs. Sissy Carter." Bena made a weak effort to smile. "God bless you, baby."

After they left, everybody but Eddie was in tears. Ellie and Leslie, happy that their sister had found love and that she would stand by her man against all odds—like an odd mother, for example. Bena went to bed and cried like her heart was breaking. Leslie and Ellie brought her in a cup of tea with honey—in one of her new white cups with a new white dish towel draped on a cookie tray.

"It's going to be okay, Mama," they said. "She loves him."

God, Bena thought, why couldn't it be that simple?

BENA WAS PRONE to crying jags on and off the next few days. She barely got out of bed, but did manage to make her way down to the empty mailbox, just to be sure. Every time she imagined the life Sissy would have with Barrett she was filled with such an ache that there was no relief. She guessed it was the way all parents must feel when they watch their child make a bad choice and they know the sorts of prices you can pay in this life for a bad choice. It's like you're sending your beloved child off to war, but once she's gone you realize that you failed to provide her with any weapons with which to fight back. Like not only didn't you teach her how to dodge bullets, but you also failed to give her any bullets of her own, so that she'll be destined to fire blanks all her life—or worse, resort to hand-to-hand combat. There were so many things she should have tried harder to explain to Sissy. Even though Sissy'd never been much of a listener. She'd always been the kind of child who learned by doing—and she had done some hard lesson learning in her short life, and now, it seemed to Bena, she had just signed up for more of the same.

Bena should've read to her more. Lots of stories with happy endings so Sissy would've learned to expect a happy ending for herself—not to settle for less. These were the sorts of things Bena was thinking. She should have discouraged Sissy's baton twirling in that little French-cut sequined outfit—marching out in front of hundreds of spectators half naked and totally naive, looking like some of God's finest work. That was what probably got to Barrett in the first place, Sissy marching along, head held high, wolf whistles coming from everywhere. She'd only been fifteen when she started that, marching with the band. What does a girl know at fifteen?

Barrett had been a senior then, a holdover hippie who couldn't seem to recover. Probably never would recover enough to actually make anything of himself. What would make Sissy choose a loser like Barrett? Was it poor home training? That's the only thing Bena could think. This situation with Barrett had all started just about the time Bobby died too. Maybe if he'd lived he could have done better by Sissy.

WHEN THE PHONE RANG Bena jumped for it because she was hoping against hope that it was Sissy calling to say she'd changed her mind. So far Bena'd spent the day sprawled over her bed with a bunch of house magazines and the channel changer to her portable TV. She'd watched every possible talk show—you know, hoping there was a message out there somewhere especially for her.

"Bena?" the voice said. She'd know that voice anywhere, even if it did sound like something run over in the road, flat, flat.

"Lucky? Is that you?"

"What's left of me. Look, you think I could come over?"

"Now?"

"I need to talk to you."

"Come on, then." Bena got up and tried to put herself together, but she'd cried so much her eyes were puffed like two boiled eggs and anything she did to them just made them look worse. She wondered what Lucky would think if she answered the door in sunglasses. She'd done that when Bobby died, worn sunglasses all day every day because grief had a way of making her look like a monster of some kind.

Lucky arrived in his own truck, not the post office van. He rang the doorbell and stood with his hands in his pockets, kicking one boot into the other. When Bena opened the door he said, "Your kids home?"

"Ellie is somewhere," Bena said. "Come on in." Lucky said nothing about the dark glasses she was wearing. "You want a cold drink?" Bena led him to the kitchen, where she poured them each a Dr Pepper.

"Something looks different in here," Lucky said.

"I hope it's me." Bena smiled.

"What's with those sunglasses?" Lucky asked.

"It's a long story, but you go first," Bena said. "Tell me everything. Don't leave out a single detail." She led him into the living room, which was almost never used, and they sat on the sofa facing each other. "Okay," she said. "Tell me."

Lucky sighed and searched the depths of his Dr Pepper as if the story floated there among the ice cubes. "Sue Cox is not coming home."

"But I thought she was making such good progress," Bena said.

"That's why she's not coming home," Lucky snickered. "Seems being around me will just undo all that progress she's made. That's what she said."

"Oh." Bena reached for his hand, but stopped herself.

"The truth is." Lucky put his glass on the coffee table and leaned back, his arms resting on the sofa cushions. "She met somebody."

"You mean, like, a man?"

"God knows it's not the first time. This happens sometimes, you know, when she goes to rehab. All that true-confession shit, next thing you know she thinks she's bonded with some guy in her therapy group. She thinks he has listened to her like I never do and he understands her like I never will. It's the takes-one-to-know-one thing. You know, like Elizabeth Taylor and that Larry Forbes or who the hell ever. Well, her Larry is named Corby. Damn if he's not more than fifteen years younger than she is too."

"So where is she then?" Bena asked.

"She's still at Hastings. She's going to stay until Corby finishes his treatment and then they'll leave together. Go straight to hell in a matter of weeks most likely. That's what usually happens."

"Maybe not," Bena said. "I mean . . . maybe . . ."

"Like I said, I been through this more than once, Bena. Sue Cox will go off with this guy and be all eat up with bliss and enlightenment. Then, you know, a couple of weeks to a month later things will get screwed up. One of them says something to the other one, one of them takes a drink, one of them starts to lie. About this time is when Sue Cox will start calling me up. She'll cry and the whole kit and kaboodle, wanting me to be understanding. And damn if I'm not. Then when she hits rock bottom with this guy—generally it don't take all that long—she calls me to come get her and bring her home and I do and we act like a couple of sex maniacs, you know, just to prove our love to each other and then, after a while, that wears off and we get back to being who we are.

"And who exactly are you?"

"Sue Cox is the best-looking drunk in Alabama, a little more messed up every year that passes. And I'm her fool of a husband. A has-been who carries the mail and jumps through hoops trying to keep Sue Cox happy enough not to leave me."

"So what are you going to do this time?" Bena asked.

"As I see it, my selection of choices is pretty damn slim."

"She'll probably get tired of this guy, Corby, and want you back."

"That's what I always count on. But I got to tell you I'm pretty damn sick of this shit. When I got to Atlanta I went straight to Hastings Hospital and she'd left me a goddamned note saying, *Sorry, I'm not going home with you.* And that was it. She wouldn't see me. I couldn't get in to talk to her damn doctor either. I waited eight to five for three days, just refused to get out of their hair over there, until she finally agreed to talk to me if I'd promise to go home afterwards."

"What'd she say?"

"That I'm part of her problem. I'm a damn enabler. I forgive her too easily. Make it too easy for her to mess up again. Shit like that."

"So it's your fault she's an alcoholic?"

"Hell, yes, it's my fault. That's why she's kept me around as long as she has, so things can always be my fault."

"What did you say to her?" Bena asked.

"I said, *Cut the crap, Sue Cox. What's his name this time?* And she said, *Corby. He might be young but he is the most sensitive guy I've ever known. He's good for me, Lucky. I'm sorry. But it's the truth.*" Lucky took a drink of his Dr Pepper. "*And I'm not good for you, right, Sue Cox?* I said. *No, Lucky,* she said, *you're not.*" Lucky shook his head and looked at Bena. "Same damn conversation we've been having all our marriage. Pitiful, ain't it?"

Bena was trying to understand what Lucky was saying. It was outside the realm of what she knew. Even when Bobby got caught dying with another woman in tow Bena had told herself the other woman was probably a one-time thing. She told herself Bobby was probably sorry for it and would never have done it if he'd known how much it would hurt everybody. That's the sort of thinking she understood. What else was there to think? What good would it have done her to think otherwise?

"If forgiveness gets you into heaven, Lucky, then you're on your way." Bena shook her head. "Me? I try hard to forgive Bobby for what happened, but I'm never really sure I do. I just let wanting to forgive him be enough. But you're like a saint or something. Is there anything Sue Cox could ever do that you couldn't forgive?"

"I'm not a saint, Bena. I'm a fool. There's a difference."

"You didn't answer my question."

"I guess I always thought I'd rather forgive her than lose her. I couldn't see my life without her. We been together since high school. We been to hell and back more times than I can count, and I don't know, don't ever let anybody tell you misery don't bond people. The more miserable we got the more set I always was on us staying together. I believe she'd of left me a long time ago if I'd have let her. There's been no lack of trying on her part. That's for damn—"

But before he could finish his sentence Ellie stuck her head in the door. "Who's truck is that outside, Mama?"

Bena sat up straight and Lucky leaned upright too and put his hands on his knees. "It belongs to Mr. McKale," Bena said.

Ellie looked totally confused. "Is everything okay, Mama?"

"Sure," Bena said. "We're just talking."

"You don't need those sunglasses in the house, Mama. And if you're telling him about Barrett, all I can say is that he is nowhere near as bad as Mama says."

"Who's Barrett?" Lucky turned to face Ellie.

"Aren't you our mailman?" Ellie asked.

"At your service." Lucky smiled.

"I don't get it."

"There's nothing you need to get," Bena said. "We're talking. We have things to talk about. That's all."

"I remember you from Joe's baseball games," Ellie said to Lucky. "Wasn't that you that always used to be there?"

"I was pretty regular," Lucky said.

Ellie took a couple of steps into the room, crossed her arms, and stared at Bena. "So, is this a date or something going on in here?"

"Ellie!" Bena said.

Lucky laughed. "No, honey, this is just a bunch of talk going on in here now. The date is tonight." He looked at Bena. "Ain't that right, Bena, sweetheart?"

Bena glared at Lucky. "Ellie, could I see you in the other room, please." She took Ellie by the arm and led her into the kitchen. "Since when do you cross-examine people that way?"

"Just tell me one thing, Mama," Ellie said. "All that whispering in there. The way y'all jumped when I came in. Are you having a thing with that mailman?"

"I don't believe that's any of your business," Bena said.

"I knew it, Mama!" Ellie squealed. "That's so great."

Bena was startled. "I'm not having a *thing* with him—and I'm not having this conversation with you either."

"Sure, Mom." Ellie grinned. "Whatever you say."

"Shouldn't you be at work?" Bena asked. "Aren't there some people about to drown out at the country club pool today?"

"Does Eddie know about the mailman?" Ellie asked.

"His name is Mr. McKale," Bena said. "And there is nothing to know. Now go find something to do and don't come back into the living room unless you're invited."

"Fat chance," Ellie smiled. "Getting invited into the love nest."

"You're ridiculous." Bena shook her head and went back to where Lucky was waiting. She was unnerved and embarrassed. Lucky was standing at the window looking out. "Sorry about that," Bena said. "Ellie has a wild imagination."

"Me too." Lucky grinned.

Bena stood and looked at him. One minute ago his heart had been breaking and he'd been confiding in her in the most private way. Now he was teasing her.

"How about you, Bena? You got a wild imagination?"

"No." She wanted to get back to the way things were before Ellie came in. Wanted to finish luxuriating in each other's betrayal.

"Something tells me you're lying," he said. "Something tells me you got an imagination that works overtime."

"Stop it." Bena waved her hand as if to erase his silliness. She sat back down on the sofa. "Come sit down. Finish telling me about Sue Cox."

"You know what? I'm sick of talking about Sue Cox." Lucky walked over and sat beside her. "I've wasted too much time talking about that woman. How about let's talk about you instead?"

"Me?"

Lucky reached over and took the sunglasses off Bena's face. "Like you could tell me why you got these sunglasses on. What you been crying about?"

It came back to Bena like a swift boot to the ribs. "It's Sissy," Bena said. "She ran away and got married. Barrett, her husband, is as no good as they come."

"You sure about that?" Lucky asked.

"More than sure," Bena said. "They left for Miami last night. There was nothing I could do. I've been sick over it ever since. She has no business being married."

"Funny," Lucky said. "That's the way I'm feeling myself right about now."

"This is different," Bena said.

"Different how?"

"Just different," Bena said. "That's all."

Lucky picked up Bena's hand and put it to his lips to kiss it.

"What are you doing?" She pulled her hand away.

"We got a date tonight, right? I'm just warming up a little. Getting you warmed up a little."

"Hush." Bena punched his arm.

"How about if I pick you up about seven?" Lucky said. "You know, like a real date. I'll come to the door to get you and the whole thing. We'll go to a nice restaurant. You can dress up if you want to."

"I don't know. It seems a little crazy to have a date with a man who is all torn to pieces over his wife. His wife, W-I-F-E. You know?"

"Take a chance." Lucky winked. "I swear I'm going to do my best to make it worth your while."

"Has anybody ever told you you're nuts?" Bena said.

"Has anybody ever told you you're sweet?" Lucky smiled.

"It's my curse." Bena grabbed the sunglasses from Lucky and put them back on. "I'm sick of people thinking I'm sweet, harmless Bena Eckerd, bless my heart."

Lucky laughed. "There's worse things folks could say. But listen to me. Tonight Bobby is dead and in the grave, Sue Cox is as good as dead and off with her teenage heartthrob. But me and you—we're alive. You understand me, Bena? We are alive and this right here is our lives—yours and mine." He took her by the shoulders and shook her gently as he spoke. "We don't have to be dead just because Bobby is and Sue Cox wishes she was. Ain't that right?"

"You're sort of scaring me," Bena whispered.

"Sorry." He kissed her forehead.

On his way out the front door he said, "See you at seven. I'll be the guy in the necktie." Then he yelled, "Good-bye, Ellie. Your Mama is an angel."

"Hush." Bena put her hand over his mouth. "My kids are the last people on earth who are going to believe that."

THIS IS THE TRUTH. Bena didn't have one thing to wear out on a date to a nice restaurant. The minute Lucky was out the door she went straight to her closet to start the search for something she knew perfectly well wasn't in there. Something she'd look great in. Something that would take Lucky by surprise because it would reveal a side to her that he hadn't suspected. Her beautiful side.

Why hadn't she cleaned out her closet before she cleaned out the kitchen? It looked to Bena right now like every single sorry item hanging in her closet needed to be pitched. That's what she began to do. She saw those women in the magazines who looked great, tried to make you think it was no trouble to look great. She didn't even have a simple black dress—unless you counted the one she'd worn when Bobby was buried. She wasn't about to wear it. If Sissy hadn't left town with everything she owned stuffed in the trunk of Barrett's sad excuse for a car then maybe Bena could have borrowed something from Sissy. But now even that was out of the question. Should she run out to the mall and see what she could find there? No, that was impossible because she'd already run up her credit card buying those dishes and glasses. She'd have to make do with what she had. Or maybe she could call Lucky and get a rain check, you know, postpone the evening until she'd gotten another paycheck and had had time to shop until she dropped or whatever women with social lives do.

"What is going on, Mama?" Ellie said. "What're you doing with all your clothes?"

"Throwing them away," Bena said. "They're awful. Look at this." She held up a dress she'd had before Ellie was born. It was psychedelic with bell-bottom sleeves.

"Wow," Ellie said. "That's sort of cool."

Bena tossed it over her head. "Don't say I never gave you anything."

Ellie draped the dress around her shoulders and flung herself on Bena's unmade bed. "So, Mama," she said, "do I detect a case of predate jitters here?"

"You detect a woman who has no business going on a date. Look at this—I don't have anything decent to wear. Nothing."

"Sit down, Mama." Ellie pulled Bena to the bed. "You sit and I'll find you something. Trust me." So Bena obeyed and curled up on the bed and watched Ellie, her baby girl, comb through her closet in search of something that might pass for decent. "Not this," Ellie said thoughtfully after studying each garment. "Put this one in the trash pile," she said with authority. "Good grief. Mama, where did you get some of this stuff in here?" She laughed at Bena's lime-green double-breasted suit with the blouse to match. It had been her Easter outfit a hundred years ago, back when she'd wanted to believe in the resurrection—or, at the very least, in spring. "Please tell me you never wore this in public," Ellie said. "But this"—Ellie held up a pale blue dress with a lace collar—"has possibilities."

"I'm not wearing that," Bena said.

"We'll take this collar off, Mama. And shorten it. It'll be great. Try it on."

So Bena did. It was several years old. She'd bought it to wear when Sissy graduated from high school. After which she sort of forgot about it. "It fits," Ellie said. "It looks good, Mama."

"You think so? It's not too sweet, is it? I don't want to look too sweet."

"When I get through with it, you won't." Ellie folded the hem and stuck bobby pins on it to mark the length. "Take it off, Mama," she said. "I'll fix it for you."

Bena slipped the dress off and handed it over.

"It's not every night your mama has got a date," Ellie said.

Bena kissed Ellie's ear, loud smacking kisses like when she was little and so dear that Bena wanted to eat her alive. "And thank you for not making fun of me."

"Actually he's pretty cute, Mama. Your mailman."

"He's not my mailman," Bena corrected.

"*Mr. McKale, he carries the mail,*" Ellie sang.

IT WAS CLEAR Ellie had passed the word that Bena had a date because before she knew it both Leslie and Eddie were home looking her over with suspicious expressions. "So, Mama," Leslie said. "What's this I hear about a man?"

"I can only imagine." Bena looked at Ellie.

"His name is Happygolucky," Ellie said. "For real. He's our mailman."

"I know Mr. McKale," Leslie said. "He used to go to Joe's games all the time."

"You all are making too much of this," Bena said. "Really."

Eddie didn't say much, just kept Bena in his line of sight in case she was about to do anything crazy. He didn't mention the date. He never liked to reduce himself to the emotional level of his sisters.

That night both Leslie and Ellie sat on the bed and watched Bena get ready. Ellie had removed the lace collar from the dress and hemmed it so that it was just above the knee. "You got to show a little leg, Mama," Ellie said.

The dress was simple and the color was nice, blue like Bena's eyes. Bena let Leslie pin her hair up too, something she never did. Bobby had liked Bena's hair long and never wanted her to cut it or pin it up. "That's an old-lady hairdo," he used to say. "And you're not an old lady yet." Somehow he'd convinced her that she didn't look good with her hair up. But Lord, how long had it been since she'd had a haircut? And the Alabama humidity was instant death to any hairdo other than exactly what you were born with. So pinning her hair up made sense. And Leslie was good at it too. When she was finished it had that natural look, like Bena had made the sudden decision to pin it up and just jabbed one magic bobby pin into her hair on the spur of the moment. Nobody would know Leslie had spent a good fifteen minutes making Bena's hair look like she had not spent even fifteen seconds on it.

Bena slipped on a pair of low-heeled sandals borrowed from Leslie and tied a cotton sweater over her shoulders and wore her only good earrings, a pair of gold hoops Bobby had given her one Christmas. She stood in front of the full-length mirror and was generally satisfied with what she saw. A woman who had once been eighteen but wouldn't go back and do it over for all the money in the world.

Eddie came in to look at Bena when he heard his sisters gushing, "Mama, you look great. Lucky-boy will fall out when he sees you, won't he, Eddie?"

"You look pretty, Mama," Eddie said.

"Thank you, baby." She smiled, turning to try to look at the back of her dress in the mirror. "Lucky's wife is a real beauty," she said absentmindedly. "There's no way to compete with Sue Cox's looks. But this is about the best I can do."

"His wife?" Leslie said.

"What wife?" Ellie asked.

"The man has got a wife?" Leslie shouted.

All three children turned to Bena and waited for some retraction or something. "Look," Bena said. "You all are making too much of this date thing. I told you that. Yes, Lucky has a wife, but they're— separated. They've been separated awhile now. Besides, this is not like you think. This is just a date. It's not a *date* date."

"Oh my God." Leslie slapped her hand over her mouth.

"Don't say *God,* Leslie," Bena corrected. "Don't take the Lord's name in vain, because if you do then sometime when you really need Him He won't come because He'll have stopped taking you seriously." It was a speech Bena had learned from her mother, and her kids had it memorized. Now she hoped a small sermon might distract them. "Don't cry wolf to the Lord," Bena said. "You know better."

"Oh my gosh!" Leslie wailed. "I know his wife. She came to our health class to talk about how drugs can ruin our lives and all. She had all these stories, but I remember she said, *My husband's name is Lucky. Can you imagine how hard it is to live with somebody named Lucky?* She was a recovered drug addict."

"Alcoholic," Bena corrected.

"She was real pretty too," Leslie said.

"I'm sure you're much sweeter, Mama," Ellie said.

"No doubt," Bena said sarcastically.

Then everybody went momentarily silent. Bena looked at the faces of her nearly grown kids and tried to read their minds. She used to be so good at it when they were little. Back then she knew what they were thinking before they did. But they stood staring at her like she'd suddenly become a very mysterious woman. And she knew for a fact that they were three of the great mysteries of her life. Now and then she accidentally unearthed one of their dark secrets —and usually ended up suffering through it worse than they did. And here, it seemed, they thought they had unearthed one of Bena's secrets. A married man named Lucky. Bena, their mother, who by all rights should not be having any secrets at all.

"I can't believe this," Leslie finally said.

Before Bena could think of a reply the doorbell rang.

"Oh my God," Leslie whispered. "It's him."

"Saved by the bell." Bena managed a weak smile. She grabbed her purse and headed for the door. When she opened the door there stood Lucky's upscale twin. A handsome man in a dark suit with polished shoes, not boots. He had on a crisp white shirt and a tie that no doubt Sue Cox had chosen. He looked like a lawyer or a stockbroker, only interesting. And his hair was wet and freshly combed.

"Hey," Bena said.

Lucky whistled and took a step back. "Lord, woman," he said. "Is that you?"

"More or less." Bena smiled. "Come in." Bena tried to signal Lucky with her eyes that there was something in store for him when she opened the door wider.

He caught on instantly when he saw her three bodyguards standing there in a row, staring at him. "How's it going?" he said to the troops.

Only Ellie responded. "Fine."

"Ellie, I got something for y'all out in my truck, on the front seat. You mind running out there to get it?"

"What is it?"

"You'll see." He smiled. Ellie went reluctantly, as if she didn't want to miss whatever might happen next.

"Lucky, I think you've met Eddie before, right?" Bena said. "And this is Leslie. She was just telling me that Sue Cox, *your wife,* spoke to her health class. Gave a real inspirational talk, right, Leslie?"

"Well, I hope you listened good," Lucky said. "Sue Cox wouldn't want anybody else to go through all that she's been through."

"For sure." Leslie was boring a hole in Lucky, her disapproving eyes narrowed into pencil lines.

If Lucky was nervous Bena couldn't tell. But she knew her palms were beginning to get sweaty, and if they stood around much longer trying to make chitchat with her kids she'd sweat underarm rings on her blue dress.

"So where is Mrs. McKale anyway," Leslie asked. "Your wife?"

"Atlanta," Lucky said. "She had to go over there to tend to some things and next thing you know she liked it so much she decided to stay. Seems she loves the bright lights and all those ten-story cement parking decks and that five o'clock traffic where everybody just sits in their stalled cars and looks at everybody else while life is passing them right by. She's into it," he said. "She always has liked strangers better than folks she knows."

Just then Ellie came busting through the door with a cardboard box in her hand and a second box, of Krispy Kreme doughnuts, balanced on top of it. "You'll never guess what this is?" she said. "Wait till you see." She sat the boxes on the floor just inside the door.

"Let me take a wild guess," Leslie said. "Could it be doughnuts? Could it be sweets for the sweet?"

"No, stupid," Ellie said. "Look." She reached into the cardboard box and pulled up what looked like a little wet rat wrapped in a dirty hand towel.

"Oh my God," Bena said. "What is it?"

"Cats," Lucky said. "Baby cats."

Leslie, the supreme animal lover in the family, was instantly on her knees and reaching into the box too, counting. Two, three, four. She lifted a kitten in her hand and put it against her face. It opened its mouth and let out a cry that barely made a sound, like a terrified whisper.

"Found them in a sack on the side of the road," Lucky said. "Their mother was run over right where you turn off to my house, and when I got my shovel to get her moved off the road I saw this old Hardee's sack—you know people are bad to throw their trash out on the highway like that—and the sack was sort of moving around and I looked inside and there was a bunch of little cats in there. I guess their mama liked the smell of ham biscuits in that sack, put her babies in there with all those paper napkins and crumbs. One little cat was dead, the runt, so I buried it with its mother. Brought y'all the rest." He looked at Bena just in case she was considering throwing a fit. Whatever made him think she needed a house full of cats?

"They're so little," Ellie said. "Look, their eyes aren't even open."

"I can't guarantee you they'll make it," Lucky said. "But I knew for damn sure they wouldn't make it out at my house with me gone all day and nobody to look after them but Tom."

"Tom?" Leslie said.

"Tom is his dog," Bena said.

"Tom don't have the best of intentions where cats are concerned."

"Oh my gosh," Ellie kept saying.

"I'm not saying you got to keep them all," Lucky said. "I just thought maybe if y'all could nurse them along a little bit, then maybe you could give them to your friends and neighbors. Nothing like a good yard cat. Folks like having a cat around."

"These aren't yard cats," Leslie said. "Yard cats end up getting scraped off the highway. These are going to be house cats."

"That's up to your mama, I guess," Lucky said. "If she won't let you keep them then I'll carry them with me on my mail route, stick them in folks' mailboxes with a bow around their necks. They make a nice surprise for a lonely person."

Eddie just watched this scene without uttering a word. Bena looked at him and remembered the way he'd cried over losing Elvis. After Bobby died, Elvis had gradually become Eddie's dog. Elvis slept with him every night and ate half of anything Eddie ate. When he limped to his death two years after Bobby it was Eddie who buried him and gathered all the family to come to his dog funeral. It was Eddie who made the cinder-block marker that said, *Here lies Elvis, the King of dogs*. That marker was still out there now, although the edge of the woods had crept closer to the house in recent years without Bobby to keep it at bay. Last Bena looked, the marker had a bunch of blackberry brambles growing all over it and probably some snakes lurking too.

"What do you think, Eddie?" Bena asked.

"I like dogs," Eddie said.

"Well, you can like both, can't you, son?"

"Eddie thinks dogs are boys and cats are girls," Ellie said. "That's his problem."

"Shut up," he said. "I do not."

"Get Mama's heating pad," Leslie ordered Eddie.

"Get it yourself," Eddie said.

Leslie lifted the box of cats and headed for the kitchen. Ellie followed her, cradling a cat in the hem of her T-shirt. Eddie looked at Lucky. "They don't know anything about cats. They'll probably kill them just by worrying them to death."

"Shut up, Eddie," Leslie yelled. "I heard that." She came around the corner and said, "Don't get the idea you fooled us or anything, Mr. McKale. We know these kittens are a bribe. You're just trying to make us forget you've got a wife."

"You got it all wrong," Lucky said. "The cats are like a favor you're doing me. The doughnuts are the bribe."

Eddie picked up the Krispy Kreme box and headed down the hall to his room.

"Let's get out of here while we can." Bena lead Lucky to the door.

WHEN THEY GOT into Lucky's truck Bena took her first real breath of the night. "If this is a date," she said, "I see how come I don't go on many."

"You got good kids," he said. "They're just trying to look out for their mama. It's not every night she goes out with a married man."

"It's not funny," Bena said. "I don't know what I'm doing here."

"Yes, you do," he said. "We both do."

"So tell me then, what are we doing?"

"Well, darling, we're stepping out of the past." He grinned. "Trying to see if there might actually be a future out here somewhere that we could stick our toes into, you know. Test the waters."

"So, this is a test?" Bena said.

"Shoot. Bad choice of words there. No, this is not a test. This is a thrill—at least for me—to get to be in your excellent company for a whole evening. Where you want to go?"

"It doesn't matter."

"Why do women say that? Of course it matters. Everything matters to women. I've learned that the hard way. So let's try again. What you want to eat? You want steak or catfish or some of that fancy sort of food you can't quite recognize that comes off a menu you can't actually read?" Lucky started up the motor and backed the truck around to head down the driveway.

"Where around here is a fancy place like that? Or are you planning on taking me all the way to Atlanta?"

"Shoot, woman, you don't get out much, do you? There's a place in La Grange, got the whole menu in a foreign language. French, I think. Or maybe Italian. You just point and take your chances. And they got several such places in Montgomery too. Stick with me, honey. I've learned a few things dragging the mail up and down the back roads of God's country."

"I think I'd like a menu I can read, if it's all right with you. I'll have to work my way up to the foreign-language menu, unless it's Spanish. I took Spanish. Arroz con pollo. That's chicken and rice."

"I tell you what." Lucky paused at the end of the drive and looked like he was debating whether to turn left or right, but he was really just waiting for the road to clear. Seemed like lots of folks had places to go on a hot Alabama night, which surprised Bena, like maybe she thought the two of them might have the road and the night all to themselves. "How about let's drive across the Georgia line, over to West Point Lake," Lucky said. "They got a nice place over there right on the water. Got those white Christmas lights strung up everywhere on the trees. They keep them up year-round. It's real pretty."

"Suits me," Bena said.

"They got live music too, starting at ten. Some R&B boys that come up from Mobile. Some Brothers, you know. That's the name of the group. Mostly it's white folks that come and eat their steak and onion rings, then head home before the dancing starts and things get lively. You know, they got to get home and watch the ten o'clock news or something. And mostly it's black folks that wait until the white folks clear out, then they come and put on their dancing shoes and raise the roof off the place. It's a good time. It really is."

"Okay," Bena said. "I'm easy."

"Now, that's a lie if I ever heard one." Lucky gunned the truck out onto the highway and started fiddling with the radio, looking for a good station.

"You talk like you're such an expert. On women."

"Damn," he said, "we both know that's not true. I know my way around every back road in this county and probably in the state of Alabama. I can't get lost if I want to. But a woman now, I never have known my way around a woman. I start out lost and stay lost the whole time. And you know what else? That don't bother me. Being lost. I guess I've got used to it and now I've come to where I like it. So if I start down the wrong road with you, Miss Bena, then you just got to say, *Hold up there, Lucky. You best back up and turn around, 'cause you are heading nowhere fast.* It won't hurt my feelings or discourage me either one. I'll just do what you say. And you can count on that."

"It's been a while since I counted on anything to do with a man."

"Well, we're fixing to change that." Lucky smiled. "I know it's the corniest thing you ever heard, but damn, I want you to count on me, Bena. I want it worse than anything. Does that sound stupid?"

Lucky settled on an NPR-type station that played jazz—not New Orleans–type jazz, but the other kind, you know, New York type or something where you get the feeling that everybody playing an instrument went to college someplace fancy and studied music until they just about ruined all their natural instincts. He turned the station real low so it gave the same nice effect as if you got a bunch of crickets and cicadas organized into a real well-controlled choir.

Bena leaned back in her seat and looked out the window at the darkening world zooming past, distant house lights dotting the countryside like fireflies. It felt so good to be going someplace. It felt like the whole world was out there waiting for her, and up until this very moment she'd forgotten all about the world—that there was one. That maybe she could be a part of it. At least this one night. She looked over at Lucky, his square hands on the wheel, his hair already curling in the damp night air, his silhouette suddenly so familiar to her. She reached over and punched his shoulder. "Hey there," she said. He grinned, his teeth shining in the headlights of an oncoming car. "Look at us," Bena said, "out here going someplace."

"Idn't it something?"

They drove in silence, then Lucky said, "What you say we take the scenic route?"

"It's pitch-dark," Bena said. "Can you have scenic in the black of night?"

"Hell yes," he said. "You can have scenic any time." At the next sad excuse for an intersection he turned off onto a dark two-lane road that to the naked eye did not look very promising. "You in for a treat," he said. And Bena believed him.

THE RESTAURANT DID look like an electrical white Christmas happening all by itself in the middle of the summer where the road met the water. The reflection of the lights was so pretty the way it shimmied on the lake, like something alive. The name of the restaurant was Larry's, and it was under new management. Before, it had been called Uncle Frank's. "It's a family operation," Lucky explained. "And overall they ain't too original in thinking up restaurant names. When Larry's boy, Buddy, grows up and takes over, then I guess this place will be called Buddy's, what you bet? I guess it don't matter what they call it long as the food stays good."

They had tables outside on a deck, but Bena and Lucky didn't want to worry with mosquitoes so they sat inside at a table pushed up against the window, practically as good as outside since they looked right out on the twinkling water. Lucky ordered Bena a glass of white wine and himself a beer. There were crackers and garlic-cheese spread on the table, which Uncle Frank's had been known for, and now it seemed Larry's aimed to keep it going, but neither of them ate any—although Lucky did pick up an occasional cracker and snap it into bits without thinking what he was doing until he saw the mess he'd made. Bena brushed the crumbs into the palm of her hand and piled them at the edge of the table. She just did it out of habit.

Lucky was on his second beer. "Bena, I'm about as nervous as a sixteen-year-old kid. I swear to God. You got me practically breaking into a sweat here."

Bena laughed. "Take off your jacket," she said. "It's a hot night."

They ordered salads and steaks. Their waitress was as nice as she could be. She seemed to really like her job, which Bena thought was a good quality in a person. There was an orange flickering candle on their table, which was a fine touch in the dimly lit place. It put a sort of golden glow on their faces. Bena liked that and sort of settled into letting herself feel pretty, you know, like nearly any woman can when the lights are low. At tables all around them seemed like people with nice lives, not too many troubles, or at least their troubles put on hold while they paused to eat a nice supper at Larry's. Bena wondered if at any of the other tables was a couple where one person was married and the other was not. She had a feeling there were plenty of couples like that. You know, with reasons of their own.

"I'm a little bit out of practice." Lucky leaned toward Bena like he was going to whisper a confession. "You know, taking a good-looking woman out to dinner. I swear to God, it's like I'm afraid to look away for a minute for fear you might just vanish or something and then I'll find out I dreamed this whole thing up."

Bena smiled.

"Say something," he said.

"Like what?"

"I don't know. Reassure me. Say you're not about to vanish. Tell me it's safe to go to the men's room, that you'll still be here when I come back."

"You're crazy."

"Crazy about you." He grinned.

Bena rolled her eyes. "You can do better than that. Don't you know any *Roses are red, violets are blue* . . . or anything?"

"You're making fun of me." Lucky grinned. "But I don't care. I hadn't felt this way in so long."

"What way?" Bena bit into a cracker.

"You know, silly and ridiculous like this. I'm talking too much. Saying every damn thing that pops into my head. Like everything around me seems so damn funny — you know. Like the stuff I've been doing all my life suddenly seems new to me and I feel sort of awkward about it. It's a wonder I could keep my truck on the road on the way over here. Man." He looked at the beer he was holding and shook his head in disbelief. "Jazzed, I guess. That's what I mean. I hadn't felt this alive in so long, Bena. I've been like that movie, *Dead Man Walking.* I mean it. You should have seen me taking a shower this evening. I was so excited about seeing you tonight I scrubbed myself plumb raw. There is not one surviving germ on this body of mine, I guarantee you that. I am clean as a whistle and doused in cologne, which I don't even believe in — men wearing cologne. Smell right here."

He leaned toward her so Bena could sniff his neck. "Nice," she said. "I like it."

"See what I mean? Just when I thought I'd forgotten how, here I am happy again. Damn if I'm not sitting here spit-shined with this silly grin on my face being an out-and-out happy son of a gun. And I got you to thank for it."

"The pleasure is all mine." Bena smiled. "Scary, isn't it—feeling happy?"

"Hell yes, it's scary. Why you think I'm sitting over here crumbling up these crackers all over the table and sweating like a damn mule. Because I'm happy, that's why. Because I am scared half out of my mind I'm so damn happy."

They started laughing like fools then, both of them. The boy came by and filled their water glasses and Bena thought for a minute, the way he was looking at them, he might just tip his pitcher and soak them both with ice water and say, *Y'all settle down. This is a nice establishment here.* It seemed funny to Bena how disapproving the young sometimes were of the not-so-young. Like maybe they thought laughing and having fun was something decent people were supposed to outgrow. And the sad thing was that for the most part—in Bena's particular case—she had.

"We're annoying the waterboy," Bena said.

"Shoot, that's just an old man in a kid's body."

"Sort of like you," Bena teased.

"Are you kidding me? I got a lot of kid in me still. Too much, according to some people. That's what Sue Cox says: *Damn it, Lucky, grow up.* That's her theme song about half the time."

Bena smiled and took a drink of her wine.

"Oops, sorry," he said. "Promised myself I wasn't saying the W word tonight."

"It's okay," Bena said. "Old habits die hard. Next thing you know I'll probably be buttering your bread and cutting your meat into bites for you, saying, *Use your napkin, don't talk with your mouth full, finish your vegetables.*"

Lucky laughed. "You can mother me all you want to," he said. "I got the feeling I might like it."

"A woman with five kids," Bena said, "that's usually enough to scare most men half to death. I'm impressed you haven't taken off running yet. Especially the way Leslie was looking you over. She's on to you, you know. You're not going to get anything by her."

"She'll get to like me," Lucky said. "Most people do sooner or later."

"Oh really?" Bena laughed. "And why is that?"

Lucky grinned. "I got a certain way with kids and dogs. I won't deny it. It's a gift. But I'm also humble as humble can be. Especially when it comes to women. It's women that made me humble, and it's women that keep me humble." He lifted his beer as if he were going to make a toast, then tapped his glass to hers harder than he meant to, sloshing beer out all over the table, making Bena reach for her napkin and begin sopping up the beer like it was spilt milk and Lucky was another one of her messy children.

"Give me that napkin." Lucky took it from her. "You're off duty tonight. You just sit back and let folks wait on you. I don't want you lifting a finger, you hear?"

Bena blushed like somebody who didn't know how to act in a nice restaurant. They didn't make the customers clean up after them-selves in a place like this. They didn't cry over spilt milk or beer. You were just supposed to relax and be happy and eat some good food you didn't cook yourself. That's all. How hard was that?

The whole idea of just relaxing and being happy got Bena sort of amused and choked up and she couldn't stop hiccuping and gasping for air because the place inside where she stored her laughter, saved it up for later, for holidays and special occasions, for the two or three funniest jokes in the whole world—that place, usually under lock and key, had had the lock picked and the door left hanging open. The feeling was just as real as when you have to sneeze, only it was laugh-ter. And the harder she tried to stop, the worse it got.

"What's so funny?" Lucky asked. "Say?" But before she could tell him she didn't know, had no idea, he was laughing too. They were doubled over, laughing so hard they were crying, tears in their eyes. "I'm sorry," Bena tried to say, but it was all just too comical, the two of them out on a so-called date together, like they were normal people who had a right to some happiness, him with a wife drying out someplace in Atlanta for the hundredth time and her with a dead husband that she half expected to float into the room like a ghost, like a ball of fog rolling in off the dark lake saying, *Okay, Bena, that's enough. Time to go home.*

Mascara tears trailed down Bena's face. And Lucky was red-faced, the lines around his eyes deep and wet. They'd almost calmed themselves down when the waitress came. She set two hot plates before them. One steak well-done. One rare. "Something funny over here?" she asked.

Bena saw the puzzled look on the waitress's face, the sizzling his-and-her steaks with the little plastic markers in them—red for rare, black for well-done. Everything adequately explained. And it was like for that split second the world almost made some sense. "You must be a heck of a funny fellow." The waitress smiled at Lucky. "Must be a pure riot."

When the waitress left, Lucky reached for Bena's hand, which was still gripping her napkin. "Look at you," he said. "If you aren't a sight. I swear to God, Bena, I'd rather listen to you laugh than die and go to heaven." His chin quivered when he spoke and Bena saw that the emotion had come up in him too, was perched right at the edge of what he could deal with. It made her smile to think he was almost as overcome as she was with the tiny lights that reflected and multiplied in the rippling water, making one small thing seem like so much more.

All through dinner it seemed that maybe Bena was pretending to be somebody she wasn't. That she was pretending to be a woman out on a summer night with a handsome man who made her laugh, instead of the mother of a brood of fatherless kids left at home looking after a litter of orphaned cats. Suddenly she was not a sixth-grade teacher with the grade book and the answer sheet but a student of life again, the way she probably used to be sometime so far back that she couldn't even remember it. Life had never been something Bena studied and analyzed and filled up with dreams and questions. It was more just something that had happened to her and she had done her best to deal with it. To stay ready for anything that might go wrong. She'd been faithful and brave and maybe even completely stupid. The more wine she drank the less she cared about who she was or who she was pretending to be. It was good the way wine filled your head with little sparkling stars just like the ones outside the window, floating around on the dark water with no real purpose except just to shine.

TRUE TO LUCKY'S WORD, when the band began to set up, lots of the white people took off for home and lots of black people started filing in. By the time the music started Bena and Lucky were just finishing their lime sherbet. She'd told Lucky all about Sissy and Barrett and he had listened. She said she could hardly stand to let go of her child when she clearly saw that Sissy was barreling head-first down a dead-end road with Barrett. It wasn't the first dead end Barrett had led Sissy into either, and left her to get out of all by herself. Bena told Lucky some of that story, but not every detail because she hated the details too much to tell them to anybody. She said that letting go was only natural when you saw a person headed off into a better life. Not headed off the edge of a cliff.

Lucky said he understood because he was the world's worst at letting go, that that was about 99 percent of his problem. He said he guessed that was one reason why God never let him have any kids. He said he respected Bena for loving Sissy enough to let her make her own mistakes. And maybe it was good Sissy was off on her own to do it, so Bena didn't have to watch and go behind her with a table napkin, cleaning up her spills.

"Maybe Barrett isn't as bad as you think," Lucky said. "There were folks who thought Sue Cox would do better to cut off her head than to marry me. I like to think now that at least some of those folks believe they were wrong in their thinking."

"Maybe," Bena said.

The music was good, the kind Bena had grown up with, black folks singing their hearts out into a too hot world and those songs just melting into you. She liked the sort of music that entered you by way of blood—not ears.

"I'm a nervous wreck dancing around black people," Bena confessed. "Look at those white people out on the dance floor. It about breaks your heart, doesn't it?"

Lucky looked out at the white couples gyrating, their arms up in the air. "Good thing about it," he said, "is that black folks got low expectations of white folks on the dance floor. Which I appreciate."

"Me too," Bena said.

"Come on." Lucky reached for Bena's hand. "Let's me and you twist and shout. Can't waste good music." The music was so loud it was like an ocean that could suck you way out over your head. It's natural and all, the pull of the ocean, but still you know you could die from it easy. The dance floor was crowded and people's skin glistened. She could shag pretty good and so could Lucky, but it seemed like not many people danced that way anymore. In college Bena had liked the way a room full of people all danced like detached individuals, set free from the confines of coupledom—aiming for a no partners-necessary, free sort of life. They stomped and shook and jerked, their heads bouncing, their hair flying. They fought with the music in a way that had thrilled her then. But not anymore. She liked holding Lucky's hand, the way she could read his next move through the touch of his fingers.

But it was the slow dances Bena liked best. Lucky's arm around her, the closeness of his body, the sweat that ran down the side of his face, and hers. She liked the holding on and being held on to, the way Lucky was breathing and singing along and biting his bottom lip, and the way he would peel his face from against hers and look into her eyes and smile so serious. This would last her a long time, she thought, this night.

To Bena, everybody at Larry's was a total stranger, and she took comfort in that. But Lucky knew a handful of the folks out on the dance floor and some standing at the bar. One pretty black woman who'd had almost as much wine as Bena came over and kissed Lucky's cheek, "Hey, baby," she said. "Listen here. You bring me something nice next week, okay? I don't like none the shit you been bringing me lately. Idn't nothing but a bunch of bad news."

Lucky laughed. "I'll see if I can't bring you a sweepstakes notice next week, Ida. You can win you ten million dollars—me and you will split it."

"Now you're thinking right, honey," she said.

"Ida Gamble, meet Bena Eckerd here."

The women smiled at each other. Ida turned to Lucky, "You deliver her mail?"

"Yes, ma'am."

"I bet the mail ain't all you delivering, is it, honey?" Then she laughed hard and swung off into the arms of a sweaty man. They danced like they were the two people on earth who invented dancing in the first place. Like they were born to it.

"The Gambles," Lucky shouted over the music. "Live on my route."

"Look at them," Bena said. "That's how I dance in my dreams."

"About those dreams?" Lucky said. "Who you dancing with in those dreams? Anybody particular?"

WHEN BENA AND LUCKY sat at a table a minute to catch their breath and drink something to try to cool off, some men over at the bar hollered to Lucky, "Didn't know the government gave the mailman no time off to chase women." And they laughed like they were the funniest bunch in Georgia. They hollered like men do when they get in a pack with nothing to do but drink and howl.

"Your mail route too?" Bena asked.

"That biggest guy, I played football with him at Auburn. He tore his knee up too, but not until he got about five years in with Tampa Bay. Two of those boys I went to high school with. The rest of them, I deliver their eviction notices and divorce papers on a regular basis."

The Some Brothers lead singer started singing "You've Lost That Loving Feeling" and threw Bena right back to the days when she used to slow dance with Bobby at parties held in unlit carports when somebody's parents were out of town. It was where she got her first inkling of desire.

Lucky practically jumped up from his chair. "We got to dance to this. I love this song." Then he looked at her. "Not that I think you lost that loving feeling, you understand." He put his arms around her and twirled her in little semicircles right onto the dance floor.

It was not like dancing at all. Lucky held Bena close and all they did was sway just barely. Their faces were pasted together with sweat. It reminded Bena of what they say about being baptized— that a feeling comes over you and claims you. And it can change you forever. Bena was not a religious woman, but dancing with Lucky, Lord, it made her want to believe things.

BY THE TIME the band took a break everybody was drenched to the bone. The room was a deep ocean, the swimmers, barefoot in their good clothes. People drifted outside to try to cool off and smoke and talk. Bena went to the ladies room, where the line for a stall was a mile long, so she just tried to patch herself together the best she could, powdered her sweaty face, pulled the wet strands of hair out of her eyes, clumsily rearranged her bobby pins, and put on fresh lipstick. Good enough. When she went back to find Lucky he took her hand and said, "Let's get out of here, okay? If we stay much longer they're going to have to hang us out to dry."

It wasn't much cooler outside than in. They climbed into the truck and Lucky said, "Let me get this AC going. Shit, I guess I'm more of an old guy than I thought. I was about to have a heat stroke in that place." He aimed a vent so that air would blow in Bena's face, and she was grateful.

"I hadn't been dancing in a hundred years," she said.

"You looked eighteen out there on that dance floor. I wish your kids could have seen you tonight."

"Shoot, my kids would be horrified. They embarrass easy. Hope I didn't trample your feet too bad. I'd hate you to deliver the mail with a limp."

"Are you kidding?" Lucky said. "I'd pay money for you to trample me."

"You are a smooth talker," Bena said. "I know that."

Lucky turned the truck around and headed down the restaurant's gravel road out to the two-lane. He reached for Bena's hand, put it up to his mouth, kissed it, and pressed it hard against his sweaty face. It could have been the wine, or the music, or the late hour, but something made Bena feel dizzy and she leaned her head back on the seat and closed her eyes. She stayed that way a long time, opening her eyes now and then to look over at Lucky, who was singing along with the radio.

"You awake?" Lucky asked.

"I'm watching you drive," she said. "Thinking about what a fine night this was."

"The night's not over yet," he said. "I'm taking the long way home and staying with the speed limit just to make this night last as long as I can. I'm trying to think of a way to get you to slide over here and sit close by me. You should know I'm considering making a sudden sharp turn or maybe running into a shallow ditch or something. You think that would work?"

For a second Bobby flashed through Bena's mind. He was in his flying car on Highway 82 saying something almost exactly like that to Lorraine, just seconds before their car went airborne. Maybe they'd crashed and died when all Bobby had really wanted was Lorraine to be close to him. Maybe if she'd scooted over they would still be alive today.

Lucky put on the brakes and pulled the truck off the side of the road, onto a dirt turnoff. He turned off the headlights and the night went absolutely black. There was nothing but the shriek of crickets to let Bena know she was still in the world. Lucky sat still a minute, she could hear him breathing, but he didn't say anything. So she waited, quiet too. Anything could happen to people on a deserted road like this, on a black night like this. It was like in high school, the story of the maniac with the hook hand who stalked lovers parked in cars. It was like that same exact maniac could be hiding in the bushes or behind a stand of trees. He might be old as the hills by now, but he could still be a maniac with a mission. He could be watching them right now.

"Lucky?" Bena said.

"Give me a minute," he said. "I'm trying to figure out what I want to say to you." He began to tap his hand on the steering wheel. The best Bena could tell he was staring straight ahead into the nothingness in front of them, concentrating, while he tapped the steering wheel and bounced his knee up and down.

She didn't care how long they sat there. She liked being closed up in the darkness with him. She liked sensing his body and hearing the shaky way his words came out when he spoke. He was nervous in the most wonderful way. She liked the silence too, and the thought that for once—like her—he was at a loss for words.

"I don't want to botch this up," he said finally. "I swear to God I want this to come out right, Bena. Pretty soon we'll be pulling up in your driveway and you've got that houseful of kids."

"And cats."

"And cats." He let out a deep breath then and his voice came out hoarse and dry. "I been trying to think about right and wrong and good and bad and all the complications, but mostly I been thinking about you, being close to you like this, and I swear to God if I don't put my arms around you and hold you and kiss you—then I think I'll just have to go home and shoot myself. I mean it."

"I sure would hate that to happen," Bena said. She could feel all the blood run to her head. Her head was just swimming in blood, and her blood was full of the music from the restaurant—it had rhythm to it, her blood. It had an electric guitar and all these perfect lyrics, and it had a man's pleading voice just wailing away with one part love, one part heartache. If somebody had cut her open right then, music would spill out. She would bleed a song, a rendition nobody had ever heard before. "So, I guess you're saying it's up to me to save your life then?"

"I guess that's one way to look at it."

"Well, let me think about it." She reached to touch his face, which she couldn't see. The clear thing was his voice, as gravelly as the road they'd just turned off of.

He pressed her hand against his mouth and kissed it, then placed her hand on the side of his face again, on his scratchy five o'clock shadow that was really an after-midnight shadow, slid toward her on the seat, and put his arms around her and his mouth on hers and kissed her hot and slow and with a desperation as honest as her own. He kissed her nearly forever. It was spiritual resuscitation designed to save her life. She closed her eyes. He leaned against her, and the heat of his breath on her face, her neck, the way he nearly crushed her in the power of his embrace, was not something she'd forgotten but something she'd never known before.

She held him too, ran her hands over the smooth muscles in his arms, put her fingers in his curly hair, touched his square chin and his damp neck where he had let her smell his cologne—which he didn't believe in. She kissed his face, his eyes, his neck, his fingers. She pressed herself against his chest and listened to him breathe and sigh. "Damn, Bena," he whispered. "Where did you come from?"

When the kissing became frenzied and urgent, when his hands felt so hot against her skin that she thought they would leave burn marks, that she would wake up tomorrow and have his sooty fingerprints all over her face and arms but she would see that they were beautiful—and if she ever forgot this night, this joy, the police could study the evidence on her skin and trace it back to Lucky McKale, the man who touched her like no other man ever had. She was dizzy and feverish and maybe Lucky knew that, because he stopped himself then. She wouldn't have known how to stop. She didn't let herself think about tomorrow or next week or the rest of her life. For once Bena Eckerd was in only one moment in time. This moment. This truck, this dirt road, this night, this man. It was not Bena who pulled back and whispered, "God, I don't want to mess this up. I want this to be right." And so he held her and stroked her face, his hands so hot and shaky and sure. He kissed her hair and whispered, "I swear to God, Bena."

3

It wasn't daylight when Leslie cried out, "She's dead." Before Bena could get up from her bed to go see, Leslie came into her room with the tiny dead cat wrapped in the tail of her pajama shirt. "I did everything," Leslie said. "I fed her. I checked on her. She was fine. The others smothered her, Mama. They were on top of her and she was the smallest one. Look." Leslie lifted the kitten out of her shirt. It curled perfectly into the palm of her hand.

Ellie came in then, her hair and face puffed with sleep. "At least she died loved." Ellie touched the little corpse. "At least she didn't die inside a Hardee's sack with that half-eaten ham biscuit."

But Leslie couldn't be comforted easily. Leslie was Bena's child who most resisted death—and was most drawn to it. She was the child with the pictures of her daddy on the wall above her bed, on her nightstand, and in her billfold. It was his face in the locket she wore around her neck. All these years later she had not let go of him, handed him off to heaven like the others had struggled to do.

When Leslie had been a little girl, death had been part of what bonded her to Bobby. She was barely old enough to walk when she learned to squeal at the sight of any limping four-legged thing, any drowned earthworm washed up by the rain, any bloody carcass attended to by buzzards. Over time the backyard became a cemetery. It had been Bobby who entered into the ritual of these deaths with Leslie, each requiring ceremony and grieving and the guarantee that the afterlife would be better than the actual life. Bobby had been the grave digger. He'd chosen the burial sites and the rocks to mark them, while Leslie wrapped the creatures in dish towels, tin foil, or leftover Christmas paper, telling them about the wonders of heaven.

From the beginning Leslie'd brought home stray animals destined for short, painful lives. The pet goat a man down the road gave her that died from yellow diarrhea in less than a week, starved dogs and cats that wandered up from the road ugly and sick, baby possums that fell off their mother's back without the mother even noticing, endless trash-can raccoons, birds with broken wings that Elvis had sunk his teeth into, turtles trying to cross the highway, rabbits that escaped their pens, baby Easter chicks that grew up to peck and bite and got so mean that even Elvis was afraid of them.

Year after year Leslie's pink and blue Easter chicks had grown into red-feathered attack chickens — squawking, their wings flapping, pecking at hands and legs, leaving dots of blood and tiny bruises. The children became too terrified to go out in the yard. Only Leslie was brave enough to feed them, put on dungarees to do it, carry their cup of corn, dump it on the ground, and run away as fast as she could.

In a moment of surrender, Bobby gave the chickens to the same old man who'd given Leslie the dying goat. But that didn't stop her from grieving for them. It didn't stop her from thinking the next batch of pastel chicks would turn out differently. That they'd rise above their nature and become cuddly and house-trained and sleep at the foot of her bed. Leslie thought enough love could do that. Change the nature of a creature.

Even now, in high school, she had a habit of bringing home the most troubled, outcast kids—those too poor, too fat, too mean, too miserable, too injured to ever fit in. Girls who had had babies in the ninth grade. Girls whose boyfriends were in prison or married or drug addicted and dangerous. Girls with green spiked hair and pierced faces, holes punched into their eyebrows, lips, tongues, and noses. Girls beaten by furious mothers, who came to school purple and puffy with stories to tell. Skinny young girls who had given up, who were already too tired to be angry anymore. And sad, matronly girls whose spirits were lost somewhere in their generous flesh. These were the girls Leslie brought home for supper. The girls she lent her clothes to and her homework and whose birthdays she always remembered.

And boys too. The ones who had been to juvenile detention a million times. The kind of boys who didn't mind going to detention because it was better than home. Boys who attempted suicide on a regular basis, like some kind of weird hobby. And other boys who memorized song lyrics about the thrill of dying, rented movies full of murder and blood, read books about true crime. Death enthusiasts of a different sort. Angry boys who carried guns and grudges and hoped Leslie might consider being their girlfriend.

But luckily for Bena, Leslie didn't aspire to be a girlfriend so much as a savior. Thank God. Very early on, Leslie had sense enough to know the difference. It was like Leslie was born knowing things. A wise old soul in a young girl's thin, freckled body. Still, outcast boys who needed saving instinctively knew that Leslie was the girl most suited to the challenge. They flocked to her and presented their sad stories, confided terrible tragedy as if their misery were an offering of some kind, laid at her feet. She listened. She asked questions. She made them grilled-cheese sandwiches. She tried to understand. She longed to suffer with them. Leslie was always grateful to anyone who could break her heart in a new and interesting way.

Leslie believed that Bobby—more than the rest of the family—understood the mystery of death. That he was like her that way. And when he died—it was like terrible proof. It also left her all alone in the understanding.

Later, when Elvis died of old age, Leslie insisted that he'd pined away for Bobby. Eddie got in a crazed fistfight with Leslie because she kept saying, "Now Elvis can be with Daddy. Isn't that wonderful?" Eddie listened until there was nothing to do but smack his sister and threaten to send her to their daddy too if she said one more stupid word. Death was not wonderful to Eddie—whatever else it was, it wasn't wonderful. He didn't want to hear a bunch of stuff about heaven either. Which just served to prove Leslie's point about the spiritual deficiencies of her family.

"Give me the cat, Les," Bena said. "We'll get Eddie to bury it later." She put the cat in an old shirt she'd pitched into the give-away pile the night before and laid it on the bed beside her.

"Hey, Mama," Ellie said. "Why didn't you wake us up last night?"

Lucky had brought Bena home very late to find a scrawled note on the door that said, *Mama, wake us up when you come home.* But she hadn't. She had watched Lucky's truck go down the drive, his headlights looking wild-eyed and startled as they wove their way through the black trees. She had looked in on the sleeping girls and the box of sleeping cats—she couldn't look in on Eddie because he slept with his door locked. Then she had washed her face and gotten into bed, not to sleep but to replay the night in her head, every detail, until she was lulled into a dreamy state, which she clung to as long as she could.

"Details," Ellie said. "We need details, Mama." Ellie was imitating Bena, the way she hovered around her daughters gathering details after big events in their lives. "Don't leave anything out," Ellie mimicked. She climbed into Bena's bed. Leslie sprawled out too, careful not to disturb the dead cat, her eyes on Bena, watching for whatever her mother might leave unsaid.

"Well, we went over to Georgia," Bena began, "to a place called Larry's. It's out on West Point Lake."

"Larry's?" Leslie said. "That's a black place. The black kids at school are always talking about Larry's."

"It's not black," Bena said. "It's both. It's mixed. Anyway, we had a real nice table looking out over the water. We ate steaks and we talked about things."

"Like what?" Leslie asked.

"Everything," Bena said. "Then after dinner we danced."

"Mama, you're not telling us anything," Ellie complained.

"One to ten, Mama?" Leslie said. "What was your night with Mr. McKale?"

Bena smiled. "Let me see. I guess it was somewhere between . . . " She paused. "Twenty and thirty!"

"My gosh." Ellie picked up a pillow and slung it at Bena in a fit of false laughter.

"You really like him, don't you, Mama?" Leslie asked. "Do you like him more than you liked Daddy back when he first came along?"

"I was fifteen when I first met your daddy," Bena said. "I thought he was the most exciting boy in the world."

"And now?" Leslie asked.

"Now I'm the old woman in the shoe and I think Mr. McKale is pretty nice."

"*Pretty nice,* my hind foot," Ellie said.

Leslie stroked the dead cat with her finger. "Mama, aren't you even the least bit bothered that the man has a wife?"

LATE THAT AFTERNOON when Lucky called it was Leslie who answered the phone. "One of your cats died," she told him.

He said he was sorry and he'd like to come by the house if that was all right. Maybe he could bury the cat for her. But she said no, Eddie had already buried the cat. So then he asked if she thought there was anybody at the house who might not like the idea of him stopping by?

Leslie was silent a minute. "I guess it's all right," she said. "Now that we know you're between a twenty and a thirty."

"Excuse me?" he said.

WHEN LUCKY PULLED UP Bena was sitting in a lawn chair studying a Sears sale catalog. She had on shorts and was barefooted. She waved to him. He got out of the truck with a sack in his hand and walked toward her with a smile on his face.

"It makes me nervous to see you coming up here carrying a sack," she said. "I hope there's nothing alive in there. We've already had one funeral today."

"Hello to you too." He grinned. He looked like he was thinking of bending down to kiss her, then he glanced toward the house. "Where are your kids?"

"They're in the house staring out the window, waiting for you to throw me to the ground in a fit of passion right here in broad daylight."

"I like the way they think." Lucky grinned.

"So what's in the sack?"

"Barbecue."

"So you think the way to a woman's heart is through her kids' stomachs? Is that the plan?"

"You making fun of my technique?" he said. "Look, I told myself not to come over here today. You know, to act cool about things. Give you a day of rest. Like the Bible says. But damn if I could do it."

Bena smiled. "Come on, let's go in and say hello to the members of the jury."

In the kitchen Ellie was making a devil's food cake from a mix. Eddie was sleeping through a baseball game on TV. Leslie was back in her room.

"Look what Lucky brought." Bena waved the sack. "Barbecue."

Eddie didn't look up or respond in any way. Bena thought maybe he'd just play dead, which seemed to be his preferred method of dealing with most things. Ellie waved her chocolate spoon at Lucky and yelled down the hall, "Les, Mr. McKale brought food."

While Bena fixed ice tea Lucky went over and stuck his finger in Ellie's cake batter. "Hey," she yelled and tapped him on the hand with the spoon, "get out of there."

"What's the occasion?" he asked.

"I was having a craving," Ellie said.

"I have those myself," Lucky said.

"So Mama tells us."

Lucky turned beet red and looked at Bena.

"She's teasing you," Bena said. "You know, *ha, ha, ha.*"

"It's not nice to make fun of an old man," he said. "We're inclined toward heart attacks and stuff when our hearts get racing."

"Just this morning Mama was talking about your heart racing. Right, Mama?"

"You better quit while you're ahead," Bena said.

"What sort of tales you been telling your kids, Bena? Next thing you know I'm going to have a reputation. Have to spend the rest of my life living it down."

"Or living it up." Bena smiled. "Depending on how you look at it."

Leslie came into the kitchen carrying the medicine dropper she'd been using to feed the cats. "What's going on in here?" she asked.

"Mr. McKale is here," Ellie said. "Be nice to him, Les. He's nervous."

"Nervous?" Lucky looked at Bena. "Am I nervous?"

Leslie began rinsing the dropper in the sink. "So what? Are you going to be coming over here every day from now on or what?"

"Leslie," Bena said. "Lucky is welcome here anytime."

Leslie shook the dropper and laid it on a paper towel. "It's just a question."

Outside, Bena and Lucky settled into a couple of flimsy lawn chairs Bena had dragged into the shade earlier. "How are you holding up?"

"Don't worry about me. I'm pretty hard to run off."

"Good," Bena said. "I like that in a man."

WHEN LESLIE CAME outside an hour later Lucky was leaning toward Bena with his tea glass resting on her knee. He was showing her some photographs. Bena was in such a trance over them that she didn't see Leslie coming, but Lucky sat up like a soldier snapping to attention, "Hey there, Leslie."

"What y'all doing?" Leslie asked.

"I'm dragging your mama down my memory lane."

"I was just wondering if you wanted to take time out to look at the cats?"

Lucky looked at Bena, checking to see if this might be a trick question. Before she could say anything he stood up. "Sure I would."

"Follow me." Leslie led him through the kitchen, down the hall to the back bedroom. Bena couldn't help herself. She went to Leslie's room too and stood quietly in the doorway, unnoticed.

"Over here." Leslie sat on the bed and lifted the box so Lucky could look inside. The tiny cats were whining with their legs swimming. Leslie had put a heating pad and a ticking clock in the box like people did with puppies. "They don't like evaporated milk," she told him. "They like sweetened condensed milk better."

Lucky sat down beside her and took the box and set it on his lap. "*Little* rascals, aren't they?" He ran his finger over them.

"The one that died," Leslie said, "I think it smothered underneath the others."

"I hope I hadn't made a mistake handing these cats over to you. It might be too much of a job to save them."

"I hate it when people don't even try," Leslie said.

"I'm grateful to you," Lucky said. "Either way."

"We named them," Leslie said. "This one is Roy Orbison. This one is Otis Redding. And this one is Dolly Parton. See how her fur looks sort of peroxided right there? If she doesn't turn out to be yellow, then we'll change her name later on. The one that died, that was Tina Turner."

"They got a lot to live up to," Lucky said.

"We always name our animals after singers. Our daddy got us started doing that." She took the box from him and set it back on the floor. She kept her head lowered while she arranged the cats in smotherproof positions. "Your wife, she's really pretty. Did she really go through all that stuff she talked about?"

"What you heard was a drop in the bucket."

"So why is she in Atlanta then?"

"Searching," he said. "For the meaning of life—if you know what I mean."

"Is that where the meaning of life is? Over in Atlanta?"

"I guess she thinks so."

"Maybe she's trying to get away from you."

Lucky laughed. "Just come on out and say what you think, girl. Don't hold nothing back."

"Do you still love her?"

Lucky scratched his ear. He looked puzzled, like he didn't know the answer to the question—or maybe he did, but thought he shouldn't let on. He looked at Leslie, a girl nearly grown, long legged and red haired, pretty in a modern sort of way, who he probably guessed could already do what Sue Cox could, and Bena too, which was practically know what he was thinking before he did. No need to try to lie to a woman who will know a lie the minute she hears it.

"Look here," he said. "Me and Sue Cox, our marriage was like— I don't know—a head-on train wreck or something. No survivors. Somewhere in there might be love, I guess. But we couldn't hardly recognize it at this point. It's just mostly a heap of tangled-up memories or something."

"That's sad."

"Things get messed up sometimes. You're old enough to know that. Things go bad wrong. Nobody wants it to happen. But it happens."

"We don't want anything going bad wrong for Mama." Leslie looked at Lucky.

Bena bit her lip. They hadn't noticed her in the doorway.

"Me neither. That's the last thing I want."

"Does your wife know you're taking Mama dancing and stuff?"

"Probably not."

"You should tell her then," Leslie said. "Maybe she'll get mad and divorce you. She should. I know I would."

Leslie was the only redhead in the family. Lucky might have thought maybe she hadn't gotten all the spankings she needed once her daddy died and that was why she had a rudeness to her that the others didn't. But he seemed to like it, her direct insults. It seemed to Bena that something made Lucky think more of Leslie because she had the raw nerve not to think much of him.

Lucky reached over and picked up a picture of Bobby from Leslie's nightstand. Bobby was young in the picture, with long side-burns and a wide necktie. "I knew your daddy," Lucky said. "We played ball together. He was a good guy."

"The good—they die young." Leslie took the picture and put it back.

"You look a little like him," Lucky said. "People tell you that?"

"Sometimes," she said. "They used to."

BENA AND ELLIE were setting out food on the kitchen counter. Ellie's chocolate cake was lopsided but sat on a pedestal plate and looked poised to reward members of the clean-plate club. They fixed plates of barbecue, slaw, and corn sticks and sat around the den in front of the TV, watching the last two innings of the Braves game. It gave them something artificial to concentrate on so that they wouldn't have to concentrate on the absurdity of the situation. A stranger—a man—in the house.

"Mama says you like baseball." Ellie was trying her best not to let Bena down, not to let the evening suffocate itself in dead silence. Leslie and Eddie weren't helping. They sat like two lumps. "We're Braves fans." Ellie said. "Are you?"

"I voted for Hank Aaron for president a couple of years back," Lucky said. "I'll probably vote for him again in the next election."

"Shoot," Bena said.

"You know what?" Lucky said. "Here's an idea. We ought to drive over to Atlanta and see the Braves play one night. All of us. You know, like a family outing or something. What do you think?"

The room fell silent. Everybody turned to stare at him chewing the meat off his barbecued rib. Maybe he was even crazier than they'd originally suspected. Even Eddie turned to look at Lucky like it was the first time all night he'd realized that there was a man in the house, sitting on the sofa next to his mother, eating supper with them as if he had a perfect right to.

It took Lucky a minute to notice that the room was quieter than church. He looked around at Bena and her kids. "Damn. What? Was it something I said?"

MOST EVENINGS LUCKY came to Bena's house and tried his best with her kids. Sometimes it seemed to be working, his efforts to make them laugh or talk. But other times it was like they forgave him for being a fool, but wished to God that their mother had better sense.

Lucky persevered. Sometimes he held Roy, Otis, and Dolly on his lap, their eyes open now, their teeth sharp, and stroked them while he pretended to watch TV. Or he sat outside with Bena and they talked late into the night, whispering and slapping mosquitoes. Bena hadn't returned the photographs Lucky had brought her to look at. They were old family pictures, mostly of his mother and brothers and sisters. But one photo was of a happy couple, fresh-faced and hopeful. "I want you to look at this," he'd said. "Tell me what you see."

Bena had studied the photo. A dark-featured, good-looking man with his arm around a clear-skinned blond girl. The man was gazing at the girl with what looked like intense love. She was smiling at the camera, but was clearly caught up in the glory of the moment. "It's your parents," Bena said. "Your daddy is your spittin' image in this picture."

"What else?" Lucky said.

"Well, they look real happy."

"It's their wedding day," he said.

"They look deep in love, like they can't wait to get started on their life together."

"Mama looks like an angel, doesn't she?" Lucky said. "Looking at this picture you never would guess how bad things would turn out, would you? I don't think they had any idea they were headed into a shitload of misery. I never saw this picture until after Daddy had stopped living with us. I used to get it out of Mama's bureau and stare at it, just to try to believe that there was a happy time between them, even if it was just that one day, their wedding day. A kid needs to believe in a thing like that, don't you think?"

"Sure," Bena said. "I guess so."

"My daddy was as sorry as they come, Bena. I reckon you heard the stories. I reckon I'm not telling you anything you don't already know. But looking at the man in the picture, would you have any way of knowing he was destined to be so sorry?"

"He looks like the nicest man in the world in this picture."

"See, I think that was what my mama was thinking when she married him. They had seven kids in nine years. I'm the youngest, so I don't have some of the worst memories the others got. My sisters, thank God, they were blessed with good looks, so they managed to get away from home early, just as soon as they could. Got one sister down in Ocala, Florida. And one up north in Washington, D.C. They both married pretty good—men with good-paying jobs, you know. And my third sister, DeeDee, she's all the way out in California. She took a Greyhound bus out there all by herself when she wasn't but seventeen. Lord, Mama cried. But DeeDee was always dreaming about getting in the movies and being famous. She's been married three different times now. She never has come back to Alabama since Mama died, but I get a card from her now and then. She always puts *War Eagle* on there," he grinned. "That girl loves football."

"I remember her a little," Bena said. "She was real pretty."

"Looked just like Mama." Lucky clapped his hands as if he was trying to chase away the thought the way you chase away a mosquito. "My three brothers now. They're a different story. Shorty, you know, he's off in prison. Six more years. And Buck and Jerrell, they're both bad to drink, same as Daddy. I hate to say it, but they're just about Daddy made over, both of them. Got kids scattered around that they don't do nothing for. Got a string of women that love them for about ten or fifteen minutes, then proceed to hate them the rest of their lives. I won't defend them either. They're sorry dogs, the both of them. I love them the same as I ever did, but damn, they didn't learn nothing from watching Daddy go to ruin."

"But you did," Bena said. "Why you and not them?"

"People were always saying athletics turned my life around. The scholarship."

"But you don't think so?"

"It helped, sure. But the difference between my brothers and me wasn't football. It was that they had their minds on Daddy all the time, how bad they hated him, how they were going to get even with the old man someday, torture him like he did us. There were times they'd find out where he was living and drive by there and shoot out his windows or something. Everybody in his house would start hollering and crying, kids running everywhere. His old lady would call the police on them. They slashed his truck tires. They siphoned all the gas out of his truck. They spray-painted a bunch of vulgarity on the side of his old lady's house. That time, he called Mama and told her what they done. Oh, Lord, you talk about a scene now. Mama trying to whip Buck and Jarrell and they were both already bigger than she was. She was yelling that she was not raising her boys to behave like trash. But there was nothing she could do to stop them really. They were obsessed with Daddy.

"But me, I had my mind on Mama mostly, watching her heart get tore up—her own boys getting as sorry as their daddy—and how she held on the best she could—tried hard to hold us all together too. I used to dream about the nice places I was going to take Mama and all the things I was going to buy her when I grew up. Me and Mama would thumb through the Sears and Roebuck catalog for hours, putting marks on all the stuff she wanted that I promised I was going to buy her someday."

"And did you?"

"Hell yes, I tried. That was one thing Sue Cox was real good about. She liked doing for Mama too."

"You must miss her something awful," Bena said.

"That's why I drug all these pictures over here for you to see. Because I'm trying to make you understand something that I ain't even sure I understand myself. When Daddy left us, you might think Mama would of said good riddance like people thought she should. But no, she just pined away for him. We'd hear her in there crying herself to sleep at night. We were always getting a story that Daddy was off living with some other woman somewhere, drinking up all her money and slapping her kids around, same as he done us. But even so, it hurt, you know. Why was he off with some other family when he had a perfectly good family of his own, right? I know he was sorry as the day is long, but still, it made us feel like something was wrong with us, the way he was always wanting to be off with some other lady and her kids—and not at home making us miserable like he should be. See, it gets messed up like that, your mind does, when you're a kid."

"I know," Bena said. "I got sixth graders who come from that same kind of thing. You can just look at them and see that their hearts are busted to pieces. Some of them will probably grow up to kill somebody."

"Here's what got me," Lucky said. "Sometimes we'd glimpse one of these women Daddy was living with. We'd see them at the grocery store buying some pork chops, or at one of my brother's ball games when they played against the sons of these women, or just riding down the road in Daddy's tore-up truck, a bunch of hungry-looking, riffraff kids squatted down in the truck bed. Daddy'd just sling a beer bottle out the truck window and keep on going like he didn't know us. And I swear to God, Bena. I don't mean this hateful, but damn. Those were some rough and nasty-looking women Daddy took up with. They looked like something the cat dragged in—most of them. Some of these women were so fat they couldn't hardly move around, just sit in a chair on their lopsided porch all day fanning themselves with a picture of Jesus. And it like to killed all of us, most especially Mama. If he'd have left us to move up in the world, then we might have stood it. But he just turned to pure trash. No other way to say it." Lucky shook his empty glass for emphasis, the ice cubes rattling.

"Your mama ever meet anybody, you know, and get a second chance herself?"

"Never did," Lucky said. "Some people don't want a second chance, Bena. You know that? Rather have the mess they've got than anything better. They get attached to their misery. I learned that. Some men tried to be nice to Mama, but she wouldn't have it. She was loyal to Daddy right up until the end, no matter how crazy we thought that was. The rest of us got to where we hated him so bad it felt sort of good, you know? It freed us up some. But she never did. She swore if it wasn't for liquor he'd have been as fine a man as you could ever hope for. I guess she needed to believe that, but none of us did." Lucky shook his head and looked into his empty ice-tea glass. "Damn."

Bena reached over and poured some of her tea into his glass, same as she would do if he was one of her kids sitting there. "I guess no woman likes to think her whole life stems from one big mistake made in the name of love," Bena said. "Believe me, I know that feeling —where you can't stand for people to think the father of your children is no good. You get dedicated to promoting his finer qualities, and it kills you because you can't hardly get anybody to believe you."

"You know what Mama said to me when she was dying?" Lucky sat his glass on the ground, folded his hands, rested his elbows on his knees. "She said, *Son, promise me this. You've married you a girl you love, and so you stay with her no matter what happens, you hear me? There's nothing so bad you can't make your way through it. God means a husband and wife to stay together until death do they part.* She was holding up the little Bible she kept in the bed with her at the end."

"So what did you say to that?" Bena asked.

"I promised her I would. I swore on the Bible in her hand."

Bena looked at Lucky's face and for a minute she could see the boy he used to be. The boy in the pictures with the big eyes and cowlick —thin as a rail. She could see him at his mama's bedside, helpless as a young man could be, promising to devote *his* life to undoing the mistakes of *her* life—so maybe she could die in peace.

"Mama wasn't but fifty-two when she died," Lucky said. "But she looked every day of one hundred. She got us all raised—she did sewing for people and took in ironing, but mostly we scraped by on public aid. Mama wouldn't let us call it *welfare*—made us call it public aid like maybe we wouldn't be as ashamed that way. Sometimes if one of us needed something real bad and couldn't find a way to get it, then Shorty would go out someplace and steal it. He was the oldest, you know. He took us as his to look after."

"Why you think you're telling me all this?" Bena asked.

"Two reasons. One, I want you to know what I come from."

"Okay," Bena said.

"I made my mama a promise, Bena. So far I've been able to keep it."

"And now?"

"And now I don't know."

⟪◉ I I ◉⟫

THE GIFT OF WEEPING

4

For the rest of the summer, a couple of days a week Bena met Lucky down at the road where he stopped to put her mail in the box. She got in the van with him and rode along on his route. She liked to double-check his trays to be sure he was putting the right mail in the right boxes. She nearly always found a few stray letters stuck in with the wrong batch and took pleasure in saving the U.S. Post Office that small embarrassment.

When Lucky had to walk the mail through the Baxter Heights housing project or the Dogwood Village apartment complex she sat in the van and sang along with the radio while she waited for him. In just a few short weeks she'd learned the names of neighbors she'd been waving to for years, traveled roads she didn't know existed, and read through an assortment of circulars, junk mail, and postcards. She figured that anybody who sent a postcard didn't actually mind if strangers read it since it seemed designed for that. And she also marveled at the fact that the world was so full of folks who couldn't spell. She decided to stress spelling more than ever when school started up again. It was a wonder to her that as many letters reached their destinations as did.

Some days Bena brought a sack lunch with her and she and Lucky ate egg-salad sandwiches out in a cow pasture or at the edge of the woods or beside a stocked fishpond somewhere that Lucky wanted her to see. Other days they stopped for Krispy Kreme or Kentucky Fried. Sometimes they got egg rolls from the Golden Dragon, a little restaurant next to the car wash that Bena had never noticed before. The Golden Dragon also sold tacos that tasted exactly the same as the egg rolls. Lucky said he guessed Ben Choi was intending to make his menu seem worldly and exotic to the discerning Baxter County consumers. He told Bena that at one time the Golden Dragon also served little slabs of Italian pizza and sauerkraut and bratwurst—and every bit of it tasted like egg rolls. He said he'd suggested that Ben Choi change the name of the place to Egg Rolls Fifty Nifty Ways. Bena thought this was funny.

Ben Choi, the Chinese man who owned the Golden Dragon, spoke with a heavy Southern accent, saying, "What y'all have today?" and "It's coming up a cloud out yonder." Bena loved the way he insisted on delivering the unexpected. She wondered if he might be the only ethnic person in all of Baxter County, in which case she hoped folks were friendly to him, and that his business was making a go. She also wondered if folks had hounded him to death to give up Buddha and get right with Jesus, and judging by the way he was talking she supposed they had. She wouldn't be surprised if he didn't teach a Sunday school class somewhere where he convinced people that Buddha was a false idol, unlike Jesus, who was the living, breathing son of God and the only direct route to heaven. She wondered if deep down he really believed it or if he just said so for a minute's peace.

Bena especially loved Ben Choi's fortune cookies. He wrote the messages himself with a red ink pen. Her favorite so far said, *Yes is the answer you are looking for*. It gave her a chill when she read it. The most worrisome said, *He who lies to himself lies to God.* This message bothered her so much she threw it out the window.

TWICE WHILE THEY were on the mail route it rained those fierce summer rains designed to cleanse the world and everybody in it. The second rain was the worst—or best. The sky was black as night. Lightning shot across the treetops, beautiful and threatening, as if the trigger finger belonged to someone not so much angry as careless—totally irresponsible. Bena jumped at every blast of thunder, as if in their own way, she and Lucky were actual witnesses to the bottom falling out of kingdom come.

The wipers slapped at the van's windshield fast and furious, but it was mostly useless. The van floated down flooded roads and through red clay lakes that formed at low spots and intersections. Bena was overcome by the thrill of the storm's destruction, the stalled trucks everywhere, cars minus drivers upended in gullies or slammed into trees, soaked people in knee-deep water, skirts held high, pants legs rolled, shoes in hand, sloshing along the roadside, sometimes smiling and waving at passersby. The nuisance of it all seemed like a strange sort of pleasure, like all the serious adults in Baxter County had been allowed, one more time, to play under a frenzied sprinkler, to ruin their good clothes in the rain and red clay, to be late to work or to never show up at all and either way be forgiven.

Bena watched the fallen tree branches, the way they crushed parked cars and rooftops, barricaded the roads, and brought down the telephone lines in one tangled fell swoop. She imagined the leaking roofs of the houses they coasted past, the people inside scurrying to set out pots and pans, calling for their cats and dogs to come in, counting their children, keeping the soap operas going nonstop on their companionable TV sets, which beeped out cheerful storm warnings.

Lawn furniture, plastic toys, and trash bags floated in the ditches.

Near-drowned dogs searched for cover, shivering their way up under trailers and homemade toolsheds, whimpering at each bolt of
lightning that stabbed earth or sky. It's a sight to see a yard dog cry.
Some folks have never seen it. They don't know the true fear and
sadness dogs are capable of. Lucky had left Tom in the house, but
told Bena he knew Tom was under the bed in a knot of terror, waiting for Lucky to come home and turn off the thunder the same way
he could turn off the smoke alarm or the stereo when the vibration
of the bass started to drive Tom crazy. "Tom thinks I got the pow-
ers of God," Lucky said.

Bena remembered Elvis. The way he scratched at the door and
cried every time a jolt of lightning sawed through the treetops. How
Joe and Eddie would cut class, catch a ride, or set out on foot, get
home any way they could to let Elvis in the house. No threats of de-
merits or zeros or school suspension could keep them from it. Later
Bena would come home from school to find Elvis in Eddie's lap,
Eddie feeding him ice cream out of the carton with a serving spoon.
Elvis's claw marks were still on the door to this day, the wood raw
with the desperate message he'd scratched there.

The thing Bena loved about water was the way it forced things to
the surface. Fears and feelings too. Whatever she was feeling inside
was magnified when it rained. Water was as powerful as love that
way. She supposed anybody who lived in Alabama for long came
to know that. Rain could make people change their minds, change
their plans, and seek a higher plane. Water tricked nature into revealing its mysterious side. Hidden things came out in the open,
things that ordinarily depended on darkness for safety. Buried things
floated upward. The same was true with things buried deep in Bena's
blood. The rain unearthed them. Her desire to live a true life over-
came her fear of making a foolish mistake or a fool of herself. Even
if she couldn't swim a lick—she'd rather try than drown.

Around the van snakes skimmed across the water, their telescope
heads poked up. They swam for front porches or clotheslines or the
roofs of trucks. Poisonous or not they curled themselves around TV

antennas, road signs, rusted basketball hoops. When Lucky came upon a mile-long black snake knotted around a mailbox, Bena's feet instinctively flew up off the floorboard and she held them in midair, trying not to let out the scream that was swelling up inside her. If you didn't know better you'd think the snake was trying to get in the van and find himself a dry place among the undelivered letters. Lucky struggled with it, two-fisted, saying, "Would you look at this. This damn snake is crazy."

"God, I hate snakes." Bena dug her nails into Lucky's thigh. "Let it go."

Lucky slammed the mailbox closed and flung the snake into the flooded ditch. Bena took a leftover Golden Dragon napkin and patted Lucky's face dry.

High above, trees canopied the road and swayed, waving their limbs, sort of dizzyheaded, and drunk in their distress. The lack of rhythm was frightening. The cracking limbs like breaking bones. Any minute an oak could uproot itself and fall on the mail van, crushing them. They would die together that way. It was almost a comforting thought. Bena figured Lucky would know his way around the afterlife just as well as he did Baxter County. She could hardly think of anyplace she wouldn't be willing to go if Lucky was by her side. Even hell, which she suspected did not frighten him as much as it did other people, since he had experienced so much of it here on earth already.

She thought then of Bobby, and how glad she suddenly was that he had not died alone. That Lorraine had come right behind him, bringing enough forgiveness for both of them and knowing the way. Bena thought that as sure as Bobby had been of this life on earth, he'd been just as unsure of what came next. Heaven had always been a hard thing for him to believe in. Even after he got saved and cried in church, scaring his children, their daddy weeping like that in front of everybody they knew, his head bowed to keep them from seeing, he was not as sure of heaven as he wanted to be. But maybe once Lorraine came along she managed to convince him of heaven by taking him there herself.

Bena noticed stunned birds perched in dark couples on the low limbs, silent as pairs of rolled socks. Lucky took Bena's hand, "You okay over there?"

She looked over at Lucky, leaning forward in the driver's seat, swiping at the windshield with his open hand, trying to see out, while the rain slammed down on them harder and harder, so hard you could just about drown in the noise it made. Lucky looked steamy and blurred. To Bena he was practically beautiful—a square-jawed man, worried about the weather, about where he was going, taking her with him. Bena loved the moments when the black-and-white world went so soft and gray. "I love you," Bena whispered. "Right now I do."

"What'd you say?" He was concentrating on keeping the van afloat on the road, which had vanished under a good foot of water.

"I love a good rain," she said. "I really do."

It was true. Bena loved storms. All her life she had loved the feeling that something powerful was happening and there was nothing she could do about it—except submit to it. Even if she was slightly afraid she was also relieved when the sky busted open and spilled everywhere. It felt sort of like a spontaneous holiday. Like the heavenly father might be angry again or might be celebrating something remarkable—but either way was trying to get a certain point across to the world. So Bena tried to listen out for one of those messages from on high that other people claimed to have gotten. Maybe it would be brought to her by a dove with an olive branch in his mouth—but in Baxter County more likely it would be a blue jay with a dogwood twig. It was like the rain washed away some of her doubt and she became a clean slate in case God Almighty wanted to use her in one of his mysterious ways.

Bena imagined huge falling pines, oaks, gums, and pecan trees turning her house into a stack of kindling like she had seen in pictures after tornadoes touched down. How she'd have to start over then with nothing to her name except her children and her second chance. She got excited thinking about how free they'd all be then to change their lives, to have some small say in their personal histories. She always imagined that life would be better if she had to start over, although she wasn't sure what exactly she would do differently.

She fantasized lightning striking her, the way it would enter through her feet and pierce her heart and what would happen then? Could the rescue squad bring her back to life? While they worked on her, would she come loose from her body, float up above, and get a glimpse of Bobby and Lorraine waving for her to let go of her small life and to come with them into that vast other realm where people fly around in a state of enlightenment, all questions answered, all mysteries solved?

Storms were about as close to danger as Bena came on any regular basis. Afterward there would be a bad mess to clean up, some damage done, but it seemed worth it. Storms reminded Bena that sometimes you had to give in to the forces of nature.

LUCKY STEERED THEM along the familiar route, made surreal by the way the sky was masquerading as a river. More than once they had to stop and wait out a deluge before easing on. They didn't talk much but looked at each other, and sometimes Lucky touched Bena's hand or her hair. Her face was flushed and her body ached like she had the flu, only it was an excellent feeling. If anybody asked she would have said she was running a fever, that was why she felt so hot to the touch. She stayed busy wiping fog from inside the windows, using up a box of Kleenex tissue.

They couldn't make it to Baxter Heights, the housing project, because the road was washed out, which meant that people there would be spared their past-due notices with the compounded late fees. There was nothing for Lucky to do but give up. Try again tomorrow. When the brakes went out and the muddy red water started seeping in the doors Bena said, "You got to give up." And so he did.

With the van stalled there was nothing to do but wait it out. Let the brakes dry out a little. "This has happened before," Lucky said. "Nothing to worry about."

"I'm not worried," Bena said.

"You can swim, can't you?" He leaned toward her and pulled her to him and his breath on her face felt as hot as her nervous blood. The way he was breathing made her crazy dizzy too. She was thinking that maybe all the electricity in the air, the threat of momentary electrocution by lightning, had done something to their hearts. Magnetized them or something scientific like that. She swore it felt like the pull between them, the way her chest slammed against his so forcefully, was something bigger than simple desire.

His kisses were hot and desperate and she welcomed them. She kissed him back with what was neither courage nor curiosity—the way it had been when she'd kissed other men she'd found herself alone with since Bobby died. She'd kissed men because they sort of expected it, or because she was using the kiss as a way to apologize for feeling nothing for them, or because it might soothe their hurt feelings, or because she didn't know what else to do in a miserable moment. This was different. She spoke her heart to him with her kisses and he answered her and answered her and answered her.

When he tugged her shirttail loose and slid his hand underneath, his hot fingers touching her hot skin, she liked it. She unbuttoned her shirt and pulled him to her, his hands, the rough beard of his face, the sweet unspoken words he breathed. The place inside her head that ordinarily issued warnings and kept her careful was on vacation. All the little internal police that patrolled her blood and brain, trying to maintain bodily law and order—had quit. They sensed, like Bena, that if she was lucky, trouble was at hand.

Lucky locked the doors and helped Bena climb into the back of the van, where he cleared enough space for them to lie down on the carpeted floor. The rain came down in sheets, making the van sway and lean. It sounded almost as nice as rain on a tin roof the way it turned the outside world away and made speaking useless. They undressed each other slowly and silently, just eyes and mouths and trembling fingers talking. Bena guided his hands over her body, only pausing once, wishing she hadn't worn a bra with broken clasps, held together with a stupid safety pin that he fumbled with. Wishing she'd worn lace panties and not her usual industrial-strength cotton underwear. But those thoughts were fleeting. She was older now, thank God. Gone was that old feeling that she was trying out for a part in some grand two-character performance that called for a persuasive stage presence, a special costume, and maybe even the ability to convince the audience to believe some particular thing. No props necessary anymore. Just her warm skin—and his.

His nakedness was as thrilling to her as her own. She could not even remember this kind of nakedness. To lie with him, both of them hotheaded and hot-bodied, the van steamy, fog weeping down the windshield, was something she hadn't known how to dream. To be held by him, to feel loved by him—it was not like when she was young and nervous, not having learned her own body yet, not sure how she would like loving a man, wondering if she would know what to do, wanting to find out. This was better. Her body knew itself so well that it could be turned loose to know his body—this man she loved.

He whispered her name. He clung to her and told her he loved her. He needed her. He wanted her. And she believed him because he was speaking her own feelings too. And the first time he pushed himself inside her she nearly cried. She dug her fingernails into him, trying to be sure he was real, trying to mark him as hers, her man, her lover. She didn't care if the floodwaters rose so high they floated the van off to some strange new place far away.

They loved each other with total desperation and tenderness. So much of Bena's life she hadn't lived in her own body. Her body had seemed to her more of an accessory to the life she lived mostly in her head. She took it with her everywhere, of course, like her purse, or her driver's license—because it helped explain who she was in case anybody wanted to know. But she had never really been quite at home in her body. This day maybe that changed. Maybe her mind married her body at last and the union was mighty. Her heart beat so strong and sure that Lucky lay his head on her breasts just to listen to how alive she was.

She loved him because he was the reason why.

THAT EVENING WHEN Lucky finally delivered Bena up her driveway to let her out in the shelter of her carport, he spoke like he was suddenly shy. "I swear to God hadn't nothing like this ever happened to me before. I get scared to take my eyes off you, Bena. Scared I'll look around and you won't be there. I don't think I could take that. I swear I don't."

"I'm here," Bena said. "I'm not going anywhere."

"I'm going to do right by you. I swear to God I am." Lucky reached for her the way he had the whole way home, to touch her hand, her face, her hair, which she had tried to put up with a rubber band off one of the mailers, into something that resembled a ponytail. She was a mess, wrinkled and damp and sticky, but she felt wise and beautiful.

"I'll call you," Lucky said. "Maybe you can come out to the house tonight, help me coax Tom out from under the bed?"

"Maybe," Bena said.

"What's happening here—with me and you—it's nothing ordinary."

"I know," Bena said.

Bena waved as Lucky drove off. All around her the world was wet and green. It smelled clean. But above her the sky was bruised. The clouds black and swollen.

IT WAS EDDIE who pointed out that what Bena was doing was against the law, a civilian riding around in a government vehicle. "You could get arrested, Mama," he said. "Everybody sees you."

"There are worse things than jail," Bena teased. "I could get a lot of reading done in jail, catch up on all the soap operas and my letter writing and my sleep."

"Yeah," Eddie sneered, "I always wanted a jailbird for a mother. That would cap things off just right."

"You don't begrudge me a little fun, do you?"

"Is it too much to ask for you to confine your fun to the realm of what's legal, Mama? Before long you'll be running bootleg whiskey or dancing on tabletops. You're getting a little crazy on us."

"I'm not crazy, baby. I'm just happy."

"Looks to me like Mr. McKale is leading you to hell in a handbasket."

Bena smiled. That was an expression Bobby used to use. *To hell in a handbasket.*

"That's what they said about Moses when he was trying to lead his people to the promised land," Bena said. "You got to have a little faith, honey." She kissed Eddie with loud smacks, the way he used to like when he was little. He rolled his eyes and pulled away from her.

"Is that where y'all go every day?" Eddie said. "The promised land?" He looked like he would gag and went back to his room and slammed the door shut.

BENA SPENT AN HOUR soaking in the tub. Twice she drained the cooled water and replenished it with hot. She was reliving the afternoon. Replaying the words Lucky had spoken. Believing them over and over again.

The phone rang as she stepped out of the tub. She wrapped herself in her robe and dripped her way to the phone. Outside you'd think the world was coming to an end. The wind was blowing so hard the rain was going sideways. It sounded like a spray of bullets when it hit the windows. People said you could get electrocuted talking on the phone in a bad storm like this. The line crackled the way it always did in the rain, making the other voice sound a million miles away, like somebody calling from a far-off planet or the back side of the moon.

"Hey, Mama." It was Sissy. There was a cheeriness in her voice that stopped Bena in her tracks. This was the way Sissy had always delivered bad news, as if she were thrilled with it, as if she were just the luckiest girl in the world to have something else to suffer.

"Sissy," Bena said. "Is everything okay, baby?"

"I got good news, Mama." Sissy's voice was too happy-happy, like somebody who has forgotten the original joke but just remembers the punch line, the part where you're supposed to die laughing. "I'm pregnant, Mama."

"Oh my God, Sissy."

"Be happy for me, Mama. Please." Bena felt Sissy's words swell as she spoke.

"Are *you* happy about it, Sissy?"

Outside lightning slammed across the sky, turning the air momentarily pink. In that flash the world looked raw to Bena, and hopelessly tender.

"I couldn't tell you when I left, Mama. I knew you'd blame Barrett for everything."

"Where is Barrett? Let me speak to him."

"He got a job working on a cruise ship, just like we planned. He works in food services and they pay him pretty good. They're training him, you know. He's going all the way to Barcelona, Spain. He left two days ago."

A scream was lodged in Bena's throat.

"He's going to fly home when it's time for the baby. He promised."

"Barrett is good at making promises," Bena said.

"Mama, don't."

"Come home, Sissy. I can send you a ticket."

"I can't *come* home, Mama. I *am* home. I've got a part-time job at a Kwik Copy. I answer the phone and take the orders and stuff. You can't work on a cruise ship when you're expecting. But the people at the Kwik Copy are really nice."

"So Barrett is off living *your* dream, while you sit home pregnant with *his* baby?"

"It's my baby too, Mama."

Bena was silent, wishing every impossible thing.

"A baby is real, Mama," Sissy said slowly. "But a dream is just, you know, a dream. And I'll get myself another dream. Later on. A better one. I promise."

When Sissy paused, Bena knew it was because she thought she was explaining a foreign concept to Bena, one too advanced for her mother, who as far as anybody knew had never bothered to come up with even the smallest little nothing dream of her own. It was just like Sissy, Bena thought, whose life was just one catastrophe after another, to pity Bena. Sissy thought even a tacky dream, even a totally messed up dream that might get you sent to prison was better than no dream at all.

For a minute Bena was angry at Sissy, her immaturity, her insistence on messing up her life every chance she got. For a split second Bena considered just hanging up the phone and letting Sissy luxuriate in this latest shattered dream all by herself. Sissy might think Bena didn't know the first thing about dreams, but it wasn't so. Hadn't Bena watched Bobby and all her children dream themselves half to death, hadn't she been the one who comforted them when their dreams went to hell? Who did Sissy think they'd all turned to whenever they were caught in between dreams? Bena had been dragged into more dreams than one person could stand—she knew as much about dreams as anybody. So what if they had mostly belonged to other people. They were people she loved. That must count for something.

"Dreams are free, Mama," Sissy explained. "A person can have as many as she wants. It's okay if every single one doesn't come true."

It would not do for Bena to scream on the phone. Wasn't Sissy calling to tell her what Bena had feared all along, that Barrett would make Sissy miserable all the days of her life? As long as he lived and claimed to love her—Sissy would suffer. If anybody was going to scream it needed to be Sissy, who was too busy trying not to cry; the catch in her voice told Bena that much.

Maybe Bena had done wrong by Sissy over the years, suffering for her if she could, robbing her of her pain like it was money and Bena needed it worse than Sissy did. Like she would tuck it away in a secret pain account, where it could accrue interest, save it for a rainy day when Sissy might really need pain and not have any. Maybe all of this was Bena's fault after all. Maybe it was because of her that Sissy had to keep looking for more and more pain, just so she could have some of her very own—that nobody else could take away from her. Maybe pain is a basic human craving of some kind and there are certain people who never really get enough.

Bena thought of Sissy when she'd started first grade, wearing saddle oxfords and a barrette in her hair, catching the school bus so fearlessly, when the other children on the bus had looked to Bena like potential bullies, all of them. And how Sissy had waved good-bye to Bena, so proud of herself, so sure that the future was a good place, so excited to go into it with nothing but milk money in her pocket. How Bena had watched the bus jerk away, taking her beautiful firstborn into the cold hard world and how she'd cried her eyes out. Even then she'd suspected the world would disappoint Sissy. That Sissy was a child who'd always dream a finer world than she'd ever find. It's something that cannot be explained, how a mother senses the sort of heartache that lies ahead for a certain child, how she can glimpse it and try to prepare for it—but cannot prevent it no matter how hard she tries. It's her powerlessness that makes a mother cry the way Bena had cried that day. Bobby had teased Bena because he didn't know what she knew. There was no point in explaining it to him either. It wasn't the sort of thing he'd have been able to believe.

"Mama?" Sissy said. "Are you still there?"

"My first grandbaby." Bena tried to sound like the weight of the news wasn't crushing her to the bone.

"Juanita—she's Mexican, she lives in the apartment next door, she has three kids—says it will be a girl. She says you carry girls high."

"I carried you high. You were up in my rib cage, sort of like a little bird caught in there." Bena looked out at the rain-soaked world and felt tired. Thunder hammered away. Lightning shot through the night, leaving everything sort of snakebit and quivering. "Mexican?" Bena said. "I didn't know they had Mexicans in Miami."

"They do, Mama. They have everything. Anyway, Juanita says babies know if people want them or not." Sissy was whispering now— as if she could talk so quietly the baby inside her wouldn't hear, would never have to know her mother's troubled heart. "They can tell if the mother is glad. Do you think that's true?"

Bena's anger and aggravation were gone. "Sweet baby," she said, "sometimes it just takes a little time for the gladness to settle in. It happened to me that way all five times." Bena was reading from a script of lies. She knew what Sissy needed to hear. "This baby is lucky to have you for a mother, Sissy. I know that for sure. You have all the right instincts, honey."

"That's what Barrett says."

"Nobody will love this baby the way Barrett will," Bena said. "Barrett is a lucky man." It was the first time Bena had ever called Barrett a man.

"He will, won't he, Mama?" Sissy said. "He'll be happy?"

"Sure he will. Babies change everything for the better, honey. You'll see."

Sometimes people needed lies in the worst ways. Lies could actually save their lives when the truth might kill them. Bena was not a liar, but had learned the practical value of a useful lie to help get somebody from point A to point B. It worked with her children, her students, her secret self. Later on, once it's served its purpose, the lie can be retracted and put away, like a stepladder or something. A timesaving tool that has done its work. There'd been times in her life when Bena would have traded all the truth in the world for one really good lie.

"A baby is just what Barrett needs, Sissy," Bena said. "I bet it brings out the best in him, honey. Like it did your daddy."

In the little wave of silence between them Sissy let go and cried into the phone. She cried the same way she had when her daddy was killed and his secrets had spilled out everywhere and there was nothing anybody could do about it.

5

It was Sunday morning and the rain had finally stopped, after nearly two weeks. Everything that hadn't washed away was soaked and ready to rot. The county had crews out picking up limbs, drowned animals, and debris. The radio was issuing germ warnings and instructing people with wells to boil their drinking water.

Bena was trying to get the dirty dishes hidden away in the dishwasher. For more than two weeks she'd thought of almost nothing but Sissy's news. A baby coming. It changed everything. At breakfast she had issued a declaration that they were all going to church together this morning. Her children had looked at her, then at one another, buttered their toast, eaten their eggs, and excused themselves. They didn't argue. Maybe they were afraid to. Or maybe they were thinking it might be different this time — church.

Bena thought of herself and her children as church people even if they almost never went to church anymore. Once a church person always a church person. Once religion had hammered your soul into shape when you were a little kid, even if you were too young to hardly know what was going on—then it was pretty much done. Forever. To Bena, a church person was simply a *good* person, who knew right from wrong, who tried hard all the time, but didn't actually have to go to church to be that way. Also, there were lots of folks at church who, to Bena's way of thinking, were not actual church people. Their reasons for going to church were not God related as far as she could tell. She had some good friends like this who never missed a Sunday. In the end she thought maybe God might have to resort to giving some people a spiritual diploma and others just a certificate of church attendance —sort of like they were talking about doing over at the high school.

Even so, she and her children would go to church today—all of them. They would do it partly for Sissy and the baby and partly for themselves. Even if it didn't help anything, what could it possibly hurt?

Bena was dressed and searching the house for her Bible, the one with her name embossed in gold. It used to be there was a Bible in practically every drawer in their house. What had happened to them? When Bobby got saved, for Christmas he'd given each child a personally inscribed Bible with his or her given name on the cover. Bena wouldn't be surprised if he had given Lorraine Rayfield one too, as long as he was at it, worrying about the souls of those he loved. She wondered if in Lorraine's Bible Bobby had scratched out that sentence that says *Thou shalt not commit adultery*—changing it from the King James Version to the Bobby Eckerd Version. And now, technically speaking, she had converted to the Bobby Eckerd Version too.

The Bibles Bobby had given the children were in addition to all the ones the average Baxter County child accumulated just by virtue of growing up Baptist in Alabama. The truth was you shouldn't be able to take a step in their house without tripping over the Gospel in some form.

If Bena didn't know better she'd swear a thief had snuck in the house and stolen all their Bibles — and nothing else. Maybe she should call the police and report that there was a Bible thief on the loose, one who had ransacked their home and stolen the word of God right out from under them — without their even noticing.

"This is crazy," she said. "How do you lose a Bible? Who steals a personalized Bible with the owner's gold name on it?" She was tearing through the kitchen, looking in all the most unlikely places when she heard Eddie in the laundry room dialing the phone. She stopped to listen, thinking he was probably talking to a girl.

"This is Eddie," he said. But it was not his girl-calling voice. It was his formal voice that he used with teachers and law-enforcement types — and his grandmother, who lived more than an hour away. "I was wondering if maybe you could meet us at church today. Sissy's pregnant and Mama isn't taking it good. I guess she wants us all to pray for Sissy's soul or something. But church, you know — Mama goes all to pieces at church. Ever since Daddy. So I was thinking, maybe you could come."

Bena was stunned. How dare he call Bobby's mother that way. She hadn't even told her about Sissy's baby yet. Bena had the urge to slap Eddie's face. Talking as though Bena needed her former mother-in-law to come to the rescue, which she did not. And now, to make matters worse, the poor woman would probably drive over, worried sick, and make things twice as bad, which was the only way she really knew to respond to trouble. It would take her an hour and forty-five minutes to make the trip, as cautious as she drove. Her nerves weren't what they used to be either. Eddie needed to learn to mind his own business.

"Who'd you call?" Bena demanded when Eddie came out of the laundry room.

"Anna Kaye. A girl from the pool. She's meeting me at church."

Bena didn't say a word as Eddie walked back to his room to find his dress shoes, which probably wouldn't even fit anymore, it'd been

so long since he'd had occasion to wear them. All she could think was
that her youngest son, the one who kept his bedroom door locked,
could lie like a dog. Even though she knew he was lying it was all she
could do not to believe him too. He was that good a liar. Like his
daddy. All the more reason to get everybody to church. At worst
every one of them could all just fall to their knees and repent.

It wasn't until they were in the car, Leslie driving, Eddie manning
the radio, Ellie and Bena in the back, that Leslie said, "Mama, what's
with church all of a sudden?"

"I feel like we need it," Bena said. "I don't want things to get away
from us."

"What things?"

"I don't know," Bena said. "Anything." This was the way Bena
talked when she only knew the feeling she had, but not the words
that went with the feeling. She looked out the window at the
drenched land around them, the red clay and black mud and grass so
green it hurt to look at it. She looked at the leaning fences blown
nearly over and the roofs with sheets of plastic covering them and
the dogs tied up on the porches and the ravaged soybean fields, a
world of weeds ready to shoot up any second and take the place over.
Everything messed up or ruined was calling out to be patched, re-
built, replanted, fixed—or else thrown away once and for all. You
could feel it, everything longing to be made good again.

Bena saw that Leslie and Ellie had managed to rustle up Bibles to
bring to church, and she had a moment of feeling she was a success
as a mother. But she doubted Eddie had even bothered to look for
one. Maybe he was counting on this girl, Anna Kaye, to provide him
with the word of God. Maybe he was looking forward to their looking up the verses together in her small palm-sized Bible, reading
them aloud with their fingers touching and hearts pounding. Bena
wondered if Anna Kaye knew that Eddie was a liar—and that *she*
was one of the things he lied about.

. . .

BENA HADN'T SEEN Lucky in over two weeks, not since she got the distress call from Sissy. He'd called her every day, left on her machine increasingly distraught messages, which she didn't return. She couldn't. The news about Sissy's baby had yanked Bena back from being a woman with new possibilities and turned her—again —into the mother they all depended on. She was supposed to set them a good example. She was supposed to put their needs first. She was supposed to remain sane and sensible long enough to get them properly reared and out into the world on their own. Then she could have a nervous breakdown if she wanted to. But she had a ways to go. Last night's message said, *I don't get it, Bena. You're scaring the hell out of me.* This morning's said, *Was it something I said? Did you die?*

As long as Bena was praying for a miracle for Sissy, maybe she could just pray for one for herself too. It was like a law of nature that if a child is miserable, the mother of that child is miserable too. A good mother could look at the ways her children messed up their lives to see how she had messed up hers. Children's lives were like mirrors at the crazy house where everything was twisted out of shape—but still, a decent mother could look at her distorted re-flection there and see clearly all the mistakes of her life.

What had Bena been thinking? Lucky McKale was a married man. Barrett might be as low-life a boy as there was in this world, but at least he wasn't married to anybody besides Sissy. At least he was willing to make her suffering legal in the eyes of the law—and in the eyes of Baxter County too—which was more than Bena could say for Lucky McKale.

So she'd make a deal with God today. She would trade loving Lucky—which was bound to be a sin no matter how she tried to look at it, it was just too wonderful, the way she felt when she was with him, to be anything Christian—for Sissy's happiness. Maybe giving up Lucky would set a good example for Sissy, who later would see that she needed to give up Barrett too. Maybe if they both could just focus on Jesus and shed these earthly men, then God would be well pleased and reward Sissy and her both with peaceful minds and hearts—and life everlasting.

Sissy was still young, still beautiful, so maybe God could hand-choose her a man later on too. One of those good ones who are next to impossible for a woman to find on her own without some divine intervention. It might be too late for Bena, but not for Sissy. It was worth Bena coming to church—risking the humiliation that might await her, suffering the pity of people—if it could get some good results for Sissy. Make God aware of Sissy's urgent needs.

Her children thought it was because of Bobby, of course. Bena knew that. But it was only because they'd never really noticed when they were younger, in the nursery or sitting with their friends in the back pew passing notes. It had always happened to some degree, the crying. She remembered when she and Bobby were newlyweds at church and he'd whisper, *What's wrong?* and she'd say *Nothing* while she sobbed into a tissue. After the service Bobby would ply her with questions: *Why was she sad? What had her upset?* But she never had any real answer. In time, he got used to it, the crying, and stopped asking her about it.

But then after Bobby died—it got worse. Her uncontrollable weeping drew such attention that the other people at church circled around her offering her biblical comfort, trying out their memorized verses on her, touching her laying-on-of-hands style, offering to take her out to lunch after the service—all five of her children too, as if some good fried fish could feed her soul and give her peace of mind.

The kindness they aimed at her was the most painful thing of all. Kindness can kill. It's true. After church she would drive home thankful to still be alive, having nearly died from such an intense dose of Christian concern.

Over time the situation got more drastic. Sometimes Bena began to cry the minute she pulled into the church driveway, the minute she heard the organ, when the usher handed her the bulletin, when she sang the first line of the first hymn. At one time she'd known nearly everybody at church. Even now she knew most of the faces and the stories that went with the faces. A handful of teachers from her school went to Baxter Fellowship Baptist too, including Mayfred Piper.

Bena was crazy about Mayfred. When Mayfred wanted to she could make a scene in the sanctuary twice as dramatic as anything Bena could do just sitting like a lump in a pew crying her eyes out. Mayfred could get filled with the Holy Ghost and twirl up and down the aisles with her arms in the air or fall momentarily unconscious in her pew, scaring people. Or she could sing a spontaneous verse to an otherwise ordinary hymn. When she got started the rest of the choir would just close their hymnals and listen to Mayfred wail out a message direct from the Holy Spirit. Sometimes she went off into tongues too. Some folks liked that, but lots of folks thought it was wrong and wished she'd go back to her black church if she was going to put on a wild show like that. Mayfred had singlehandedly introduced the congregation to the unpredictable nature of the Holy Ghost. In Bena's experience white people—herself included—didn't really take to the unpredictable.

After Bobby died, after his funeral, when things got quiet and strange, Mayfred had come to call on Bena, and when Bena's children told Mayfred that Bena was resting and didn't want to see anybody, then Mayfred just came in Bena's room and lay down beside her on the bed. Mayfred told Bena about when her own mother died from diabetes. And how her mother had appeared to Mayfred later on, like an angel, whole again with her amputated leg put back and all that weight she lost put back too. And what a joy it was to see her mother like that. When Mayfred saw that Bena was listening, then Mayfred told Bena about the nature of men and God-the-Father, who made men the way they were. Mayfred knew this because she had three children by three men and hadn't married any of them—but had studied them hard.

"Honey, my college education was nothing compared to what I learned from trying to love those men," she said. "God was setting me up to do his work way before I had sense enough to know it."

It was funny that Bena hadn't minded being the focus of Mayfred's religious fervor. Mayfred had said, "All dying is is getting reborn. Only here on earth we're watching the wrong end of it. We think something is being lost, when really everything is being gained." Mayfred talked Bena's ears off and it had worked better than taking tranquilizers. She told Bena that God sent her with these messages and Bena knew beyond a shadow of a doubt that it was probably true. Ever since then Bena and Mayfred had loved each other the best two women could in Baxter County, Alabama, when one was white and one was black.

There were six other black members of Fellowship Baptist—all women—with a dozen children among them. Mayfred and her sister, Hexie, were the only two Bena knew. They both sang in the choir. Solos sometimes. Bena could not imagine what black women would want with a white church—not to mention a white choir—especially since not everybody in the congregation welcomed them wholeheartedly.

But Mayfred didn't care. She confided in Bena, "You know how everybody sends missionaries to Africa to get those people right with God. Well, Africa is not the only place where people's souls need a little work." Mayfred said she wanted white folks to get used to seeing her black face up in the choir week after week. She wanted them to shiver when she sang her songs. You know, to help them get rid of any sort of bad attitudes they had about people like her and her kids. Her sister, Hexie, was the same. They were on a mission.

For once God's mysterious way had made perfect sense to Bena. Mayfred had the power to trigger Bena's tears too when she belted out *He walks with me and talks with me and tells me I am his own*—meaning God, because it was something no real man had ever done for Mayfred. Bena's weeping usually began with tears going down her cheeks, which she would dab away with her fingers, but soon the sadness would work its way into sobs and she would be wracked with grief that she couldn't explain, her terrified children patting her, whispering, "Shhhhhh, Mama. It's okay."

Nearly all her life Bena had brought her *reason* to church with her and had taken it home with her when she left and never actually known what it was. *The reason.* It got so bad that Bena had stopped going to church almost totally. She did it to save herself. But also for the rest of the people, who could hardly keep their minds on their own sins with her crying a river the way she did.

This Sunday Bena and her children sat in a pew toward the front because most of the back pews were already taken. A boy Bena used to keep in the nursery sat beside Leslie. He was the preacher's nephew and was as gay as the day is long, but maybe Leslie didn't know it—maybe nobody there knew it, not even the boy himself. Maybe Bena was the only person with the radar to know and the willingness to trust her radar. Something seemed to come over her at church. It was like she could see into the souls of certain people around her and know things she had no real right to know. The only soul that eluded her completely was her own. By the time Tucker was eight or nine and leading the singing at children's church, Bena had known his future just as sure as if he had been one of her own. But it was like the whole congregation was dedicated to not knowing what Bena knew. Bena imagined the life that loomed before this boy, one of pretending always not to be who he really was. Maybe he would marry an unsuspecting or desperate girl and they would have a child just to prove to the world that he deserved to be let alone— after which he could get to work on his secret life.

"Hey, Tucker, honey," Bena said. "How are you?"

"Hey, Mrs. Eckerd. Glad to see y'all back at church."

Before they finished the opening hymn a pretty girl nudged her way down their pew and sat next to Eddie. She was dark haired, dark eyed, and petite. "Mama," Eddie whispered, "this is Anna Kaye."

The girl beamed a hello smile. Bena reached across Eddie and patted Anna Kaye's tan arm. Sure enough she was gripping a tiny white leather New Testament with a little zipper around it. Eddie had been right to count on Anna Kaye after all.

As the service began Bena noticed that Eddie was constantly turning to look behind him. And she knew why. "Who are you looking for, Eddie?" she whispered.

"Nobody," he said.

As it was in the beginning, is now, and ever shall be, world without end, Amen, Amen, Bena sang. The first tears appeared. She wiped them away with her fingers.

By the time the collection was gathered, Anna Kaye had reached into her purse to get Bena a handkerchief. Eddie was swivel-necked, searching the church for his grandmother. The more emotional Bena got, the more Eddie's search intensified.

"Is your mama okay?" Anna Kaye asked.

"Yeah," he whispered. "Church gets her upset sometimes."

During the silent prayer Bena went all out. She bowed her head and unleashed as much thanks as she could and then moved on to her prayer requests. She had them catagorized according to degree of urgency. Sissy was first, then the baby — she even prayed for Barrett. Her plan was to go over each child and then end up on herself. But the preacher ended the silent prayer time before Bena was finished — and that sort of threw her off.

The preacher started in on his sermon. It was about developing *a personal relationship with Jesus Christ.* Bena had never had *a personal relationship* with Jesus. Not like the preacher was talking about. Nobody had ever wanted to turn her life over to Jesus more than Bena had, but it was like He wouldn't take hold of it. She didn't think Jesus was supposed to be allowed to refuse to accept a life when somebody was trying to turn it over to Him. It wasn't right. So then Bena'd had to pretend. She'd invited Jesus into her life a good thirty or forty times at least — to no avail. The awful truth was *a personal relationship* with Jesus simply had never happened to Bena like it was supposed to, and suddenly it seemed the saddest thing in the world that she had missed her chance to know Jesus—the one man in this world you were supposed to be able to count on—in a real and eternal way.

It is not enough to believe that Jesus walked this earth and gave his life for you, the preacher proclaimed, *but you must turn your life over to Him. Let him be your Lord and Savior. Develop a personal relationship.* Every time he said the words *personal relationship* Bena choked on her tears and people turned to look at her.

"Oh shit," she heard Eddie say under his breath.

"What's wrong?" Anna Kaye asked. "Why is your mama crying?"

Eddie was turned almost backward in the pew, his eyes searching for help. Bena thought it would serve him right if his grandmother didn't come. But she imagined that her mother-in-law was en route this very moment, delayed by the bad road conditions, maybe hopelessly lost on a poorly marked detour. So Bena said a prayer for her safe travel. This was a gasping sort of prayer, because the tears were full force now. Bena lowered her head to her knees as if she were about to faint.

Ellie leaned forward and patted her mother's back, which only served to drive Bena further into this unnamed sorrow. She was shaking the pew with her sobs. Worshipers were turning to stare. People who knew Bena shook their heads in sad recognition of the grieving widow who needed desperately to pull herself together after all this time. The sanctuary got hot with tension; Bena was sweating as bad as she was crying. Her children were hot-skinned too with their helplessness. When it looked to everyone like Bena Eckerd might just collapse from her all-consuming grief a figure rose up from the back of the church.

The preacher, who did not miss a beat in his prepared sermon— *personal relationship with Jesus, personal relationship, personal relationship*—looked up as the figure started down the aisle. The man was tall and tan and had on a white dress shirt and a necktie that looked like it was choking him to death. He had on boots and jeans and a War Eagle belt buckle. People turned to see Lucky McKale, not even a member of this church, maybe not even a Baptist, make his way to the pew where Bena was folded over, sobbing.

"Excuse me." He pushed his way into the pew. Bena was too wracked with grief to notice him. "Scoot over, Eddie," Lucky said. "Let me sit by your mama." Eddie was happy to edge closer to Anna Kaye, who looked bewildered and enthralled.

Lucky sat down beside Bena and put his arm around her and leaned down to say something no one could hear. She lifted her head then, startled, like someone who has been called out of a dream. Lucky kissed her wet cheek and tucked her damp hair behind her ear. She leaned against him in a collapsed posture and he put both arms around her and hugged her like they were parked in a car at a drive-in movie. Everybody stared except Bena's children, who were doing their best not to look.

"Come on," Lucky said to Bena. "Let's get you out of here."

Bena stared at him as if he were speaking in tongues like Mayfred. She knew her eyes were blackened with mascara. He took her hand and pulled her up, saying, "Everything is going to be okay." He nodded to Leslie and Ellie. "Let's go, girls." He patted Eddie's shoulder and said, "Come on, son." All the Eckerd family stood up and in single file slid out of the pew. Lucky held Bena's hand and led her down the aisle, never taking his eyes off her. Her children followed. Tucker and Anna Kaye did too, like a couple of innocent bystanders caught up in a wave of irreverence. All eyes were on Bena and Lucky. The sanctuary went nearly silent, except for the droning of the preacher who didn't know he had witnessed a miracle just now—firsthand.

When they got outside the sun was out. The air was so yellow you had to squint to keep from going blind. Lucky put his arms around Bena again and said, "I love you, Bena. Damn if I don't." For a minute it looked like he might cry too.

"Who is that?" Anna Kaye asked Eddie.

"My mother's boyfriend," Eddie said.

"He's married," Leslie clarified.

Then Lucky turned to look at Bena's children, who were all staring at him hard. "Y'all hear me? I said I love your mama."

Leslie was the one who spoke. "We hear you," she said.

"Anybody who's got a problem with this—you can take it up with me later. Eddie, you and your sisters take your mama's car and follow me out to my house."

"Now?" Eddie said.

"Yes, now." Lucky spoke in a tone of voice that didn't invite questions. He held Bena and she cried on his shoulder, messing up his white shirt. He held her a long time, like he was afraid if he let go she would fall to pieces right there in the church yard, just come unglued like they say and then he would have all the loose pieces of a broken-up woman. It was only when Eddie honked the horn and signaled that they were waiting that Lucky led Bena to his truck. She walked lopsided, blowing her nose into the knotted handkerchief Anna Kaye had given her.

Lucky started the truck and was easing through the parked cars when Mayfred ran out toward them in her choir robe. "Lucky!" she shouted. "You wait a minute."

"You know Mayfred?" Bena asked.

"It's a long story," he said.

Mayfred came up to the truck on Bena's side and stuck her head in the window. "You okay, girl?"

"I made a fool of myself, Mayfred," Bena said.

"You got the gift, child."

"What gift?" Bena rubbed at her smeared mascara with the clenched handkerchief. Her eyes were puffed up like biscuit dough.

"Weeping, honey. The Holy Spirit got you weeping for all the folks ain't got the sense to weep for themselves. You weeping for those too mean to weep. You weeping for those too weak to weep. See what I'm saying?"

Bena looked at Mayfred like she was crazy. "Maybe I'm just crying for my own messed-up self. And praying I hadn't messed up my kids too bad already." She managed a halfhearted smile and rolled her eyes heavenward.

"For real, girl," Mayfred said. "You crying one tear for your own self and ten for the rest of this spinning-around world. That's what God Almighty got you doing."

"You're an angel," Bena said.

"Yes," Mayfred said. "Thank you, Jesus."

THEY WERE SEATED around the table at Lucky's house. He'd stopped to get a bucket of chicken, but only Eddie was eating anything. "Look here," Lucky said. "I got some things to say."

Leslie was petting Tom, who had taken a liking to her. He put his head in her lap and she fed him bites of chicken while Lucky talked. Ellie was watching Bena for signs that she was back to normal. Eddie ignored them all and ate like a starved man. "Slow down, Eddie, honey," Bena said. "We got plenty."

"I know I'm not the sort of guy you all think is right for your mama," Lucky began. "I know she deserves better. But this past week when I knew something was wrong and she wouldn't let me help her out—man, I'm telling you." His eyes filled up then and he had to stop to keep from crying out right.

"Damn," Eddie whispered without looking up.

"It made me know how much your mama means to me," Lucky said. "Y'all too. I know I can't make you accept me right off the bat, but damn if I'm not going to try. Because your mama needs that— me to be okay by you all. I never had any kids, so it's fair to say I don't always know the right way to go about things. So I'm just asking you to give me a chance."

No one said a word. Lucky kept looking at Bena like he was about to fall to his knees and kiss her feet—and nobody wanted to see that. "You think you can do that?" He looked at Bena's children, who avoided his eyes. "Give me a chance?"

"If Mama wants us to," Ellie finally said, "we will."

"Thank you, Ellie, honey." Lucky took her face in his hands and kissed the top of her head. "I appreciate that." He looked at Leslie and said, "Leslie, look at me a minute." And Leslie raised her eyes to him. "You were right, what you said to me. I been trying to get ahold of Sue Cox. We had the papers drawn up a long time ago so all we got to do is sign them."

Leslie buried her face in Tom's fur, making him whine.

Eddie rolled his eyes.

"Eddie," Lucky said, "I appreciate you calling me this morning. It meant more to me than you'll ever know." He patted him on the back the way he'd done in church. Like he was acting out being a dad or something. Eddie didn't like it much.

IT SOUNDED LIKE a police siren was coming up the drive, like somebody was on their way to a fire and pounding on the car horn so people would get out of their way. "What the hell?" Lucky said.

Tom jumped up and ran to the front door, his toenails scrambling on the hardwood floor. He started barking frantically. Outside a car came to a screeching halt with the radio blaring some sort of rap music. Two car doors slammed shut. Before anybody could get to the front door, it swung open, banged against the wall, and somebody sang out, "Yoo-hoo, anybody home?"

"Damn," Lucky said. "That's Sue Cox."

Bena thought of snatching up her kids and running out the back door. She thought of running to the bathroom and patching herself together a little better. She thought of trying to explain to Sue Cox how it had happened, how she'd fallen in love with Sue Cox's very own husband. But before Bena could make a move Sue Cox came into the kitchen with Tom leaping in circles around her and her baby-talking to him. "Hey my little precious baby," she cooed. "You miss Mama?"

When Sue Cox looked up and saw everybody sitting around her kitchen table, staring at her—stunned—she grinned. "Well hey," she said. "Looks like I've walked in on the Waltons' Sunday dinner."

Lucky stood up and walked toward her and she threw her arms around him and hugged his neck and kissed his face. "Hey there, Lucky," she said. "Looks like you got company. I hope I hadn't come at the wrong time and disturbed anything."

Lucky nodded toward the table, "You remember Bena Eckerd, don't you?" Bena stood up just then and Sue Cox came over and hugged her too, like Bena was just the person Sue Cox was hoping to see. "Hey," she said. "Lord, it's been ages, hasn't it? Bobby's funeral was the last time." Then she glanced at the others, who were gawking at her. "I know these can't be your kids, Bena?"

"Some of them," Bena said. "I got more where they came from."

"My God, they look grown. Good-looking too. Hey." She went to the table and stuck out her hand. "I'm Sue Cox. Lucky's wife. Y'all just call me Sue Cox, hear?"

Lucky shot over to the table right behind Sue Cox to make the introductions since all three kids looked too dazed to speak. "This is Leslie," he said, "and Ellie." They nodded hello. "And the handsome guy at the end, that's Eddie."

"Nice to meet you." Eddie was trying to wipe the grease off his fingers with a paper napkin before he shook her hand.

"Y'all go ahead and eat," Sue Cox said. "Don't let me interrupt."

"I didn't know you were coming," Lucky said.

"We decided to surprise you." Sue Cox smiled and hooked her arm through his and put her head on his shoulder.

"We?" Lucky said. "Who's *we*?"

"Me and Corby. You remember Corby, don't you?"

"Hell yes, I remember Corby. Where is he?"

"He's waiting out by the car. I wanted to make sure the coast was clear first."

"We were just leaving," Bena said. "Weren't we, y'all?" She nodded to her kids, who looked like they were in the front row at a horror movie just when it was starting to get good.

"No, no, no," Sue Cox said. "Y'all don't go. Let me go get Corby and we'll just all get acquainted. Corby's great. Y'all will really like him." She turned and smiled at Lucky. "Luck, will you go tell Corby to come on in. He's waiting out there."

"Sure." Lucky looked at Bena and shrugged his shoulders.

"Who's Corby?" Ellie asked. "Your dog?"

Sue Cox clapped her hands and threw her head back in a hearty laugh. "Oh my God, Ellie honey, Corby is not a dog. He's my—"

Right then a blond boy who didn't look much older than Leslie walked in behind Lucky. From the looks of him you'd think he was about to head for California because he'd heard the surf was up. You'd think the Beach Boys would burst into song at the mere sight of him. He was tan with long yellow-blond hair and a face nice enough to be on a magazine. He was wearing a tank top. It was obvious he worked out a lot and spent his share of time in the tanning bed. He had the kind of male good looks that crossed over the line into downright pretty. Somewhere inside he must have known that and decided to work with it. The only thing that was not right with him was his eyes. They seemed cautious, the way they were flashing around, this person, that person, like he was on the lookout for possible danger.

"Corby, sweetie, come on in here and meet these nice folks." Sue Cox hooked her arm through his the way she had done with Lucky minutes ago. "This pretty lady is Bena. She's a widow. She used to be married to Lucky's buddy Bobby. Bobby was a sweetheart. Idn't that right, Luck?"

Lucky went over and stood by Bena, who looked sort of numb.

"These are three of Bena's kids," Sue Cox said. "Bena doesn't look old enough to have such grown kids, does she? Leslie is the redhead. Ellie is the brunette. And Eddie here is the baby, isn't that right?"

Eddie turned so red it made Sue Cox laugh. "You're the cutest thing."

Corby said his hellos, and it was clear he was in the twilight zone almost as much as the rest of them.

"Y'all sit down and have some lunch," Bena said like it was her kitchen they'd wandered into. "There's plenty left. We're just finishing up and getting ready to go."

"I could stand to eat something." Corby pulled out a chair and sat down. Bena got him a clean plate and he began serving himself. "Sue Cox never eats," he said to Leslie. "She forgets us mortals got to eat to stay alive."

"Where are you from?" Leslie asked.

"You think I'm not from Alabama?"

"I know you're not," Leslie said.

He grinned and pointed his fork at her. "Smart girl."

Bena studied Sue Cox as much as she could without making a fool of herself. Sue Cox was taller than Bena, and thinner. She wore tight black slacks and a white T-shirt and sandals. Her hair was pulled straight back in a ponytail. She was the same head turner she had always been, only with crow's-feet and laugh lines now. Maybe in Sue Cox's case they shouldn't be called laugh lines, Bena thought. Not in Bena's own case either. Who was it that thought women got wrinkles from laughing so much? Even Eddie was gawking at Sue Cox like she was a movie star. Sue Cox seemed to be in a good mood too. Not moody like Bena had seen her in the past.

Sue Cox rummaged through her bag for a cigarette and then got a match out of a kitchen drawer. "I know, I know." She smiled at Bena and Lucky. "Smoking kills. But damn, I got all this nervous energy that'll kill me faster than any cigarette. Everybody needs to be allowed to hold on to at least one bad habit. Idn't that right? If I give up smoking then I guess I'd be damn near perfect." She winked at

Bena. She inhaled deeply and blew the smoke slowly up at the ceiling. It looked like a pose she had rehearsed many times.

"So." She looked at Bena. "You and Luck are friends?"

Bena must have been taking too long to come up with an answer because Lucky spoke up before she did. "Good friends," he said. "The best of friends."

"Good," Sue Cox said. "That's real good. 'Make new friends but keep the old, one is silver and the other's gold,'" she sang. "Y'all remember that song, don't you?"

"Girl Scouts," Bena said.

"Training Union too," Sue Cox said. "I always liked that song. But those fools at First Baptist threw me out of Training Union. Did Lucky ever tell you that story?"

"Not yet," Bena said.

"Sue Cox," Corby said, "can you smoke that thing someplace else. We're trying to eat over here."

"Sure, baby." She motioned for Lucky and Bena to follow her.

"Any more of that slaw?" Corby asked. Ellie passed him the container. "So, if you don't mind me asking"—he looked at Leslie—"how'd your old man go out?"

Bena had never heard her children explain Bobby's death to anyone. She would like to have listened, but they waited until she and Lucky followed Sue Cox into the living room before answering.

Sue Cox threw herself down on the sofa—the one Bena didn't like to sit on because she worried it would wrinkle so bad. "Y'all sit down," Sue Cox said. Bena and Lucky stood and looked at her like they were thinking the offer over. "I bet I messed up your afternoon, didn't I? I just thought it would be fun to surprise Lucky. There used to be a time when Lucky liked surprises."

"Well, I'm cured now," he said. "You pretty much cured me."

"See, I guess that just proves you *can* teach an old dog new tricks." She winked at Bena. "No telling what sorts of new tricks you can teach our boy Luck here. If I were you, I'd start by teaching him to beg. That's always a good starting place with an old dog, don't you think?"

"Far as I can tell, Lucky doesn't need much improving," Bena said. "He's pretty great like he is."

Sue Cox smiled. She had that great mouth that stretched all the way across her face. When Sue Cox smiled, mostly everybody else did too. She aimed her smile at Lucky. "She's nice," Sue Cox said. "She really is, Luck. She's very nice."

"Well, I know Bena is glad to get your stamp of approval," he said. "That means a lot to us, doesn't it, Bena?" His sarcasm made Bena nervous. She wasn't used to it, this anger seeping out of him.

"I hate that description," Bena said. "Nice." She looked at Sue Cox, trying to neutralize Lucky's remarks. "Some people are born smart or talented or rich—but me, I was born *nice*. Been nice all my life. When I die they'll write on my headstone, *Here lies Bena Eckerd. She was nice.* It's like a curse."

"I wouldn't know," Sue Cox said. "So far nobody has ever accused me, you know, of being nice."

"I guess it's the only thing you hadn't been accused of," Lucky said. Bena glared at him.

"I'm just kidding," he said. "Sue Cox knows I'm kidding."

"He doesn't bother me," Sue Cox said. "When you've been through all we've been through you get immune to each other."

"So what exactly brings you back here to the scene of the crime?" Lucky asked. "I don't guess they've run you out of Atlanta already?"

"Don't you love him?" Sue Cox said to Bena. "They say a good sense of humor is what women are most looking for in a man. I read that somewhere."

"You didn't answer the question," Lucky persisted. "What are you doing here?"

"I take it from your tone that you're not exactly thrilled to see me."

"Just answer the question, Sue Cox. Okay?"

Bena should leave and go home. She should collect her children, say good-bye to surfer boy, and get out of here. But she couldn't make herself go. She wanted to hear what Sue Cox had to say. She wanted to see how she and Lucky were in the same room together. Bena was too curious to leave.

"Y'all sit down," Sue Cox said. "Please."

Lucky took Bena's hand and they sat on the sofa across from Sue Cox. She was staring at Bena. "I can't help but notice — you been crying, haven't you?"

"That's none of your business," Lucky said.

"Well, don't blame me," Sue Cox said. "I just got here. It can't be my fault."

"You assuming I made her cry?" Lucky said.

Bena patted Lucky's arm and looked at Sue Cox. "I don't know if you'll understand this, but I think maybe I've got the gift of weeping. Whenever I go to church, I cry. I mean I *really* cry. My friend Mayfred says I weep for people who can't weep for themselves. People I don't even know. But also me. And my kids too. And everybody in the world. Does that make any sense?"

Sue Cox was staring at Bena, studying her hard.

"Because if it doesn't," Bena said, "then I think maybe something is seriously wrong with me." She tried to smile. "Maybe I'm crazy." She folded her arms so Sue Cox wouldn't notice the sweat rings under her arms.

Sue Cox set her ashtray on her knee. She got very serious. "I used to have just the opposite problem. I couldn't cry. Remember that, Lucky? I would need to and try to, but I just couldn't. My energy was blocked back then."

"I guess I was probably blocking it," Lucky said.

"I didn't say that, Luck." Sue Cox took a drag from her cigarette. "It was awful not being in touch with myself. Hastings made me see what my problem was. So it makes sense what you're saying. Maybe you used to be crying for me back then."

"It's out of my hands," Bena said. "That's the thing."

"I don't want to interfere with the sisterhood here," Lucky said. "I'm glad we're all in touch with our feelings and we got our energy unblocked. Shit, I can get with that. But Sue Cox, you still haven't said why you're here?"

"I come bearing gifts," Sue Cox said.

"Why does that make me nervous?" Lucky said.

"Did you or did you not leave messages on my machine saying you thought it was time we made our split legal? We've had our divorce papers drawn up for a long time. You're right about that, Luck. So I'm here to say okay. Sure. If you want me to I'll sign the papers."

"You mean that?" Lucky said.

"Have you ever known me to lie?" She grinned. "Lately?" She looked at Bena and winked. "We both got new chapters waiting for us, Luck. I take it your chapter is sitting right there beside you. And mine, bless his heart, is in the kitchen with that bucket of chicken."

Bena stood up. "Y'all should talk this over by yourselves. This should be a private conversation."

"Bullshit," Sue Cox said. "Me and Lucky never have had any private life. Everything about us has always been in the public domain. We like it like that, don't we?" Sue Cox stood up and smoothed her hair with her hands. "This is like the Fourth of July. Lucky and me are about to sign our own personal declarations of independence! Come on, let's go in the kitchen and make the big announcement."

Lucky looked lost in the sudden series of events. He watched Sue Cox stroll into the kitchen and shook his head. "I'm not sure what's going on here."

"I think Sue Cox is going to set you free," Bena said. "Isn't that what you want?"

"You know I do. But Sue Cox is up to something. This ain't the real her."

"Maybe she was right about Hastings Rehab. Maybe she got cured over there."

"Don't we wish," he said. "Just remember this, Bena. What goes up, must come down. And down, that's the killer."

BENA DIDN'T KNOW what Sue Cox was expecting from Corby and the others when she announced that she and Lucky were signing the divorce papers. Maybe she thought they'd lift her on their shoulders and parade her through the house. Maybe she thought they'd leap up and hug her neck and thank her for the generous gesture, which would change their lives forever. But all they did was look at her, silently.

"Go, Coxie," Corby finally said.

AFTER LUNCH CORBY discovered the big-screen TV and Lucky's stash of videos. He and Bena's kids settled into Lucky's football-watching room with a movie. Now and then you could hear them laugh at a good part. A movie was good, Bena guessed. It kept them from having to make any substantial conversation.

Sue Cox went to lie down. "I guess the beds have been reassigned around here." Sue Cox took off her sandals, pulled the rubber band out of her ponytail, and disappeared into the guest room.

"Beauty rest," Lucky said.

Bena wanted to go home and knew her kids did too. But Lucky wouldn't hear of it. "Don't let Sue Cox and her boyfriend run you off," he said. "Let's me and you take a walk out where the pond is going."

They hiked through the stickers and underbrush in silence. Bena watched for snakes every step she took. Her mother had trained her that way when she was a small girl with endless stories of people stepping on snakes and having heart attacks on the spot, or else getting bitten on the ankle and dying of venom before they hit the ground like a rock. It was even possible to step on a knot of snakes all balled together and get bitten, say, twenty times before you could ever untangle yourself. It was a terrible way to die. Fear of snakes had messed up Bena's pleasure in the out-of-doors. But she followed Lucky through the thorns and briers, saying a half prayer every step she took until they finally found a tree that had been blown over by the storm, a decent place to pause and sit. Bena walked all that way in her Sunday clothes. Her shoes were a muddy mess. Lucky still had on his noose of a necktie. It was hot as Hades, the way it usually is after a bad storm blows through.

"Hear me out, Bena," Lucky said. "I think I been around you enough to know how you think about certain things." He stood up and rested one foot on the log where Bena sat to take her ruined shoes off. He'd already sweated all the way through his white shirt. "Like, for example," he said, "I bet after we made love that day in the rain—I mean damn, I was a happy man and it seemed like you were happy too—and then you went home to find out Sissy was all alone and pregnant down in Miami, you did some of that old-time Baptist math."

"What are you talking about?" Bena said.

"Baptist math. I know about it because my mama used to practice it. It's based on the belief that there are never enough blessings to go around, never enough happiness for everybody. Like each family is allotted just a little bit and you got to be careful not to use it up too fast, you know? So a mama has got to divvy things up. Not too much happiness for this one because then there won't be enough for that one."

"I'm not your mother," Bena said.

"No," he said. "You're not. But damn if you don't think like she did. You figured that something good coming into your life—and I know I'm something good in your life, don't even try to tell me I'm not good for you—that you being happy somehow caused Sissy to be sad. Am I right? You got to subtract your own happiness so she can get hers back, right? You know, like you've got to keep things always adding up to zero. But you know what zero is, Bena? Zero is nothing. It's not a damn thing."

"I know that," Bena said.

"So you telling me I got this figured wrong?"

"You don't have kids, Lucky. You don't know how it is."

"You tell me how it is then."

Bena slapped at the gnats that were biting her ankles. Her shoes had rubbed raw places on her heels. "You know how they have those advertisements on TV. Don't leave your child alone in the bathtub, not for even thirty seconds, cause that's all it takes. Don't leave a bucket of mop water in the kitchen, or let your kids play near a toilet, or take your eyes off their wading pool. Don't let them anywhere near a pond." Bena waved her hand at the imaginary pond. "Don't take your eyes off them—ever. Because if you do, then like that"—Bena snapped her fingers—"they can die. They can kill themselves while you're busy brushing your teeth or something. While you are busy getting naked with the mailman in the middle of the afternoon—when you're old enough to know better."

"The mailman?" Lucky said. "That's me? The mailman?"

"You know what I mean," Bena said. "It's just that if you forget to be responsible and you go off and . . . and . . . start acting like a crazy woman . . ."

"Crazy?"

"Not crazy. Just, you know, carefree or something."

"Like Bobby did?"

"Yes," she said, "like Bobby did."

Lucky picked up a stick and threw it as far as he could. Ordinarily Tom would go after it, but today Tom was in the house with Leslie, watching a movie in her lap. "So let me get this straight," he said. "Either you can be happy or your kids can be? But not both at once? And it's up to you to make sure you never get any happier than you already are because then they'll have to get *unhappier*. Is that it? That's the way the good Lord's got motherhood set up?"

"Bobby is dead, Lucky. I don't have a backup person to stay sane so I can have a time-out to go crazy. It's all mine to do. The kids are *my* kids. That's how it is."

"Bena, don't give me that shit." Lucky was leaning over where Bena sat, breaking a twig into little pieces and tossing them into her lap. "I watched my mama play this same damn game. Always ready to trade any scrap of happiness that might come her way so that we could have that extra scrap. And you know what? All we wanted in this world was our mother to be a happy woman. That would have done more for us than all the sacrificing and denying she ever did. To see her smile, damn it. To see her get tickled and just bust up laughing. To see her dress up and go someplace and come home full of gossip and secrets. If you ask me, you got it all wrong, Bena. Every time you deny yourself, you deny your kids. Don't you see the way they're cheering you and me on? How bad they want us happy."

"No," Bena said. "I think that's your imagination talking."

"Eddie calling me to come to church and get you? Ellie making that cake that first time I came over? Leslie, yeah, she's a hard-ass, but she's looking after my cats, idn't she? She's dedicated to them surviving. And she keeps tabs on me, trying to be sure I got the best of intentions where you're concerned. Lord, woman, don't you think it would take a heck of a lot off their minds if you didn't have to be worried about—if your happiness wasn't their job?"

Bena was staring at Lucky. His shirt was stuck to him the way it had been in the mail van that rainy day. Gnats circled his face and he kept shooing them away. "You got to take that necktie off," she said. "Before you strangle yourself."

Lucky tugged at his tie and sat on the log beside her. "Don't do it, Bena. Damnit. Don't divvy up the happiness until you got it spread so thin there's not any to notice." He was folding his fingers together as he talked. Bena watched his hands, the way they were rubbing together. "I can help you with your kids, Bena. I want to. You got to let me. I'm no daddy, but damn if I can't learn to be." He took Bena's hand and held it in both of his. He sqeezed so tight it hurt and she pulled her hand away.

"My ring." She rubbed her fingers.

"I wish you'd take that damn thing off," he said. "You hadn't been married for a long, long time."

"And you have," she snapped. "You still are."

He looked at her a minute, then stood up and started to take off his wedding band. He struggled with it the way you do a pickle jar when the lid's too tight, just sort of unscrewing it. His skin was white as a baby's butt where he'd worn that ring all these years. "Now you," he said, showing her the ring in his open palm.

Bena didn't have a diamond. Bobby had promised her one, but they had never seen their way clear to get it. She had a gold band. They'd exchanged a matching pair at their wedding. She'd insisted that Bobby be buried wearing his wedding ring. Now as she fumbled to take her ring off she felt mean-spirited about having done that. *Sure, maybe he loved this Lorraine person, but he is married to me.* Was that what she'd been thinking?

"Okay." She held her ring in her hand. "What are we going to do with these?"

"Throw them in the pond." Lucky stood up and slung his ring where the pond was supposed to be — you could hear it hit a tree and fall to the ground like an acorn. Bena stood up and threw her ring too. Hers went silently, landed making no sound.

"Now if we just had water in the pond we could jump in and celebrate this occasion," Lucky said.

"Are you just going to talk about that pond the rest of your life?" Bena said. "I get worried that maybe you're all talk and no action."

Lucky looked startled. "Is that what you think?"

"Not really." Bena saw it was the wrong thing to say.

Lucky put his hands in her sweaty hair and rested his chin on her head. She could feel his heart pounding. It sounded good to her — like a good, steady heart.

THEY STAYED OUT at the pond a long time. Then it took them a while to walk back up to the house because Bena had to go barefoot. Lucky held her hand and carried her shoes while she patrolled for snakes and sandspurs. Before they were halfway there Bena's legs were covered with brier scratches and bug bites. Lucky had finally taken his tie off. He looked like a man who'd just escaped a hanging. When the house came into view Bena said, "It's kind of strange, isn't it, Sue Cox showing up today? Just out of nowhere."

"Not if you know her, it's not."

"You're so mean to her."

Lucky shook his head. "Naw, that's not it. We've got an ugly pattern, me and Sue Cox. I hate like hell for you to witness it. Don't know what's left for Sue Cox to do that she hadn't already done, but I don't put nothing past her. She's got to have excitement twenty-four hours a day. That's her real addiction. The booze, it just helps her along, because you know if Sue Cox can't find enough excitement to suit her, then she'll make some of her own."

"And that's what scares you?"

"Damn straight."

WHEN THEY GOT back to the house Sue Cox was wide awake and making grilled-cheese sandwiches in the kitchen. "So how was the nature hike?" she asked.

"It's hot." Bena hooked her frizzy hair behind her ears. "Bugs are out."

"Hot as hell," Sue Cox said. "Excuse me for saying so on Sunday." She pretended to fan herself with a plate. Sue Cox was cooking with her cigarette hanging from her mouth and her eyes squinted in the smoke. Sweat was trickling down the side of her face, same as it was Bena's.

"Sue Cox hates nature." Corby stood behind her, nuzzling her ear. "Everything gets so dirty out there in nature. Idn't that right, Coxie?"

Leslie thought this was funny. She began to laugh.

"Sit down and eat your sandwich." Sue Cox kissed at Corby's face, handing him a plate. She was smiling ear to ear. "Ignore Corby," she said to Lucky and Bena. "He knows I don't have a thing in the world against nature. I like nature just fine. If it weren't for nature, where would we be?" She took a drag off her cigarette. "How about you two? Y'all want a grilled cheese?"

"No thanks," Lucky said.

"Your stomach is not acting up again, is it?"

"I'm just not hungry."

"Bena, you know Luck has a delicate stomach. You can tell when he's upset over something because his stomach turns on him."

"My stomach is not bothering me," Lucky insisted.

"You sure?" Sue Cox held her cigarette in one hand and a spatula in the other.

"Coxie, let it go," Corby said. "The man says his stomach isn't bothering him."

It surprised Bena that Corby would talk so straight to Sue Cox and that Sue Cox would listen and modify accordingly.

"Lord, it's hot in here," Sue Cox said. "Are y'all hot? Eddie, honey, are you hot?" Eddie barely glanced up from his sandwich. "I'm about to faint I'm so hot," Sue Cox said, fanning herself with the greasy spatula.

"You know what they say?" Corby looked at Leslie. "If you can't stand the heat . . ."

"Get out of the kitchen!" Leslie said.

"I believe I'll do just that." Sue Cox swatted Corby playfully, then picked up his paper napkin to wipe the sweat from her forehead. "Lucky, the air-conditioning isn't broken, is it? I don't ever remember this house being this hot."

"Nothing is broken," he said.

It did look to Bena like Sue Cox was hot as a firecracker. Her skin was bright red and she looked sort of wilted around the edges. She kept wiping her sweaty palms on her pants. "You sit down, Sue Cox," Bena said. "I'll get us some ice tea."

They sat directly under the ceiling fan in the main room. Sue Cox was barefoot and folded her legs under her Indian style. She nursed the ice tea like it was medicine. Lucky was too restless to sit down. He paced.

"Lucky, you don't care if Corby and I spend the night, do you? We'll take the guest room." Sue Cox patted Bena on the leg, "Bena, you don't care, do you?"

BEFORE BENA LEFT to go home Lucky pulled her into the bathroom and gave her a distracted kiss. "You're not mad, are you? I'd kick her out if I could. I swear."

"Hard to kick her out of her own house, isn't it?" Bena said.

WHEN BENA AND her kids drove home that evening they rolled down the car windows and let the damp air slap their faces and tangle their hair into knots. The crickets were shrieking their heads off. For some reason Eddie didn't bother with the radio like he usually did. Nobody had much to say at first. Nobody had anything at all to say about the divorce announcement—which, to Bena's way of thinking, had been the one saving grace of the long, half-miserable afternoon.

Once they got out of sight of the house and turned onto the main highway Leslie and Ellie perked up. "Corby met Sue Cox in rehab," Leslie announced. "Did you know that, Mama? They were both strung out. He wants to be a musician, but right now they have this sandwich shop in a la-la office building in Buckhead. Buzzy's or something. Or Bucky's. They just do lunch. He makes the sand-wiches—gourmet stuff—and Sue Cox works the counter."

"He calls her his *old lady*," Ellie said. "That's so redneck."

"He says all the suits flock in there every day to get a look at Sue Cox. As long as they're in there gawking they go ahead and buy a sandwich and a cold drink. They're doing a good business, he says. At night he practices his music. He's got a tryout with a new band this fall. If he makes it he might go on tour. His whole life could change. He writes his own music too. He's going to send us a tape."

"So, you all like Corby?" Bena asked.

"Not really," Eddie said.

"He's pretty cool," Ellie said. "If you're into blonds."

"What about you, Les?"

"I don't know," Leslie said. "I haven't made up my mind yet."

"And how about Sue Cox?" Bena asked. "Did you all like her?"

Leslie was driving. "How's that for a loaded question?" She held one hand out the window, grabbing at the wet air.

"She's good-looking," Eddie said. "Sorry, Mama. I mean, I don't like her or anything, but she is pretty good-looking."

"So I've been told," Bena said.

"You want to know the truth, Mama?" Leslie looked at her in the rearview mirror. Her hair was whipping across her face, giving her a wild look. She pounded on the car horn and shrieked, "This has been the day from hell!"

Bena laughed. She laughed until she nearly choked. Maybe it was the tensions of the day finally busting loose, maybe it was that silliness that comes when you're dog tired, but suddenly something seemed hilarious to Bena. She laughed so hard that it made the rest of them start up too. "Mama's gone crazy," Ellie shouted. "Look at her." Bena was in a ball in the backseat, howling like a maniac. She was practically hysterical, hee-hawing so hard she was crying. "Mama," Ellie screamed in the midst of her own fit of laughter, "stop it! You're going nuts."

"I hope to God Mama doesn't have the gift of laughter too," Leslie said.

"If she does," Eddie said, "we're going to have to stop the car and shoot her and put her out of her misery."

• • •

THE PHONE WAS ringing when they walked in the house that night. It was Joe. His weekly calls had turned out to be monthly calls instead. "What's up, Mama?"

"Not much," she lied. "If you're calling about that money, baby, I sent it on Wednesday."

"It's not about the money. It's something else," Joe said. "Do you believe in predestination, Mama?"

Bena thought he must have come directly from a philosophy class or something—asking such a strange question. He usually just wanted to know if he should wash his underwear on hot or cold—or how long to heat up a pot pie.

"What do you mean?"

"You know, do you believe that certain things are meant to be? Like they might seem like a coincidence, but you sort of know they're not. You know, do you think things happen for a reason?"

It was a strange night for Joe to go cerebral on her. Maybe this was what college did to kids and she should be happy to know his education was taking. But he was asking her questions she needed time to think about—especially after a day like she'd had. "I guess so," Bena said.

"You guess what?"

"Things happen for a reason."

"Good," Joe said. "I was hoping you thought so."

"Why are you asking, honey?" Bena was too tired for this conversation.

"You know I told you I met this girl."

"Right. What was her name again?"

"Lisa."

"That's right. I remember."

"Well, Mama, she's not just any girl. And Mama, promise me you won't freak out or anything, okay? But her name is Lisa Rayfield."

Bena didn't get it. What did the girl's name have . . . "Rayfield?" Bena repeated.

"Yeah," Joe said. "She's Lorraine Rayfield's little sister."

Bena leaned against the wall and slid down to a sitting position on the floor.

"Mama, are you still there?"

"You're calling to tell me this, Joe?"

"Lisa is refusing to have anything to do with me until I tell you who she is and see how you take it."

"I see."

"You're taking it all right, aren't you, Mama? You don't have a problem with it, do you?"

BENA WAS HOME ALONE. She was grateful for the solitude. Her kids had all gone to work and she was planning to sort out her linen closet, such as it was. She'd just dumped everything out on the floor when the doorbell rang. "Who in the world?" she thought. The nice thing about living off the beaten track was that you didn't get a lot of nusiance interruptions; a person had to go to a lot of trouble to *just stop by.*

Bena looked out the window and saw Corby sitting on the hood of his car, peeling an orange. The doorbell rang a second time before Bena got to it. There stood Sue Cox. "Any chance a girl could get a cup of coffee around here?"

Bena was not in the mood. She still had on her bathrobe. At least it was a new one—thank God—white, that she'd bought recently after she threw most of her clothes away. "Sure," she said. "Come on in."

Bena didn't really want Sue Cox to come in. It was the last thing she wanted. This house with four unmade beds that would probably stay unmade all day long, until everybody reclaimed them later. With a cat litter box that should have been changed this morning, but hadn't been. And three adolescent cats roaming the house in search of rodents or roaches or half-eaten sandwiches left on the floor in front of the TV. Now Sue Cox would see Bena's life, the ugly mingled carpet that hid dirt as long as it could, but had been forced, at last, to give up. The brown plaid sofa. The La-Z-Boy with the broken lever, so you could never fold your feet down. You just had to lie in the chair and look between your shoes to see the TV. It had been Bobby's chair in the beginning, where he liked to recline in the evening and watch the news with a couple of kids straddling his belly. Now the family fought over who got that chair. It was the best seat in the house.

Right this minute Bena would like to set a match to it. And to her Early American coffee table too with the wobbly leg. And the hand-me-down desk Bobby's mother had given them that Bena never wanted in the first place. And her curtains, which would not close anymore since Eddie had tied the drawstring into some sort of Boy Scout knot, which ruined the whole pulley mechanism.

"I wasn't expecting anybody," Bena said. As if *if* she had been expecting somebody then the house would be carpeted in that new white carpet she saw at Sears and all the furniture would be new and expensive too. And she would be looking like a vision of loveliness first thing in the morning.

"I should have called," Sue Cox said. "I was afraid you'd make an excuse, you know. You might not want to see me."

"Excuse the house," Bena said. "It's a mess."

"Looks lived in," she said. "That's the whole point, right?"

Bena turned to look at her. "And what's the point at your house?"

Sue Cox laughed. "The reason my house looks like nobody really lives there, is because, you know. In a way, nobody really does."

"I bet Lucky and Tom will hate to hear that," Bena said.

"I'm kind of a control freak about a house," Sue Cox said. "After all these years it sort of rubbed off on Luck. I know he keeps it cleaner than your average hospital."

"I get jealous about that," Bena said. "A clean house. I dream about a clean house. But as Eddie told me once, 'Mama, you're not a control freak. You're just a regular freak.'"

"Hard to believe an alcoholic can be a control freak, isn't it?" Sue Cox said. "My psychiatrist told me it's because our lives stay so chaotic—when we drink—that we cling to what little control we have left. In my case, it's my house. I'd rather clean a house than make money. My mama always thought it was my one good quality."

"Come in the kitchen," Bena said. "I'll make coffee." She tightened the sash around her robe and led Sue Cox to the kitchen table, where newspaper was strewn everywhere and there was evidence that earlier cereal had been poured and toast jellied by her semiconscious offspring. Bena pulled out a chair. "Sit down."

"You got an ashtray?" Sue Cox said. "I mean, do you mind if I smoke? I get jumpy sometimes. A cigarette helps."

Bena opened a drawer to get an ashtray. One of her students had made it for her last Christmas. It said, *Peace on Earth*. "Here," Bena said.

Sue Cox sat down and lit her cigarette. Bena shoveled little scoops of coffee into the coffeemaker and got cups from the cabinet. "So, what brings you to see me?"

"Lucky and I went to see a lawyer yesterday. I guess he told you."

"He did. An old friend of your daddy's? Right?"

"He's done work for me before. You know, when I had the accident." Sue Cox took a long drag of her cigarette, sucking in and sort of holding her breath before blowing the smoke back out. "So things are under way. I just wanted you to know that I'm not standing in Lucky's way. Or your way."

"Isn't a divorce what you want too?"

Sue Cox picked a piece of tobacco off her tongue. "We should have done it a long time ago. We'd have both been better off."

"That's what Lucky says."

"Here's the thing," Sue Cox said. "I don't want to get corny or anything, Bena. But I hope you'll understand what I'm about to say."

Bena braced herself for what was to come. Was Sue Cox going

to warn her about Lucky's dark side? Reel off a list of all his bad habits? Explain why he was impossible to live with?

"It's just that my mama and daddy are both dead. You know that. And I'm an only child, right? So Lucky is all the family I got left. See? I just need to think that even if we're divorced that Lucky and I can still be—you know—family. I'm hoping you can understand how I feel. I'm sort of scared of having, well—nobody."

"What about Corby?"

"I'm crazy about him," Sue Cox said. "Look out there at him. He's a beautiful person, isn't he? But damn, I know the future goes just so far with a boy like that. I'm not stupid, Bena. I know we won't get married and live happily ever after. But if I thought it was possible I'd marry him tomorrow."

Sue Cox's legs were crossed and she was swinging her foot as she talked, her sandal flapping back and forth. Before Bena thought to warn her about the cats Otis Redding sprang for her ankle and clung to it with his sharp toenails. Sue Cox shrieked and jumped up from her chair, kicking Otis across the floor and knocking a cereal bowl to the floor. "Damn," she said. "What the hell was that?"

Bena started to go after Otis but he'd darted out of the room in pure terror. "We have cats," Bena said. "They're everywhere. I should have warned you."

"I love cats," Sue Cox said. "I swear." She took a puff from her cigarette and Bena could see her hand was trembling. "I would never hurt a cat—or anything."

"It's okay." Bena stooped to get the cereal bowl and wipe up the milk. "You didn't hurt him. You know cats. They like to learn everything the hard way."

Sue Cox sat back down, putting her feet on the seat of the chair. "My nerves are jumpy in the morning."

"It's okay," Bena said. "You were talking about Corby."

"He's got dreams." Sue Cox crushed her half-smoked cigarette into the ashtray. Bena noticed that she rubbed it out a long time, like maybe she had a secret fear of leaving a tiny ember burning, of accidentally setting things on fire if she wasn't careful. "I'm perfect for a man with dreams because I can always see just what he's after—the life he's looking for. I start to think I can see the way to get him there—get us both there. Life's beat the shit out of Corby, but it hasn't killed his dreams."

"And you didn't feel that way with Lucky?"

"A fishpond is not what I call a dream, Bena. No offense."

Bena smiled. "Coffee is ready." She got up to pour it.

"Don't get me wrong, Bena. I love Lucky. I always have loved him. But not like that. Not love love. Lucky wants a kind of happiness that bores me to death. Peace and quiet. Car running. Bills paid. Pond stocked. Chicken for Sunday dinner. Lord help me, but I got to have more than that."

"I see." Bena set a cup of coffee in front of Sue Cox.

"You know what my psychiatrist told me once?" Sue Cox fumbled in her purse for another cigarette. "He said that happiness is not for everybody, Bena. Some of us need excitement or even pain instead. I don't mean we *want* it. I mean we *need* it. We got to take risks. We got to cause trouble. Because that's how we know we're alive. Crazy, huh?" She fiddled with her lighter a few times before she got the flame to appear. "He said that's my problem. I start feeling sort of dead inside and then I got to make something happen, you know, to bring myself back to life. I take something now to take the edge off it. These new pills keep me from having to wreak havoc just to keep myself from dying."

"Well, that's good then," Bena said. "That new medicine."

"You know they say an unexamined life isn't worth living. Right?" Sue Cox blew smoke in Bena's direction. "Well, my life must *really* be worth living. People can accuse me of a lot, but nobody can accuse me of living an unexamined life."

Bena smiled. "I got plans to examine my life just as soon as Eddie goes off to college."

"I'm saying this all wrong, aren't I?" Sue Cox said. "I just came over here to say I hope we can be friends, Bena. You and me."

Bena picked up her spoon and dipped it into her coffee like a paddle, like she was going against the current, trying to cool her coffee. "I guess we could try," Bena said. Here was another person practically begging her to lie to them. And here she was, trying her best to do it.

"Good." Sue Cox glanced around the kitchen into the den, like she had never been in an ordinary house before, never witnessed authentic domestic life. "You got any toast?" she said. "I usually eat a piece of dry toast in the morning."

"Sure," Bena said. "Toast I can manage." She went to the counter to get the bread and walked to where the toaster was plugged in. She could feel Sue Cox's eyes on her, like she was just staring a hole in her. Bena felt herself begin to sweat a little. "You and Lucky got a lot of history," Bena said, trying to break the spell.

"Sad but true." Sue Cox smiled. "You know, Bena, I hope it's okay saying so, but you make me think of Lucky's mama a little bit. You don't look like her. I don't mean that. But you got her ways."

"I got a thousand kids like she did." Bena smiled.

"And a husband that ripped your heart out."

Bena looked at Sue Cox. "And that too." Was that the way people perceived her—a woman with her heart ripped out?

"I wish you could have seen Luck with his mama," Sue Cox said. "That's what made me love him back in high school. It was how much he loved her. How much he wanted to do for her. I thought, if only a boy could ever love me like that—like Luck does his mama." Sue Cox laughed. "I sure was young and stupid then."

Bena thought of Joe and Eddie. She hoped to God she hadn't ruined them for the next women—the ones they would choose for themselves. What if she'd overloved them? Overindulged them?

Overforgiven them? Would they spend their adult lives looking for another woman to do the same? Would they finally be forced to give up and move back in with her—grow old sharing bunk beds in their boyhood bedroom? While she grew old picking up socks and heating up their TV dinners?

"My drinking and everything." Sue Cox shook her head. "I made Luck miserable some of the same ways his daddy did. He hates me in that same complicated way. It was like, in a way, he ended up married to his daddy—not his mama like he hoped." She flicked ashes into the Peace on Earth ashtray. "Life's a bitch, huh?"

"I wish I'd known Lucky's mama," Bena said.

"You know, he made his mama a promise that no matter what happened we would stay married forever."

"He told me," Bena said.

"I guess she's turning over in her grave about now. I never wanted to be a promise to anybody's dying mama." Sue Cox picked cat hair off her blouse.

The toast popped up. "You want any butter or jelly?" Bena asked.

"Just dry," Sue Cox said.

Bena put the toast in front of Sue Cox. She could hear a second car come up the gravel road. She looked out and saw Leslie in the car the doctor loaned her to haul his kids around over the summer. The three kids were with her and the radio was on too loud. "It's Leslie," Bena said.

"Well, we need to get on our way." Sue Cox bit into her toast. "Corby's got to rehearse tonight. His band is starting to pick up some jobs. They're pretty good."

Bena watched Sue Cox eat her toast. Everything she did seemed graceful. She made eating a piece of toast look like a scene from *Swan Lake* or *The Nutcracker* or any of those ballets Bena had never been to but had seen on TV. She'd never admit it to a soul in this world, but Bena basically didn't get the point of ballet. She was one of the few mothers she knew of who'd never encouraged her daughters to take lessons. She secretly thought there was something silly about it—all that tiptoeing around and twirling. It was very graceful though, she would say that much. Sue Cox might have made a good ballerina, Bena thought. Long legged and limber and her hair in a knot just like the ballerinas on TV.

"Can I ask you something?" Bena said.

"Sure," Sue Cox said. "Shoot."

"Do you look at me and wonder what Lucky sees in me?"

Sue Cox looked up from her toast. "What are you talking about?"

"Look at me." Bena twirled around in a clumsy pirouette. She hadn't had a shower. Her hair was still uncombed. She was barefoot. Under her robe she had on a pair of Ellie's boxer shorts and an ancient T-shirt of Bobby's that she still slept in. Wisps of gray hair were at her temples. She'd bitten her fingernails to shreds Sunday night when she finally got home after the day from hell. Didn't a woman like Sue Cox look at her in bewilderment? Didn't she wonder what on earth her husband saw in a woman like Bena?

"I *know* what Luck sees in you," Sue Cox said. "You're real."

"Oh great. That's great. I'm real."

"It is great," Sue Cox said. "I was always the woman who might have been, who used to be, who never was. But you, Bena. You're a woman who is. You are. You always have been. You will be tomorrow. You're real and Lucky is crazy about you because of it."

"It's just that you're always—you know, *Miss Baxter High*," Bena said. "I still halfway expect to see you wearing your rhinestone tiara."

Sue Cox laughed. Her voice was unusually low and sort of gravelly. "Good looks are the least God could do for me, considering the rest of the mess I got stuck with. God owes me something for all the shit I have to put up with." She smiled. "But Bena, good-looking is something different from beautiful. I'm not beautiful. Those young girls in the magazines—the ones who are nothing but lips and teeth—they're not beautiful. You got to be real to be beautiful. See? Don't you get it?"

"You're pretty hard on yourself," Bena said.

"You're pretty hard on *yourself*," Sue Cox answered. "What women do you know who aren't hard on themselves?"

BENA WALKED OUTSIDE with Sue Cox to where Corby was waiting in the drive. "If Lucky talks bad about me, Bena, promise me you won't take it to heart. The stories he might tell—you don't have to believe them."

"We don't really talk about you that much," Bena said.

Leslie had parked her car behind Corby's and let the children out. She was leaning against Corby's car listening to him pontificate. He used his hands when he spoke. He paused for a minute and got a pen and paper out of the glove compartment and wrote something down and tore it in half and handed part of it to Leslie. The youngest girl, Abby, was curled around Leslie's leg, begging for something. She tried to grab the paper out of Leslie's hand but Leslie pulled it away and stuck it in the pocket of her shorts. Corby and Leslie were so engrossed in their conversation they didn't see Bena and Sue Cox coming from the back door.

"You're really good with kids," Corby said. "I love kids, too."

"Maybe you and Sue Cox will have some kids then?" Leslie said.

Corby grinned. "Sometimes I think I'm as near to a kid as she really wants."

"If you ask me, you're lucky she puts up with you," Leslie said. "She could probably have anybody she wanted."

"Tell me about it," he said. "Sue Cox is as near to a stroke of luck as I ever had."

"Then I think you ought to count your blessings."

"What makes you think I don't?"

Abby saw Bena and pointed to her. She tugged at Leslie's shorts.

"Speaking of blessings," Leslie said. "Here she comes now." Corby turned to see Sue Cox and Bena walking toward them.

"Hey, Mama," Leslie said. "We just came over so the kids could play with the cats. They like to change the litter box. I know it's sort of sick. But I'm always on the lookout for cheap, wholesome fun. Hey, Mrs. McKale."

"Hey there," Sue Cox said.

"Is everything okay?" Leslie's eyes searched Bena's face for some sign of trouble.

"If you mean did we get in a fistfight or anything—no," Sue Cox said.

"You probably don't remember this, Mrs. McKale," Leslie said. "But when you spoke at my high school, I introduced you. I thought your talk was really great too."

"I hope I said, *Do as I say, not as I do,* because I was so out of it back then that I don't remember a thing. Sorry, honey. You ready to go, Corby?" Sue Cox lifted the sunglasses she had on to look at him in the bright light.

"Say the word, Coxie."

Before getting in the car Sue Cox hugged Bena. "You take good care of Lucky for me. If he gives you any trouble, you just let me know."

As Corby drove them down the long drive he tapped the horn and they both stuck their arms out the windows and waved.

"Tell me that's not a strange pair there," Leslie said.

"I think Corby likes you, Les," Bena said.

"Yep." Leslie grinned. "That's how I know he's a disaster waiting to happen."

"What was that piece of paper he gave you?"

"Mama, you're so nosy." Leslie reached into her pocket and pulled out the paper. "We exchanged addresses. He's going to send me a tape he made. I'm supposed to write him back and tell him it's wonderful. You know the drill, Mama."

"Just remember," Bena said, "Sue Cox loves that boy."

"I guess she's desperate now that you've stolen Luckyboy away from her."

"It's not like that," Bena said.

"I'm teasing, Mama." Leslie punched her. "Lighten up."

6

Thanksgiving was Bena's favorite holiday. It was the one meal every year that she threw her heart and soul into preparing. She started getting in the mood weeks ahead, beginning with her class. They reenacted the original Thanksgiving dinner, Indians and settlers eating corn and pumpkins and sliced turkey from Kroger. Most of her students were black but it didn't seem to deter their enthusiasm for the event. Half of them dressed up like Indians and the other half like Puritans. They made feather headdresses and Puritan hats and collars. Bena let the Indians paint their faces with red tempera paint and the settlers with white tempera. That seemed to her an African sort of compromise. Her students ran with it too, imitating the peculiar habits they attributed to Indians and white people. It was clear they considered both groups strange, and the exercise made them more than glad to be of African descent. Bena'd been in the classroom for years and was required to teach a yearly American history unit revolving around Thanksgiving. She figured she wasn't tampering with history any more than most textbooks were.

This was her year to teach the slow learners—kids who usually had so much *life* on their minds that school seemed frivolous in comparison. But the notion of a big outdoor cookout where a bunch of people who didn't really like one another sat down together to eat a bunch of odd food fascinated them. The concept fascinated Bena too. Those had been the sort of family Thanksgivings she'd known as a child.

Mayfred had the classroom across the hall. She'd started going out with a white man from church. It had her three kids in a stir. "We keeping it a secret best we can," Mayfred said. "Long as Jesus knows, then I figure it's nobody else's business."

Joe was planning to bring Lisa Rayfield home for Thanksgiving dinner—*to meet the family,* as he put it. "Y'all are going to love Lisa," he kept saying, "especially you, Mama. Wait and see." He offered these comments as instructions, not predictions. Bena sensed the panic in him. Another of the Rayfield girls, Bena thought. Who were these people anyway? Where did they come from? How many more would be sneaking their way into her life? Was this God's idea of a test? Maybe if there were enough people at Thanksgiving dinner Lisa Rayfield would just blend in and sort of go unnoticed. That's what Bena was hoping.

Without asking anybody, Leslie invited Corby and Sue Cox for Thanksgiving too. Sue Cox startled Bena when she called to accept, saying, "Sure, we'd love to come."

Corby had spent the fall sending Leslie band tapes, so she'd gotten interested in the music scene and had started going to concerts over in Atlanta and Birmingham and even out at Larry's with some kids from school. Sometimes Ellie went with her.

Eddie surprised everybody and invited Anna Kaye to dinner too. Ordinarily he liked to keep Anna Kaye out of the fray of his mother and sisters. Bena could count on one hand the times he'd brought her to the house. Even then Bena thought Anna Kaye had probably had to beg to come. And they were always in Anna Kaye's car too—

since Eddie's turns with the family car were precious few. He'd gotten so he could jog all the way to Anna Kaye's house in less than an hour and did so a couple of nights a week. He'd even started going to church regularly just so he could sit by her and praise the Lord for the wonders of this world. Sometimes Leslie drove him to church, sometimes Mayfred picked him up on her way, and once he'd run all the way out to Anna Kaye's house, changed his sweaty clothes, and ridden to church with her family. Mayfred reported to Bena that Eddie sat all through church with his arm around Anna Kaye. "That boy is rejoicing," Mayfred said.

When Lucky was around on Sunday mornings he was good to let Eddie take his truck for most of the day, which had done wonders for their basic relationship.

In an enlightened moment Bena invited Mayfred and her new white man from church and her kids too to Thanksgiving dinner. She called to invite Bobby's mother and Kyle just like she always did, and Bobby's mother declined just like she always did. She would spend the holiday with Bobby's brothers as usual. But it was a ritual they'd kept up since Bobby's death. You would think Bena lived a thousand miles away considering how nonexistent their visits were.

Sissy was too far along to travel home for Thanksgiving. Her baby was due any time. She told Bena she'd have Thanksgiving with Juanita and her kids and swore it would be fun. Bena wondered what Mexicans had for Thanksgiving dinner. She imagined something with jalapeño peppers.

Even though Bena suggested it, Lucky didn't really want to invite his brothers Buck and Jarrell to Thanksgiving, for fear they might actually come.

ELLIE AND LESLIE helped Bena spit-shine the house. Besides the dining room table, they set up card tables and borrowed Mayfred's white tablecloths. For once in her life Bena had enough matching plates and silverware to go around. It embarrassed her how totally satisfying that was. Ellie tied the napkins with ribbon and colored leaves. It looked as good to Bena as something you'd see out at the country club.

Eddie and Lucky cleared out the carport and set up the new smoker they'd bought at Wal-Mart so Lucky could smoke the turkey outside. It was his idea. Lucky brought Tom over for the day and he dashed around the yard, terrorizing the cats. Mayfred insisted on bringing her mother's corn-bread dressing recipe, enough for an army, and also collard greens and sweet-potato pies. For some reason Ellie set out to make the tuna casserole she learned in home ec. Nobody could talk her out of it. Leslie made the ice tea and put the pickles and olives on a plate and kept the cats off the counters and out of the kitchen. Bena made the mashed potatoes and green beans. Anna Kaye brought a plate of deviled eggs and celery sticks stuffed with pimento cheese.

Sue Cox and Corby arrived early with fresh flowers—a trunk-load. It seemed there was a flower shop right next to Bucky's—and the guy who ran it liked Sue Cox. A lot. Ellie swore she'd never seen anything so wonderful. She held the flowers the way you do a baby and buried her face in the petals. She forgot about her casserole and began to arrange the flowers in anything she could find that resembled a vase. When she was through there were flowers on all the tables, on top of the TV, and in the bathrooms, and she even made bouquets for people to take home after dinner.

Lucky manned the smoker along with Mayfred's white man, whose name was Jerry Lee. He'd been married to two white women and it'd been a big mess both times he said. "I might not necessarily be crazy about every black person who walks the earth," Jerry Lee told Lucky, "but I am crazy about Mayfred. She goes beyond color." Later he would say to Bena, "Did Mayfred tell you we met at church?"

Mayfred's kids did like kids always do in a stranger's house: act paralyzed at first, then bust loose with all kinds of energy and wildness. Mayfred kept telling them to go outside, but they mostly stayed in the den, watching TV and tasting anything they saw wrapped in tinfoil. They let the cats in every time they opened a door. Sue Cox settled herself in the den with her cigarette and ashtray and asked Mayfred's kids all sorts of questions, especially her son, LaVonte, the oldest. "So you like Jerry Lee out there? Is he good to your mama? Where is your real daddy?" Stuff like that.

"Why you all the time asking so many questions?" LaVonte said.

"I'm nosy," Sue Cox said.

"Don't be asking me all them questions."

"All right then," she said. "You ask me some questions. Questions don't bother me. I like questions. Ask me anything?"

"Okay," LaVonte said. "Who are you anyway?"

THE PLAN WAS to have dinner coincide with the Auburn-Alabama game. For a lot of people the game was the real reason for the holiday — something most folks in Alabama were grateful for. When everything was ready, they held off eating awhile longer because Joe and Lisa hadn't gotten there yet. Bena was a little worried, but there couldn't be much chance of them being in an automobile accident, could there? She hoped there was no jinx on the Rayfield women, you know, where anytime they got into a car with an Eckerd man, the car crashed.

It wasn't like Joe not to call. He'd acted like this was about the biggest event in his whole life — this Thanksgiving dinner in which he would unveil his family, in hopes they'd pass inspection. He'd given elaborate instructions on how everybody was to behave, how they were to make Lisa Rayfield feel welcome — and not say anything stupid. Everybody had promised to try to act civilized and enlightened. The only thing stopping them was that Joe and Lisa hadn't shown up yet.

It was Anna Kaye who insisted everybody write down something they were thankful for. She and Mayfred's daughters, Tasha and Jazzmond, passed out pieces of paper and made everybody do it— even people like Eddie and LaVonte, who didn't want to. "If you can't think of nothing to be grateful for, boy," Mayfred told LaVonte, "then you mize well go on out and sit in the car till we through eating. You don't have no business at a Thanksgiving if you don't have no thanks in you." LaVonte snatched a piece of paper from his sister and sat down with a scowl on his face, trying to think up one tiny blessing he wouldn't mind mentioning in front of all these white people.

Sue Cox took her piece of paper and went outside. She sat all by herself in a chair out by the pecan tree with Tom panting at her feet. Corby went outside too, where Lucky and Jerry Lee were at the smoker. Eddie followed him. It was like all the men wanted to collaborate or something—and they did it in near-perfect silence. "Whose idea was this anyway?" Corby finally asked.

"Sounds to me like Mayfred's idea," Jerry Lee said, apologetically.

"Naw," Eddie said. "It's Anna Kaye's idea. She comes from a real religious family." It was like he was defending her. "You can just put down what comes to mind. You don't have to sign your name to it."

Bena overheard all this when she went to call them to the table.

First, they all gathered around and held hands. Mayfred's orders. Then Mayfred launched into a nice prayer about friends and family—such great blessings in this life. She thanked God for sending a fine man like Jerry Lee into her life too—which Bena noticed made Jerry Lee's lip quiver. LaVonte snorted and kept his eyes down during that part. Then everybody said *Amen*. Anna Kaye passed the written-down blessings to Lucky—the man of the house—so he could read them each out loud before everybody sat down to eat.

Lucky cleared his throat. "*I'm thankful for . . .*" he began unfolding the papers, then read aloud:

Freedom——coming this June. The big world out there waiting for me.

Darryl Owens. That time at Bible Camp last summer. Sorry, Mama.

My job at the Country Club——where I met Anna Kaye.

Miles Davis, Patsy Cline, John Lennon, Janis Joplin. The universal language.

Daddy's memory. Sissy's baby. Everybody getting along.

God's love.

A couple of old dogs like me and Tom learning a couple of new tricks.

The gift of weeping——which I hope is really a gift. And my good Luck.

Mama and Baby Jesus and that coconut cake right there.

Good health. Good food. Good people.

My personal relationship with Jesus Christ.

When this day gets over with.

The last paper Lucky struggled to read. "This one has got so damn many cross-outs." He turned it sideways. "Shoot," he said. "Wait. Here it is." He squinted, then read "*Change.*"

"That's a good one," Bena said.

"Amen," Eddie said. "Let's eat."

THEY HAD NEARLY finished dinner when Joe's truck plowed up the driveway. Bena went to the door and waved but saw imme-

diately that Joe was alone. Joe got out of the truck slowly, carrying
a couple of big bottles in his hand. Wine, it looked like. His face
showed the ravages of heartache. It looked like maybe he'd been
crying.

"Where's Lisa?" Bena asked.

"Decided not to come," Joe said. "Chickened out."

Bena hugged him, felt the pain coming off his body. "Any turkey
left?" he said.

He got a royal welcome—and all the obvious stupid questions
too. *Where's Lisa? Where's Lisa? Where's Lisa?* He looked at everybody
and said, "Looks like I'm late for a prayer meeting." Then he set the
bottles on the counter. "I brought champagne," he said. "Just in case
there was cause to celebrate." Bena looked at Lucky. They couldn't
have champagne in the house, could they? Not with Sue Cox here.
Besides, Joe was too young to buy liquor, wasn't he?"

"I'll put that in the refrigerator," Bena said.

"Joe looks awful," Ellie whispered. "Where's Lisa?"

"She changed her mind," Bena said.

"I bet she's scared to face you, Mama," Ellie said.

THE AFTERNOON WAS full of pie and football. Nobody was
neutral about either thing. Even Sue Cox got into it, cheering for
Auburn, going outside to do a cartwheel in the grass every time the
Tigers scored. Joe and LaVonte, Tide fans, not to be outdone, did
their own version of cartwheels when Bama put points on the board.
They made the afternoon crazy and kept everybody loud and happy.
Bena watched Joe on and off all day for signs of sadness. He was able
to laugh. He was able to concentrate on the game. He'd been able to
shake Lucky's hand and say, "I've heard a lot about you." He wasn't as
skeptical as the other children had been about this man in his
mother's life. Maybe he was tired, like Lucky said, and ready to send
in the replacements. *If you'll take Mama off my hands, I sure will appreciate it. More than you know.* Was that what was he was thinking? He

was the only child to call Lucky by his first name too. "You must be Lucky," he'd said.

Alabama beat Auburn. LaVonte celebrated by eating nearly a whole can of Reddi-wip, which he sprayed directly into his mouth —and then at his sisters, who screamed like the house was on fire. It was nearly dark when Mayfred and Jerry Lee began to round up Mayfred's kids and load the car. Mayfred hugged Bena and said, "Wooooo, we gon' have to talk, girl. After a day like this— I'm about to fall out I got so much to say. I'll be looking for you on Monday."

"I'll be the fat lady. Don't you ever come near me with another one of your pies."

It was only after Mayfred and her family left that Bena noticed she hadn't seen Corby in a while. Or Leslie either. "Where's your sister, Ellie?" Bena asked.

"Don't ask me." She shrugged.

Sue Cox had fallen asleep on the sofa in the den. It amazed Bena that she could sleep through the second football game Joe and Eddie had blaring on TV. Anna Kaye and Ellie were talking a mile a minute too. Bena was glad Sue Cox was sleeping. Maybe Corby and Leslie would be back before she woke up.

Bena and Lucky put on jackets and sat out in the carport, drinking hot coffee and enjoying the peace and quiet. They sat by the smoker, which was still putting out heat. Tom laid half under Lucky's chair. "I'm worried about Joe," Bena said.

"He's okay," Lucky said.

Already the trees had begun to drop their leaves. It made the sky seem bigger and brighter. The moon seemed twice as large too, looming through the branches above them like a big yellow eye. It wasn't cold, really. Only cool enough to be sweater weather, but still, it seemed cozy to huddle near the smoker and contemplate the future. "Christmas will be here before you know it," Lucky said.

They'd been sitting alone for a while when Ellie hollered, "Sissy's on the phone."

"Come on," Bena said to Lucky, and Lucky followed Bena into the house just as Eddie and Anna Kaye were headed out. "I'm taking Anna Kaye home," Eddie said. "Okay if I take your truck, Mr. McKale?"

Anna Kaye hugged Bena. "Thanks for everything," she said.

Bena saw that Sue Cox was still asleep in the den. "We'll get the phone in my bedroom," she whispered to Ellie.

IT WAS GOOD to hear Sissy's voice. They talked a long time, Bena giving an update on everybody and a rundown on today's menu. Then Sissy did the same. Bena'd learned the names of all Juanita's kids over the past couple of months. Jose, Jesus, and Carmelita. It seemed like maybe being around them was good practice for an expectant mother. Juanita got on the phone too to give Bena a report. "Your girl is very fat," she said. "So healthy. A fat baby is good."

Sissy took the phone away from her. "I'd rather you two not discuss how fat I am," Sissy said. "Especially after Juanita just stuffed me with dinner."

"I got somebody who wants to say hello to you." Bena handed Lucky the phone.

"So," he said, "I hear the days are numbered until you make Bena here a grandmother." Bena lay down on the bed and listened to Lucky talk to Sissy. He was easy at it once he got going, teasing her a little bit, exaggerating the hard time her sisters and brother had given him when he came courting their mother. She could hear Sissy's muffled voice on the other end of the line. She imagined how strange it must be for her talking to this stranger—her mother's boyfriend. Especially when Barrett was on another continent and according to Sissy—couldn't call much because he was saving his money, for the baby. Bena knew the truth was Sissy hadn't heard a word from Barrett in months.

"I never had kids of my own," Lucky told Sissy. Bena couldn't hear what Sissy said, but she could imagine. They talked a long time and it made Bena happy.

Before she finally hung up Sissy said to Bena, "He seems nice, Mama." Then she said, "The doctor told me I'm dilated a little. It shouldn't be too much longer."

Those words sobered Bena right up.

BENA AND LUCKY lay in her bed and talked until they drifted off into semisleep. They might have slept through the night if it weren't for hearing Eddie charge back up the drive in the truck and slam the door shut. Bena nudged Lucky awake and they went down the hall to the den. It was empty except for the chatter of the TV. Eddie came into the kitchen in his usual post–Anna Kaye daze. He didn't even see them standing there.

"Where is everybody?" Bena asked.

"Ellie's gone to bed, and I'm on my way," Eddie said. "Joe and Mrs. McKale are outside talking."

Bena and Lucky walked across the dark yard toward Sue Cox's cigarette tip. They could hear muffled laughter. When they got nearer, Joe spotted them. "Y'all pull up a chair. We're out here toasting *love gone wrong.*" He raised his glass.

"Mama knows about love gone wrong," Joe assured Sue Cox. "She knows about getting your heart busted to hell. Ain't that right, Mama. You're the expert." That was when Bena noticed the empty champagne bottle in the grass at Joe's feet and the one in Sue Cox's hand.

"Hey." Sue Cox waved the bottle. "Joe and me here—we're just getting acquainted. Seems we got a lot in common."

Lucky went over and took the bottle out of Sue Cox's hand.

"Uh-oh," she said. "We're making Luck mad."

"No need to get mad. Just get even," Joe laughed. Bena had never seen him drunk before. "Or, of course, you could *just get sad.* How's that? *Just get sad.* Naw, don't have a ring to it."

"Where's Corby?" Lucky asked Sue Cox.

"Now, there's a good question for you. I like that question. Do you like it, Bena?"

"Joe," Bena said. "Sue Cox can't drink. You can't give her champagne."

Sue Cox reached over and patted Joe's arm. "I have a drinking problem, honey, didn't you know? I'm a fall-down drunk. I can prove it too—if you don't believe me."

"Well, we all got problems, don't we," Joe said. "Nobody's perfect, right? Isn't that right, Mama? Nobody's perfect."

"Did you know your boy here has got a first-class broken heart, Bena? You're so busy dishing out the turkey and dressing maybe you didn't notice his heart is shot to hell. Some little bitch is giving him a real bad time. Tell your mama, honey," Sue Cox said to Joe. "Tell her what that little bitch did."

"Don't talk about Lisa like that," Joe said. "I don't let nobody talk about Lisa like that. You're a damn drunk," he said. "Your wife is a damn drunk," he said to Lucky.

"Joe." Bena grabbed his hand. "This is not going to help anything."

Joe got up and put his arm around Bena. "I love you, Mama. You know that, don't you? Mama wouldn't hurt a fly, would you, Mama?"

Lucky pulled Sue Cox to her feet too. She sort of fell against him in a way that Bena imagined was very familiar to both of them. Lucky looked at Bena. "Where the hell is Corby anyway?"

Bena wished he'd stop asking that. "You stay here with Sue Cox," she said. She turned and walked with Joe toward the house. He was a good foot taller than Bena and was draped around her shoulder. "Let's get you to bed," Bena said, feeling very small beside him. They had to pound on Eddie's door to get him to unlock it. He looked more irritated than surprised when Bena led Joe inside and helped him sprawl out on the lower bunk—Eddie's bed.

"Ain't love grand," Eddie said.

"Shut up," Joe mumbled, rolling over on his side. "Don't talk about Lisa like that. I don't let nobody talk bad about Lisa."

"If he gets sick," Bena said, "try to get him to the bathroom."

WHEN BENA GOT back outside Lucky was walking in circles with Sue Cox propped against him. "What the hell was Joe thinking," he said.

"He didn't know."

"He poured liquor into her glass," Lucky said. "Damn."

"He never laid eyes on Sue Cox before today. It's not his fault she's a drunk."

"Uh-oh," Sue Cox said. "You're making her mad, Lucky. And she's the nice one too. Remember?"

"Shut up, Sue Cox," Lucky said.

WHEN BENA SAW the car slinking up the drive, its headlights like two cat eyes in the night, her heart began to pound. Lucky had his arms around Sue Cox, trying to keep her moving. It looked like some sort of sloppy dance. Bena stood with her arms folded. The car doused them in light when it came into the yard—clearly they could see what they were coming home to.

Leslie was the first out of the car and came running toward Bena. "What's wrong?"

"You tell me," Bena said.

Corby came up right behind Leslie. He saw Sue Cox wobbling in Lucky's arms. "Oh, damn." He darted for her, lifting her away from Lucky. "What happened?"

"Guess," Bena said. "Guess what happened."

"Where the hell have you been?" Lucky asked him.

Sue Cox pulled away from Corby and stumbled to the nearby picnic-table bench. "This ought to be good," she said. "Let's see if he can make us believe him."

"The car broke down," Leslie said. "We had to wait for somebody to jump the car. Nobody had cables. It took forever. I swear."

"They didn't have any phones where you were?" Bena asked.

"Where were you?" Sue Cox said. "Think carefully before answering."

"We tried to call, Mama. The phone was busy."

"Look, I'm sorry about this." Corby said. "This is the last thing I wanted to happen. Believe me."

"You left me here," Sue Cox said.

"I'm sorry, Coxie. I was trying to get back to you. The car stalled. Had to wait for a guy with jumper cables. Come on." He reached down for her. "I'll take you home. We'll go home. Me and you."

"I'm mad at you," Sue Cox said, hugging him.

He kissed her forehead. "I'll make it up to you. I promise. But first, let's get you home. Let's get you straight."

"Maybe you should wait until morning," Bena said. "It's so late."

"I'm stone sober and wide awake," Corby said. "The sooner we get home, the better." He led Sue Cox to the car. "Will somebody grab her purse and stuff?" Leslie darted off to get it. She came back with a bouquet Ellie'd made and laid it across Sue Cox's lap the way you place flowers on a corpse in a coffin.

When Corby had Sue Cox seat-belted into the car he came back and said, "Look, I'm real sorry about this. None of this is Leslie's fault. I was the one that wanted to ride around and listen to some CDs. She didn't do a thing wrong."

Bena looked at Leslie, who was wet-eyed and distant.

"We had a great time today," Corby said. "Me and Sue Cox. Thanks for having us. And don't worry about Sue Cox," he said to Lucky. "I'll take good care of her."

He glanced at Leslie as he walked away and mouthed, *Sorry*.

LUCKY SPENT THE NIGHT. It was late and he was obviously unnerved seeing Sue Cox drunk again, seeing somebody else trying to do his job—trying to take care of her on the downslide. "That punk is a drunk himself," Lucky said to Bena. "How's he going to do her any good?"

It bothered Bena, lying beside a man who was worried sick about his wife. A man who thought nobody else could possibly do right by her. It wouldn't have surprised Bena if Lucky had leaped from bed and taken out after Corby and Sue Cox, just to supervise. To be sure Sue Cox didn't shift her dependence—ever.

"It's not your problem," Bena said.

Lucky and Bena hadn't been in bed long when they heard Leslie knock at the door. "Can I come in?" Usually Bena's children avoided her bedroom like the plague when they knew Lucky was in it. Leslie came in and crawled up into the bed between them like she used to do when she was a little girl and Bobby was the man in the bed. She hugged her mother and for a minute Bena thought Leslie might actually cry. "Don't be mad at Corby," Leslie whispered.

Bena felt her heart lift out of her for a minute the way it does when it has to make room for something. She looked at Leslie's face in the darkness, and in that instant she knew. "Oh my God, Les," she whispered.

"Shhhhhhh," Leslie said. "Please don't say anything."

IT WASN'T BENA'S own idea really. It just happened that she came into the kitchen when Joe was making a call. "Corby," he said. "This is Joe Eckerd. Look, man. I'm calling to say I'm sorry about getting Sue Cox messed up with that damn champagne. I was pretty messed up and feeling sorry for myself—but I sure as hell didn't mean to bring Sue Cox down with me. Tell her I'm really sorry, man. Sure thing. Yeah, maybe so. Okay, sure. I will. I'll give her the message." Joe hung up the phone and went out to the truck, where Eddie was waiting for him. They drove off, two brothers in search of some common ground.

When had Joe learned the art of apology?

IT WASN'T THE SORT of thing Bena thought over. It was instinctive, like monkey see, monkey do. As soon as Joe and Eddie were out of sight she called information and got the phone number, and before she could talk herself out of it she'd dialed the Rayfields' house and asked to speak with Lisa. She only had a matter of seconds to think what to say before Lisa picked up the phone. "Hello." Lisa's voice made Bena think of a whippoorwill. It had a sort of melancholy lilt to it. Bena's stomach churned a second and she wanted to hang up the phone, but she barged ahead. "Lisa, honey, this is Bena Eckerd, Joe's mother."

There was silence on Lisa's end.

"Joe was so disappointed you couldn't come for Thanksgiving dinner," Bena said. "We all were. Joe thinks the world of you and really wanted us to get to know you better." She paused and waited for a response, but there wasn't one. "So, you know, that's all. I was just calling to say, you know, we missed having you here and hope that maybe later on we'll get the chance to meet you."

It felt to Bena like she was talking to a ghost. She couldn't see or hear anybody but could sense the girl's presence almost like she was in the room instead of miles away at the end of the line. "Lisa, honey, are you there?"

"Yes, ma'am."

"Okay then," Bena said. "Well. Good-bye."

When Bena hung up the phone she felt wound up, like something about to spin in fast circles. She felt like she needed to run five miles or chop down a tree or wash the car. Something. So she put on a sweater and went out for a walk.

JUANITA CALLED. "It's a boy," she said. "His hair looks little bit red."

Bena could hardly breathe. "And Sissy?"

"The first baby, you know. It comes slow. You got plenty time to be scared. But Sissy did very good. She was wishing for her mama very much. They not so nice at that hospital. Not to the poor girls. It's better she come home."

Bena didn't like her own daughter being referred to as one of the poor girls—Sissy treated like a poor girl. It made her think of girls in her class, mostly poor, and how little they had to look forward to in terms of institutional courtesy and concern.

"I give Sissy the phone," Juanita said, "she tell you herself. She's trying to nurse. I tell her there's no milk yet."

Bena heard Juanita speaking Spanish to her kids and then, finally, "Hey, Mama."

"Everything is going to be okay," Bena said.

"I'm happy, Mama. Really I am. He's a sweet baby." Sissy began to cry.

"I love him already," Bena said.

"I named him after Daddy," Sissy sobbed. "That's okay, isn't it?"

"Your daddy would be proud." When Bena hung up the phone she wanted to cry too. But no tears would come.

LUCKY HAD SENT plane tickets for Sissy and the baby to come home as soon as Sissy could travel. Nobody was expecting to see a rusted-out green Dodge Dart putter up the drive before the baby was barely a week old. Bena glanced out the window thinking it must be some of Leslie's friends—that maybe they'd stolen a car or something. It wasn't until she saw Juanita, a small, dark-haired woman with a long ponytail, get out of the car and open the back-seat door, speaking Spanish to her three tired, brown children, that she realized Sissy was home. She ran into the yard with Ellie and Leslie right behind her—just in time to see Sissy ease her way out of the front seat with the baby in her arms. Ellie and Leslie went straight for the baby. "Be careful, y'all," Sissy said, handing him over.

"Oh my God," they kept saying. "Oh my God."

Bena went straight for Sissy, her own baby. She hugged her gently because Sissy's breasts were so full of milk they were leaking everywhere.

• • •

LUCKY CAME OVER the minute he got Bena's call. He still had on his uniform. "Look who's here," Bena said. "This is Sissy."

Sissy smoothed her hair with her hands. "I look so bad."

"If you ask me, a new mama is always a beautiful sight," Lucky said. "So is an old mama for that matter." He put his arm around Bena. "Lots of folks glad to have you home, Sissy, myself among them."

Sissy tried to smile.

"Come look at the baby," Leslie insisted.

Lucky walked to where Leslie stood with the baby. "Sit down," she ordered him. "You can hold him."

"I don't know," Lucky said.

"Don't be a sissy. People hold babies all the time. Sit right there." So Lucky did, and Leslie handed him the baby. "Just relax," she said. "Support his head."

The baby fit in the curve of Lucky's elbow. "See," Leslie said. "There. You're not a natural. But you'll get the hang of it."

"Maybe," Lucky said.

"His name is Bobby," Ellie told him.

It was like Lucky was momentarily lost in the information. He studied the baby in his arms. "Red hair," he said, and his hands shook as he ran one finger down the baby's leg. The baby's tiny foot wasn't as big as Lucky's thumb. "Hey there Bobby-boy," Lucky said.

"He likes you," Bena insisted.

Lucky sat stone still, barely breathing, holding the baby, until Leslie couldn't resist any longer and lifted Bobby from Lucky's arms.

"That's a fine baby," Lucky said. "I never saw a better baby."

The baby's full name was Robert Barrett Carter. All evening long, all through supper and the dishes and making up beds for the night, awake or asleep, Bobby was passed from person to person, kissed, whispered to, studied, and rocked. Even Jose and Jesus wanted turns to hold Bobby and sat in the reclining La-Z-Boy to do it. "Sissy let us," they said. "We know how."

That night Juanita and her kids settled into Eddie's room, and Eddie dragged his sleeping bag onto the sofa in the den. Bena insisted that Sissy and the baby sleep in her room at least the first few nights. This didn't go over well with Leslie and Ellie, who begged to have the baby in their room. After all, they were the ones who'd gone to Wal-Mart with Lucky after supper to get a Portacrib for Bobby. At Lucky's insistence Leslie and Ellie had gone a little nuts in the baby department, buying disposable diapers, blankets, toys, bibs, and little footie pajamas. Later, when Bena saw how much they'd bought, they told Bena that Lucky had insisted, that he'd kept looking at the shopping cart and saying, "I'm no expert, but I swear I think a baby needs more than this little bit we got in this cart. What else we need? Let's just get him one of everything they got." When Bena heard the story she gave Lucky a kiss in front of everybody. "Well," he said, "we don't want Bobby going without, do we?"

Sissy left the room then. She took the diaper off her shoulder and laid it on the kitchen counter and walked to the back of the house. "Damn," Lucky said. "I got a knack for putting my foot in my mouth."

"If you ask me," Leslie said, "Bobby doing without Barrett is a blessing."

"Shhhhh," Bena said. "Don't let Sissy hear you say that."

"I don't care if she does," Leslie said. "It's true."

It was late when Lucky left to go home. Bena was exhausted by the time she got to bed. Sissy wasn't asleep yet. "Do you want to talk?" Bena asked.

"No," Sissy said.

"You sure?"

"If anything happened to me, Mama, you'd take care of Bobby, wouldn't you?"

"Don't talk crazy. Nothing is going to happen to you."

"Just tell me yes or no, Mama."

"Of course I would." Bena kissed Sissy's cheek like she used to do when Sissy was a little girl. "There's nothing to worry about." Bena held Sissy in her arms until Sissy fell asleep. Bena didn't sleep a wink all night. She was too worried about Sissy worrying. Too busy getting up with the baby.

7

Lucky came to Bena's sixth-grade Christmas party. It was nice the way Bena's students said, "That your boyfriend, Mrs. Eckerd? Do you go with him?" She answered yes to both questions. The children ate Christmas cookies and drank punch and pasted together red-and-green construction-paper chains to wrap around the gifts they'd made their parents—bird feeders out of peanut butter jars and tin pie plates, filled with popcorn. Bena'd tried to incorporate the bird feeders into their nature unit. *If you take care of Mother Earth, Mother Earth will take care of you.*

Sixth graders approached Christmas differently than younger children. Already the futility of asking for what they wanted had become apparent to them. They modified and trimmed their wish list with every year that passed. *I'm getting a jacket for when it gets cold. My mama said she don't have money to get me nothing. I don't want nothing anyway. Mama is getting my outfit out layaway for Christmas. She won't let me wear it to school though.*

It was not sad to Bena that her students had learned to minimize their dreams. She admired them for it and took a certain comfort in their realistic expectations.

"What you want for Christmas, Mrs. Eckerd?" they asked her.

"I got a new grandbaby," she said. "That's my present."

"Ask me what I want," Lucky said to the class.

"What you want, mister?" they yelled.

"A grandmother—just about like this one here." He put his arm around Bena, making all the kids squeal and whistle.

Even though it was against the law, they all sang "Joy to the World" and "We Wish You a Merry Christmas" before leaving to catch the buses home. Nearly every child in her class had been born and raised in Baxter County. The odds of offending anyone with an overt dose of Christianity was next to none. Bena gave each child a small wrapped gift and a kiss on the cheek as they left the classroom.

THE TREE WAS TOO BIG. Lucky and Eddie had taken Jose and Jesus with them to get it. Naturally it would have been too simple to buy a nice tree off a lot. Lucky insisted they troop all over his six acres until they came upon just the right tree to cut themselves. It was an ordinary pine, sort of ball shaped, and a good twelve feet high. When they dragged it out of the truck and up to the house Bena was speechless. Jose and Jesus were filthy from running all through the woods, and Lucky had bought them grape Popsicles, too, which made them look like little old men with purple mustaches.

"We get the best one." Jesus's eyes sparkled. "Look here, Mama."

"We'll trim it up a little," Lucky said to Bena.

When Lucky and Eddie were finished with the so-called trimming, the tree looked like they had simply cut it in half. It was seven feet tall and eight feet wide—and took up almost the entire living room.

"What kind of Christmas tree is that?" Leslie asked.

"I told Lucky it was too big," Eddie said. He'd started calling Lucky by his first name since he'd heard Joe do it.

"We got a little carried away. At least won't nobody else have one like it." Lucky grinned.

"That's for sure." Leslie looked at Bena and rolled her eyes.

By the time the lights were strung and the ornaments hung it looked a little better, but not much. "A real tree the best," Juanita said. "No matter."

"We get gifts piled up under there," Lucky said, "it'll be damn near perfect."

BY THE TIME Christmas rolled around there were so many presents under the tree that Jose and Jesus were not allowed to go into the room by themselves. They'd already opened half a dozen gifts, which Juanita had quickly rewrapped the best she could. At night, one by one, people gathered in the dark living room, just sat around on the furniture or the floor and stared at the lighted tree. Lucky especially loved to sit in the dark and watch the tree lights flash. He talked to Jose and Jesus, who barely understood a word he said, but sat as close to him as they could get and listened anyway. Every time they said anything to Lucky he nodded his head and said, "*Sí, señor.*" It was almost as good as if they understood each other.

Lucky'd gotten better about holding Bobby too. Now he wanted his turn just like everybody else. Sometimes when he couldn't hold Bobby, Carmelita would plant herself on his lap and stare at him. This was good because in the beginning she'd been scared of him and ran from the room whenever he came in. Now he'd bounce her on his knee and say, "*Qué pasa, Carmelita?*" She'd look at him in silence and hold on to his leg like she was riding a horse.

Sissy had given in to her sisters' begging and moved back into her old room with Bobby and the Portacrib. "They're spoiling that baby rotten," Eddie complained. "They don't put him down long enough to give him a chance to cry. They're going to ruin him if you let them, Mama."

Lots of nights now Lucky stayed over. He waited until the house was still and dark, then he locked all the doors the same way Bobby used to do. He got in bed beside Bena and stared at the ceiling like he was lying beneath a heavenly host of stars. "I love this," he said. "Kids make Christmas, don't they? All these years me and Sue Cox been missing out on all this. Heck, half the time we'd take off for Panama City over Christmas, check into a hotel or something—just to get away where we didn't have to notice how alone we were."

"Well, you're sure not alone this year," Bena said.

"Reminds me of when I was a kid," Lucky said. "Everybody excited and wound up. It didn't take but a few Christmases that didn't quite materialize—you know—to cure us of the Christmas spirit. But I got it this year, Bena."

"Good." She kissed him.

"For all I know this could be my last Christmas on earth. I want it to be a Christmas to remember. You just never know, Bena. Anything could happen."

"No, it couldn't," she said. "*Anything* has already happened. God won't let *anything* happen again. Neither will I."

Lucky rolled closer to Bena and put his arms around her. "You're right."

PEOPLE DRESSED UP on Christmas Eve because Joe was bringing Lisa Rayfield for dinner. Juanita had cooked tamales, enchiladas, rice pudding, and a lot of stufff nobody recognized. It smelled spicy and foreign, like hot chilies and cinnamon, and if you came into the kitchen Juanita would shoo you out with a big spoon. The house was decorated with holly branches and green twigs Jesus and Jose had gathered from the yard. The dining room table and card tables were draped with white bedsheets for tablecloths and Bena's set of matching dishes. The girls had put candles, poinsettias, and pinecones on the centers of the tables, like Ellie had seen in *Southern Living* magazine. Christmas music blared on the stereo, but you could barely hear it over the volume of voices. Lucky put on a tie, but Eddie refused to. Bena wore a red dress that belonged to Sissy. She'd been so busy all day that she hadn't had time to dwell on Lisa Rayfield at all. Now that they would arrive any minute she had a low-grade fever and a queasy stomach.

Joe blew the horn to warn everyone that they were coming up the drive. "Nobody mess this up," Ellie ordered. "Try to make her like us." When the door opened and Joe led Lisa inside, it was the moment from which all moments would extend. It was the beginning of something. Bena felt it in the pit of her stomach.

Joe held Lisa's hand and said, "Okay, y'all. This is Lisa." Bena could read Joe's eyes. He really loved this girl. It was a weighty moment for Bena—knowing Joe, her oldest son, had fallen in the kind of love that could change his life forever. Joe looked at Bena and raised his eyebrows, as if to say, *See, Mama, I told you. Isn't she the greatest girl in all of Alabama and maybe the world?*

Bena walked over and took Lisa's hands. "Welcome."

Lisa looked at Joe.

"See," Joe said, "I told you."

DINNER WAS CHAOTIC. Bobby needed to nurse in the middle of things. Carmelita cried because Jesus spilled milk all over her starched dress. Every few minutes Leslie would have to get up and take Dolly or Otis or Roy out of the room. "Hope you're not allergic to cats," she said to Lisa. "*Los gatos son muy malos,*" she whispered to Jose. Spanish and English were both going at once, more talkers than listeners. People who didn't know better were biting into tamale corn husks and burning their mouths on hot peppers. Lisa was quiet through dinner. More than once Bena felt Lisa's gaze on her, and she looked up and smiled at the girl. She didn't allow herself to study Lisa too closely—her looks, her manner, how much she ate, the degree of pleasure she seemed to derive from the evening. If someone had asked Bena, *Is Lisa pretty?* she wouldn't have known how to answer. *She has brown hair,* she'd say. *It's curly.* Later—maybe when she finally got into bed—she'd try to put together a whole impression from the tiny glances she collected through dinner. She would invent Lisa from a collage of split-second glimpses.

Lucky was in a great mood, urging seconds on everybody, asking Lisa about herself, how she'd had the great fortune to meet Joe. She answered his questions politely. Joe grinned from ear to ear as if each answer Lisa gave was original—a pearl of wisdom. "Lisa's really smart. Makes you wonder what she's doing with a guy like me, don't it?"

"Doesn't make me wonder," Bena teased.

"Joe is Mama's favorite," Leslie said. "Can you tell?"

AFTER DINNER JUANITA and Sissy insisted on clearing off the table and doing the dishes. Leslie, Ellie, and Anna Kaye—and Eddie by default — volunteered to get Juanita's kids bathed and in bed. It had the effect of the circus coming to town. Small, wet boys running through the house naked with shampoo horns on their heads shrieking in Spanish while the girls chased them with towels. Eddie was warning them—in English—that Santa was making a list and checking it twice.

"We don't concern," they squealed.

Carmelita was cooperative in her girl way. Anna Kaye carried Carmelita out to say good night. She was dressed in angel pajamas and her wet hair was finger-curled. The only thing missing was a halo. Anna Kaye instructed her to give everybody a good-night kiss, and she did it on cue. Kisses—the universal duty of little girls. "Look what a good girl Carmelita is," Leslie said to Jesus and Jose. "Santa Claus is so proud of Carmelita." She looked at Ellie, then Bena like she couldn't believe the things coming out of her mouth. The little boys shouted and ran from her, and their wild laughter filled the house and spilled out into the yard. Bobby slept on Bena's swaying lap through all the confusion.

"He's a pretty baby." Lisa Rayfield looked at Bobby. She and Joe remained at the table with Bena and Lucky, as if by grand design. Sissy poured them coffee and said, "It's not every day Joe brings a girl home. Isn't that right, Mama?" Sissy shot Bena a *Behave yourself* look —the same one that Bena'd given her a million times.

"Would you like to hold the baby?" Bena asked Lisa.

"Won't it wake him up?"

"He sleeps like a rock," Lucky said.

Bena passed Bobby gently to Lisa, who slid her chair back to make room in her lap. "I love babies." She leaned to kiss Bobby's forehead. "I always wonder about Lorraine's baby, you know. They said it was a boy too."

It took Bena a minute to actually hear what Lisa was saying. Her blood heard first—and understood instantly. "Lorraine's baby?"

Lisa looked up from where she was fixed on Bobby's perfect, sleeping face. She went pale. She looked at Joe. He had gone pale too. Lisa turned to Bena. "You didn't know?"

"Know what, exactly?" Bena said.

"I thought you knew." Lisa's eyes darted from Bena to Joe. "Mama said you came to the hospital. So I assumed." She bit her bottom lip and spoke quietly. "They were trying to keep Lorraine alive as long as they could, you know, to see if maybe they could save her baby."

Bena held her coffee cup in both hands and her hands shook so that coffee sloshed out onto the white sheet tablecloth. She fumbled to right the cup in its saucer. For a few seconds it was like putting the round peg in the square hole. Lucky reached over and took the cup out of her hand. "Here," he said.

"I thought you knew," Lisa whispered. She looked at Joe. "I thought she knew."

"Lorraine was pregnant?" Bena's voice was hoarse.

"The baby is buried next to Lorraine," Lisa said. "She never got to name him. It says Rayfield, Baby Boy. That's all. Mama still says a rosary for him—and Lorraine too." She looked at Bena helplessly. "And Bobby, your husband, of course."

FOR THE LONGEST TIME after Bobby died Bena couldn't remember ever having made love with him. Every memory she thought she'd saved became distorted, and Lorraine's face from the newspaper replaced Bena's own face in all her intimate moments with Bobby. It was like losing your internal photo album and having somebody you don't know give you a bunch of photos of her life instead. As if the few photos you managed to hold on to got rained on and destroyed, turning all the people into strangers. Bena's whole sexual past was erased somehow. She'd thought that over time it'd all come back to her, fall into place properly, let her have her sweeter memories back, but so much time had passed that Bena'd stopped trying to remember. It wasn't right. Five children later and Bena had no real memory of Bobby's nakedness, his hands, his whispered words. Lorraine had stolen it from her.

"Are you okay, Mama?" Joe asked. "Lisa didn't mean to upset you. It was an honest mistake."

"All this time I thought you knew," Lisa said.

"Excuse me." Bena stood up abruptly and sent the cup of coffee Lucky had just rescued flying to the floor, where it shattered. Now her new set of dishes would be one cup short. As of tonight she was down to service for fifteen. Already it was happening. The undoing that always happens. She left the room hurriedly. Before she was out of earshot she heard Lisa say, "No, I'll do it. I'll talk to her."

Bena had barely gotten her bedroom door closed when she heard Lisa knock. "Mrs. Eckerd, please. Can I come in?"

"I'd like to be alone, Lisa." Bena spoke through the closed door. She wasn't good at sounding angry.

"I feel terrible," Lisa said.

"Funny." Bena made a sound like a failed laugh. "I feel pretty ter-rible myself."

"Please let me in. I'd like to try to explain to you. About Lorraine."

"I think you've explained enough, Lisa. I'd like you to leave now." Bena turned the lock on the door then.

"Lorraine was a person too," Lisa said. "You didn't know her. She was a good person." Afterward Bena could hear Lisa walk down the hall toward the kitchen.

Thank God, she thought. Bena leaned against the door, telling herself to breathe.

"Mama, open up." It was Joe pounding on the door with his fist. Bena cracked the door just enough to be sure he was alone. He pushed the door open and came into the bedroom. "Mama, you can't get mad at Lisa. It's not her fault."

"Of all the girls in Alabama, this is the one you like?"

"I don't like her, Mama. I love her."

"Fine. But don't expect me to love her, Joe. It's too much to ask."

"That's exactly what I'm asking, Mama."

Bena sat on her bed. She remembered when they got the news that Bobby was dead, how Joe had understood instantly—before the other children—that Lorraine was not just a random woman in his father's car but a significant woman. The way he'd cursed Lorraine with such conviction—and how Bena had insisted he stop it, thinking that such rage in a young boy would only lead to trouble. She had talked him out of his rage, tried to interest him in forgive-ness. Now she wished she hadn't.

"Do you know how hard I've worked to get your daddy buried and put to rest, Joe? Say?" Bena gripped the bedspread in her fist like she was trying to uproot something. "And this girl comes waltzing in and raises him from the dead or something. Now I have the trouble of trying to get him back in the grave again, and I don't want to have to bury him a second time, Joe. You understand me?"

"Don't you think it was hard for Lisa to lose her sister? We're not the only people who got hurt in all this. For God's sake, Mama. Lisa is the accidental messenger. She's not the damn message."

"She is the *damn* message, Joe. Don't you get it? Every time I look at her there's the message, as ugly as ever. Is Lisa going to bring me a new chapter of the Bobby-and-Lorraine saga every holiday? Is that what I have to look forward to?"

"I can't believe you're acting like this." The veins in Joe's neck were like ropes—the way Bobby's used to do when his anger was strangling him.

Bena stood up and walked to where Joe had planted himself like a tree in the middle of the room. She put her hand on his shoulder more to steady herself than anything. "Lisa is not the right girl for you, Joe. I think she knows it—even if you don't." Joe looked at Bena like he'd never seen her before in his life—like she was doing a terrible impersonation of his *real* mother. "This so-called love you feel is just something you're working out for yourself," Bena said, "something about your daddy. Can't you see that?"

"Bullshit." He jerked away from her.

"If you want this girl in your life, then fine. There's nothing I can do about that. But I don't want her in mine, Joe."

"You don't mean that, Mama. You don't even know her."

"I don't want to know her, Joe. That's what I'm saying."

Joe looked at Bena with such revulsion that she stepped back. How dare he be so indignant and judge her this way. How dare he bring this girl home and insist that everybody adjust to her, everybody like her no matter how impossible that was. Joe had so much to learn about life. She wondered if he would learn any of it before she lost him altogether—the same way she'd lost his father. It was painfully obvious that Bobby and Joe were both pitiful fools when it came to love.

. . .

BENA WATCHED FROM her window as Joe and Lisa stormed down the driveway, the truck kicking up a cloud of dust, Joe driving like a crazy man. She was thinking about what might happen to him, wondering if his fury would make him take the curves too fast too in his hurry to get away from her. The Rayfield sisters were evil to Bena, the way they swooped down on men and took them away from their families. There was something wicked about it.

Bena tried not to think about Bobby's son—unborn, unmourned—buried next to Lorraine. His headstone with no name. Bena's children had a brother—dead. They'd never seen him, or touched him, or cried for him when he was laid to rest in a miniature grave and covered with dirt. From womb to womb. And now it was too late. He was just another missed moment in their lives. One of those buried secrets that come to light too late. He didn't even get the ceremony Bobby used to lavish on Leslie's runt kittens or baby birds that fell from their nests too soon.

LUCKY WAS UNDAUNTED. "What's the holidays without the occasional fistfight or brawl," he teased. "When I was growing up we counted on the fuss and uproar as much as the jingle bells and fruitcake." He coaxed Bena out of her room with the promise that Joe would probably call or come back tomorrow to make things right. "A boy hates to hurt his mama over Christmas," he said. "The guilt eats him alive."

Bena tried her best to believe Lucky and to pretend to be jolly. Not that anybody was convinced. "What did you say to Lisa, Mama?" Ellie asked. "You made her cry."

Bena knew the new information about Bobby and Lorraine had made the rounds—that each of her children would take it in and do his or her best to work with it some way. *There was a baby. Daddy's and Lorraine's. He was our brother.* There was no need to prescribe a healthy response for them the way she tried to do when they were younger. They were all too old now to take whatever medicine she might want to dish out. Besides, at this point it was probably clear to them that Bena didn't actually know as much as they once thought she did.

Lucky poured wine for everybody old enough and Kool-Aid for the little ones and ushered them all into the dark living room, where the ball of a tree looked like a miniature world lit up. "To a fine Christmas." Lucky raised his glass. "And to a fine family. I thank you for letting me be a part of this."

Lucky's toast almost killed Bena. She'd messed things up, hadn't she? Lucky's dream of the best Christmas ever? Lorraine Rayfield had nearly ruined their lives. Bena was not about to let Lisa Rayfield ruin their holidays too. She watched Lucky survey the tree and the packages. "I say we let each one of the little guys open one present before bed," he said, picking up a present and shaking it.

Nobody loved the frenzy more than Lucky, watching Jose, Jesus, and Carmelita rip into their gifts, their dark eyes as bright as candles. Jose got a set of race cars on a little track and Jesus got a bow and arrows with rubber tips guaranteed to put an eye out within days. Carmelita got a stuffed white lamb that would bleat when she squeezed it. Their joy revived everybody. They shrieked and ran in circles, raising their toys high in the air for everyone to admire. Then Sissy opened a present for Bobby, a tiny baseball cap with a red A for Alabama. "It's from Joe." Sissy put the cap on Bobby's small, unsuspecting head. It fell down over his eyes and nearly swallowed him. Lucky laughed. But it made Bena sad, thinking how many other things would try to swallow him up the same seemingly harmless way. Eddie moved the cap from over Bobby's eyes and shouted, "Roll Tide!"

Anna Kaye took pictures of all the children. It was perfect, really. Except for the ache Bena felt in the spot usually reserved for Joe. Bena wouldn't think about the mess now. She'd live through the holidays first. Make it a happy time if she could. Then later, when the new year slammed down on her, she'd think about how things had gone wrong and try to figure out what to do.

After the children were put to bed, sleeping with their toys, the others sat around the tree thinking private thoughts and listening to the Christmas music on the stereo, Elvis singing "White Christmas." Bena felt sure Elvis had never had a white Christmas in his whole life. None of them had. Bena wished he wouldn't sing about something he knew nothing about. It bothered her.

Leslie sat beside Bena and looped her arm through Bena's. "I love you, Mama," she said. "No matter what happens, never forget that, okay? Promise me."

"I'll never forget if you won't," Bena said.

"Mama, just because we do things you don't like, you know, make you think we're messing up our lives or whatever—it doesn't mean we don't love you."

"I know that, Les," Bena said.

"Good," Leslie said. "I just want to make sure."

WHEN BENA AND LUCKY got to bed Lucky was as happy as a child. He wrapped himself around Bena and hummed in her ear.

She had to smile whether she wanted to or not. "I don't want to talk about Joe and Lisa—you know—Bobby and Lorraine and all that. Not until after the holidays."

"Fine," he said.

"Joe blames me."

"People fuss," Lucky said. "It'll all blow over."

"More people commit suicide over the holidays than any other time," Bena said. "Did you know that?"

"More people make love too. More babies born in September than any other month."

Bena rolled over to face Lucky in the dark. "So what's your point exactly?"

JOE DIDN'T SHOW UP on Christmas day the way Bena'd hoped. But Sue Cox and Corby did. They came with presents, pound cake, and pecan divinity. Sue Cox came in shouting, "Merry Christmas" and hugging everyone in her path. Corby followed behind her like a shadow. "Hey," he said to each person. "What's up?" His eyes scanned the room.

Sue Cox went crazy over Carmelita in her Christmas dress, carrying her bleating lamb. She picked her up and kissed her startled face. "This is pure sugar right here." Carmelita didn't like strangers, so she started to cry. "Oh, don't cry." Sue Cox bounced the child up and down. "You'll make me cry too. Look here, look what Aunt Sue Cox brought you." She picked up a piece of divinity and gave it to Carmelita. "She can eat nuts, can't she?" she asked Juanita. "Does she have teeth?" She put her finger in Carmelita's mouth and felt for teeth.

"How'd you like to come home with me?" Sue Cox asked Carmelita. "Wouldn't you like to be my little girl?"

Carmelita stuck out her bottom lip and began to scream.

This brought Jesus and Jose running to Carmelita's rescue. "Leave alone our sister, lady," they said. "Don't say to her." Sue Cox handed Carmelita to Jesus and she hushed right up.

"*Como se llama?*" Sue Cox asked the boys. "Jesus?" she shrieked when they told their names. She looked around like they were all witnessing a miracle. "Did you hear that, y'all? We got Baby Jesus right here among us."

"She called you Baby Jesus." Juanita smiled.

"I am no the *bebé,*" Jesus said.

THE CHRISTMAS DAY chaos was the good kind. The cats went crazy over the wrapping paper and ribbons. TV announcers kept everyone apprised of the line of scrimmage. Bena's kids were playing the homemade mix tapes they'd given each other for Christmas. Every kind of music took its turn blaring. At least fifty times Bena said, "Can you turn that down a little? You're about to raise the dead."

Sue Cox had brought a present for Bena. It was an antique hand-held wooden mirror like women used to keep on their vanities. She had attached a note that said, *To a beautiful person. Look in here if you ever doubt it.* Bena was flabbergasted. She'd only gotten Sue Cox a gift certificate at Books-A-Million. She was ashamed.

"This is beautiful." Bena hugged Sue Cox, and everybody in the room stared.

All day Bena kept an eye on Leslie and Corby, making sure they kept their distance. Leslie helped Juanita and Sissy with the children. Corby listened to music with Eddie and Anna Kaye. At one point Corby sat in the den with Lucky, and Bena listened to them try to talk.

"So, Lucky, tell me, man, is it true?

"Is what true?" Lucky was only half listening to Corby.

"Your name. Are you lucky?"

"I never won the sweepstakes, if that's what you mean—or the lottery either. I won a couple of quinellas, though, over in Macon County, betting the dogs. So I guess I've had my share of luck."

"What other kind of luck you had?" Corby scratched at a hangnail on his guitar-strumming hand.

"Well, for a couple of years I ran around inside Jordan Hare with eighty thousand folks screaming my name. You ever had eighty thousand strangers love you half to death?"

"Not yet," Corby said.

"It's something. I had kids lining up for my autograph and women I didn't even know hugging and kissing on me. I was feeling pretty lucky right about then."

"Anything else?"

"The sun's come up most every day of my life. I'm not dead yet. I can still get up and walk around and see and hear, and that's pretty damn lucky. Got the best dog in the world. A job I like that keeps me out of the poorhouse. I got Bena in there with all her swarm of kids. I got my truck paid for. The way I see it, I got everything a man needs. I think maybe my old man—fool that he was—knew what he was doing naming me Lucky." His thumb was on the remote control, switching TV channels while he talked. "How about you?"

"I hadn't had all that much luck yet," Corby said. "But I believe that's about to change. I believe I got me some good luck coming."

"Good," Lucky said. "Just keep your eyes peeled because sometimes luck sneaks up on you and you don't even recognize it. I've seen that happen to people."

"No," Corby said. "I ain't about to let that happen."

ONLY ONCE DID Bena see Leslie and Corby together. They stood outside talking beside the car Sue Cox had given Corby for Christmas. Bena was afraid they might go off together like before. "Les," Bena yelled to her. "Can I see you a minute?"

When Leslie came to the kitchen door Bena said, "Do you think it's a good idea to be out there alone with Corby?

"Mama, we're standing there talking in broad daylight."

"Well, don't," Bena said. "You need to stay away from him."

"Good grief, Mama, I'll stay away from Corby if you'll stay away from Lucky."

"I beg your pardon?"

"Well, they both belong to Sue Cox, don't they, Mama?"

TWICE BENA NOTICED Lucky in deep conversation with Sue Cox. The conversation looked so personal it bothered Bena. "What was that all about?" she asked later.

"Divorce talk," he said.

"On Christmas day?"

"'Tis the season to be jolly."

BEFORE THEY SAT DOWN to dinner Sue Cox cornered Bena in the living room. "Ellie told me you had a fuss with Joe's girlfriend. That Lorraine was pregnant."

"She shouldn't have told you," Bena said.

"Ellie worries about you."

"Well, she doesn't need to."

"Some people just won't die, will they? My daddy was that way. To this day I still hear him saying, *Sue Cox, you are worrying me right into the grave.* He said it so much it came true."

"This is different," Bena said.

"Maybe. But you got to find something to say about the situation that you can live with. If you say it enough, then maybe you can actually start to believe it."

"You saying if I lie to myself enough—I'll be fool enough to believe the lies."

"Yep, that's pretty much what I'm saying." Sue Cox smiled. "I paid a hundred dollars an hour for that advice."

"You got robbed," Bena said.

BENA SAT NEXT to Lucky at dinner, "You told Sue Cox about Bobby, didn't you? Don't deny it. I saw all that whispering."

"I haven't mentioned Bobby's name today. The man is on your mind. Not mine."

"Bobby is not on my mind."

"Well, good," Lucky smiled. "Because I got a surprise for you."

Everybody was seated. Leslie volunteered to sit at the children's table. Juanita fixed their plates and they were already eating. Carmelita was in the new high chair that Bena's kids had pitched in on for Bobby for Christmas.

"Shhhhh," Leslie said to Jose and Jesus. "Listen to *el hombre*."

Lucky stood up and tapped his glass with his fork. "Let me have your attention here," he began. "In all the gift giving going on this morning there was one gift got overlooked. I happen to have it right here with me." He reached into his pocket and pulled out a small box. "Let's see." He pretended to read the tag. "Says, *to Bena.*"

Bena looked around at all the faces, a sea of smiles, all glistening eyes on her.

"So, Miss Bena, here you go. Why don't you open this up and see if it's anything you like?" Lucky handed her the tiny box.

Bena's mind was racing. She fumbled with the paper, scratching it off nervously. Inside the box was a diamond ring. Bena sobbed. She'd never had a diamond.

With everybody watching Lucky got down on one knee and took Bena's hand. He was trembling as much as she was. The room fell totally silent; even the small children seemed to understand the power of the moment. "Bena Eckerd," Lucky said. "I love you. I want to spend the rest of my life with you—if you'll have me."

Everybody clapped and hollered. Even Sue Cox.

"Put on the ring, Mama," Leslie said.

"Lucky" was all Bena could say.

Before Lucky slid the ring on her finger he said, "Did I hear a yes?" Bena nodded yes. He put the ring on her finger and stood up and hugged her long and hard. There was not a dry eye in the house.

"*Qué pasa?*" Jesus kept shouting. "*Mamá, qué pasa?*"

"The man loves the lady," Juanita said.

THAT NIGHT WHEN Lucky and Bena went to bed, things looked new to Bena. With the ring on her finger everything felt different. Better. Maybe she'd been brought up to think like that. Or maybe it was true.

"I was going to pop the question last night," Lucky confessed, "but then the thing with Joe. So I wanted to do it today, but didn't want to get Sue Cox stirred up or anything, you know. It's not every day you propose to your new wife with your old wife watching."

"You're a brave man," Bena said.

"I thought so." Lucky pulled Bena close to him.

Sometimes joy is nothing more than lying quietly beside the person you love most, listening to him breathe. Joy can be so silent, one of those rare, satisfying moments when the right time, the right place, and the right person collide perfectly and you drift off to sleep with everything unspoken absolutely understood.

Sue Cox's scream was blood-curdling. At first Bena thought it was one of her girls, but with the second scream she knew for certain that it was Sue Cox. She was screaming the word *No,* making it an endless, nonstop, forever word. Lucky shot up in bed like he had been stabbed by the word. "What the hell?" he sprang from bed.

Bena grabbed her robe and ran toward the screaming, which seemed to come from outside. It made her think of Mayfred, the way she grieved at funerals. Her cry that led to swooning, that pierced the most doubtful soul. The way Mayfred's pain brought her to her knees in a pose of imitation gratitude. Her body in the thank-you-Jesus stance, her voice in some other hellish place.

"What's wrong?" Juanita ran down the hall in her nightgown. "Who it is?"

Sissy came next, carrying Bobby, waking him up and making him cry. It didn't surprise Bena that the first people up were mothers. Childbirth changes the way you hear things for the rest of your life. Leslie and Ellie didn't know those sounds yet, the way they swim through your blood like a school of startled, fast-finned fish, darting into all the deep places.

Lucky was the first one out the back door to where Sue Cox was screaming like somebody in a fire-ant bed. She waved pieces of paper and stumbled to her knees and back up again. She kept looking behind her like maybe something was sneaking up on her. Lucky grabbed her. She pounded her fists against him and her legs buckled. "They're gone," she wailed.

"Who's gone?" Lucky held Sue Cox off to look at her face.

Bena knew instantly. She looked for Corby's car, the one Sue Cox bought him to drive her around in style. It was gone.

"What's this?" Lucky tried pulling the note out of Sue Cox's fist. "Let me see it, Sue Cox. Let go."

"Corby and Leslie," she said. "They left."

Bena could feel her own knees nearly buckle.

Lucky got the papers away from Sue Cox. One was an opened note to Sue Cox. The other was a sealed envelope with *Mama* written across the front.

"I think this is for you." He handed Bena the note. She put it in the pocket of her bathrobe and tried to help Lucky get Sue Cox to sit down on the picnic-table bench. "Damn them," Sue Cox mumbled. Then she looked at Bena with such fury that Bena let go of her arm and stepped back. "Your daughter is a white-trash slut." Sue Cox spit her words. "She is a fucking little bitch."

Before she could even process the words, Bena raised her hand and slapped Sue Cox as hard as she could. It was instinctive and excellent. As many times as she'd wanted to, she'd never slapped anybody, never known the satisfaction. "Don't you dare talk about Leslie that way."

Sue Cox seemed stunned, unable to speak. She stopped shrieking momentarily, as if Bena had slapped some sense into her. But it wasn't that. There was no sense to be had, none at all. Lucky was staring at Bena like she was a total stranger. Sissy was frozen in place too, rocking Bobby back and forth in her arms.

They didn't understand how it was to always be the sane woman in a world where other women allowed themselves to go crazy, the calm woman when other women acted wild and ridiculous and sometimes stupid, the one who held it in when all around her the others let it go. Slapping Sue Cox had been as automatic as slapping a mosquito, but as out of character as slapping a baby, as slapping little Bobby. Only Sue Cox wasn't a baby. That was part of it, wasn't it? Why wouldn't she grow up and stop carrying on like a spoiled child? Was it because she never had any children to push her all the way into adulthood? Was she was just going to linger forever in her eternal adolescence? Do people only grow up if there is somebody around to make them do it? Did Sue Cox think she was the only woman who'd ever lost a man? Did she think her pain was greater than that of other women? That she deserved her pain less? Did she think the whole world owed her an apology of some kind because something else in her life had gone wrong? Why didn't she stop her sobbing and look around her?

Even when she was a child, Bena had never made a spectacle of herself, never thrown a tantrum to dramatize her personal dilemma —except maybe that time with the marijuana and, in recent years, at church, which was not really a tantrum and not even of her own doing, but more like the mysterious work of God, so altogether different. Bena had never even allowed her own children to carry on the way Sue Cox was, expecting everybody to come running and be audience to her grief. When Bena's kids suffered any kind of heartache, they went to their rooms and closed the door and tried to cope with it quietly, by themselves. Maybe that was wrong, but Sue Cox's antics were just too much to stomach. It made you forget what caused her pain and just want to put a stop to the show. No wonder Bena had slapped her. It felt good, too. If she could get away with it, she'd do it again.

"Bena, you go in the house," Lucky ordered. "I'll take care of this."

Ellie and Eddie had come outside. Jesus, Jose, and Carmelita were behind them in their pajamas, their hair was standing up straight on their heads the way it did every morning.

"You heard me," Lucky said to Bena. "Go in the house."

Bena couldn't convince her legs to move. She turned to leave but it was like she was magnetized to the spot where she stood. "Leslie's a good girl," Bena said. "Leslie's a wonderful girl."

"Come on, Mama." Ellie took her arm. "Let's go inside the house." With Ellie pulling, Bena was able to take steps, to be led away.

"Did you know anything about this?" Bena searched Ellie's face.

"I knew Les was in love with Corby, if that's what you mean," Ellie said. "Anybody with eyes could see that."

"Not Sue Cox," Bena said.

"She could have seen it if she wanted to see it."

"You should have stopped Leslie. She's your sister. Why didn't you stop her?"

Ellie looked amazed. She looked at Bena the way Sissy used to when she was explaining something so basic that it would seem anybody's mother should already know it. "You can't stop love once it gets going, Mama. You know that. Maybe you're not even supposed to try to."

"This is terrible," Bena said. "Look at Sue Cox." They turned to see her sitting bent over with her face in her hands.

"You really smacked her good, Mama."

BENA DRESSED AND put a pot of coffee on. The others drifted into the house, Juanita to feed and dress her children. She mumbled something in Spanish. Sissy came inside to nurse Bobby, who'd begun to scream. Eddie just to get out of all the drama. "Count on Leslie to pick a winner like Corby," he said. "What makes Leslie think he's going to treat her any better than he did Sue Cox?"

"Love is hopeful," Bena said absentmindedly.

She poured a cup of coffee and took it out to Sue Cox, who was calmer now, sitting beside Lucky on the picnic bench, still gripping the note in her hand. Bena sat down and handed Sue Cox the hot coffee. "I shouldn't have slapped you."

Sue Cox took the coffee and tried to sip it. "What am I going to do?"

"You'll stay here." Bena looked at Lucky. "For a while. Until you feel better."

"Lucky thinks maybe he can go after them and bring them back."

"Sue Cox is pretty sure Corby is headed west," Lucky said.

"West is awfully vague," Bena said.

"It would make Sue Cox feel better"—Lucky nodded to Bena— "if I at least tried."

Sue Cox was studying her hands, the note crumpled and sweaty. "Sure," Bena said. "Okay then."

Lucky had managed to get a few days off from the post office. Not an easy thing during the holidays, and now he'd spend them driving Lord knows where looking for a couple of lovesick fools. It wasn't what he had in mind. "I'd like to get my hands on that punk Corby. How you guess he talked Leslie into going with him?"

"I don't think it was hard," Bena said. "I think Leslie believes she loves Corby."

"Then she's as big a fool as Sue Cox," Lucky said.

"She loves love," Bena said. "She always has."

Lucky threw his shaving kit and a change of clothes into the cab of his truck. "Look," he said, "I know Sue Cox can be a pain. But she's got her heart busted. She's fixed on the fact that she's too old anymore for anybody to really love her."

"Except maybe you?"

Lucky ignored the question. "Sue Cox has some ideas where Corby might go. Take me a couple of days to check it out?"

"If you find them," Bena said, "what then?"

"I'm going to try to stepdaddy Leslie into coming home. See if I can talk both of them into going about this the right way."

"What's the right way?"

"Damned if I know." Lucky smiled. "All I got to work with is reason, and reason ain't what it used to be."

Bena watched Lucky's truck until it was out of sight. She went in the house, dug through her bathrobe pockets, and took Leslie's note out. Ever since *the news* about Bobby, Bena liked to be alone when any news came her way. Sometimes she waited to open the mail, bills and all, until she had the house to herself. Sometimes she locked herself in the bathroom to do it—or waited until late at night when she was alone in bed. She tore the note open.

Dear Mama,

By the time you get this note Corby and I will be on our way to our life together. I hope you don't hate me. We never wanted to hurt anybody. It doesn't seem right that one person's happiness is another person's misery, but I guess maybe that's how the world is. Corby feels terrible about Sue Cox, but neither one of us has ever felt the way we feel about each other. It's not right to waste feeling this way since it might never happen again. We think God means us to be together. No matter what happens I will never regret loving Corby. He is not like you think, Mama. He is tender and good. I swear.

Don't anybody worry about us. We will make it just fine. I have my baby-sitting money from the summer. We can get jobs. Corby has so much talent, Mama, I just want to help him make the most of it. I know his future is bright. As time goes by I promise I will be in touch to let you know we are okay and to make sure you are. Please forgive us our trespasses,

I love you, Leslie

P.S. Please tell everybody I'm sorry and I love them all.

Bena put the letter back in its envelope and put it away in her underwear drawer. She imagined there'd be times ahead when she might want to read the note again, just for a minute's peace. Bena wasn't as frantic as she might have been because she imagined Bobby up in heaven, hovering over Leslie, watching every move she made, protecting her. When she said a prayer for Leslie, it was not to God. It was to Bobby.

• • •

JUANITA KEPT SUE COX busy holding Carmelita, which seemed to soothe Sue Cox a little. Juanita even asked Sue Cox to feed Carmelita her supper and bathe her and get her ready for bed. Sue Cox went at it nervously. No matter how miserable she was about Corby leaving, she didn't let on to Carmelita very much— except when she gave the child a gingerbread man she said was named Corby and told Carmelita to bite his head off first thing.

"I should have suspected something," Sue Cox told Juanita, "when Corby didn't want to go out to Lucky's last night. He said he was too tired. We slept on the sofa in our clothes. I never heard him get up."

"You too old to let a man surprise you," Juanita said. "Nothing no man does surprise me some more. I guess it before he do it. Whatever it is."

"I thought Corby was different," Sue Cox said.

"That's what you get then," Juanita said.

SISSY MOVED BOBBY's Portacrib back into Bena's bedroom so that Sue Cox could sleep in the room with Ellie—and the cats. If Sue Cox was bothered by the cats she never said so. That night she rocked Carmelita to sleep and then went to bed herself, still wearing her clothes from the day before. She slept hard, like a woman who'd fallen off a cliff and hit the bottom so hard she was knocked unconscious. She slept in Leslie's bed.

Eddie had gone to Anna Kaye's to watch TV, so Bena left the back door unlocked for him. Sissy'd nursed Bobby and he was fussing his way to sleep. Bena dug through her underwear drawer for Leslie's note and handed it to Sissy. "Read this."

Sissy read it twice before looking at Bena. "Leslie's as bad as me, isn't she?"

IT WAS TWO-FOURTEEN in the morning when Ellie shook Bena awake. Bena knew because she looked at the red-light numbers on her alarm clock. "It's Sue Cox. She's scaring me, Mama. She's crying so bad she sounds like she's about to choke or something. I can't get her to stop."

Bena got up. She could hear Sue Cox's sobs before she looked in the room. It was a frightening sound, half crying, half gasping for air, like somebody drowning.

"You go sleep with Sissy," Bena said. "I'll stay with Sue Cox."

Ellie didn't argue.

Bena stood in the doorway until her eyes adjusted to the darkness. Sue Cox was curled into a ball in the bed. Bena walked over and touched Sue Cox on the arm. "Move over," she whispered.

Sue Cox opened her eyes as if she hadn't heard correctly. She squinted, trying to be sure who it was. "Scoot over," Bena said. "I'm getting in beside you."

Sue Cox moved over, making a space for Bena. She held up the sheet so Bena could put her feet under. Bena positioned herself behind Sue Cox, making spoons, like couples do. She pulled Sue Cox's wet hair out of her face and whispered, "Everything will be okay." She put her arm around Sue Cox and held her gently, the way she did Sissy her first night home, the way she would love to do Leslie now —if only she could. Sue Cox's skin was hot and sweaty. Bena patted her and whispered anything she could think of. "Lucky will be back in a couple of days. Just hold on."

Bena remembered a moment when Sue Cox's breathing went soft and she fell into a peaceful place, her arms going limp, her fists unclenching. It was then that Bena finally closed her eyes.

THE NEXT FEW DAYS Sue Cox baby-sat Carmelita while Juanita went to put in some job applications. She was hoping for a job at the mall but was not going to be picky. Sue Cox played checkers with Jesus and Jose and taught them Go Fish, which wasn't easy. She went to the grocery store with Bena and Sissy, watched football with Eddie and Anna Kaye, washed the dinner dishes, fed the cats.

Nobody was sure what inspired Sue Cox to thoroughly clean Ellie's room—which, technically speaking, was also Leslie's and Sissy's room. She took the beds apart, washed the windows and the woodwork. She organized the bedside table, and the dresser drawers, which was a mistake because in the bottom drawer were all the tapes Corby had sent Leslie. Sue Cox held them like they were made of fragile glass. She took one at random and put it in the tape player on top of the dresser. In seconds Corby's voice boomed out through the house, "Hey, Leslie baby. Man, do I ever miss you. I think about—" Ellie was in the room in a flash. She hit the stop button and ejected the tape. "You can't do that," she said. "Those are private."

Sue Cox looked ghostly standing there listening to the recorded voice of the boy she was longing for. "I'll be damned," she said. "I used to mail these things for Corby. Took them to the post office myself." She picked up one of the tapes from the drawer and threw it across the room.

"I'll get these out of your way." Ellie dumped the drawer's contents into a laundry basket on the floor.

"You think I want to listen to those things?" Sue Cox shouted.

"I know you'll listen to them," Ellie said. "I did. And I don't even like Corby. Who said you could nose around in all the drawers anyway?"

"I'm cleaning up your room."

"I like my room the way it is." Ellie hauled the laundry basket out of her room.

"I don't want to hear the stupid tapes," Sue Cox yelled. "I wouldn't listen to them if you paid me!"

After that Sue Cox was like a streak of lightning shooting around Ellie's bedroom. She mopped and waxed the hardwood floor, took the braided rug out to the line to beat it with an old baseball bat, then gave up and put it in the trash pile. She even took it upon herself to clean out the closet, which, to Bena's knowledge, had never been cleaned out since they'd moved into the house almost twenty years ago.

"Mama, make her stop," Ellie pleaded. "She's going through everything, messing everything up."

Bena understood so well Sue Cox's need to clean up a mess and organize the chaos, and she appreciated both the need and the results so much, that she couldn't bring herself to interfere. In time Ellie might understand too.

Several times Sue Cox paused to smoke a cigarette and drink some ice tea or play with Carmelita. She tried to get Ellie to come look at how she'd rearranged her room. Without asking, she'd taken the third bed out of the room and put it out in the carport until Eddie could haul it to the Goodwill box at Wal-Mart. But Ellie refused.

Sue Cox got Sissy and Juanita to take her to the mall. All the children went too. They came back with the most stuff anybody ever saw. New bedskirts and comforters and matchstick blinds for the windows. New pillows and sheets and lamps and straw rugs. By this time Sissy and Juanita were in the spirit of the thing, and as soon as they got the children fed and put to bed they helped Sue Cox revamp Ellie's room. Out with the hodgepodge of bright colors and in with the neutrals and natural fabrics. Even Bena got a little excited seeing the room transformed. They all conspired to keep Ellie out until they were finished. Twice they had to make a run out to the mall for one more thing, a throw pillow, another lamp.

It was almost midnight when they finished. They'd hauled a truck-load of stuff out to the carport. Gone were the stuffed animals with their ears ripped off, gone were the bulletin boards with the wilted corsages and deflated balloons and memorabilia whatnot. Gone were the faded spreads and mismatched sheets and lint-covered throw rugs. Gone was the desk nobody ever used and the chest of drawers full of discarded clothes too good to throw away. Gone was the picture of Bobby and the old Rolling Stones poster and all the rest of the posters. Gone were the flyers from when Sissy ran for homecoming queen and Leslie ran for Student Council. Gone was the cat litter box and the cardboard box the cats called home.

When Sue Cox finally gave the okay and Sissy led a very reluctant Ellie down the hall to the bedroom it was Christmas day all over again. There were matching twin beds with beige paisley comforters and checked sheets. The hardwood floors gleamed, the matchstick blinds were partly opened, the windows shone. The furniture was polished, the lamps gave off nice light. There was a new wicker chair and an old trunk Sue Cox had moved from the hall. It looked like a room in a house out at Baxter Country Club. Maybe better.

Ellie was momentarily stunned when she saw it. It looked like a room where a very substantial girl would live. It looked designed for the woman she'd always wanted to be, had hoped she was on her way to becoming. It was like Sue Cox knew that or something. Ellie went over and sat on the bed. "I love it."

The others swooped down on her in their enthusiasm and said, *Look at this, look at this, look at this.* Sue Cox stood over in the corner smiling and smoking a cigarette. Ellie walked over to her. "I'm sorry I yelled at you."

"No problem."

"I guess you're a better roommate than I thought."

"You can change anything you don't like."

"I like everything. Except . . . I might put Daddy's picture back."

"Great," Sue Cox said.

"And also, there's no smoking in here."

"Right." Sue Cox snuffed out her cigarette.

LUCKY CAME HOME exhausted and clueless. He'd checked out all the leads Sue Cox had given him, but said he guessed Corby had sense enough not to do the obvious. "Waste of time," he said of the search.

Bena made him a sandwich and he took a hot shower, and by then Sue Cox and Ellie and Sissy were home from apartment hunting with Juanita. She was looking for a starter apartment where Jose and Jesus could walk to a good school. Every day she studied the *Baxter County Bulletin* in search of a decent job and a decent place to live. Sissy was looking for a job too, but not with the same determination.

It was obvious they'd seen Lucky's truck when they pulled up. Sue Cox was the first one in the door, "Well?'" she asked, breathless. "What happened?"

"Nothing happened." Lucky shook his head. "I looked where you told me to look. No sign of them, Sue Cox. So nothing to do now but wait to hear something."

Sue Cox dropped into a chair in the den like she'd been shot. "If only I could find Corby I know I could talk sense to him."

"Meanwhile," Lucky said, "you need to get on with things, Sue Cox. No need to pine away after him. Life is too short."

"He'll be back," Sue Cox said. "As soon as he sees that Leslie is just, you know, a young girl, he'll start to miss me."

"Don't count on it," Bena said.

"Mama!" Ellie glared at Bena.

"I just mean that Leslie is not that easy to dismiss. Did it ever occur to anybody that Corby might actually love Leslie?"

"This is a no-win conversation, right here," Lucky said. "We don't need to have this conversation."

BENA HAD NO WAY of knowing that night after night Sue Cox and Ellie were sitting up late talking in Ellie's revamped bedroom. She had no way of knowing what sort of ideas Sue Cox was planting in Ellie's mind. The first clue should have been when Ellie came home with a new haircut that made her look sort of like Sue Cox. Her hair was dark like Sue Cox's, and she'd always worn it long or in a clasp on top of her head. Suddenly she comes in from the mall with shoulder-length, blunt-cut, shiny hair—knowing she looks great. "It was Sue Cox's idea," she said. "She says a good haircut makes all the difference in the world."

Ellie could hardly keep her eyes off herself, swinging her hair, looking in the mirror or at her reflection in the windowpanes.

"You look like a million bucks, El," Lucky said.

"I look like Sue Cox, don't I? People at the salon thought she was my mother."

"I'm flattered," Sue Cox said.

"I never had a good haircut before. Sissy and Leslie always cut my hair for me." She turned to Bena. "Mama, you ought to go over there and get your hair cut sometime. It's expensive, but you only live once. Right?"

Bena stood in a stupor, watching Ellie. Since when had Ellie become disgruntled with the haircuts her sisters gave her? Since when had she noticed that Bena was in such bad need of a good haircut? Bena could hear Sue Cox's words coming out of Ellie's mouth. It unnerved her. "I think you're beautiful, haircut or no haircut."

"See," Ellie said to Sue Cox, "I told you Mama would say that."

THE SECOND CLUE came days later when Sue Cox took Ellie to the after-Christmas sales at the mall and bought her expensive clothes that Bena could never afford and that Ellie didn't really need. Sissy and Juanita took interest too, pulling stuff out of the shopping bags and going crazy over it, nudging each other to look at the prices.

"You have the fairy mother," Juanita said. "She waving her magic stick at you."

After supper Ellie tried on her outfits and modeled them for everybody. Her feet didn't touch the floor as she glided around the room. She tossed her head so her hair would fly just right. She spun like she was on a runway. Bena barely recognized her. "I told Sue Cox this was too much, Mama," Ellie said. "I said I didn't need all this."

"It was on sale," Sue Cox said.

"So much black," Juanita said. "You look like the funeral."

"It's what they wear in Atlanta," Ellie said. "They don't dress like hicks there."

"Hicks?" Sissy said. "Since when are we hicks?"

"You know what I mean," Ellie said. "I can mix and match everything."

"I see a few things I'm borrowing," Sissy said, "soon as I get my waist back."

"I don't know where you're going to wear all that in Baxter County," Bena said. "Kids here wear jeans and T-shirts to school."

"There is more to life than Baxter County, Mama." Ellie put her arm around Sue Cox, each of them wearing black wool slacks and matching black sweater sets.

Sissy looked at Bena. "Are you going to let her keep all this, Mama?"

"Of course she is," Sue Cox said. "It's a gift. My way of saying thank you."

"Shoot," Sissy said. "Remind me to do you a favor sometime."

ON NEW YEAR'S EVE Bena and Lucky stayed home and baby-sat the kids. Sue Cox talked Sissy and Juanita into getting dressed up and going out for the night—Ellie too. They were having a dinner dance at the Holiday Inn out by the interstate. Sue Cox saw it advertised in the paper and she was picking up the cover charge for everybody.

Bena had been thinking that she and Lucky might go out someplace—maybe back to Larry's to dance. She'd have settled for a quiet night at Lucky's house, just the two of them and Tom and the whippoorwills. Maybe a bottle of wine. But before she knew it, everybody else's plans depended on her not having any. "Sure," she told Sissy and Juanita, "go ahead. Lucky and I will keep the kids."

She rocked Bobby in her arms and watched the rest of them get ready for the night. The makeup, the hairspray, the giddiness that accompanies temporary escape from the ordinariness of day-to-day life. It made Bena yearn a little. It was the first time since Sissy came home that she'd done anything with her hair or put on any makeup. She was wearing a pair of Bena's black pants and a sweater she borrowed from Sue Cox. Even Lucky paused when he saw the transformation. "Damn," he said. "What we got here? Miss America?"

"I feel funny going out," Sissy said, "since—you know—I'm still married."

"So what?" Sue Cox said. "A little dancing never hurt anybody."

"Forget Barrett," Juanita advised. "He forget you."

Sue Cox walked out with her arm around Ellie, who looked twenty-one instead of seventeen. She wasn't old enough to get into the Holiday Inn, but Sue Cox said, "Just leave that to me." Bena hadn't put her foot down either. The four climbed into Bena's car and took off in a cloud of perfume and high spirits. "Don't wait up," Sue Cox yelled.

Bena half wished she were going too. A night out with the girls. She couldn't remember one—ever. Instead she and Lucky would get the little ones bathed, read to, and tucked into bed, and then they'd collapse in front of the TV and play Go Fish with Jesus and Jose until they fell asleep on the floor and needed to be carried to bed. Then maybe the two of them would watch the New Year arrive amid a sea of loud New Yorkers operating in a totally foreign time zone.

BENA AND LUCKY were asleep on the sofa when the others came home, blowing their pink snake horns and wearing little pointy hats. They kicked off their shoes and attacked the last of the pound cake.

"Sissy is back in town," Ellie said. "Word will travel fast now."

"Sissy got too much friends," Juanita said. "All the mens, they like Sissy."

"Local girl makes bad." Sissy smiled.

"Nobody even asked me for an ID, Mama," Ellie bragged.

"Alabama mens," Juanita said, "they more polite than in Miami."

"You'll never guess who I saw, Lucky." Sue Cox was breaking bits of cake and tossing them in her mouth. "Edward Lincoln. Remember him?"

"Sure," Lucky said.

"He loves me," Sue Cox said matter-of-factly. "He always has."

Two DAYS LATER, Ellie came out to the carport, where Bena and Lucky were drinking their after-supper coffee. "Mama," Ellie said. "The coolest thing is happening. Sue Cox wants me to come to Atlanta with her. To live with her."

Bena was struck dumb.

"I'll have my own room and they have great schools there. Sue Cox will pay my tuition. I can work at Bucky's on weekends if I want to. It's my chance, Mama."

"What chance?" Bena asked.

"You know, Mama. To get away from here. I've lived in Baxter County all my life. It's totally boring. Now I have a chance to live in the city with Sue Cox. I'll just keep her company, you know? I can drive her around some. And Atlanta is totally cool. Everybody at school swears that as soon as they graduate they're moving to Atlanta—so I'll just be one step ahead of everybody."

"We need you here, Ellie," Bena said.

"Why, Mama?" Ellie looked determined. "Sissy's back. You still got Eddie. Now you got Mr. McKale too. Y'all are getting married. Why do you need me?"

"Because," Bena said. "I do. It's not time for you to go yet."

"Is it because Sue Cox used to drink? She doesn't drink anymore.

She swears if she ever takes a drink I should pick up the phone and call you to come get me. And I will. I promise. But with Corby gone, Sue Cox will be lonely. She needs me."

"This is crazy, Ellie honey," Bena said. "Sue Cox can't invite you to move to Atlanta without talking to me first."

"I wouldn't let her, Mama. I knew you'd be like this."

"Like what?"

"Selfish. All you think about is yourself and what you want. Well, what about me? I've got this chance for better things, and I'm going to take it too. You can't stop me. I can run away the same as Leslie if you make me, Mama." Ellie turned then and ran back to the house.

Before Bena could catch up with her Sue Cox came outside to run interference. "I was hoping you might like the idea," she said.

"Why would I like it? Do you think since Leslie took Corby from you then you'll just take Ellie from me? Is this your version on an eye for an eye?"

"You know what, Bena, maybe Ellie needs me just as much as I need her."

"Because you bribe her with clothes, you think that means she needs you?"

"When was the last time you paid Ellie any special attention? I'm not judging you, I know you got five kids needing your time. But I can give Ellie attention and opportunities that you can't, Bena. Don't spoil that for her."

Lucky walked up then. Maybe he thought a fistfight might break out. "Talk to her, Lucky," Sue Cox said. "She'll listen to you."

"Bena's going to do what's best for her kids," Lucky said. "She always does."

"I'm not trying to steal Ellie from you. I'm just sort of borrowing her," Sue Cox said. "You'll still be her mother."

"How generous of you," Bena said.

"We'll need to leave soon so we can get Ellie enrolled in school."

"No," Bena said. "Absolutely not."

"Think about it," Sue Cox said.

SUE COX RENTED A CAR and she and Ellie left for Atlanta on Bena's first day back at work. Bena had agreed Ellie could go—on a trial basis—but didn't want to watch her leave. Sissy drove out to the school to tell her they were gone. It reminded Bena of when she had her wisdom teeth pulled and the dentist flooded her head with novocaine so she wouldn't feel the pain. He'd convinced her it was the right thing to do, then proceeded to dig her teeth out of her gums with a sharp instrument. She stayed in bed two days afterward.

"I know you're upset, Mama," Sissy said. "Ellie said to tell you she loves you. And Sue Cox sent you this." She handed Bena a piece of paper. "It's the address and phone number. The name of Ellie's school and all."

Bena didn't think she could stand another note—of any kind. She took it and folded it into a small square.

Mayfred came out of her classroom to see what was going on. "What y'all whispering about out here in the hall?"

"Ellie is moving to Atlanta to live with Sue Cox," Sissy said.

"Lord, is the child pregnant?"

"No," Bena and Sissy snapped.

"Thank God for that," Mayfred said. "That's a blessing."

"I think you did the right thing, Mama," Sissy said, "letting Ellie go."

JUANITA GOT A JOB working for Ben Choi at the Golden Dragon. She'd make tacos and burritos and also run the cash register. On the side, she put out flyers to cater Mexican food. Somebody had already booked her for a home wedding.

Juanita had also put a deposit on an apartment at Dogwood

Village. The school bus picked up right out front and would take Jesus and Jose to school. Carmelita would go to work with Juanita at the Golden Dragon every day. Ben Choi didn't mind. He set up a playpen in the kitchen. He told Juanita his own parents had raised him in the kitchen of their restaurant back in China. Juanita would make minimum wage plus tips. Already she was dreaming of opening her own restaurant someday and buying a little brick house with a fenced yard and an automatic dishwasher.

THE HOLIDAYS HAD come and gone. Sissy heard nothing from Barrett. "He can't call me, Mama," she said. "He doesn't know where I am."

"He knows where I am," Bena insisted. "He knows I know where you are."

"He knows you hate him too, Mama. He's not going to call you since you hate him so much."

Sissy rarely cried. Even growing up she wasn't much of a crier. She'd never seemed willing to admit to herself that any problem was *really* a problem. She pretended so convincingly that when she was little Bobby used to say, "That one ought to be an actress. She loves make-believe." He had meant it as an odd sort of compliment, but he hadn't lived to see it become a curse.

With Juanita and her kids in their new apartment, Sissy couldn't depend on Juanita to help her look after Bobby. Now she was Bobby's mother every single minute, day and night. The house was so quiet too, without Juanita's kids tearing through it. Sissy had time to be lonely. Also, seeing Juanita move into a life of her own made Sissy want to do the same thing. But it was harder for Sissy. She wasn't as confident as Juanita. And Bobby was barely two months old.

Just as Ellie had predicted, after New Year's Eve at the Holiday Inn word had traveled fast that Sissy Eckerd was home with a baby but no real husband—only Barrett Carter, who was off in Europe somewhere doing who knew what. Her friends from high school had begun to call and come by to see her. Sissy turned down most of their invitations. She didn't like to go anywhere she couldn't take Bobby. The girls she used to share an apartment with invited her to move back in with them, but they were single and social, two things Sissy really wasn't anymore.

Bena watched Sissy spend her evenings studying the classified ads in search of that nonexistent Baxter County job that required few skills but paid a livable salary. She'd nearly decided to take a part-time job helping out at the Fellowship Baptist day-care center. She would make next to no money, but at least she could take Bobby with her, and she' be getting out of the house every day.

Eddie was the one who told Sissy they were hiring a hostess out at the country club. They wanted somebody to work lunch and dinner six days a week. All she had to do was dress nice, smile, and show people to their tables. Almost anybody could do it. Sissy took Bobby with her when she went to put in her application. They hired her on the spot. For one thing, she was good-looking. For another, she was Bobby Eckerd's oldest girl.

For the first month she continued to live at home with Bena. After school Bena picked up Bobby at Fellowship day care and kept him until Sissy came home. Bena held Bobby, talked to him, fed him, bathed him, got him into his warm pajamas, and rocked him to sleep. By the time Sissy got home from the country club Bobby was tucked into bed and Bena was too. As tired as she was, Bena thought this was a good plan. A day of sixth graders, an evening with an infant — she was exhausted. Lucky managed to make do with ragged scraps of her time. Some nights he rocked Bobby to sleep singing "Proud Mary" or "House of the Rising Sun," so Bena could take a hot bath and grade papers.

When Sissy took Lucky and Bena to see the trailer she was planning to rent they were horrified. It was tiny. The sort of thing retired people hauled behind their car up until the wheels fell off. It was old, too, the chrome ripped off, leaving raw nail heads poking out. There was nothing good about it that Bena could see—except that it was not too far from Dogwood Village and if she wanted to Sissy could walk over to see Juanita. There were six tragic trailers in a circle. Bena thought it looked like a gypsy camp. The manager said most of the people there paid their rent with their welfare checks. As hard as Bena tried to convince Sissy not to move into the rusted tin can of a place, she was wasting her breath.

Lucky helped Sissy pack some stuff in his truck and move it over to the trailer park. She was excited about it too, as if she were moving into perfectly decent accommodations. One of the kitchen workers from the country club would pick her up each day, stop so she could drop Bobby at day care, and then take Sissy to work. Juanita would keep Bobby in the evenings. "A perfect plan until I get a car," Sissy said.

It was a nightmare for Bena to watch Sissy spiral downward, taking Bobby with her. After meeting some of the other residents of the trailer park Lucky was so unnerved he gave Sissy a handgun for protection. Sissy acted like she appreciated it, but Bena was furious.

"I'm just doing what Bobby would do if he was here," Lucky said.

"If Bobby is going to be your model," Bena snarled, "then let me know now so I can call this whole thing off before it goes any further."

LESLIE CALLED ONCE, left a brief message on the phone. *Hey, Mama, we're doing fine. Hope everybody there is okay. We miss y'all. Corby has picked up some club jobs. So things are looking pretty good. I love you a lot, Mama.* And the message was over.

THE HIGH SCHOOL track coach had spotted Eddie running up and down the highway and mistaken it for a love of running instead of the simple desire to get somewhere fast. He talked him into staying after school to run cross-country. Bena was surprised that Eddie agreed. Up until then Anna Kaye was Eddie's primary extracurricular activity. "Coach thinks I got good endurance," Eddie explained.

III

ONE THING

AND THEN THE OTHER

8

They settled on a Friday night for the wedding. That way they could take a two-day honeymoon and go someplace nice. Lucky had rented them a cabin over at Callaway Gardens. It would be perfect.

Bena called Joe immediately to try to convince him to come to the wedding. She left a message on his machine because he never answered his phone anymore. *I'd love you to be here,* she said. *It'd mean a lot to me.*

In return Joe left a message on Bena's machine while she was at school. *Mama, how can you ask me to be happy for you when you refuse to be happy for me? I won't come without Lisa. Would it kill you to invite her too?*

Bena erased the message.

Her luck wasn't any better with Ellie. *Mama, you know I want to come, but I can't go off and leave Sue Cox. Do you care if she comes too? She's happy for y'all, I swear she is.*

So in the end it was a small affair in the living room at Bena's house. The preacher from Fellowship Baptist agreed to perform the ceremony. Bena was pretty sure she wouldn't cry since she wouldn't be in an actual church. Mayfred and Jerry Lee came. And Eddie and Anna Kaye. And Sissy and little Bobby. They lit candles all around the room and Sissy brought home some flower arrangements from the country club, which she planned to take back afterward. Mayfred made a carrot cake. Eddie was Lucky's best man. Sissy was Bena's matron of honor. Mayfred held Bobby. Anna Kaye read a little Bible verse about a man cleaving unto his wife.

Bena wore a cream-colored pantsuit and boots. The week before, she'd gone to get herself a good haircut like Ellie suggested. At the salon they talked her into coloring her hair too. It was redder than it'd ever been and shorter too. They sold her some gel in case she wanted to stiffen her hair up for special occasions. So far she hadn't used it. She wasn't sure stiff hair would be a good thing. Lucky said he loved Bena's new look, but she didn't know if he meant it. She put on makeup and fixed her eyes and thought she looked sort of pretty, all things considered.

The ceremony was short. They'd forgotten to ask the preacher to take out that part about a woman obeying her husband, so they just ignored it and kept on going.

Mayfred said the part she didn't like was that about *better or worse.* "Who you know that gets married for the worse?" she said. "My mama told me no need to marry nobody if he can't make your life better. You can make it worse by yourself."

When the preacher said, *You may kiss the bride,* Lucky did. Anna Kaye made everybody pose for pictures. Afterward the preacher left, but the rest of them drank champagne and ate carrot cake and toasted Bena and Lucky with good wishes. At one point Lucky raised his glass. "I'm as happy right now as I ever been. I thank God for Bena."

"Amen," Mayfred said. And they all drank to that.

• • •

LUCKY WOULDN'T LET Bena take any papers to grade at Callaway Gardens. He said all she needed was a pair of jeans, some good walking shoes, and a jacket. He packed up a cooler with food and loaded it into the car. It was weird to Bena, like they were a couple of teenagers sneaking off for a weekend. Not like they were actually married in the eyes of God.

Here she was a woman with five practically grown kids and a new husband promising to love her to the end of time. It was a lot to comprehend.

It was late when they arrived at their cabin. They slept through most of the first day. The second day Lucky woke up with a terrible case of the flu. He threw up so much Bena begged him to go to the emergency room. But he wouldn't. She drove back to Baxter County with Lucky sprawled out in the backseat throwing up into a plastic garbage bag. "This ain't no kinda honeymoon, is it Bena? I'm gonna make up to you for this. I swear." He was drenched in a film of cold sweat and his eyes were bloodshot. Bena kept looking in the rearview mirror as she drove. Lucky was folded up like a bent lawn chair.

BENA AND LUCKY took sick leave the following week. Lucky was so sick he could hardly lift his head for the ice chips Bena tried to spoon into his mouth. He couldn't keep down more than a sip of soup or ginger ale. He got the shakes so bad sometimes that Bena had to wrap him in a warm blanket and lie on top of him to get him quieted down. Other times he was so hot she kept a cold cloth on his head while he went in and out of sleep. He kept his shaving kit in the bed and fumbled for pill bottles he kept in there, choking down pills with water he sipped through a straw.

"What is all that?" Bena asked.

"For my stomach," he said.

Bena pushed away the thought that marrying her had triggered something in Lucky that could make him this sick. Mayfred had told her once that illness was just fear acting itself out in the body. What was Lucky afraid of? It couldn't be her, could it?

BY THE END of the week he seemed a little better. He ate some Jell-O and kept it down and kept asking for more Sprite. By then Bena was so worn-out she thought she would probably come down with the flu too, but she didn't. All she needed was a couple nights' sleep and she was almost glad to get back to school.

Lucky's first day back at work he was pale as a ghost but swore he was feeling fine. The other postal workers teased him like crazy— faking a week of sick leave to prolong his honeymoon. Clearly he hadn't left the dark of his bedroom all week, which must be what gave him that pasty look. They would slap him on the back and laugh, "Our boy, Lucky, damn if he's not a lover. Ain't that right, Luck?"

"Didn't get out of bed all week long," he said. "Too sick." They didn't believe him for one minute, envied him like they had back when he was a star running back.

It wasn't until Lucky was back to his old self that Bena realized how scared she had been seeing him so sick. Every terrible thought had gone through her head. "Don't you ever scare me like that again," she said. "I was all but ready to pick out the music for your funeral service."

"Sorry," he laughed. "You know men are sissies. That's why women are the ones that give birth, ain't that right?"

"All I know is I got long-range plans for you—for us, son."

"Me too, lady," Lucky said.

Just to be on the safe side, Bena bought Lucky some once-a-day vitamins for middle-aged men and set out one red tablet each morning by his coffee cup.

THEY'D DECIDED THEY'D live at Bena's house—until Eddie finished high school. Out where Lucky lived was too far for

Eddie to catch a ride to school or to run either. Eddie didn't like to be dropped off by his mother every day, because besides being uncool it put him at school almost an hour early. So Lucky and Tom had moved into Bena's temporarily. Once Eddie was gone off to college Bena and Lucky would move back to his place permanently and—finally—put in a pond on the place. Maybe add a couple of extra bedrooms too. Lucky liked to fiddle around with a pencil and paper, drawing up a floor plan.

Bena kept thinking about a job description that had been in her box at school, advertising for a human-resources clerk at the school-board office. It was a nine-to-three job that paid better than teaching and let you sit all by yourself in a little air-conditioned room with a calculator and a computer and a bunch of government forms. You could drink coffee at your desk. Go to the bathroom when you needed to without having it scheduled into your lesson plans. Eat lunch alone, or with adults of your choice, with no fear that a fistful of flying peas would hit you in the face. There was nothing or nobody to aggravate you to death or break your heart to pieces. Bena was thinking maybe she would apply for that job. It couldn't hurt anything just to fill out the application and see what happened.

FOR A COUPLE of months things went along fine. Tom learned more or less to get along with Otis, Dolly, and Roy, so he was let in the house regularly now. At night he slept in Bena's and Lucky's room on the foot of their bed. He took up so much room they could never stretch their legs all the way out. So they both slept sort of balled up and tangled together—which was nice.

Bena and Lucky never missed one of Eddie's track meets if they could help it. It was something to see Eddie out there stretching and deep breathing before he set out to run three thousand meters. It wasn't the ideal spectator sport, but Bena would stop at Hardee's on her way and get coffee and some French fries, and Lucky would meet her there when he got off from work. It was exciting to

Bena—she screamed and stomped for him and waved her arms the same as she'd done when Joe played baseball. Anna Kaye was just as bad. Eddie's coach told Bena that if he worked hard Eddie had a chance to run his way to college—maybe even get a free ride there.

On weekends sometimes Eddie and Anna Kaye played cards with Bena and Lucky. Bena made chili dogs or cheese-smothered tortilla chips with jalapeño peppers. Sometimes they went out to the mall and roamed around, maybe ate some Chick-fil-A. Once they all went to a movie. Sitting in the dark holding Lucky's hand, Bena hadn't felt any older than Eddie and Anna Kaye.

Sissy had only asked Bena and Lucky to baby-sit twice. There was a divorced golf pro at the country club who'd asked Sissy out to dinner a couple of times. He'd gone to college at the University of Georgia on a golf scholarship and now he thought golf was sort of like a religion. He was very devout that way. Bena thought that once Cole saw the trailer Sissy and Bobby were living in it would make him think twice about the sort of girl Sissy was. But so far, that hadn't seemed to happen. Sissy liked him too. "Cole is nice, Mama," Sissy told her. "He doesn't mind if we take Bobby everywhere with us."

Once, Bena and Lucky even baby-sat Juanita's kids overnight while she went to a Wedding Fair in Montgomery, where she passed out her catering menus and set up a tasting table to see if she could get any customers interested in signing up for a Mexican-style wedding reception. Juanita was born to be a businesswoman. She even had cards printed up—*Juanita's Fiestas*—and business was trickling in.

On Sundays Bena and Lucky liked to stay in bed, drink coffee, and read the *Atlanta Journal* and the *Montgomery Advertiser*. Now and then Bena made pancakes. Lucky had trouble keeping his weight up. His appetite wasn't very good, and sometimes he'd lose five pounds in a couple of days—and on him, it showed. So Bena tried to fatten him up on the occasions when he seemed hungry and willing to eat. He'd been known to eat ten pancakes at a sitting and half a bottle of syrup. Other times Bena couldn't even get him to nibble toast.

It's funny, all the little things you never really notice until you marry a person. Even with all the time they'd spent together before the wedding, she didn't know Lucky then the way she did now. It must be something about becoming united in the eyes of God that makes all your little quirks show up and blur together all at the same time.

Sometimes they didn't get dressed all day on Sundays. Lucky lay in bed and watched a game on TV with Tom sprawled beside him, while Bena graded papers and wrote out her lesson plans. They were happy in a way that made them fall asleep easily and often. And wake up and reach for each other instinctively and gratefully. On Monday mornings parting really was sweet sorrow.

It was on April Fool's night that Lucky came home and told Bena he was leaving the following day for California. She thought it was a joke.

"It's my sister DeeDee," Lucky said. "She called me at work. She's got to check herself into the hospital for some treatments. Female trouble, I think. She needs me to come out there. I'm all she's got."

The look on Lucky's face made it clear he was not kidding around. He looked practically stricken. "How long?" Bena asked.

"Long as it takes," he said. "It's hard to say."

When Lucky got worried about something he got distant, went into the back room of his mind, where he stored stuff he hoped he would never need. He packed that night like a man in a trance, a man going into the unknown and imagining the worst. Bena did her best to hold on to him all night, but he tossed and turned and barely slept a wink. By morning he seemed exhausted.

At breakfast Lucky gave Eddie the keys to his truck and a list of instructions, the most important of which was to look out for Tom and be good to his mama. Bena couldn't tell if Eddie was really listening. He seemed so happy to have a set of keys in his hands—a truck of his own—for a while. "Sure, Lucky," he said. "Sure thing."

Bena took off from school to drive Lucky to Atlanta to the airport. He seemed a million miles away already. "What are you thinking about?" she asked him.

"I don't know," he said. "How life has got a mind of its own, I guess."

"How long since you've seen DeeDee?"

"Too long. Way too long."

"You love her a lot, don't you?" Bena said.

"She was the next youngest to me. We was a lot alike in some ways. Only she always had more guts than me."

"She must be pretty great." Bena smiled.

"DeeDee's had about all the bad one woman can stand. I swear to God I wish none of this was happening."

"Doctors know a lot more than they used to," Bena said. "I'll say a prayer for her every day. We all will."

Lucky looked at Bena. His eyes were sort of bloodshot and tired, but he smiled and ran his knuckles over the side of her face. "You do that."

Lucky refused to let Bena park and come inside the airport with him. He insisted she let him out at the curb. He leaned over and kissed her, buried his face in her neck a minute, then hurriedly got out of the car, grabbed his suitcase out of the backseat, slammed the door shut, and walked off without even looking back. Maybe Bena was crazy, but it looked to her like he might be crying.

"Don't let DeeDee die," Bena whispered. "Please, God."

Bena was thirty minutes down the interstate before she realized that Lucky had forgotten to give her DeeDee's phone number and address like he promised. She didn't even have the name of the hospital. Lucky was too worried to remember, but how could she forget a thing like that? Lucky promised to call her when he got to California—and he was a man who kept his promises. She would probably have the information she needed by morning.

. . .

WHEN BENA PULLED up in her yard that afternoon there sat Mayfred on the picnic table filing her fingernails. "Hey girl," she said. "They told me you called in about family illness, so I got worried. Lucky sick again?"

"His sister DeeDee," Bena said.

"I remember her," Mayfred said. "When we were sixteen we worked at the Hardee's together. Between us we ate enough of them biscuits to just about put the place out of business. She was just dreaming her life away back then."

"She moved to California," Bena said. "She's got female trouble and called Lucky to come out there and see about her."

"She got any kids?"

"I don't think so."

"Oh, you hate that," Mayfred said. "Somebody to have female trouble before they have a chance to have any kids."

"I don't know." Bena sat down on the picnic table beside Mayfred and looked at her own ragged fingernails. It hardly ever crossed her mind to look after her nails. Every couple of weeks she went at them with a pair of clippers, but that was it. "Sometimes I wonder if it isn't better to imagine what kind of wonderful mother you would've been—rather than to have to face what kind of mother you actually are."

"Hush up. You a real good mother."

"That's why I got one son who won't speak to me. A daughter off who knows where who—if I'm lucky—leaves me a phone message once a month to let me know she's still alive. A daughter who'd rather have Sue Cox Miller for her mother. And a daughter and grandbaby camped out in a trailer park with a bunch of what seem like prison escapees."

Mayfred laughed. "That's what they don't tell you, now."

"What?" Bena said.

"They don't tell you isn't no telling who you gon' get to be your child. Sometimes you might get an uncommonly hard child—or you might even get downright impossible. I just say to myself, *God means you to have whatever child you got.* You just got to work with it."

"I guess," Bena said.

"LaVonte, he's my trial. If all I did was look at the way that boy acts to see what kind of mama I am, well, then I'd just have to give up on it. But I look at it like this: he came stubborn. I'm not the one that made him that way. Some of the mess he gets hisself into, it has more to do with who he is than who I am. A mama has got to think like that because if she don't she'll run herself crazy."

"Stay for supper," Bena said. "Can you? We'll go over to Ben Choi's and get some of Juanita's tacos."

"I guess so." Mayfred blew on her fingernails. "Let me call Jerry Lee to stay with the kids. You know what I like most about Jerry Lee? He is wild out of his mind over me. He thinks I am the answer to all his questions. Sort of like Lucky thinks about you."

"Don't we wish," Bena said.

SINCE IT WAS so early they were the only customers at Ben Choi's. Bena told Mayfred about the desk job she was applying for at the school board. Mayfred thought it was the worst idea she'd ever heard. She thought it was terrible. "We can't have all the good teachers give up and move to the better-paying jobs, just because it's easier," Mayfred said. "We need to keep the teachers with the heart and soul in the classroom, Bena. You know that."

"You ever feel like you might be running out of heart and soul, Mayfred? You ever leave school and cry all the way home?"

"Hell yes." Mayfred was the only person Bena knew who put ketchup on her egg rolls. "Any teacher worth anything has got to cry her eyes out now and then just from the sheer frustration of it all. A decent teacher is going to have her heart busted pretty much all the time. But we got too many teachers in there now whose hearts gone icy and turned to stone. Where you think all those administrators come from?"

"Nothing changes," Bena said. "You work yourself to death in your classroom, but still, when the bell rings, your kids go right back out into the world, which tries to undo everything you're trying to do."

"Girl, you need a vacation," Mayfred said. "You gon' eat that other taco?"

WHEN BENA GOT HOME she put the tacos she'd brought for Eddie on the counter and checked the answering machine. A message for Eddie from Anna Kaye. Nothing else. The house seemed so empty it was eerie. She fed Tom and the cats, took her bath, put on one of Lucky's T-shirts, and got in bed to watch TV and wait for the phone to ring.

Next thing she knew it was morning. The TV was still going and the lights had been left on all night. She shot up from bed and looked at the phone, tugged the wires to be sure it was plugged in. He hadn't called her. Lucky had promised to call and he hadn't done it. She felt nearly sick, the way you do after you eat some fried oysters when you know perfectly well the current month doesn't have an R in it.

BENA TRIED TO ACT cheerful and enthusiastic in the classroom, but kids are so much smarter than that. "Why you sad, Mrs. Eckerd?" they asked her.

When Mayfred saw her she said, "Lord, what is it, Bena?"

"Lucky didn't call me last night. I don't even know where he is. Maybe something happened to him. Maybe there was an accident."

"Maybe you just need to have a little faith," Mayfred said.

A LONG, SLOW WEEK passed and still there was no word. Even Eddie got a little worried watching Bena worry herself sick. "Why don't you call Lucky's sister," Eddie asked. "Get her number from information."

"I don't know her last name," Bena said. "She's been married three times."

Eddie knew when he was in over his head. He called Anna Kaye to come over and she arrived excited, the way she always was when something was spinning out of control at the Eckerd house. Bena guessed they provided the only real excitement the poor girl was ever exposed to. Her lawyer-style church family seemed to prefer control and order and nonstop sanity. It was what Bena preferred too, but she'd just never attained any of it. "Let's call Sue Cox," Anna Kaye said. "Just explain the situation and ask her DeeDee's last name. I bet she knows."

Twice Bena picked up the phone with Anna Kaye cheering her on, but both times her stomach churned so she had to hang up before anybody answered.

"I'll call Sissy," Anna Kaye said. "She can come over when she gets off work. She'll call Sue Cox for you."

Bena saw the way Eddie was looking at Anna Kaye. Just lost in a swamp of admiration for her clear thinking and good ideas. It was interesting to see Anna Kaye in the take-charge role—and Eddie so grateful for the chance to follow her lead.

Sɪssʏ ᴄᴀᴍᴇ ᴏᴠᴇʀ around ten o'clock, carrying Bobby, who was sound asleep in his carrier. "Mama, why didn't you tell me you were so worried about Lucky?"

"No need for everybody to worry," Bena said.

In a few seconds Sue Cox was on the line. "What's wrong with DeeDee?"

"She's real sick," Sissy said. "Lucky's with her."

"The last guy DeeDee married was named—I think it was Irving. Monty Irving. Dee Dee Irving. Long Beach. That was it. They got divorced, I think. DeeDee moves around a lot."

"Thanks," Sissy said. "That's a start."

Sɪssʏ ᴀɴᴅ Aɴɴᴀ Kᴀʏᴇ tried long-distance information, every configuration they could think of. But no luck.

"Damn," Eddie said. "What's Lucky's problem? Why doesn't he call?"

"Maybe he wants to, but he can't." Anna Kaye went silent at the thought of that.

NIGHT AFTER NIGHT Bena tossed and turned and tried to coax herself into sleep. Some nights she imagined awful scenarios where Lucky was in danger and needed her desperately and she was trapped in a slow-motion life and no matter how hard she struggled she couldn't get to him in time. Other nights she imagined crazy stuff, like maybe he'd met a woman on the plane and decided that she, not Bena, was the woman of his dreams. Maybe he was secretly an FBI agent, masquerading as a mailman, and had gone off into an undercover job, or been relocated and assigned a new identity for his own safety. Maybe when the truth finally revealed itself Bena would see that Lucky had sacrificed everything for the good of others — that he was, after all, a hero. Maybe he was dead. California had all that violence going on, right? Maybe he stumbled into a gang fight and got shot for being in the wrong place at the wrong time. Maybe he disturbed a drug deal and they had to kill him to keep him from talking. Maybe his worry and grief over DeeDee had caused him to lose his mind and he was institutionalized against his will until he came to his senses.

Bena called the post office and spoke to Lucky's supervisor, who told her that Lucky'd taken a year's medical leave of absence from his job. "A year?" This gave Bena no comfort at all.

WORD PASSED THROUGH Baxter County that Lucky McKale had gone missing out in California. Left his new bride and her five kids and grandbaby to mourn his absence. Now when Bena went places people lowered their eyes when they saw her, spoke to her in whispers, and touched her shoulder or arm in a gesture of compassion. Sympathy was rampant.

Mayfred was the one who talked Bena into hiring a private detective to track Lucky down. It seemed to her the wrong kind of thing to do, but Bena was so worried she was willing to try nearly anything. Mayfred went with Bena to Atlanta to meet with the detective agency they'd selected out of the yellow pages. They gave the detective a photo, Lucky's social security number, and told him the sorry story. Even the hardened detective, who said nothing they could say would shock or surprise him in the least and so they shouldn't be embarrassed or hold anything back, even he—it seemed to Bena—felt sorry for her. Would the pity never end? In her worst moments Bena thought the only way she could ever forgive Lucky for bringing all this pity down on her head was if he was stone cold dead and helpless to save her from it.

After the meeting with the detective Bena and Mayfred went down to Peachtree to Bucky's Gourmet Sandwich Shop to see Ellie. She looked like she'd lost weight, but she was happy to see Bena. She kissed her and Mayfred too. "Y'all sit down and I'll get us all some raspberry tea. You want a sandwich or something?"

Bena and Mayfred declined the sandwich and sat at the front of the shop, where they could look out on the street. "Bunch of busy folks around here," Mayfred said. "Looks like they running a foot race out there."

Ellie brought them ice tea with mint sprigs and vegetable chips in a basket. "Here," she said. "I'm so glad to see you, Mama. I really miss you."

Bena smiled. "Me too."

"We been to see the private eye," Mayfred said. "He just like those private eyes on TV—not Tom Selleck, you know—but all the rest of them. He's real stupid looking, but probably ain't as stupid as he looks. Don't seem possible. He's gonna find Lucky for your Mama."

"This is awful," Ellie said. "It's terrible."

Bena nodded in agreement.

"It doesn't make sense."

Bena nodded *no it doesn't*.

"He'll come back, Mama. I know he will."

"I hope so," Bena said. "I miss him."

Ellie told them all about the private school she went to now. She was wearing her school uniform: plaid skirt, white blouse. She actually looked Catholic to Bena. She didn't look Baptist anymore. Her teachers were nuns. In her whole life Bena had never met a nun, and for some reason she wanted to keep it that way. Nuns seemed sort of spooky to Bena, the notion that they were sort of the brides of Christ and worshiped him too. You shouldn't actually worship the person you were married to, should you? How could that work? Besides, the nuns were only married to an idea anyway, not to an actual living, breathing man. As far as Bena could tell, nuns didn't know the first thing about real live men and weren't required to, which might have been what appealed to them about the profession in the first place. Bena guessed it might be easy to worship a man who'd been dead for thousands of years—only his wisest insights remaining.

Ellie said there were only twelve to fifteen kids in each of her classes. None of them poor either, like at Baxter High School—which was weird. Chapel every day too—where Ellie swore she always took time to pray for Lucky, that he'd come home to Bena so they could get on with their marriage, which up until now had been off to such a good start. She was reading the Bible from front to back too, all of it, every word, for her Bible class. Had a test every Friday. "The Bible is not like people think," Ellie said. "It's full of a lot of real wacko stuff, wacko people too. God has definitely got his kinky side."

"Oh, girl," Mayfred said, "don't talk that way. You making me nervous."

"You know what I mean," Ellie said. "Regular messed-up people. Not just a bunch of angels or anything."

"Make you feel better about things—or worse?" Bena asked.

"Better, Mama. So much better."

"Well, that's good then."

"Where's Sue Cox?" Mayfred asked.

"Next door at the flower shop," Ellie said. "She's got a thing going with the guy over there. Besides, she wanted us to have some time together, you know—alone."

"I don't guess you ever hear anything from Joe—or Leslie?" Bena said. "I don't hear much from those two."

"I know, Mama," Ellie said. "Maybe I can get Joe on the phone. I can try to get him to call you or something."

When it was time to leave Ellie said, "Your hair is looking good, Mama. You cut it, didn't you? You look good as a redhead."

"I went to the place you told me about. They talked me into a change."

"Change is good, Mama."

BY THE TIME the detective came up with any real information Lucky had been gone nearly two months. Bena had lost more weight than she could afford to lose, because when she lost Lucky she lost her appetite too. She could barely force herself to eat anything. Juanita had made her a big pot of black-bean soup and she had sipped on it like it was a lifesaving serum, breakfast, lunch, dinner for more than a week. Other than that, food made her sick the same way it had when she was pregnant and morning sick.

Mayfred went with Bena back to Atlanta to see the detective.

"San Diego," he said. "Your husband took a flight to San Diego and checked into the airport Hilton there. He was seen with a blond woman—his sister maybe? Together they checked out of the Hilton two days later. Still got my guys checking on DeeDee McKale Irving, last known address Long Beach, but they don't have anything much yet. Last known job the ticket office of Disneyland. Everybody liked her there. Nobody knew she was sick. We checked all the hospitals and rehabs. Checked the morgues for unidentified bodies. Checked with police and missing persons. Nothing on either of them. I'm sorry."

"Nothing else?" Bena asked.

"It takes time," the detective explained. "Lots of people in California. Easier to hide there than in Baxter County."

"You think they're hiding?"

"If they're not dead, and not hiding anything, they why wouldn't they pick up the telephone? It's just a question," he said.

"Come on, Bena." Mayfred pulled her up by the arm. "Let's get out of here. This man is charging us by the hour."

IN EARLY MAY, just before school was out, Bena got notice that she'd been selected by the school board for the clerical job she'd applied for. She'd nearly forgotten all about it. The bad thing — which wasn't clear in the job description — was that it was year-round. No summers off. Ordinarily that would seem awful, but with Lucky gone, and Bena reduced to a figment of her own overworked imagination, the last thing she needed was a big sprawling summer full of spare time to think about things. At the school board she would be mostly alone in her small, cool office — but at least she would be busy. She accepted the job.

Even Bena could see how ghostlike she'd become the last months of school. Her students never knew when she might stop what she was doing and put her head on her desk. They weren't the types to be upset by a teacher crying. They acted like she had every right. "Mrs. Eckerd's husband gone," the girls whispered, as if, young as they were, it was something they already understood. Some of them joined in with her, standing by her side, patting her back and matching her tear for tear. "My mama says it's good to cry," one girl said. "Everybody got to cry sometimes."

The boys were pretty good too. Some wrote her notes. One said:

Dear Teacher,

I see you sad. I'm sorry to hear it. I hope it is nothing I done to cause you to cry like that. If so, I am sorry.

Your friend, Jamal

Another said:

Mrs. Eckerd,

Please do not cry. Things will get better. When I used to cry my Mama always tell me this. So I believe it. Now I never cry anymore.

Love, Remmick

And one said:

Teacher,

I do not know who been making you cry but if you tell me I will take care of him for you. Me and my brother will. We make him stop what he been doing to you.

Please tell me, Marcus

Bena had never loved any group of students more than the ones she was failing day after day—lost in her own worries and unable to listen for the unspoken the way she usually did, and being too slow to respond when she did listen. In the afternoons she took home pictures her students had drawn for her, or flowers they'd snatched from the azalea bushes in the schoolyard or from the dogwood trees. If it weren't for her students Bena would never have known that spring had come and the world had burst open, right on time— bloom and color everywhere.

One girl brought her a Rice Krispies square her mother sent and one a slice of almond pound cake wrapped in a paper towel. In the afternoons before leaving to catch the buses home, certain of her students lined up for hugs—not to get them, Bena thought, but to give them.

On the last day of school Bena held each child tight to her and said, "You've helped me so much. I'll never forget you."

Some of her students cried good-bye right along with Bena, saying, "I'll come see you next year, Mrs. Eckerd. You the best teacher I ever had." It wasn't true. Bena knew that. But for some reason she believed it anyway. The way you believe the truest thing in the world.

When Bena thought of her sixth graders—some of the girls full grown and unnaturally wise, some of the boys small and embarrassed, desperate to hurry up and grow into their hands and feet so they could play basketball or get the girls with the bras on and sanitary napkins in their backpacks to notice them, when she thought of the way junior high would swallow some of them up, spit them out, wounded and lost, feeling wrong about themselves, and wrong about this world they were born into—she wanted to hold them all back, keep them safe in elementary school one more year, let them toughen up a little more before they got bused to junior high.

There, some children grew too fast and got too big, and others didn't grow at all and seemed to shrink until they became almost invisible. Some voices changed and some stayed the same. Some kids could carry a tune and knew all the words to all the hot songs, and others never could, never knew. Some kids danced just walking down the hall, some couldn't ever really dance no matter how much they practiced in front of the mirror. Some kids had the right clothes to wear, and some—even if they could afford it—didn't. Skin broke out, hearts broke open, lockers were broken into, heads got busted, kids got busted. Lies got told and the truth got told too—

and both were terrifying. The damage done, extensive and everlasting. There were always kids who were not chosen, not invited, not included, not even noticed. Kids lost their way, their gym shoes, their lunch money, lost their religion, lost their virginity, lost hope, and lost their minds. Everything happened.

Bena had watched all five of her own children enter junior high, some brave, some reluctant, and in every case she'd watched them struggle with who they were, who they wanted to be, who others wanted them to be, who they should be, who they could never be. All that vying for a place inside one twelve-year-old's startled body and soul. But these particular students, her last class of sixth graders, Bena ached for the way a mother does for children sent to fight an undeclared war. Even if they didn't get killed they'd surely be badly wounded and might never recover.

Bena stood on the breezeway in front of the school and waved good-bye until every single yellow bus had chugged away and disappeared into the ominous world. And then it was over. This chapter in her life—Bena Eckerd, teacher.

LONELINESS IS A strange thing. It's like a yellow rubber raincoat you wear twenty-four hours a day. It's hot and heavy and awkward and you can't get comfortable when you try to sleep in it, or take a shower in it, or shop for groceries in it, or watch TV or go through the drive-in window of a fast-food restaurant to get onion rings. You can't even take it off long enough to run it through your Kenmore washer and dryer—so after a while it gets a stink to it. You think you're hiding underneath that bright yellow raincoat, that nobody can see you sweating bullets, your clothes pasted to your skin, which is coming loose from your bones. You think if you put the hood up and hurry from place to place no one will notice how alone you are, how lost, how afraid.

It would take a friend like Mayfred to say, "Okay, girl, time's up, get that raggedy raincoat off. You look like a fool going around in that thing hot as it is. Not a drop of rain falling. I don't want to look at you wearing that nasty thing anymore."

So far, Mayfred hadn't said that.

It was Sissy who took Bena under her wing. Who better than Sissy to know what it is to be left by a man? To not know where he was or why. To not know if he'd ever come back—if he was dead or alive. To waver between hoping he was one thing and then the other.

"I got you something out at Books-A-Million, Mama." Sissy dug through Bobby's diaper bag and pulled out a book. "I saw them talking about it on TV. It's supposed to help people get over stuff, you know. It has all kinds of sad cases in it where people go on to find happiness."

Bena looked at the book. *The End Is the Beginning.* Bena didn't think she could possibly read anything so ridiculous, so awful.

"It's pretty good, Mama. Really."

"Thanks." Bena thumbed through the book like someone looking for pictures. As if she needed illustrations in order to understand how the end of one thing could possibly be the start of something else. As if she were a fool.

"Come on, Mama. Juanita and the kids are meeting us out at the mall. They want you to come."

"I don't feel like going anywhere."

"I gave my word, Mama. I said you were coming, so now you have to." She held Bobby up. He had drool dripping from his toothless grin. "You want Grandmama to come, don't you, Bobby?" Sissy bounced him up and down, like a yes in baby language. "See, Mama, Bobby wants you to come with us."

Bena smiled. "Lord, I'm a sucker."

Sissy laughed. "Aren't we all."

Bena ran a comb through her limp hair, but it didn't help, so she took a glob of gel and slapped it through her hair, making little points and wisps. It looked crazy, but she didn't care.

When she came out of the bathroom with her purse Sissy said, "Bobby, look at Grandmama. She's happening, isn't she?"

EVEN WEEKNIGHTS AT the mall were crowded in the summer, when school was out. They found Juanita at the food court. She'd set up Jesus and Jose at a small table, where they were eating McDonald's and talking with their mouths full. Carmelita was parked in her stroller beside them, munching French fries. Juanita sat at a neighboring table with a woman Bena didn't know. She might have been black or she might have been Mexican, Bena wasn't sure.

"Hey, y'all," Sissy called out. "Look who I dragged out of the house."

Juanita hugged Bena. "I brought somebody to meet you. She can help you."

Oh, Lord, Bena thought.

Sissy went to get chicken nuggets and Diet Cokes. Bena held Bobby on her lap and let him play with the car keys.

"This is Venus Leeds," Juanita said. "Miss Venus—Reader. You ever see that sign out on the highway by Ben Choi's?"

Bena felt the color wash out of her face. Damn. A palm reader or something? That's what Juanita thought she needed? Her tea leaves read? A game of cards to spell out her destiny?

"Don't worry," Juanita said. "She just want to meet you, you know. Maybe something come to her."

Bena could hardly force herself to look at the woman for more than a few seconds. She looked like the average secretary or insurance-claims clerk. She wore a polyester pant suit and had her hair cut real short and sensible. She hardly looked like a person who knew the future—or even had much of one herself.

"Juanita tells me your husband has disappeared? Been gone nearly three months and no word from him?" Venus leaned forward and spoke in a perfectly ordinary chitchat voice.

Bena looked hard at the woman then. This was all really none of her business and Bena had no intention of launching into the story and trying to explain something she didn't even understand herself. "That's right," Bena said.

Venus continued to watch Bena casually—as if she were trying to decide whether or not she liked her looks. She seemed to be fixed on Bena's spur-of-the-moment hairstyle. Sissy came back with their food, and Bena dipped a chicken nugget into the barbecue sauce and ate it hurriedly. Maybe if they all ate fast then this could be over with and they could all go home.

"Are you getting any vibes on Mama or anything?" Sissy asked.

Bena hated to think of Sissy and Juanita plotting to subject her to a mind reader. Didn't they know the answer was nowhere in Bena's mind—if it were, she'd pull it up herself. But it made her nervous anyway, Venus drinking a fruit smoothie and licking her lips afterward, staring a hole in Bena.

"Y'all just relax and talk," Venus said. "If I get anything I'll let you know. Sometimes I don't get anything at all the first time."

"Don't you need to sniff one of Lucky's old shirts or something?" Bena said sarcastically. "You know, to put you on his scent."

"Mama," Sissy said. "Venus is not a bloodhound. She's trying to help you. There's no harm in it."

"Does Lucky speak Spanish?" Venus asked. "I see a woman speaking fluent Spanish."

"That's Juanita." Bena nodded in Juanita's direction. "You got your wires crossed. Lucky can say *hola, adiós,* and *qué pasa, Carmelita.* That's about it."

"No Spanish," Sissy said. "Try something else."

This required another fruit smoothie. Venus got up to replenish her drink.

"Mama," Sissy scolded her, "cooperate."

"Venus have very good trail of records," Juanita said.

"Track record," Sissy corrected. "She's worked for the police before, Mama. Would the police be consulting her if there was nothing to her? Say? If the police are willing to seek Venus out and listen to her, then I think you ought to be willing to do the same."

"We pay her," Juanita said. "You don't act nice to her you waste our money."

"This is crazy," Bena said. "You're paying her? How much?"

"That's next to the point," Juanita said. "We want to get answers for you. But you acting like this."

"Okay, okay," Bena said. "It's just creepy."

"You husband gone. That's what creeps," Juanita said.

When Venus came back to the table Bena made a point of smiling at her. But now Venus was the one acting funny. She sat very quietly while the rest of them finished eating. Juanita and Sissy tried to drag things out as long as they could, but Bobby got fussy and Jesus and Jose were getting rowdy and throwing French fries at people walking by. "Stop that," Juanita yelled. "Be more nice."

Finally Sissy loaded Bobby in his stroller, clearly disappointed in the way the evening had gone. Juanita was frustrated too. Just as Bena was feeling relieved that the insanity was almost over, just as she was thinking she would insist on paying Juanita and Sissy back whatever they'd spent on this misguided idea, Venus reached out and took Bena's arm. "May I speak to you alone?"

The way she said it, her painted fingernails clamped down on Bena's arm, made Bena feel paralyzed.

"We'll meet you out front, Mama." Sissy's eyes were wide open and hopeful. "In front of Radio Shack."

When the others were gone, Venus let go of Bena's arm. She picked up a paper napkin and twisted it into a tight white rope. Bena watched her fingers—not her face. "Your husband is not coming back," Venus said. "He's dead."

Bena felt an icy finger go down her spine. It made her sit up straight and let out a breath that had sound to it. "How do you know?" she whispered.

"He's been dead for some time. But he worries about you and will try to contact you. Look for signs. A favorite song or something. Maybe three times in a row."

"What are you talking about?"

"He's trying to say good-bye. He loved you very much. He never meant to lie."

"I don't believe you," Bena said. "You're making this up."

"I just tell you what comes."

"Here's what comes to me." Bena grabbed a fistful of napkins off the table and tossed them at Venus. "Lucky is not dead! If he were dead I'd know it. I'd feel it." She got up, grabbed her purse, ran her hand nervously through her stiff hair, which was standing up straight on her head like a bunch of nails driven through her skull from inside out, and walked out into the night to meet Juanita and Sissy.

When they saw Bena they hurried over. "What?" they said. "What'd she say?"

"Lucky is alive and well," Bena said. "He's trying hard to come home. I have to be patient."

"Wow," Sissy said.

"See." Juanita waved her finger at Bena. "I told you she do very good. I told you she see the true."

EVERY MORNING BENA went to work extra early. That way she wouldn't have to run into anybody on her way to the cubicle where she was paid to feed student data into a computer. Her weeks of training had gone well enough. "Not the most exciting job in the world," her predecessor said. "If you start to go stir-crazy, let me know. Come down to the lounge and get some coffee or something." But so far Bena hadn't gotten stir-crazy. She practically loved the nothingness of the job. If you did what you were supposed to, the computer rewarded you by spitting out all sorts of interesting information. Then she was supposed to send the interesting information to Montgomery so they could send it on to Washington, D.C. What happened then, Bena wasn't sure. She suspected not much.

21% of the students in Baxter County presently have or have had a parent incarcerated.
53% qualify for free lunch.
34% have been referred to the school guidance counselor.
4% have parents earning in excess of $1 million a year.
58% of families own (or are paying on) two or more cars.

Bena liked all these facts. They were so pleasantly numerical and concrete that it didn't really bother her that they were probably also useless. She kept her cubicle so neat and nice that on the rare occasion that anyone stepped inside to speak to her they almost always mentioned how well organized she appeared.

In her bottom drawer she kept bottled water and, most days, the yogurt she brought for lunch and maybe some Oreos or vanilla wafers. Everything was so simple and quiet, and she loved spending the day dealing with provable facts about other people's lives.

It was harder at home, of course, to keep herself calm and distracted. Lucky haunted her house. His clothes in the closet. His imprint dominating every room, his voice, his loud laugh, his mail-carrier credentials on top of the dresser, his loose change in an ashtray beside the bed, his boots beside the back door. Every night Bena went to sleep with Tom at her feet. Sometimes she thought she saw Tom asking with his dog eyes—*Where is he?* She thought she knew exactly what was wrong when he whimpered and whined. She pulled him up beside her in the bed and put her arm around him and tried to tell him all that she did not know.

But Lucky had left Eddie in charge of Tom, and it surprised Bena how seriously Eddie took the responsibility. Most nights, even if

Tom started off in Bena's bed, he ended up in Eddie's. Some nights Bena woke up to the sound of Eddie stumbling in the dark to get Tom, half waking him, half carrying him into his room down the hall. Lots of evenings he loaded Tom in Lucky's truck and took him to Anna Kaye's. Sometimes they could be seen going down the road with Tom perched between them in the front seat like an eager child.

When it rained Bena ached for Lucky so much that she thought she might actually die from the pain. The rain made her take to the bed, like somebody sick, and listen to the sounds, splashing, slapping, and dripping. Sometimes machine-gunning against a closed window or hammering on the roof. The smells of the drenched earth were so pungent and raw too. She opened her curtains and looked out at the wet world—cleansed and all messed up at the same time. This was when she felt closest to Lucky, when the lightning shot through the sky. When the thunder rolled across the night like an airborne train come off its unimaginative tracks. Everything about it made her miss Lucky and try to dream him back where he belonged.

It was on such a night that Bena could not fall asleep, because she was worried about Eddie, still out in Lucky's truck, the roads slippery, the visibility awful, the ditches overflowing so much it would be easy to lose sight of the road and float off someplace. Maybe the truck would flip. Maybe it would sink. Maybe it had stalled and Eddie was somewhere way off the road waiting for help that might never come.

Bena was restless and fretful and the only reason she got up out of bed was because she was sure she heard a truck pull up in the driveway, but it was odd too, because it had come up without the headlights on. She felt her way down the hall, Tom at her heels, and went to the kitchen and looked out. The rain was so black she couldn't see anything. She would wait a minute, see if Eddie made a run for the door, getting soaked on the way. She would kiss his face when she saw him. She would say, "Thank God, Eddie."

But when he didn't come and didn't come, she opened the door a second time to look for him in the downpour, and that's when she heard the voice say, "Close that door, baby. You getting sopping wet."

Bena let out a cry, jumped around to see where the voice was coming from. It had sounded like—well, it couldn't be. "Who's there?" she said. Beside her Tom began to whimper.

"You forgot me this soon?" Then Bena saw it, a smoky sort of mist at first, like steam off a boiling pot, but when she looked harder she saw that it was Bobby.

Well, it was not exactly Bobby. It was sort of like Bobby dressed up in an Elvis outfit, that white one Elvis used to wear with the big buckle and the long white cape. And Bobby had his hair sort of Elvis style too, longer than normal with sideburns and all. "Bobby?" she said. "Is that you, Bobby?"

"Hey, baby," he said. He sounded the way Elvis did when he said *Hey, baby* to Ann-Margret in *Viva Las Vegas*.

"Why are you talking like that? What do you want?" Bena gripped the fur on Tom's neck, holding on to him to keep her balance. Her eyes darted around the room. "Did I die?"

Bobby laughed and shook his head. "Naw," he said. "I'm dead. But you're all right. Pinch your arm or something. See for yourself."

Bena pinched herself and it hurt.

"You been getting rid of lots of stuff around here. I'm glad to see you didn't get rid of my favorite chair over here. I love this chair."

"It's next," Bena said. "Everything in this room is next."

"Mind if I have one last re-cline?" She watched the Elvis vapor sprawl out in the La-Z-Boy. He looked at her and smiled. "No need to be scared of me," he said. "Nothing I can do to you now."

"No," Bena said, "guess you did enough before you left."

"You gotten sort of spunky since I been gone, haven't you? I like that."

"Are you a ghost? Am I seeing a ghost?"

"A spirit," Bobby said. "I prefer to go by spirit. It's a little more up-to-date."

"Up-to-date?" Bena said. "You used to hate anything up-to-date."

"Die and learn." He smiled.

Tom began to bark.

"You're scaring Tom," Bena said. "He's never seen a ghost—a spirit."

"Let go of his neck," Bobby said. "You're choking him."

Bena let go of Tom and walked closer to where the Bobby figure was reclined with his legs crossed. She didn't even feel afraid. "If you've come to tell me something bad about Lucky—that he's dead—or something, then you better go right back where you came from because I won't believe you."

"That's not why I'm here. I come to bring the Queen a little advice."

"Advice?"

"Bena, Baby, you got to forgive . . ." He said it like he breaking out into a song.

"I did forgive you, Bobby. Lorraine too. I swear."

"Not me, baby. Not Lorraine either. You got to forgive your-self." He said it like he was talking into a microphone. The sound of his voice vibrated all the way through the house, then made a high-pitched squeal like an amplifier does when a band is warm-ing up.

Bena was stunned. "Forgive myself? For what? What did I do?"

"You're looking real good, baby. I always liked redheads."

"I bet you did," Bena said.

"Never worry about me—not anymore," Bobby mumbled in his Elvis voice, his form sort of lifting from the chair and coming apart like a cloud in a sudden breeze. "I forgive you, Bena, honey. I always have. I always will."

"For what?" Bena cried. "Why are you forgiving me?"

But the spirit flapped his Elvis cape and vanished like some sort of spooky amateur Superman.

Before she could think what to do Bena woke up with a jolt. She was so hot she was sweating, and her T-shirt was as wet as if she'd been out in the weather. Tom leaped off the bed and ran for the kitchen, his toenails clawing the wood floor and linoleum, making a racket. At the back door Eddie was struggling to get into the house, out of the rain. "Hey, boy." He stooped to pet Tom.

When Bena came in with a dry towel he didn't see her. "Thank God, Eddie," she said. "Take off those wet shoes and that shirt."

"Mama?" He was startled to see her. "What you doing up this time of night."

"Waiting for you."

"I tried to wait the rain out," Eddie said. "But nothing let up, so I finally came on. You look a little funny, Mama. Is everything okay?"

"I had a strange dream," she said.

"About what?" Eddie asked.

"I dreamed your daddy was Elvis."

Eddie shook his head, a serious, worried expression on his face. "I don't know, Mama. You might need to get you some professional help or something."

BENA CONVINCED HERSELF that Bobby's appearance was a dream and nothing more. First of all, she hadn't been a bit afraid of him. If Bobby were really crossing over from the other side it should scare her to death, shouldn't it? Also he hadn't brought Lorraine with him—and only in Bena's wildest dreams were those two ever not together, clutching each other, pawing and gushing. He never even mentioned little Bobby, his namesake, his only grandchild. He forgot to ask about any of his children, who were not children anymore—and the true Bobby knew better than that. But mostly, Bena knew it was a dream because Bobby was so busy giving her advice that he forgot to say, "I'm sorry, Bena." The real Bobby—if he'd shown up in spirit—would have dropped to his knees overcome with remorse and regret. She'd pictured that moment at least a thousand times. She knew exactly how it should have gone.

Bena smiled when she thought of Bobby all dressed up in white and half mumbling, half humming like Elvis. He hadn't quite been the hot and handsome Elvis whose crooked smile could stop women in their tracks and cause them to keel over and faint. He was more like the middle-aged Elvis on the cusp of his decline, when all his fried bologna and peanut-butter-and-banana sandwiches had begun to do their damage—not to mention the drugs, sex, and rock and roll. Plus a loneliness beyond anything even Bena could imagine. Bobby appeared to be in Elvis's early, plump, get-me-my-sunglasses era. For some reason, that made Bena happy.

She didn't tell anyone what she'd dreamed—except Mayfred. But Mayfred didn't derive the same amusement from the dream that Bena did. She was annoyed with Bobby for trying to masquerade as the King. "Ain't it just like a man," she said, "to rise from the dead just long enough to tell you what to do and how to do it, point out your little small shortcomings when his own shortcomings are so severe they've done put the man in a early grave."

"I think he meant well," Bena said. "In the dream."

"If you ask me," Mayfred said, "death has not improved that man one bit. If you don't learn nothing from dying—then you are just too hopeless to talk about."

71% of Baxter County students report having at least one gun in their home.

29% of Baxter County families receive government assistance.

24% of Baxter County students participate in some form of organized sports.

31% of Baxter County families subscribe to at least one periodical.

8% of Baxter County students have been held back one grade or more.

THE FOLLOWING SUNDAY Bena got in the car and drove toward Montgomery. She turned off Highway 231 like you do if you're
heading for Wetumpka and the women's prison. That would take her
right by the graveyard where Lorraine was buried. She remembered
that from the newspaper obituary Lorraine's mother had sent her.
It was a long drive, but Bena didn't mind. She turned the radio full
blast to the oldies channel and sang along out loud. Hardly a song
came on that she didn't remember the words to.

The cemetery wasn't hard to find. It was just like Mrs. Rayfield
had said, "half a mile down from the Manufactured Homes Center
and across from the Burger King." Bena was hoping nobody would be
there when she arrived, but there was one car parked at the entrance, although not a soul in sight. She drove past it and parked her
car under a shade tree. Elvis was bellowing *hunk-a-hunk of burning
love*. Bena had always hated that song and snapped the radio off.

It was a pretty big graveyard. It might take her a long time to find
what she was looking for. It was a modern graveyard where ease of
maintenance was more important than honoring the memory of the
deceased. No upright markers allowed. Only uniform-sized name
plaques lying flat to the ground so that a riding mower could drive
over them with no problem. No live flowers allowed either. Only
plastic that could easily be moved aside for the grass cutting. They
had signs posted on pine trees explaining the rules for getting
buried. There was a number to call if you were interested in buying a plot.

THIS CEMETERY GAVE her the same feeling she got in the
one where her parents were buried or the one where Bobby was.
That seemed odd, because as far as she knew she'd never met a single soul buried here. But she had a feeling in cemeteries that she was
being watched—that everyone buried there understood her better
than she understood herself. It was unnerving—but nice.

It made her wonder why she hadn't been to the graves of her

loved ones more often. It wasn't creepy to her. It wasn't even sad. But she could count on one hand the times she'd gone to visit the dead. A couple of Father's Days the girls had made a pilgrimage to the cemetery to put flowers on Bobby's grave. "You want to go with us, Mama?" they'd asked. "No," she'd said. "He wasn't my daddy, was he? Y'all go ahead. Have fun." She'd actually said that, "Have fun." Then she'd stayed home and watched a Braves game with Joe and Eddie.

Bena walked until she found Lorraine's marker at the far edge of the place. It was undistinguished, identical to every other marker. She pulled up a couple of sprigs of crabgrass that were threatening to take over where the regular grass was struggling. The grass looked like a threadbare spread too small to properly cover Lorraine's resting place. Somebody should complain to the cemetery people, get them to throw a blanket of sod over her burial site. The dead deserved at least that much. But Bena hadn't really come to visit Lorraine's grave. It was the small grave beside her that Bena had come to see. Rayfield, Baby Boy.

She sat on the ground beside the marker and studied it. The grass was nearly bare here, sunburned and needing water and fertilizer. The dirt around the marker was hard red clay and you could break it off in clumps and crumble it in your hand. In Lorraine's flower holder was a plastic white tulip and in Baby Boy's was a little clump of plastic violets. She guessed Mrs. Rayfield must be the one who put the plastic flowers here. Or maybe it was Lisa.

Bena wasn't sure why she needed to see the grave of this never born child. She wasn't sure what made her want to sit beside it and run her finger over the dusty etched name and solitary date. Was she expecting something to happen? A vision to appear? A moment of clarity to descend upon her?

In her years of teaching sixth grade Bena had had six students deliver babies. Four babies lived and two died, and she had never been able to make up her mind which scenario was worse. Nobody in this world should have a twelve- or thirteen-year-old mother. But it happened. No child should be buried unborn, unnamed, and unloved. But that happened too.

Bena stayed at the grave for nearly an hour. She leaned against the chain-link fence that circled the place and let her mind roam. If it hadn't been so hot and if the bugs hadn't been so bad she might have just lain down right there and fallen asleep in the sun.

WHEN BENA GOT home Eddie had scrawled a note: *Mama, call Joe. He wants to talk to you.*

Bena was nervous when she dialed the number. Joe answered, and for a minute Bena didn't recognize his voice.

"I'm calling about Lucky, Mama. Any news?"

"Not yet."

"How you doing?"

"Okay," she said. "Trying to stay busy."

"You'll call me if you hear anything, won't you, Mama?"

"Sure, I will."

"And Mama." Joe cleared his throat. "I just want to say something, you know, for you to think about. Will you hear me out?"

"Go ahead." Bena dreaded whatever Joe was about to say. She felt her spine tense and her throat go dry. She wasn't in the mood for an argument.

"I've been thinking a lot lately, Mama. About Daddy and all." Joe paused for a signal that Bena was listening.

"Yes," she said.

"All my life I been mad at Daddy. I came close to hating him for what he did. But now, you know, I'm starting to see things different. What Daddy did, he did out of love. He never meant to hurt anybody. You used to say, *Daddy made a mistake, Joe. Everybody makes mistakes.* But, Mama, what if it wasn't a mistake? What if love is never a mistake?"

Bena let out a breath. "I don't know the answer to that, Joe."

"See, Mama, Daddy was operating out of love when he hurt us. But you, Mama, the way you are with Lisa, that's not out of love. So, I guess, you know, that makes it seem worse."

"I'm sorry, Joe," Bena said. "I don't know what else to say."

"Well," Joe said, "just think about it, Mama."

IT SEEMS THAT in Alabama all so-called saved and decent mothers secretly hope their firstborn sons will become preachers. Every good mother watches for and can see that moment when her firstborn son gets the calling. Bena had never thought that way though. Until now. Joe might not be religious, but he definitely had a streak of preacher in him. Bena wished she felt better about that.

> *21% of Baxter County married couples have four or more children.*
> *34% of Baxter County children are born out of wedlock.*
> *41% are accepted to four year-colleges.*
> *18% have faced criminal charges.*
> *12% leave the state of Alabama after high school.*

Eddie still worked at the country club snack bar in the mornings. Afternoons he had cross-country practice at the high school. When Eddie came home late one afternoon a Salvation Army truck was backed up to the carport and a couple of guys were loading his daddy's La-Z-Boy into the truck. Bena tried to catch Eddie before he got inside the house and saw that she'd given away everything in the den except the TV set. She thought it'd seem cruel and unusual to make Eddie do without a TV.

"What's going on, Mama?" he called to her. "Where are they taking our stuff?"

"I'm giving it away," Bena said. "Come look at this?" She took Eddie's arm and led him through the bare den and into the bare living room and then on into her own bare bedroom. Nothing left but the clothes in the closet and a couple of cardboard boxes sitting on the floor.

"What's going on? Where you going to sleep, Mama?"

"Maybe in Ellie's old room," Bena said.

"I don't get it."

"I couldn't stand it anymore, honey," Bena said. "Everything such a mess all the time. Sometimes it's better to have nothing than all the wrong stuff."

Eddie looked at his mother with the same look he got when one of his sisters tried to explain their so-called logic to him. It was a terrified look.

"What about my room?" he asked.

"Didn't touch a thing." Bena smiled.

Eddie walked down the hall and looked inside at his unmade bed. Sure enough, everything looked junky and untouched, just as he liked it.

"See," Bena said. "Nothing to worry about."

Eddie was glancing all around, like he half expected somebody else to appear, a translator maybe, a sane person who had wandered into his crazy life that he lived with his crazy mother.

"So what are we going to use for furniture?"

"I've been thinking," Bena said. "You got Lucky's truck, right? Until he comes back. You got a way to get back and forth. So what's to stop us from moving out to Lucky's place? Sooner seems just as good as later."

Tom went crazy his first week back at home. He searched the house and the surrounding acreage for some sign of Lucky. It about broke Bena's heart because that was exactly the same way she felt on the inside, like a dog chasing her own tail, searching her heart and soul for some clue, some unturned memory that held the answer to it all. The cats were less exuberant. They roamed the yard cautiously, attacking crickets and squirrels. Maybe Leslie hadn't wanted them to be yard cats——but Bena convinced herself that fresh air and freedom were good for them.

Her first night in the new house Bena slept like a baby. She'd forgotten sleep. When grief set in a strange thing happened. Bena found herself sleepwalking through her waking life, blind with her eyes wide open, deaf when she listened, numb to everything she touched and everything that touched her. Grief let go of Bena only at night, when she dreamed a world even stranger than the one she was trapped in. In the dream world everything strange seemed comforting and familiar, the details stayed with her, the words made sense, the feelings were intense and real. After Lucky left, most days Bena couldn't remember what day it was, what she'd had for supper, or who'd called on the phone. But when the night claimed her and her dreams came she remembered everything. The colors, the sentences, all the impossible things that could never really happen but did. In grief she slept through every long, slow day——awakening only when, at last, she fell out of this world into the place where dreams happen.

The months of grief had left her exhausted that way. So Bena was surprised that sleeping in Lucky's bed in Lucky's house she could actually experience the old kind of sleep and wake up less tired than when she went to bed. It was a small thing. But it was something.

Eddie stayed nervous the first few days at Lucky's. Bena noticed that he took off his shoes and left them at the door so he wouldn't track up the house. He wiped up the counter after he made a sandwich. He draped his wet towels over the shower door instead of slinging them on the floor for the Good Fairy to pick up later. He even talked quietly and kept the TV turned low. Sometimes Bena had to go and look to be sure Eddie was in the house. He seemed as nervous as company until he brought Anna Kaye over and she made herself at home instantly, demystifying the place for Eddie. It was almost like an exorcism watching Anna Kaye explore the house, open doors, drawers, cabinets——and comment on everything. She

claimed the house so easily, which is something most women understand and do naturally. But Eddie didn't understand houses—
that they're more than houses. He thought they were random places
where you put random furniture so that you could sleep and eat.
The spirit of a house, the thing Anna Kaye was in instant communi-
cation with, escaped Eddie on the conscious level. But Bena suspected that might not always be true. She suspected, in time, he'd
learn a lot from Anna Kaye.

*91% of Baxter County students report having a Bible in their
home.*

14% of Baxter County residents have never seen a doctor.

11% of Baxter County students play a musical instrument.

23% of Baxter County babies are born prematurely.

6% of Baxter County students are home schooled.

Bena bought a trunkload of white paint. In the afternoons when
she got off work she went to the old house, put on old clothes, and
spent the evening painting the rooms. It was amazing the difference
it made. So far she'd only painted the woodwork in the living room
and dining room, but it felt better than professional therapy—which
she didn't really believe in, and which was too expensive anyway.

There were only two psychiatrists in Baxter County. One had
moved to the county from New York City, which never made any
sense at all. People said they guessed he'd gotten run out of New
York City—like he might be a fugitive or something. But then people said, no, New York City doesn't run off crazy people because if
they did then the entire city would have to be evacuated. There had
to be another reason. Maybe something terrible. It was a popular
pastime in Baxter County, trying to guess why a psychiatrist from
New York City would move to Baxter County, Alabama, unless he
had something to hide or was running away from somebody. It didn't
occur to anybody that he could actually like it down here, where

nearly everybody was totally resistant to his chosen profession. Bena was not sure about any of this because she had never been to New York City—and to this day didn't have the slightest interest in ever going.

The New York City psychiatrist's partner was a local boy who had gone off to school at Emory and come back home to try to help all the crazy people in Baxter County face the fact that they were crazy. This would be a pretty tall order for anybody. Bena didn't know what compelled him to devote his life to this purpose. He'd have done better to make a preacher. It was the easiest thing in the world to convince people in Baxter County that they were all no-good sinners—people embraced that notion freely and enthusiastically and ran with it all their lives. The notion of sin was so powerful and rampant that some of the modern Baptist churches had set aside time at the beginning of the service for sinners to stand up and confess the darkness of their hearts to one and all in the congregation—sort of like the Catholics do in dark closets. It had become the favorite part of the service for lots of folks—both those with the deep desire to confess as well as those with the deep desire to know the sins and personal business of their friends and neighbors. Some people said it was the best free entertainment in the county, especially when it served to turn a rock-hard heart into putty in the hands of God. By all accounts the sinner concept was extremely popular in Baxter County.

But at the same time it was the hardest thing in the world to convince anybody at all that they were even the slightest bit crazy. For some reason, confessing to being crazy had just never caught on in Baxter County. Bena was no exception. She might be a lot of things, but crazy wasn't one of them.

Several family members of Bena's students had been sent by court order to see these psychiatrists, and one of the teachers at school had gone of her own free will. People said she did that just because she heard one of the psychiatrists was single, and he made an excellent salary by Baxter County standards. He was about the nearest thing there was to a rich bachelor in the area, which seemed to have done wonders for his business.

By all reports what these psychiatrists were good at was helping you figure out the main things wrong with you—which most folks pretty much knew going in. What the psychiatrists were really bad at was helping you figure out what to do about it. Bena'd had a student, Gary, who was arrested for shoplifting and got sent by the court to see the New York City psychiatrist. Gary's social worker got him out of class once a week for twelve weeks and took him to his sessions. When they were over Bena asked, "What did the psychiatrist tell you, Gary?"

Gary had looked at her, puzzled that she would have to ask. "He say I got a problem with stealing."

As far as Bena could tell, it wasn't that hard to be a psychiatrist.

Most women don't really need psychiatrists anyway—not if they have a true friend. Bena believed this. Women naturally and instinctively serve as one another's counselors. Bena thought that as long as she had Mayfred to pour her heart out to—for free—that was the best guidance she could ever hope for. Mayfred would never lie to her or give her stupid advice or try to talk her out of knowing what she knew. Mayfred was never too tired or too busy to listen if Bena wanted to talk. There was no appointment to make. No outrageous bill at the end of the month. And for every story Bena peeled loose from her heart Mayfred peeled one too, from hers, that matched or exceeded Bena's. They proved to each other at every turn that neither one of them was ever really crazy—or alone. Bena loved Mayfred the way you could never love a psychiatrist. At least you weren't supposed to.

It was odd how wonderful it was to be in her old house when it was nearly empty. The emptiness was somehow exciting to her. After nearly everything was gotten rid of Bena felt, for the first time in a long, long time, that she had room to breathe, room to move around, room to think. The house echoed when she walked or talked, but mostly it was silent like a sleeping giant—or like Jonah's whale, who, having swallowed her up years before, was letting her, years later, whitewash his tired belly before he spit her out at last.

She didn't mind if she dripped paint on the carpet. As soon as she was finished painting she would rip out all the old carpet too. Maybe she and Eddie would make a bonfire of it, set a match to it and watch the past go up in flames.

SOME EVENINGS MAYFRED came by to help paint. A few times she brought LaVonte with her. After LaVonte roamed the house and looked at everything enough to satisfy his curiosity, he took up a roller and went at the walls with a fury that Bena recognized. She thought maybe LaVonte understood the thrill that came from improving something with your own two hands. Mayfred, on the other hand, mostly watched the painting and said, "Lord, this looks so good I might have to talk Jerry Lee into painting my place."

Once in a while Mayfred brought supper over—usually something she picked up on the way but once a casserole she made herself; Chicken Supreme she called it. Bena ate two helpings of casserole and could have eaten another one. It was the first thing she had been able to actually taste since Lucky vanished.

"It's the paint fumes," Mayfred said. "They aggravating your appetite."

Lots of nights Bena painted well into the night. Just Bena, alone, in the empty place that had once housed her soul, her life, and her children. She patched and painted over nail holes, fingerprints, scuff marks, faded places, scrapes, scars, and general all-purpose dirt. One clean swipe of the roller and it was all gone—almost like it had never even been there. With paint you can stroke clean right over the dirty, and clean will win. For a woman who'd spent so much of her life at war with dirt it was almost magic. It was powerful. Bena painted every room with two coats—not always because it needed it but because the pleasure of it was so unspeakable.

IF ALL WENT WELL Bena could have the entire house painted by the end of the summer. She'd invited Sissy and little Bobby to move in and save their rent money, but to Bena's surprise, Sissy declined the offer. "Mama, I'd be scared to death out here all by myself with Bobby. You could scream all day long and nobody would ever hear you. At least if I scream at the trailer park I know somebody will come. He may be one step ahead of the sheriff himself, but somebody'll come."

It was true, of course. That just showed how much the world had changed. It was the quiet, isolated location that Bobby and Bena had loved so much in the beginning when they'd moved into this house with Joe and Sissy, just babies—a little family of four with everything to look forward to.

LESLIE CALLED. When she'd dialed home to leave her usual clandestine message of general well-being and was told the phone number had been disconnected, she panicked. She called Joe at his dorm, and he told her everything. That Lucky was gone, might never come back, might be dead. And that their mother and Eddie had moved into Lucky's house way out there off the highway.

"Joe says you're not giving up hope, Mama," Leslie said. "He says you're too stubborn to give up."

"Maybe that's right."

"Joe is as stubborn as you are, Mama. He's just like you that way."

"Lord, don't tell him that," Bena said.

"I guess we're all pretty stubborn," Leslie said. "If we weren't, who knows what would happen to us."

"It's good to hear your voice, Les. I miss you a lot."

"Me too, Mama. But Corby and me, we're doing fine. People in Texas are nice. Austin is a cool place. Corby's got a regular job with a band. Dogs Never Born."

"Sounds awful."

"They're good, Mama. They really are. Corby's learning so much about the music business. He's lead singer now. Writing lots of his own stuff. We got a little place over by campus. I'm working as a temp around the university—just typing and stuff. Gotten pretty good on the computer."

"Les, we're not sending the police after you or anything."

"I know, Mama."

"You can call collect as much as you want to. You can give us your address when you're ready."

"I know."

"You could even come home. You know, for a visit."

"Soon as we get enough money together, Mama. I promise."

THE FOLLOWING SUNDAY Sue Cox and Ellie showed up unexpectedly at Bena's old house. They were on their way back from a trip to the beach and were both brown as berries and had that sandy, sunburned, sassy quality to them. They radiated that unique satisfaction that comes from doing nothing but lying in the sun, sipping something cold, slathering yourself with oil, and doing a little horizontal semi-soul-searching for a solid week. Their car was full of wet towels, crumpled fast-food bags, and half-finished cold drinks. They smelled like a couple of coconuts.

Bena was instantly jealous. Why didn't it occur to her to drive down to Panama City or Gulf Shores? Why didn't she think to take time out from being miserable to get a good suntan and eat some fried fish? A flash of anger shot through her. How had she managed to forget about the beach? She used to love the beach more than anybody.

"Sissy told us you're redoing your house." Sue Cox's skin was a high-gloss brown. "We got curious."

"It's okay, isn't it, Mama?" Ellie was barefoot, her face burned, her hair sun-bleached and pinned up on her head the way she used to wear it. "I told Sue Cox it was okay if we stopped by. You don't care, do you?"

"I'm just painting," Bena said. "I don't know what Sissy told you, but it's not much to see. White paint."

"We wanted to see you too," Sue Cox said.

"Well, here I am." Bena faked a smile, a dripping roller in her hand. "Come on in if you want to. Feast your eyes."

"Oh my gosh." Ellie stepped inside the house. "It looks so different without the furniture."

"You mean so much better," Bena said.

"And bigger." Ellie walked down the hall and ran her fingers over the freshly painted walls. "Now you have to get new carpet, Mama." She wandered to the back to look at her room, which remained untouched since Sue Cox had redone it.

Sue Cox stood in the kitchen with Bena. She seemed nervous. "Any word from Lucky?"

"Not yet."

"This must be awful for you."

"Yep," Bena said. "Pretty awful."

"Bena." Sue Cox was still wearing her sunglasses like a couple of black eyes to hide behind. "If I'd had any idea you were going to lose Lucky, I never would have taken Ellie with me to Atlanta."

"I haven't lost Lucky." Bena spoke sharply. "He'll be back. So if you're here to feel sorry for me, don't."

"No pity from me," Sue Cox said. "I don't do pity. Ellie and I just thought maybe we could help out, you know. I love to paint. I'm good at it too."

"Is there anything you're not good at, Sue Cox?" Bena's words were acid coated. Her tongue burned as she spoke them.

"Clearly I'm not good at getting you to stop being mad at me."

"Here." Bena jabbed the roller at Sue Cox. "Paint if you want to. Knock yourself out."

Sue Cox was not kidding about her love of a paint roller. She went to work with a dedication that surprised Bena. She went silent too, like any serious wall painter does when called into the inner sanctum by the wonder of what she is doing. Bena left Sue Cox to her own devices—and the thrill of an unpainted room of her own.

Ellie was unusually clingy. She was like a talkative shadow one step behind Bena every step she took. "Sue Cox says if you want me to come back home for my senior year that I should. You know, under the circumstances."

At least Ellie had referred to Baxter County as *home*. Bena took note of that. It was a small satisfaction.

"So, do you want me to, Mama?"

Bena paused where she was painting a windowsill and looked at Ellie. "You know I'd love to have you here, El. Always."

"But . . . what?" Ellie asked.

"But not because you're worried about me or think I'm lonely or something."

"Eddie says you are lonely, Mama. So does Sissy."

"I miss Lucky," Bena said. "Nobody can fix that but Lucky. I'll miss him just as bad if you're here as if you're in Atlanta."

"So you wouldn't be mad if I stayed in Atlanta then?"

"Seems like you love Atlanta. Your school sounds good—in a Catholic sort of way. What good would it do for me to drag you back here kicking and screaming?"

"I'll come if you need me to, Mama. I swear."

Bena touched a sticky, painted finger to Ellie's cheek. "I know that."

"So I can stay. It's okay?"

"You can stay," Bena said. "Lucky used to try to tell me that there isn't just one big pot of happiness that everybody has to stick a finger in or dip their empty cup into and scrape around the bottom for any little bit that's left over. He used to try to tell me that there's a millions different happinesses out there—like a bunch of pies, you know. We don't all have to line up for a tiny sliver of lemon

meringue either. People can have banana cream or pecan or blue-
berry—anything they like. I used to not believe him, but now I do."

"Cool," Ellie said. It was clear she had no real idea what Bena was
talking about.

"Maybe I talk about Lucky too much," Bena said.

"Mama." Ellie touched Bena's shirt. "What if Lucky doesn't come
back?"

"He will."

"But what if he doesn't though—"

"He will."

"But, Mama—"

"He will."

ELLIE TOOK SUE COX's car for a quick ride over to Sissy's
trailer to see little Bobby. Sue Cox stayed to finish what she'd started.
She painted her way into the bedroom, where Bena was on her
knees working on the baseboard trim. Sue Cox traded her roller for
a brush and silently went at the door trim. She and Bena didn't speak
for the longest time, each of them mesmerized by their task. Bena
liked the silence in the room. She liked looking over and seeing Sue
Cox at work. Her slacks were already ruined with white splatters,
but either Sue Cox didn't know it or didn't care. Bena watched
the way Sue Cox bit her bottom lip while she painted, the way
she stepped back from time to time and squinted to get the general
effect.

"It must seem weird to you that I moved into your house without Lucky," Bena finally said.

"It's not my house." Sue Cox never took her eyes off the spot she
was painting.

"Well, it's not really mine either."

"It's Lucky's house," Sue Cox said. "That makes it your house."

"So, it doesn't bother you that Eddie and I have moved in?"

"I like picturing you in the house. Your kids too."

"Except Ellie. You seem to like picturing her in Atlanta."

"Ellie is happy in Atlanta."

"So, you're not worried that we'll do to your house what we did to this one?" Bena was more or less in control of the sentences she was speaking, choosing her words—but she wasn't in control of their snide delivery.

"Nope," Sue Cox said. "I'm not worried."

"We probably will, you know? Mess everything up."

"Fine with me."

Bena laughed and dropped her brush in the paint tray. "Okay, I get it."

Sue Cox looked at Bena, "Get what?"

"You're being so nice—because I'm not being nice."

"And?" Sue Cox looked confused.

"You want to be the nice one. Just this once. Is that it?"

Sue Cox broke into a smile. "Fuck you."

"It doesn't suit you," Bena went on, "being nice."

"Is that right?" Sue Cox walked over to where Bena was sitting on her knees.

"I like you better the other way."

"The other way?"

"You know, bitchy, selfish, causing trouble."

"Oh." Sue Cox was grinning ear to ear now. "You mean like this?" She ran her paintbrush down the side of Bena's face and on down across the front of her shirt.

Bena grabbed her brush and slapped white paint across Sue Cox's slacks. "Oops," she said.

Sue Cox was undaunted. She put one of her bare feet in the paint tray and deliberately stepped on Bena's leg. Then she kicked at Bena like she might do it again, like she might walk all over her and leave white footprints to prove it.

Bena went into the hall, got the bucket of paint off the ladder, and came back. The can was only a fourth full, but she held it in two hands like a weapon. "Now what are you going to do?"

Sue Cox backed up against a still-wet wall. "Damn!" she shrieked. Her whole backside was white.

Bena waved the paint can like she was preparing to sling it.

"Don't you dare." It was Sue Cox's mannish order-giving voice. "I mean it, Bena."

Bena stepped toward her and Sue Cox screamed. For a matter of seconds Bena was on the verge of throwing the bucket of paint at Sue Cox. It would feel good. She knew that.

Sue Cox took Bena's hesitation as a sign of momentary surrender and slung her brush at Bena, hitting her on the side of her head, getting paint in her hair. Bena reared back and slung the can, sloshing paint over Sue Cox as she ran out of the room half screaming, half laughing. "You bitch. I can't believe you."

Bena came after her, her laughter on the verge of leaping off the edge. It came hard, like something falling down. It was so funny, the look on Sue Cox's face, the way she laughed, breathless, in a state of total disbelief. Then laughter took Bena over too. It was like if you took a block of ice and ran it through a huge blender so that it could be spit out in little bursts of hysteria. So that it could all come loose from its cold storage and spill out like hundreds of sparkling ice chips.

Sue Cox's throaty laughter was loud and soulful. She was practically howling. "I'm going to tell Lucky on you," she said. "Boy, have you got that fool fooled." Before she finished the sentence Sue Cox sobered up and tried to get it back from where it was suspended in the air between them. But it was too late.

Bena, laughing one minute, then nearly strangling. It was the word *Lucky*. Lucky'd come so close to setting her free, and he'd done it by marrying her, which made no sense at all. Now his absence kept her prisoner, locked behind a wall of questions. She had a question for every second the clock counted out on its round, startled face.

Bena looked at Sue Cox, whose expression was fearful, almost stricken with the certainty that she'd said the wrong thing. Sue Cox was the sort of person who always said the wrong thing—even when she meant well—because it came natural to her. *Wrong* was what she knew best and did best and could always be counted on to deliver in the place of what was actually needed. But the look on Sue Cox's apologetic face was as raw and naked and afraid as Bena felt every morning when she got up and forced herself to look in the mirror.

Bena and Sue Cox looked at each other the way women often look at each other, like a couple of distorted mirrors reflecting back and forth images they both recognize and both resist claiming. They see how much alike they are, sisters in their rage and bewilderment, sisters in their endless cycles of courage and fear, sisters in their ability to love nearly everyone else more than they love themselves. Bena saw herself in the terror in Sue Cox's squinted eyes—and Bena was pitiful there. Small and lost.

"Where's Lucky?" Bena's voice was childlike. "Where is he?" She was weeping like she had not since she'd said good-bye to her sixth graders, sent them too soon into the too hot, too hostile world.

"Oh God, Bena. Don't," Sue Cox whispered.

Bena buried her face in her hands, not to hide her anguish but so she could catch the gasps and whimpers as they ripped loose and broke out of her.

Sue Cox said, *Don't cry* automatically even though she and Bena both understood—maybe all women understand—that in this world there is crying to be done and sometimes you do your own crying and sometimes some other woman—one you don't even know, or wish you hated, or are afraid of—cries for you. No woman does all her own crying in this life—or ever cries only for herself.

Sue Cox rocked Bena back and forth and let her own tears come too.

"He's not dead," Bena gasped.

"Shhhhhh," Sue Cox whispered.

"He's not dead." Bena wept like a fish yanked from the water and left to drown in the dryness of the wrong world. There was something inside out about it.

Sue Cox wiped her paint-covered face with the tail of her paint-covered shirt. "Here's what I know," she said. "Death is the only thing that could keep Lucky away from you. If he's not dead then he's out there somewhere trying to come home."

"That's right." Bena nodded. "I know that."

They heard the car door slam when Ellie drove up. She barged into the kitchen the way she always did, letting the screen door bang behind her. The sight before her stopped her in her tracks. She looked at Bena, then Sue Cox.

"Oh my God," she cried. "Sue Cox, what did you do to Mama?"

THAT WAS THE LAST crying Bena did. Even the night she couldn't sleep and felt the earth rotating on its axis so certainly that she nearly rolled from her bed and floated off into the star-studded Milky Way, she didn't cry. She could feel the grinding movement of the solar system in which she was even less than the proverbial speck and she knew that somewhere something was happening—and that it affected her profoundly—even if she wasn't sure what it was. Bena got up and dressed. Lying still made her seasick. The world was going around and around so predictably, the natural order of things conspiring to keep her from sleeping.

Bena looked in on Eddie, who had—for reasons unknown—stopped locking his bedroom door. Inside he slept like the little boy he'd once been, face puffed, mouth open, Tom at his feet dreaming a dog dream.

Bena put on her flip-flops and slipped out the front door and drove away as quietly as she could. On some level she must have known where she was going, although her destination wasn't clear to her at first. She couldn't get fast-food coffee at this hour and didn't want to walk into the all-night truck stop alone. She drove by Sissy's trailer, all lights out, Cole's expensive car parked out front, and kept going.

She wanted to be alone, but not alone. When she turned onto the road to Fellowship Baptist it was obvious where she'd been going, and what she'd do.

She parked behind the church and got out and walked across the noisy gravel parking lot. It was pitch-dark except for the quivering yellow light above the back entrance, looking like a giant firefly perched there. The door wasn't locked, just as she knew it wouldn't be. Mayfred had explained to Bena that God didn't want His houses locked up so that nobody could get in to see Him in the off-hours. Mayfred was on the committee that decided the back door should always stay unlocked.

The sanctuary was smaller in the dark. Bena took off her flip-flops because they were too noisy in such silence and she walked barefoot down the aisle to the pulpit. Several years ago a church member who worked for Carpet World had donated the red-and-black swirly-design carpet runner to the congregation. It had been ordered for a Denny's restaurant that had changed its mind. Jerry Lee had volunteered to install it, which he'd done with a hammer, pounding roofing nails into the wooden floor. She'd heard him tell the story.

Bena knelt at the front of the church and bowed her head— thankful that no one was around to see her. She'd never had God's undivided attention. She'd never spoken out loud to God either. In the darkness it was easier to do. "God all powerful." She looked up toward the ceiling. "I guess you know why I'm here."

She stood up and looked around her and waited for a sign. She waited maybe ten minutes before lying down on the front pew and falling asleep.

It was the sunrise that woke her up.

THERE WAS A POLICE CAR parked in front of the house when Bena got home. She slammed on the brakes with thoughts of turning the car around and gunning back out to the highway and going as far away as she could as fast as she could. Instead, she held her breath and coasted into the drive.

Eddie hurried to open Bena's car door. "Damn, where the heck you been, Mama? The police ringing the doorbell at the crack of dawn and I can't find you anywhere." He looked distraught. "You ever heard of leaving somebody a note?"

The look on Eddie's face made her ashamed, his fear so obvious. When he was little and swore he didn't drink any Kool-Aid, his cherry-red mustache always gave him away. His inept devotion to secrecy broke her heart.

"What are they doing here?" Bena nodded toward the police.

"They're saying they found Lucky, Mama."

Bena sank back into the seat and closed her eyes.

"They're crazy, Mama. Got some photo from Mexico saying it's Lucky. But it ain't. It's some old guy in a wheelchair. Don't look nothing like Lucky."

"My God," Bena whispered. "Let me see it."

As she got out of the car Eddie grabbed her arm. "That detective guy is with them, Mama. Don't let him fast-talk you into believing anything."

Bena invited the two policemen and the detective inside. "I'll make us some coffee," she said. They followed her into the house and Tom had such a barking fit that Eddie had to lock him in the bedroom. Bena put coffee on while the men waited politely. "Nice place you got out here," the older policeman said. "Private."

"Thanks," Bena said.

They waited while Bena poured the hot coffee into mugs and handed each of them one. "There's cream and sugar right there." She pointed to the countertop.

The younger policeman scooped sugar into his coffee. "The detective here has got something he'd like you to take a look at, Mrs. Eckerd."

"It's Mrs. McKale," Bena corrected. She recognized the young policeman as a boy Sissy had gone to school with. He'd taken Sissy to a Christmas dance in seventh grade. Sissy had been a good five inches taller than he was then.

"If you want to take a look at this." The detective put the photographs out on the kitchen table. "We tracked your husband's sister DeeDee down to Guadalajara. A clinic down there."

"What kind of clinic?"

"Pretty much voodoo if you ask me. They claim to cure everything from the common cold to brain tumors. They're selling hope is all it is. Hope is damn expensive too."

Bena looked at the first photo. The quality was bad, grainy and dark. A blond woman was pushing an old man in his wheelchair. It wasn't Lucky. The old man was mostly bald and looked toothpick thin. His skin was loose, hanging from his face. Bena had never seen him before.

"You recognize him?" the detective asked.

The second photo was of the old man on a terrace. The blond woman was helping him stand up. It was out of focus, but even so Bena could tell it wasn't Lucky. Not his eyes. Not his square face. Not his hand on the blond woman's arm. "Nope," Bena said. "Don't recognize him."

"Look again," the detective said.

"It's not Lucky," Bena said.

"I told you." Eddie spoke up. "We never saw that old man before."

"The woman is DeeDee McKale," the detective said. "She identified this man as her brother when she checked him into the clinic."

"I think I'd know my own husband," Bena said.

"People can change when they get sick."

"Even sick," Bena said, "I'd recognize Lucky."

"You hold on to these photographs," the detective said. "You think it over."

As they were leaving, the detective said, "Mrs. McKale, according to our information DeeDee McKale and her companion checked out of the clinic more than three weeks ago. It's possible that the patient has died since then. If he's not your husband it won't matter to you, but if it is?"

• • •

IT WAS ANNA KAYE who told Bena that if Lucky didn't come back in due time, and if Bena had made a good-faith effort to search for him, she could have him declared legally dead. "My daddy says sometimes a family has to do that so they can get on with their lives." Anna Kaye's daddy was a lawyer. He had represented Barrett when he had those drug charges against him. He had managed to get Barrett off both times.

THE OLD HOUSE had begun to look so good that Eddie and Anna Kaye cleaned out Eddie's old bedroom too. Bena assumed it was Anna Kaye's idea. They boxed up the stuff Eddie wanted to keep and hauled the rest to the Salvation Army. They got rid of the old TV too, gave it to Sissy for her trailer. Now the only furnished room in the house was Ellie's—which, in due time, Bena was planning to paint, too.

JOE SHOWED UP at the old house on a Saturday afternoon. Bena was overcome. She ran to him, threw her arms around his neck, and kissed his face.

"Damn, Mama," Eddie said. "Don't show any partiality or anything."

"You already know I love you," Bena said. "Joe's not so sure."

Joe looked taller to Bena, his shoulders more pronounced, and his face was squaring up too, giving him a grown look—or maybe it'd just been a long time since she'd laid eyes on him.

"Eddie said you needed some help ripping out the carpet over here," Joe said. "We figured the two of us could get it for you."

"Wonderful." She put her arms around them. "When is the last time I had some time with both my boys?"

"All right then," Joe said. "Let's take a look." He walked inside to look around.

. . .

IN THE MANNER of big brothers Joe took the role of giving orders. He figured out what tools they needed, where they should start, and how they should go about it.

"Your job, Mama," Joe said, "is to run to the store and get us some cold beer."

"Beer?"

"Mama," Joe said. "Eddie is a lot older than his years. You know that better than anybody."

"Come on, Mama," Eddie chimed in. "A cold beer never hurt anybody."

Bena didn't argue. She obeyed almost like an anxious-to-please child, getting in her car and driving down to the 7-Eleven, humming as she went. To see Joe and Eddie doing something together—a man sort of thing, too—was beautiful. And it was for her—their mother, who did not have a man. Two good boys can equal one good man, can't they? Maybe two sons who love you are as good—maybe even better—than one husband who says he loves you, then comes up missing for so long that you worry yourself nearly out of what remains of your mind.

Bena hadn't felt safe since Lucky left. Not the sort of safe where you're unafraid of dark parking lots at the mall and strange noises at night and rapists on the loose. The other kind of safe—where you're unafraid of your own thoughts, what your heart whispers to you, what your dreams make you believe. The sort of safe that comes when you sleep every night and wake up every morning beside someone whose soul has made love to yours, whose soul sleeps in your menstrual blood and never minds, whose soul introduces you to your own soul in such a way that, at last, you fall in love with yourself.

WHEN BENA GOT back with the beer Joe and Eddie took a break. Joe popped a beer and handed it to Bena. "Here, Mama, drown your sorrows."

Bena took a long swig of beer and felt it scratch its way down her throat as if she'd swallowed a simple—only mildly unpleasant —truth, putting far more effort into it than it required. When had everything become so much more than it appeared to be? When had Bena started insisting that everything mean something else? Her worried mind wouldn't let things alone. Nothing was simple anymore. Especially not the truth. It lurked everywhere, camouflaged in the ordinary. Maybe the truth wasn't champagne or wine or an expensive after-dinner drink only for those who could afford it and knew enough to ask for it. Maybe the truth was the beer in her hand. She took another drink. There was enough to it to intoxicate her over time, but mostly it was unremarkable in its mild bitterness and its ready availability to nearly anyone. Lord, she was doing it again, making one thing mean something else. A cold beer on a hot day. You just pop the cap and guzzle. That was what Joe and Eddie did. Poured beer down their throats like it was the truth—at last.

THERE'S A MOMENT when a mother realizes her job is nearly done. Anything's she left unfinished will stay unfinished forever. In just the span of a few heartbeats she realizes that her children see her as someone to be looked after—just the way she's always seen them. They begin to worry about her the same way she worries about them. A rare moment of balance—when you've lost your own.

All evening Bena watched her sons rip up carpet. They looked more like men than boys when they were bent with hammer and tools, prying loose strips of carpet nails, ripping back heavy carpet, scraping up the rotted pad glued to the floor, their muscles knotting under their skin, their bare chests gleaming.

When they were playing baseball or running for the finish line it had seemed just an exhausting sort of play—a male kind of fun involving sweat and scores and stopwatches. When they'd caught pop flies or won races, she hadn't seen the men they were becoming. But seeing them now, brothers, so different, so much the same, working side by side in silent harmony, handing off tools, trading orders, tugging together, harder, harder, until the carpet yielded and ripped loose in their hands. It was beautiful in an odd way, seeing that they worked hard and well, stopping only for beer, sweating like grown men, not quitting until they'd done what they set out to do.

It was so ungodly hot in the house. Even the fans were sluggish and hopeless against the humid air and the smell of fresh paint and old carpet glue. Bena cleared her throat and asked in her most harmless tone, "How's Lisa doing, Joe?"

Joe mopped his brow and looked at his mother. "She's great."

"That's good," Bena offered.

THE GOOD THING about the smell of paint fumes is that mosquitoes hate it about as much as people do. But the crickets were hard at it, laying claim to the night as usual. Bena saw the headlights coming up the drive before she heard the horn blow.

"Who in the world?" She looked out the kitchen window.

"Probably Sissy," Joe said. "We told her to come by when she got off work."

It was a van that Bena didn't recognize. But Sissy was always catching rides in unfamiliar vehicles. Still, it made Bena nervous—a strange van this time of night. The horn blowing like that. It gave her that same creepy feeling she used to get when Barrett drove his beat-up van up and down their drive—just a lot of nonstop heartache on wheels.

"Sissy likes to let people know she's coming," Eddie said. "So they can stop what they're doing and bow at her feet."

"You love Sissy, Eddie." Bena spoke in automatic-mother tone.

"Yeah, I love her," Eddie said. "But she's still a freak."

Bena stepped out the kitchen door just as the van pulled up beside the carport. It looked like Sissy was driving. As Bena took a couple of steps closer to the van, the driver opened the door and got out. "Hey there," she said.

Bena felt her knees weaken under her. She felt the fish fast-tail through her head, a school of them darting savagely. "Sissy?" she said, knowing full well it was not Sissy. But not trusting what she knew.

"No," the woman said. "It's me, DeeDee. Lucky's sister. I brought him home."

9

It was the catlike sound coming from Bena that brought Joe and Eddie out into the yard. "What's going on?" Joe said.

"Where is he?" Bena asked.

"He's in a bed there in the back of the van." DeeDee pointed.

Bena walked slowly toward the van, as if any quick movement might chase this moment away, make it vanish the way a good dream does when you roll over in bed.

"He's medicated," DeeDee said. "He's been sleeping most of the way. He doesn't wake up much."

DeeDee opened the side door, and as dark as it was Bena could barely make out the shape of a sleeping man. It could be any man. How could she have forgotten the way Lucky looked lying in a bed? He was thin as a coat hanger and had not shaved in so long that his face was silver and bristly, making him look old and unloved. If you didn't know him you could mistake him for one of the homeless guys you saw sleeping on the streets of Atlanta. "Lucky?" Bena reached to touch his face. He was sleeping hard, his mouth slack, saliva dried on his lips. He didn't wake to her touch. Didn't even stir.

"Let's take him home," Bena said. She climbed in the van beside him, into the rolling tomb of urine-soaked blankets.

JOE AND EDDIE led the way home in Lucky's truck, DeeDee followed in the van. Bena and DeeDee rode most of the way in silence, Bena watching Lucky's face for any sign he might sense her presence, wake up, and be happy to see her. She ran her fingers over him, touching his hands, his ears, his belly where his T-shirt was tangled and his ribs showed through as if she were looking at an X ray instead of a man. She couldn't keep her hands off him.

"I was scared we wouldn't make it," DeeDee said. "Been driving day and night."

"Thank God you came."

"He thought they could cure him. He was so hell-bent on getting well he wouldn't listen to reason."

"You're here now," Bena said. "That's the important thing."

"I haven't had a cigarette since we left." DeeDee held up her trembling hand for Bena to see. "I used to smoke a pack a day."

"I'm so grateful to you," Bena said. "We all are."

"The doctors don't give him long," DeeDee said quietly. "It started out in his stomach, but now it's made its way, you know. It's spread. The doctors didn't think he'd survive this trip."

"But he did," Bena said.

EDDIE AND JOE carried Lucky into the house. It was a sight to see, the deliberate way they carried him—gentler by far than the way they carried little Bobby, bouncing him, pretending to toss him into the air. But Lucky, they held him steady and tight, as near upright as possible. They handled him like he was the most fragile sort of treasure, maybe their mother's only chance at happiness, like they would rather die than drop him and watch their mother's life bust all to hell a second time. "We got you, man," Joe said to Lucky, who didn't respond at all, his head flung back, his mouth still gaping, his eyes fluttering in a sort of drug-induced sleepiness.

They put him in his own bed and Bena rushed to open the windows and let the hot, bug-infested night air fill the bedroom, thinking the sounds and smells of home, if not enough to wake him, might at least comfort him.

"Eddie, honey," Bena said, "let DeeDee have your room, okay?"

"Mama, I don't need you to tell me that. I was already planning on it."

That was the last thing Bena remembered about the night. That Eddie and Joe and DeeDee were suddenly gone and she was alone with Lucky, her husband, who was barely recognizable. She undressed him and sponge-bathed him in warm water, lingering on his vacant face. Then she got undressed herself, turned off the light, and got in bed beside him. His smell was stale and medicinal. Even his skin had a sour chemical odor. She positioned him on his side so that his arm could wrap around her. She whispered love words to him, and stroked his unfamiliar face. Even when she heard Tom scratching at the door she didn't let him in. She'd waited too long for this moment to share it—even with Tom. A thousand times, she paused to thank God and make Him a whole new set of promises. She fell asleep easily and slept like there was no tomorrow.

THE FOLLOWING DAY Joe and Eddie helped her bathe Lucky in the tub. Then Joe lathered and shaved his face. By noon Sissy and Bobby were at the house, along with Mayfred and Jerry Lee, who had brought a Bible with certain verses underlined for just such an occasion. Juanita had called to say she would be by later with a pot of tortilla soup. Ellie and Sue Cox were on their way from Atlanta. Lucky's bath seemed to help his medicine wear off a little. He opened his eyes and began to look around, but his stare was blank, his eyes flat and dull. When he was awake enough to eat, Bena tried to feed him some oatmeal. Tom sat on the bed beside Lucky, licking his unresponsive hands and feet.

DeeDee slept all day long. Twice Bena looked in on her to be sure she was okay. DeeDee was the one who knew about Lucky's medicine. But unless Lucky took a turn for the worse, Bena was not going to disturb DeeDee.

Sunday evening Sissy brought Dr. Hays to the house. He'd been having dinner with his family out at the country club and Sissy had begged him to come home with her and take a look at Lucky. It was a rare man who could resist one of Sissy's modest requests. Even she didn't seem to understand her power yet, although Bena did, and all the rest of them too. Of course Dr. Hays would come. He would come immediately. He had been the one who'd looked after Leslie the time she was eaten alive with poison ivy and the one who gave Eddie the tetanus shot when a stray cat bit him in the stomach.

Everybody gathered to watch Dr. Hays examine Lucky. Lucky neither resisted nor cooperated. His eyes opened sometimes, but it was clear that he saw nothing—saw no one. "What medicine is he on?" Dr. Hays asked.

DeeDee brought him a manila folder full of test results and obscure medical information and the plastic bag she kept his medicines in. Dr. Hays read each label and shook his head. "Sleeping pills, antidepressants, painkillers, tranquilizers. Damn. No wonder the man is a zombie." He ordered Bena to stop all medication except the painkillers and even then to administer them only if she thought Lucky was in real pain. "Get as many fluids in him as you can," he said. "Let's get his system flushed out and see what we got then."

THE THIRD DAY Lucky was slightly more alert than he'd been. He seemed to be understanding where he was—at least in brief flashes. He didn't say anything, but his eyes followed the people who came in and out of his room, and he was able to pet Tom and shake his head no when DeeDee tried to give him his apple juice.

By the end of that week he was sitting propped up in bed. His steady stream of visitors had relaxed. His appetite was slightly better. His eyes had come back to life—there was a tiny spark of light in them. The first time he spoke it was to Sue Cox. He looked at her fussing around his room, tidying up the bed covers, and said, "Didn't I used to be married to you?"

She laughed like a crazy woman, thought it was the funniest, most wonderful thing she'd ever heard anybody say and repeated it all day to everyone she saw until she was on everybody's nerves.

BENA CALLED THE Baxter County extension agent to come out and explain to her what needed to be done to put Lucky's pond in. It was not the agent's first trip out to the place. But this time Bena was in charge, and she was determined to make Lucky's dream come true while there was still time for him to know it. He had money set aside in a savings account, plus she could sell the timber off the lot when they cleared it. The extension agent came back a second time with a crew, and using what looked like yellow crime-scene tape, they marked off the area where the pond should go. It'd be a decent-sized pond. But more important, it'd be a real pond.

THREE WEEKS AFTER Lucky got home he was able to get up and go to the bathroom himself. He held his own cups and bowls when Bena brought his food—although he ate next to nothing. He took a shower every morning and every night, just braced himself against the tile and let the spray rain down on him until Bena got worried and went in and turned the water off. "Back in bed," she'd say. "You're going to drown in there."

The night before the bulldozers and backhoes were due to begin digging the pond, Bena was so wound up she couldn't sleep. Lucky

must have sensed something. He kept his eyes on her for a long time
and finally said. "I wanted to come back to you a well man."

Bena turned to stare at him. It was the first real sentence he'd spoken to her.

"I didn't want it to be like this," he said. "You looking after me this
way."

"Would it help you to know I considered just shooting you?"

Lucky smiled. The old Lucky, with the smile Bena had ached to
see.

"I been sick a long time," he said. "I thought I could outrun it, you
know? Thought I already had."

"You're here now," Bena said. "We're together."

"I thought about you, Bena. I swear to God. You can ask DeeDee.
All I wanted was to get cured and get home. I didn't want you to
have to watch me die."

Bena ran her fingers down the side of Lucky's face. "If we all got
half of what we wanted, that wouldn't be so bad, I guess."

"The truth is, I got scared of dying alone, Bena."

Bena nodded. She understood.

"You might decide to go on and shoot me before this is over,"
Lucky said.

"Hush," Bena said. "I don't want to shoot you before tomorrow.
I got a big surprise for you tomorrow."

THE HEAVY EQUIPMENT arrived at six sharp the following
morning. By noon they had most of the trees cleared and a couple of
loads of timber hauled off the property. It was alarming, how skint
things looked. How injured the land seemed. You might think everything was ruined if you didn't know better.

Several times that day Bena tried to get Lucky up to look out the
window, see what was going on. But Lucky was gone again to that
blank space where he spent most of his time now. When he was like
this no room had any windows or doors. There was no escape from

a room like that. Bena would have to wait until he woke up in a different room one morning. When he knew it was daylight and that Bena was his wife.

Dr. Hays came by weekly now. He talked about making Lucky comfortable. He never said a word about making him well.

WHEN THEY SAW that Lucky seemed to be doing better, Sue Cox and Ellie headed back to Atlanta. Sue Cox had a business to run, after all. And Joe had had to get back to Tuscaloosa and take his summer exams so he didn't lose the credits he needed to be eligible for baseball. He'd promised to try to track Leslie and Corby down and tell them they could stop worrying—that Lucky was home.

They'd all had their private moments with Lucky. And their own good reasons for leaving.

But it was a surprise to Bena when she woke up one morning to find a note from DeeDee on the kitchen table.

I hate good-bye. Never have been any good at it. Lucky knows I love him more than life. These last months I have said good-bye to him a dozen times, thinking he was taking his last breath. I can't do it again. I hope you understand. I know Lucky does. Thank you for everything, Bena. I know I am leaving Lucky in good hands. He is where he belongs.

Love, DeeDee

Bena went to the door and looked out and saw that the van was gone. She would miss sitting out on the porch while DeeDee smoked a cigarette—her nerves, she said—and talked about Lucky and her, the crazy kids they'd been, the crazy life they'd lived, the way that craziness had bonded them forever. The fact that Lucky was the only man who ever really understood DeeDee. That was what she'd said. "Lucky was the only man."

There were remnants of beauty left over from DeeDee's high

school days, but time had done its dirty work the way time usually does. Now DeeDee was a fragile woman who'd smoked one pack of cigarettes too many, gotten one suntan too many, laughed at one bad joke too many, lost one low-wage job too many, made one low-rent move too many, dyed her hair one color too many, and married at least a couple of men too many. She was tired. She'd tell you that. Bena sensed DeeDee was shutting down from the inside out, the way you batten down a house before a tornado hits.

Bena had offered to let DeeDee move into her old house, stay as long as she liked, forever if she wanted to. But DeeDee had declined. "Got to get back." She'd smiled. "A moving target is harder to hit."

BENA TOOK A leave of absence from work. She barely even noticed when school started back. Eddie was a junior and inches taller than Bena. He turned seventeen the first week of school. Mayfred and LaVonte came to stay with Lucky while Bena dragged Eddie out to the Golden Corral to celebrate his birthday with a steak and baked potato. Anna Kaye met them for dessert and brought a cake she'd made herself. She had written on it, *Happy Birthday, Eddie, I love you.* Seeing the *I love you* scrawled there in blue icing nearly made Bena cry. It touched her that of all the boys in Baxter County, Anna Kaye loved Eddie. Her Eddie. That fact alone made Bena love Anna Kaye. Like any mother, Bena wanted the whole world to love her son. She thought he deserved at least that.

For his birthday Bena gave Eddie a gift certificate to Gayfer's so he could get himself some new school clothes. Anna Kaye could help him pick them out.

IT TOOK THE work crew nearly two weeks to dig the pond. The loud noise of the machinery was pleasant to Bena. It gave her something else to focus on, a different kind of excitement to distract her from the excitement of this involuntary letting go she was caught in. Even in terrible loss, the kind you dread most, there is a strange excitement.

Bena called the Hospital Supply and got a wheelchair and a hospital bed delivered. The hospital bed she put in the middle of the main room, facing where the pond would soon be. It had a button Lucky could push to sit himself up or lie himself down. Every morning after he doused himself in the shower, she dressed him in sweats and a T-shirt, and situated him in the hospital bed so he could watch the men and machinery while he pretended to eat Cream of Wheat or frozen yogurt. Some days Bena had to help him every step of the way, and even then he sat in a stupor, staring at the ceiling or the curtains instead of the miracle taking shape right in front of his eyes.

It was after one very frustrating day where Lucky seemed to be backing up to the place where he wasn't Lucky anymore—he had lots of days like that, when Bena could just have easily been tending to a total stranger—that one of the workmen from the pond crew rang the doorbell. His clothes were caked with red clay, as was his skin. He had sweated through the cap he wore, so he took it off and held it in his hand. Bena recognized the man because he liked to pause to eat his lunch out in the yard, where the grass was mowed, while the rest of the crew tended to eat in their parked trucks. Afterward sometimes he lay down under a dogwood tree and took a short nap before going back to work on the pond.

"You don't know me, ma'am," he said when Bena opened the door. "My name is Buck. I believe you're married to my brother."

He didn't have the McKale look. In all the ways that Lucky and DeeDee were square, Buck was round. But he did have DeeDee's blond coloring, and his hair was curled and sweated to his face like it had been glued there. He was red-faced too, like lots of the men working on the pond. Too much sun, she thought, and maybe too much liquor too.

"Come in," Bena said.

Buck sat in a chair beside Lucky's bed while Bena got him a glass of cold tea. If he ever said a word, Bena didn't hear it. Lucky looked through Buck the same no-see way that he looked through her. When Bena brought his ice tea Buck was petting Tom nervously. "He don't look a bit good." Buck nodded at Lucky. "Don't hardly recognize him."

"You need to catch him on a good day sometime," Bena said. "On a good day he'd be real happy to see you." Bena turned to Lucky and shook his foot gently to see if he would make eye contact, but he didn't. "Lucky," she said too loudly, "look who's here. It's Buck. Your brother Buck."

You could see that Lucky was breathing, but otherwise he was lifeless.

When Bena showed Buck to the door he said, "Ma'am, if you don't object, I'd like to stop by and see ole Lucky now and then. We been lost to each other a hell of a long time."

"You stop in anytime," she said. "And my name is Bena."

Buck paused at the door and said, "I don't know what kind of man Lucky become, but he was always a real good boy."

NEARLY EVERY WEEKDAY afternoon after that Buck stopped in to check on Lucky, sit with him five minutes tops, then put his cap back on and left. Lots of days Bena could smell the liquor on his breath. But she poured him some ice tea and sat him at Lucky's bedside. Sometimes she heard Buck say under his breath, "Hey there, old man." Once she heard him say, "Hell of a pond you're puttin' in out there."

ONCE THE POND was dug there was nothing to do but wait for rain. Bena found herself praying for an all-out storm. Some evenings when he was up to it Bena took Lucky for a walk out in the yard, where he could breathe the hot air and smell the upturned earth. Other times she put Lucky in his wheelchair and she and Tom pushed him around so he could see the huge red scar that would become the pond he had always dreamed of. Bena was almost desperate for Lucky to understand the wonder of it all. It was an ugly sight by any standards, the blood-red hole in the ground that Bena was already calling a pond. It looked like a giant bullet wound, the flesh around it ragged and raw. The rains would be the salve. The rains would soften the edges of the thing and make it beautiful.

THE RARE MOMENTS when Lucky came into himself were priceless to Bena. One night he woke her up and said, "Bena, God ain't going to heal me, is He? Why you think that is?" Bena had been startled and speechless at his coherence. "You think I should of gone to church more? You think it's because I never did walk the aisle? DeeDee walked the aisle—and damn, look at her mess of a life. Where is DeeDee? What the hell happened to DeeDee?"

Other nights Lucky might be mostly silent, but talked to Bena gently with his hands, running his fingers lightly over her face and arms or reaching for her hand and kissing her fingers one at a time.

One night when Eddie was home from track practice and eating his supper on the foot of Lucky's bed, Lucky said to him with all the authority in the world, "Eddie, you got to be strong, you hear me. You got to be strong because I can't be. Not anymore."

"Okay," Eddie said.

ONCE BENA WOKE UP from a stolen nap because she smelled something awful. A burning smell. She looked out to see if the men had come back to burn more debris out by the pond, but nothing was stirring there. She ran into the kitchen and found Lucky standing at the stove, smiling. "Making some soup," he said.

Bena saw that he had put a can of chicken noodle soup in a pot and turned the gas on high. The tin can was burning and the paper wrapper was singed and curling. She yanked the pot off the stove and put it under the faucet. The hissing of the water hitting the hot can filled the kitchen with steam. "If you get hungry, you tell me," Bena yelled. "Damn it, Lucky, you could have burned the house down."

He looked so puzzled. He looked like the child she imagined he had once been, anxious to please, trying to be helpful, thinking that if he was good enough then all the bad things would stop happening to him, to his family, to the whole world.

SEVERAL NIGHTS LATER Lucky got out of bed to go to the bathroom. "You want me to come with you?" Bena asked.

"Nope," he said. "I'm okay." He was as coherent as a judge, and the bathroom was only steps away. Bena woke up a while later and saw Lucky hadn't come back to bed. She panicked and leaped up to search for him. "Lucky!" she yelled. "God, where are you?"

In minutes Eddie was up and sharing Bena's panic. He ran through the house hollering, "Lucky!" Tom was barking. Bena saw that the kitchen door was hanging wide open and her heart stopped. Outside, it was the blackest sort of night. You couldn't see your hand in front of your face. She and Eddie ran outside, stumbling, calling. There was no immediate sign of him. Eddie went to look in the vehicles in case Lucky'd gotten in and fallen asleep. Bena went back to the house for a flashlight, a feeble pinpoint of useless light, which nonetheless made her feel better.

For over an hour they searched the yard and the edge of the woods. Eddie ran all the way to the end of the drive and back but found nothing. "I hope to God he hadn't wandered onto the highway."

Bena immediately thought of the cats, that Lucky had found them because their mother had wandered onto the highway.

"Mama, you go in and call Sissy and tell her to call Cole. Call Jerry Lee and LaVonte too. Call the police if you want to. We got to have some help."

For the second time in a matter of weeks Bena obeyed her son's instructions without asking questions. She went in and called Sissy, waking her up and scaring her half to death. Luckily, Cole was there and took the phone from Sissy. "We're on our way," Cole said. "We'll call the others."

Bena went through the house and turned on every single light. Just in case Lucky was wandering around out there in the night in his know-nothing condition, maybe he'd have instincts like insects do and travel toward the light. Maybe his blood would tell him to do it. Maybe a flood of light would shock him into remembering just long enough to make it into the yard, where they could find him.

Bena searched the woods like a blind woman. Nothing except her desperation to find Lucky could entice her into the woods in pitch darkness. She tripped and fell every other step, unable to distinguish a thorn from a snakebite. In her imagination she stepped on at least a hundred writhing snakes and every one of them bit her at least once. She imagined Lucky had fallen into a nest of snakes and they had paralyzed him with bites.

In blackness like this all Bena had was her fear. The rising of that fear the only reminder that she was still alive. "Lucky!" Bena screamed. "For God's sake, answer me." This must be how it was in Lucky's head, just so much blackness, and no path anywhere. It must seem like left and right are the same and up and down too and that no matter what step you take in what direction something is waiting there to hurt you—at least a little. Bena's fear-driven panic made her think she was caught in that windowless, doorless room where Lucky was spending more and more of his time. She screamed for him in a voice she had never used before. It came from some small, terrified place inside her. "Lucky, please God!"

Bena could hear Sissy calling for Lucky from the yard and Cole and Jerry Lee shouting orders back and forth. When the police arrived they shone a huge light in waves across the back of the lot, like they were signaling for an airplane to land in the yard. Lucky McKale, pilot of the nothingness of this world, could make a safe landing there if only he would. Or maybe they were signaling some unidentified flying object to swoop down and take Lucky up and away from this unimaginative planet, where the only choice left for him was one of an endless night like this one.

It was Eddie who found Lucky. "Mama!" he wailed like a siren. Bena ran toward his voice. The night had gone pale. The heavy blackness had turned to a murky purple and then that misty lavender of early light.

Eddie had picked Lucky up and was carrying him in his arms. Lucky had made his way out to the pond and beyond. He was covered in red clay like a dusting of dried blood. Lucky was so frail he barely weighed anything, but it wouldn't have mattered; Eddie had strength that a boy finds only in the very worst moments of his life. Lucky seemed lifeless. He was scratched and bruised. Bena ran to him, but Eddie didn't stop, just put one foot in front of the other until he had delivered Lucky to the house, where there were paramedics waiting. They wanted to take Lucky away in the ambulance, but Bena wouldn't hear of it. She insisted Eddie put Lucky in his own bed. She let the paramedics check for broken bones and start IV fluids, thanked them, and showed them out. Then waited for Dr. Hays, who was on his way.

There must have been twenty cars parked in the yard, the police, an ambulance, and all sorts of neighbors and strangers, who had risen from their beds to chase Lucky through the black night, where, even after his rescue, he remained. Tom was lying beneath Lucky's hospital bed, whimpering. Ordinarily he would have a barking fit at so many people crowded around. Mayfred took charge of getting folks to leave and go home. She was firm and persuasive.

Dr. Hays arrived after most people had gone. He attached morphine to Lucky's IV and told Bena how to regulate it. "A matter of days," he told Bena. When he left Bena was so alarmingly calm that it frightened Sissy and she began to cry for Bena. She cried until she made Bobby cry too. Cole had to take them both home.

Mayfred called in sick and then set about straightening up Bena's orderly house. She got in the kitchen and began cleaning out the refrigerator, cooking up what she could, making room for what food would no doubt be coming soon. Jerry Lee and Eddie sat on the foot of Lucky's bed and stared at him until Bena couldn't stand it another minute and turned on the TV so that they'd have something to look at besides Lucky's gaunt, unconscious face. She put the TV on a sports channel. Lucky would have liked that.

"I got an errand to run," Bena said. "You look after Lucky until I get back."

"Where you going, Mama?" Eddie asked.

"I won't be long."

"You shouldn't leave now, Mama. It's not the right time."

Bena let the door slam behind her and took off in the car with Mayfred and Eddie both yelling at her, "Where you think you're going?"

WHEN BENA GOT home an hour later she unloaded the coils of water hose she'd bought at Wal-Mart. She was deliberate and precise, carrying them around to the back of the house, hooking the first length to the outdoor spigot.

"What the heck is Mama doing out there?" she heard Eddie ask.

Mayfred and Jerry Lee stood at the back door looking out at her. "Girl, what you up to?" Mayfred yelled. "You got a sick husband in here that needs you."

Bena unrolled the first length of hose as far as it would go, almost halfway across the sloping yard, then screwed in the second one. "Go out there and see what your mama thinks she's doing," Mayfred yelled to Eddie. "She might of gone off the deep end. Grief drives some folks under, for a fact."

Eddie walked out to where Bena was struggling with the hoses. They looked like rolled-up garter snakes, thin, long, unnaturally green. He saw she was attaching one length to the next. "Mama, what's going on?"

"I want to do this myself," she said. "Go back to the house. Stay with Lucky."

"Mama, you ought to be the one—"

"You heard what I said," Bena snapped. "I'm not going to let Lucky die and never see his pond full of water."

"What?"

"Go in the house," Bena ordered.

"Damn, Mama." Eddie walked back to where Mayfred and Jerry Lee were standing in the doorway. "She's going to try and fill up the pond." Eddie shook his head. "She's given up waiting for rain."

ALL AFTERNOON BENA worked to hook up the hoses and stretch them all the way from the house out to the gouged, sore place waiting to be a pond. It took eight hoses weaving between bushes and trees to reach that far.

When she walked back up to the house she saw the others gathered at the window looking out at her in pity. She turned on the water full blast, listened to it spit its way down the line, hissing and spraying at the leaky joints. She would let the water run until the pond filled up. She didn't care how long it took.

"We got some supper ready," Mayfred yelled out to Bena. "Come on in here and sit down and eat something."

When Bena came inside she saw that Buck was in the main room sitting by Lucky's bed. "Never heard of nobody filling up a pond with a water hose," he said.

THAT NIGHT AFTER everybody went home, Bena took her bath and lay down in the hospital bed beside Lucky, who was moving his head side to side in morphine sleep.

"Mama," Eddie said, "you care if me and Tom sleep in here on the sofa? Just in case." They settled in on Sue Cox's linen sofa and in minutes Eddie was asleep with his arm slung over his face.

During the night Lucky thrashed and twisted like a man being chased in a dream. Bena could pat him and whisper, "It's okay," and he would relax momentarily. She slept with her hand on him to make sure he didn't get up and wander off—or worse, float away—in the night.

DR. HAYS CAME by early every morning afterward on his way to the hospital for morning rounds and checked on Lucky. Sometimes he brought a sack of ham biscuits and left them on the kitchen table. Every morning at sunup Bena and Tom walked out to the pond to check the height of the water. Sometimes Eddie went too. On certain days when Eddie didn't want to go to school, Bena didn't make him.

Bena bathed Lucky, and Eddie lathered and shaved his face. When Lucky was rocking back and forth in bed it was hard to keep from nicking him. Tom spent most of the day sleeping on the foot of Lucky's bed, guarding him. If you called Lucky's name loud and clear, sometimes he might open his eyes and look at you.

One afternoon when Juanita brought her kids over, Jesus punched Lucky's arm and said, "Me and Jose got the new boots, Lucky. Look." It seemed like Lucky understood him and smiled. Carmelita was afraid of Lucky, his emaciated body and watery eyes, but the kids left him get-well pictures they'd drawn, and Juanita left some beans and rice and green-corn tamales.

AT THE END of the week the pond was maybe one-fourth full. Bena sat on the bank for an hour, watching the water inch upward.

Afternoon and night, the house filled with people. Mayfred and Juanita took charge of the kitchen. Eddie and Sissy answered phone calls. Cole walked around the yard and out to the pond, carrying little Bobby and yelling for Jesus and Jose to stay away from the water. Sometimes he organized them into a game of tag, sling the statue, or putt the ball into the bucket, anything to keep them occupied outside and out from underfoot. Juanita thought he was being a good sport, but the truth was, he didn't like to be around the spectacle of death. He told Sissy he hated watching a man cross over headfirst.

Bena and Anna Kaye gave Lucky a manicure. They sat on his bed, each taking one of his hands. It kept Lucky still and quiet, the massage, the clipping, the warm water, their voices as they talked to each other quietly while they were touching his fingers. Another night they soaked his feet in warm water and gave him a pedicure. It was harder because his feet were jerky, but they persisted and he seemed soothed, especially when they rubbed sweet-smelling lotion on the rough skin of his feet.

Sissy sat beside Lucky and combed his thin hair. He seemed to like it, the comb gently raking across his scalp. Usually they kept the TV on nonstop, a reminder of the ongoingness of the world beyond.

Jerry Lee liked to tell stories. Buck liked to see what sorts of desserts Mayfred had wrapped up in tinfoil in the kitchen. LaVonte liked to sit in Lucky's game-watching room with his sisters and flip the channels until a fight erupted. Joe called home every few days to get a report from Eddie or Sissy.

Sue Cox and Ellie called Bena like clockwork every afternoon when Ellie got in from school. Sue Cox said, "Bena, maybe this is not the right time, but you should know that my daddy bought Lucky and me burial plots out where he and Mama are buried. They're nice and they're paid for and if you want to use one for Lucky, you know, when the time comes, then—you can."

Bena had never given a moment's thought to where Lucky would be buried. Maybe it was right that he should be laid to rest beside Sue Cox and her family. There was no law saying anybody had to be buried beside the person they loved the most in this life. Look at Bobby. He was buried sixty miles from where Lorraine and Rayfield, Baby Boy were buried. And right next to Bobby's grave was a spot reserved for Bena. Maybe it was right that people just got buried beside whoever they'd put in the most time with.

Leslie had called only once. Bena had resisted begging her to come home.

Two weeks passed. The pond was nearly half full. And the rains finally came. Dark clouds had hovered all day. At the first crack of thunder, the first jolt of lightning, everybody in the house ran into the yard and waved their arms in the air like fools. The rain came hard and swift and soaked them all to the bone. The sky stayed gray and out of focus for days. The downpour was relentless. At night Bena fell asleep beside Lucky, who writhed and kicked, but she was comforted by the pounding thunder and the blasts of lightning pointing in every direction at once.

Bena woke every morning and put on Lucky's boots and raincoat and hurried through the mud to see how high the pond was. It was a sad sort of magic, seeing the pond begin to look, at last, like a real pond.

Bena and Eddie rolled Lucky up in the bed and tried to get him to love the rain—to love seeing the pond fill up. Even during the heavy rains Bena kept the water hoses going full blast, pumping water around the clock. When Lucky opened his eyes she could never be sure what he was seeing—if anything.

Buck came by every day, paid his respects to Lucky, then walked with Eddie out to watch the pond fill up. Lots of nights he stayed for supper, which the teachers at school were taking turns fixing. Mayfred had organized the whole thing.

On the fourth day, when the sun finally came out again, Lucky seemed to sense it. His rocking back and forth subsided some. When Eddie placed him at the window, he was peaceful for a few minutes, like he hadn't been in days.

. . .

Sue Cox and Ellie arrived early Saturday morning. Sue Cox brought a trunkful of wildflower seeds that her florist boyfriend had gotten for her. "All you have to do is throw them around everywhere after a hard rain, and when the time comes they bust out and bloom like crazy," she said. "I thought they'd look good around the pond."

Jerry Lee and LaVonte loaded the sacks of seeds into the wheelbarrow for her and pushed them out to the pond. Sue Cox, Ellie, and Anna Kaye were at the pond slinging seeds when Sissy and Cole and Bobby got there, bringing lunch for everybody. Actually it was finger sandwiches, spinach dip, and a fruit plate left over from a wedding at the country club the night before.

Lucky's belly was swollen and hard. Bena was trying to get him to sip some Ensure through a straw when Joe and Lisa pulled up in the drive, a trailer with a torn-up-looking rowboat in tow. "Mama, you got to see this," Eddie yelled.

Bena looked at them coming up the drive and ran into the yard. Lisa got out of the truck hesitantly. She watched Joe wrap his arms around his mother, then she followed suit, but lightly. "We brought something for Lucky's pond," Lisa said. "It used to be my daddy's. It's in pretty bad shape, but it floats."

Bena looked at the battered boat.

Eddie and LaVonte helped Joe unhitch the trailer and drag the boat out toward the pond. Lisa went with them, maybe afraid to let Joe out of her sight, afraid to be left alone with Bena.

From the window Bena watched as they struggled to get the boat through the trees and stickers, out to the pond. It was a job. Cole got a piece of rope out of his car trunk so they could tie the boat to a tree when they finally got it out there, afloat.

Mayfred was the one who suggested that Eddie and LaVonte take Lucky's truck to the old house and load up the picnic table from over there. "It would look good out at the pond," she said. "Under that pecan tree, where it's not so hot."

Eddie was hesitant to leave, but Mayfred said, "If you get back soon enough we might could eat our supper out there."

"It's something to do, man," LaVonte said. "Come on."

WHEN JERRY LEE came by and saw what was going on, he left immediately and came back an hour later, bringing half a dozen army-surplus duck decoys and his duck call. "We get these decoys out on the pond and I believe Lucky will like that," he told Bena. "He won't know the difference any better than the ducks do." He blew his duck call. "Might even could call up some real ducks with this."

Jerry Lee waded into the pond and set the decoys out and a silence fell over everybody. The decoys floated off in all directions, and it gave people a reason to clap and cheer. The fake ducks thrilled Juanita's kids. They blew the duck call all afternoon long, trying to coax the decoys into floating over to them, trying to coax other ducks from a sky where there were no ducks. Nobody tried to make them stop. Bena watched it all from the window where she had Lucky sitting up in his bed. She knew what it was to want so badly to believe that something was real. That something was possible.

Lucky's eyes were closed and he was rocking side to side, rhythmically, like he heard some awful music nobody else could hear and it was making him keep time with these strange, repetitive motions. Even his morphine could not stop the music.

NO ONE WAS sure of the exact moment Lucky died. Bena had managed to fall asleep beside him and had not noticed when his rocking stopped. She only knew that when she awoke he was motionless and curled beside her. She didn't leap up and go tell anyone that Lucky was gone. Instead, she pulled the sheet up over the two of them, chin high, and held on to him and waited until the words finally came to her. *Lucky is dead.*

EPILOGUE

It don't seem possible that it's been nearly two years since Lucky died. Mama's hair is turning gray. It doesn't bother me, but seems like it bothers my sisters. They're always offering to color it for her. "I like it gray," Mama tells them. "It suits me."

The other thing is her name. All my life Mama has been Bena Eckerd, then Bena McKale. But since Lucky died she's started going by her given name, Verbena. On the name tag she wore at Parents' Night she wrote out her name, Verbena McKale, which sort of shocked me. Twice that night she introduced herself to my teachers as "Eddie's mother, Verbena."

I don't know what's up with that. I let it go at the time—didn't ask her why. Now I'm mostly used to it and I don't guess it matters why.

I STILL CAN'T hardly stand to think about Lucky's funeral. You talk about sad now. I had that bad crying spell in front of everybody. Not the kind where your lip quivers and your throat swells up until you think you might choke on all the sadness. No. I cried like a damn girl. All these people came

*over and patted my shoulder and put their arms around me, some of them to-
tal strangers. I felt like a fool.*

*My sisters now, Lord, they bawled their heads off. If you so much as looked
at one of them they started up all over again. I hated all that crying. You got
to be made out of steel to keep from letting it get to you. Leslie and them, I
swear it's like they like to cry. They get into it. Even Sissy. But it makes me sick
to my stomach, all that show of emotion. For real. Crying in front of a bunch
of people who are crying too. It's just too much grief. I don't think Lucky
would have liked it either—all that sobbing and carrying on. He wasn't that
type. I tried to be strong for him, you know. I knew he wouldn't have wanted
everybody all torn up like that.*

*Mama never shed a single tear. All through Lucky's service she sat between
Leslie and Lisa Rayfield, who boo-hooed into wadded-up tissues with their
smeared mascara and runny noses. But Mama was calm. She looked straight
ahead, seemed to hear what people were saying about Lucky, but never broke
down like I was expecting her to. Like I thought she would.*

*Me and Joe and Corby were Lucky's pallbearers along with Cole, Jerry Lee,
and Buck. I'd never been a pallbearer before, but I swear I liked it better than
just sitting still in all that heartache. Sadness is easier to work with if you
can move around in it a little bit. If you have a job to do that keeps you from
dwelling too much on the deathly way you're feeling.*

*When Daddy died I was just a little kid. I was sad and I guess I cried my
share. But mostly I remember being scared. I didn't understand what was going on. Everybody talking about Daddy going to be with Jesus and all that.
It freaked me out pretty bad. I got scared Mama would die too. I know it
don't make sense now, but at the time it was all I could worry about. She
don't have any idea how much time I spent spying on her, peeking at her
in the bathroom, listening to her cry behind the closed door, looking in her
bed to see if she was sleeping or not, waiting to hear her car come up the
drive after school. Back then it was like I couldn't hardly breathe if Mama
was out of my sight. I used to lie in bed with Elvis and try to come up with
a plan for my life, you know, if Mama died and left us like Daddy did. I'd*

practically paralyze myself worrying like that. Couldn't hardly get up out of bed sometimes.

With Lucky dying though, it was different. I was older for one thing. And I saw it coming, day by day. I had time to try to get ready. Daddy dying, that was sort of like getting struck by lightning when there wasn't so much as a cloud in the sky. But with Lucky it was more like knowing a flood of grief is coming, giving you some time to scrounge up some kind of life preserver if you can—or learn to dog paddle or something. So, you know. It was different. Losing Lucky was hard because I knew Lucky sort of like one man to another. He always acted like I had sense as good as he did. I felt like we made our peace, me and him. I said to him what I needed to say, which wasn't all that much. Because Lucky, he didn't require a bunch of talk. We had an understanding between us. Anna Kaye says that's a rare thing. When your feelings don't have to be expressed because the other person already knows.

LESLIE AND CORBY didn't get home until the night before Lucky's service. Leslie broke down the minute she walked in the house and didn't quit crying until she left a week later to go back to Austin. That bothered me, especially since she'd been gone for all the hard parts, missed the worst of things. But maybe that was what had her so upset, because she hated to have missed out or a tragedy or anything half as sad as Lucky dying. Leslie clung on to Mama like she was her shadow or something. She insisted on sleeping with Mama every night too, like some kind of little kid. Corby just threw a sleeping bag on the floor in my room.

I wasn't sure it was right for Corby to come home with Leslie. Not under the circumstances. But then after Lucky's service was over and people were sitting around out at the pond eating ham and potato salad and stuff— because, you know, a bunch of crying makes people hungry—people talking as quiet as zombies, and Corby takes out his guitar and starts playing some old hymns. He didn't seem to me like somebody who would know any hymns. So, you know, people can surprise you.

Mayfred got started singing with Corby and it was something to hear. I can't remember one word the preacher said, but I remember Corby singing *those songs with Mayfred. "Y'all don't stop," somebody said every time they paused. They sang until it was past dark, Jerry Lee's cigarette tip the only light there was out there. I guess if the mosquitoes hadn't got so bad we might have sat there until daybreak.*

HERE'S WHAT BOTHERS ME. *Mama swears it's all right with her, doesn't bother her, but I'm pretty sure she's lying. Mama will lie in a minute if she thinks it's in the best interest of everybody else. Maybe that's not actual lying, I don't know. But I know this. They buried Lucky in a plot beside Sue Cox's parents. Someday I guess they'll plant Sue Cox right next to Lucky. It's plain wrong. That's all. Lucky ought to have been put to rest someplace where Mama can join him when her time comes.*

"If Mama gets buried beside Lucky," Leslie said, "then who will get laid to rest by Daddy? He'll be alone."

This is the twisted way Leslie looks at things, but I think that's because Leslie didn't see Mama with Lucky, you know, at the end. She didn't see the way they slept folded together on that hospital bed night after night, the way Mama washed Lucky and talked to him and rubbed his jerky feet—when half the time Lucky didn't even know who she was.

Don't get me wrong, I don't have anything against Sue Cox. That's not it. Sue Cox shocked everybody at Lucky's service when she stood up and said, "I've never seen Lucky as happy as he was with Bena and her kids. He always wanted a family." She cried saying it and if you ask me she acted sincere too.

When Leslie and Corby showed up that first night Sue Cox said, "Glad you're home." Leslie just held on to Sue Cox and cried like there was no tomorrow. I guess that might have shocked Sue Cox, who just held on to Leslie, rocking her back and forth saying, "It's okay. It's okay." Sue Cox probably didn't know how sensitive Leslie is deep down—that anything to do with death just about kills her outright.

"Hey, handsome," was all Sue Cox said to Corby.

JOE AND LISA *brought Mrs. Rayfield, Lisa's mother, to Lucky's funeral. "She wanted to come," Joe said, like that explained anything. At first nobody was sure how it would go, Mrs. Rayfield walking in the house with a pan of fried chicken and a dish of three-bean salad. But I guess Mama was too stunned over losing Lucky to get mad at anybody. "I hate you having to go through a thing like this twice," Mrs. Rayfield told Mama. "I know how hard it is."*

Later, after the service, when everybody was just sitting around, Mrs. Rayfield said, "Joe spends nearly every weekend at our house. You can't pry those two apart. It wouldn't surprise me if Joe gave Lisa a ring sometime soon." She said it cheerful, like maybe it might lift Mama's spirits.

I don't think Mama even heard the part about the ring. I think she only heard that part about Joe spending his weekends with Lisa and her mother. No wonder he never answered his phone. No wonder he hardly ever came home to visit. I looked at Mama to see if she was as upset on the outside as I knew she must be on the inside. But I couldn't tell.

DAMN IF BARRETT didn't show up a couple months after Lucky's funeral. When he got wind that Sissy was involved with Cole he was a real asshole about it. He started telling Sissy he wanted joint custody of little Bobby, that little Bobby was as much his as he was Sissy's. He said, "A boy needs a daddy," and shit like that. I was home when Sissy came over to tell Mama. Sissy was hysterical, thinking Barrett was going to sneak into the trailer and kidnap little Bobby or something. She was saying thank goodness Lucky gave her that gun and stuff like that, which got Mama all upset too. I couldn't hardly get either one of them calmed down.

I never liked Barrett in the first place. Sissy don't deserve the shit he's put her through. But the biggest mistake Barrett made was going out to the country club and harassing Sissy on her job, making her cry in front of the dinner crowd. They said Cole beat the living hell out of him. I wasn't there to see it, but some of my buddies saw the whole thing. Said Barrett didn't know what hit him. And to tell the truth, I think more of Cole since he did that. A golfer. You don't ordinarily expect a golfer to lay somebody out like that. They called the police. Cole could have lost his job, but it didn't seem like he cared.

Mama was grateful to Cole afterward too. It was clear he intended to look out for Sissy—and that's a big relief for Mama. And everybody.

Since then nobody has seen Barrett. Some people say he's gone back to Florida. Other people say he's holed up in his mama's house drawing an un-employment check.

I know Cole is older than Sissy and all that, but I don't know what the heck Sissy is waiting for. If Sissy doesn't love Cole—she should.

For a long time *after Lucky was dead and gone Mama kept on work-ing on our old house. People tried to talk her into forgetting about it, but I thought it did her good, having something besides her job to keep her busy. Me and Anna Kaye started spending some time there too. Anna Kaye helped Mama strip and sand the kitchen cabinets, which took next to forever. After they painted them I rehung them myself. It was a two-man job, but I didn't call Joe to help out. Not this time. Anna Kaye is just like Mama in one way—she likes anything to do with a house. I see that. Now that old house doesn't even seem like the same place anymore. Mama refinished some of the wood floors and put in some new carpet and everything.*

Mama still goes over to the old house and just walks around the rooms, or sits on the steps and drinks a cup of coffee. A couple of times when I got worried because I didn't know where Mama was I drove over to the old house and found her there. Once she was asleep on the refinished living room floor. Scared the hell out of me. She told me she likes the emptiness of the place. She says it's peaceful.

Cole is trying to buy the old house from Mama. He's talking about getting it landscaped, putting in a blacktop drive, and maybe—when little Bobby gets older—a swimming pool too.

"A swimming pool?" Mama said. "We already have a pond out at the new house. We don't really need a swimming pool."

I can see that Mama likes talking to Cole about the possibilities of the house, but I'll be surprised if she actually up and sells it anytime soon.

• • •

COLE IS NOT *the only one with ideas. Mayfred and Jerry Lee want Mama to sell them an acre or two of Lucky's land so they can build a house out there near her. It might not be a bad idea since I'll be leaving for school soon, going to Mobile to run track at South Alabama. It would be good for Mama to have somebody nearby to look after her. But so far she hasn't agreed to anything.*

WHEN I LEAVE *for Mobile everything will change. I know that. Some people say when I go off to school Anna Kaye will get lonely and take up with somebody else. Get her another boyfriend. They say that always happens when somebody goes away to school and the other person doesn't. Anna Kaye is only human, people say. But I don't belive any of that. I trust Anna Kaye with my life. I never worry about Anna Kaye.*

I worry about Mama.

LOTS OF WEEKENDS *and all the holidays since Lucky died people have gathered around Mama. If it isn't Jerry Lee frying fish out at the pond with a contraption he rigged up, or Cole buying steaks for everybody and grilling them pondside, then it's Juanita bringing enchiladas or Mayfred fixing barbecued ribs and white bread and laying out a feast on the picnic tables. The pond is the gathering place. There are three picnic tables out there now, a fancy gas grill Cole bought secondhand from the country club, a world of lawn chairs and toys and a hammock or two. Me and Joe strung up a tire swing, even though LaVonte was the one who ended up climbing the tree to situate the thing. Jerry Lee put up some bird feeders. And Sue Cox's wildflowers took hold and when they come out in the spring it looks like something out of a book. Everybody goes crazy. You can't hardly believe it.*

Everything about the pond is just fine — except one thing. There's not a drop of water in it. Once Mama turned off the water hoses and the rains let up, the pond immediately started draining, day by day, until it was dry as dirt. Sure, once in a while after a good downpour a foot or two of water might build up and last a couple of days. In a rainy season the pond takes on the qualities of an uncommonly large mud puddle, hardly enough water to drown

in. Once in a while you'll see a deer in early morning or late evening getting a drink out of the little bit of muddy water. There are weeds taking root
on the sides of the pond. It's gone back to being what it had started out as,
a big red hole clawed into the earth. Empty again.

But do you think anybody ever mentions this? As far as I can tell I'm the
only one who's noticed. The big gash in the ground that Mama paid good
money to have dug is not a pond. Except maybe a day or two—it's never been
a pond. There is no pond. "What pond?" That's what I want to know. "What
pond?"

The rowboat Lisa and Joe brought sits on the bottom of the pond year-
round. Jesus and Jose, they love to play in that thing. Juanita always
checks to be sure no snakes are coiled under the seats. She doesn't trust the
cats to do their jobs. The duck decoys are still there, all six of them. You
ought to see Carmelita with those decoys. She arranges them like dolls. She
makes them talk, she makes them swim, she feeds them and puts them to
bed. It's a sight the way she carries on over those fake ducks. People get a
kick out of it.

Little Bobby is walking now too. He loves the pond. The second Sissy takes
her eyes off little Bobby he heads for the pond. He loves to push his plastic
lawn mower through the mud or drive his dump truck back and forth in the
red dirt or up and down the sides of the pond like it's a mountain or something. Mayfred says she'd hate to know how many clothes he's ruined playing in that pond.

The duck call hangs on a string out there, something Cole fixed so it won't
get lost and the kids can keep on trying to convince imaginary ducks to detour down from the sky, or Jerry Lee can signal everybody that the fish is fried
or the hamburgers are ready. Mayfred blows it when she's trying to round up
her kids to go home. LaVonte blows it just to blow it.

On really hot days Mama has been known to drag the water hoses all the
way out there again and set the sprinkler out in the middle of what she in-
sists on calling a pond. It's crazy. The kids roll in the red-clay puddle like pigs
in mud. The rest of us take off our shoes and walk barefoot in the red dirt. I
do it myself. But there is no water. Not enough for even one puny fish. Not

enough to float the rowboat or the decoys. Not enough to serve as a wildlife drinking hole. Only enough—maybe—to hatch a swarm of mosquitoes.

I swear, now that Lucky is dead, sometimes I feel like I'm the only person left living in the real world.

WHEN SUE COX *and Ellie visit they like to put on their swimsuits and lay out in the sun at the pond. Anna Kaye does too. They spray themselves with the hose or bottles of water and run ice cubes over their faces. I don't see the fun in that, but they make a day of it, cooking themselves in the hot sun and talking their heads off.*

Last Christmas Leslie was the one who made Corby string up a bunch of those tree lights out at the pond. He couldn't talk her out of it. She decorated a pine sapling out there with flashing colored lights too. Corby sprang for the extension cords himself, ran them alongside the water hose. Little Bobby went nuts, seeing the pond lit up like that, strings of white lights draping from tree to tree in the night. It looked like the Twilight Zone to me, but Anna Kaye said it was beautiful.

Christmas night we all sat out there listening to Corby play Christmas carols on his guitar, some people singing along. I'll admit it was nice, the whole thing. Except that the pond was stone dry. Except that there was no pond.

We kept those lights strung out at the pond after Christmas. Jerry Lee ran a real electric line out there with a switch so we can sparkle the place up any night we want too. Or plug in a radio or a CD player.

Mayfred invited the whole Fellowship Baptist Church to have homecoming at the pond. I never saw so much food in my life. Jerry Lee put up a volleyball net and some folding tables and chairs. Mayfred decorated the tables with balloons and whatnot. It looked like a circus come to town. Folks parked all over the yard, kids squalled and ran wild, people talked and prayed and said a bunch of Baptist-style stuff. Only one person, as far as I know, commented on the nonexistence of the pond. Between bites of deviled egg this old man said "Pond's low, huh?"

"Yes, sir," I said.

MAMA TRIED TO *get me to invite the track team to come out to the pond for an end-of-the-year thing. But I wouldn't do it. I don't want people knowing that my whole family tries to pass ourselves off as people who have a pond—when we really don't.*

Mayfred, who I can usually count on to have some good sense, said once, "I like a pond you don't have to worry about nobody drowning in." She's the only one who seems willing to ackowledge the emptiness we're all dealing with here.

But of everybody, Sissy is the worst. Maybe because she lives nearby and comes over more than the others. She'll pull up in the car Cole bought her, unstrap little Bobby from his car seat, and say, "Hey, Mama, just came by for a glass of tea."

Mama always has ice tea ready. So she'll pour them each a glass.

Like clockwork Sissy'll say, "Let's sit out by the pond, Mama. Okay?" She'll turn to little Bobby and say, "You want to play out at the pond?" He'll already have taken off across the yard for the path that leads out there. Mama and Sissy will sit at the pond for hours and talk about God knows what while little Bobby fools around in the pond with his toys. I got no idea what they say to each other or why they want to say it out under a pecan tree beside an ugly red scar in the earth. Maybe Mama is trying to talk Sissy into loving Cole. Or maybe she's telling Sissy stuff about Lucky. Woman stuff. Sometimes they sit out there past sundown.

I SORT OF HATE to go off to school and leave Mama like this. With no real grasp on reality. One minute she's sitting all alone at the old house, everything painted ghost white, sipping a cup of coffee while Tom sniffs around after squirrels. The place is as empty as a tomb. It echoes. If you yell something inside the house it'll answer you back. It's like the house can talk.

Other times Mama spends hours sitting out beside her imaginary pond. All her kids and friends pretending right along with her. Nobody bothering to tell her the truth. Nobody acting like they even know the truth.

. . .

I TRY TO TALK to Sissy about the pond. But Sissy is no better than Mama really. "Listen," I say. "Why are we all acting like we got a damn pond? You're going to mess up little Bobby's mind making him think that big hole in the ground is a pond. It's not a pond, Sissy. You and Mama can pretend all you want to — everybody can — but that still don't make that clawed-out hole a pond."

Sissy looks at me like she feels sorry for me. My sisters do that all the time, act like I don't have a clue. Well, I got more than a damn clue. I got sense enough to see what's right before my very eyes. Which is more than I can say for the rest of them.

Sissy runs her hand through my hair, messing it up like I'm still a little kid. "Of course it's a pond, Eddie," she says.

"How can you say that?"

"Because it's true."

I point at the pond. "It's a big dry hole. Do you see a drop of water?"

"No," she says.

"A pond has water in it, Sissy," I insist.

"Not this one." She smiles.

ACKNOWLEDGMENTS

I thank Abby Thomas for all the ways she has influenced and inspired me.

Thanks, again, to my agent, Liz Darhansoff, and my editor, Shannon Ravenel, for befriending Verbena. Also special thanks to Shelly Goodin, my publicist, for her valuable assistance; Dana Stamey, Algonquin's managing editor, for forgiving me my tresspasses; and Anne Winslow for the sensitivity she brings to the jacket design. I'm grateful to all the good people at Darhansoff and Verrill Agency and Algonquin Books—who do their jobs so well, go the second mile so often.

Also, my gratitude to the University of Arizona English Department and Poetry Center; to Amy Rogers, Frye Galliard, and Bob Inman for publishing an excerpt of *Verbena* in the anthology *Novella;* and to the Alabama Writer's Symposium.

I thank Lynn Siefert and Lael Smith for their friendship and support of my work, and for the dreams they have for Lucy and Dixie—and thus, all of us. Verbena too. And to Sylvie Rabineau and Liza Wachter for their enthusiasm and efforts to make dreams come true. Thanks also to Ron Bernstein at ICM.

Thanks to Rosa Cordova, who helped in me so many ways.

To our children, who challenge us to learn to love the people they love. To my mother, who, like Verbena, occasionally tried to answer a prayer when God refused. To anyone who has ever been—or longed to be—a good-hearted ex. To whoever said that forgiveness is not a feeling but a decision. And to the families who blend, merge, and blur the boundaries in an effort to make room for everybody.